ALLURING SONG

AIMEE MCNEIL

Cover designed by Emma Dolan   emmadolancovers.com
Edited by Allister Thompson   allisterthompson.com

To my husband, who has given me a love like no other.
To my parents and sister, who have always believed in me.
To my daughter, who listens to my endless
brainstorming and always gives brutally honest feedback.
To my sons, who make me laugh every day.

Chapter 1
LORELEI

Slender fingers reached out and caressed the surface of the water as it rushed over the bed of shimmering rocks. It was cool and refreshing as it cast a rejuvenating tingle over her skin. As soon as her touch left its soothing embrace, she craved it again. Water had always been a source of strength and comfort to her, and she never strayed far from its call. Her long blond hair that was almost as white as the wild flowers scattered upon the earth was loose and flowed over her shoulders, spilling down into the clear water of the narrow, noisy river. The blond tendrils wanted to be swept away in the current, and a smile played on her full lips as a few small fish swarm toward her. They brushed against her skin as she gently stroked them. She always dreamed of letting the water carry her away, swimming away with the fish. When she touched their flesh she would sometimes receive whispers and images of vast bodies of water with endless depths, stretching out to where the Sun meets the Earth.

When she was a small girl she told her mother of her desire to swim away with the river and find waters so deep and wide and full of treasures to behold. Her mother feared these words and warned her of the dangers that would find her in the open waters, away from the shelter of their beloved home amidst the protection of the trees. She loved her mother and like an obedient daughter did as she asked, but it did not stop the ache within her that grew as she did, desiring more than their secluded hideaway and the shallow waters that passed over their land. She wanted to dive into great depths and watch the sun sink into the water as night fell across the sky. She was restless and craved a life she did not know.

"Lorelei!" She turned to her mother's call in the distance, like a gentle song carried on the breeze.

"Coming, Mother!" Lorelei retreated from the river with a sigh and watched the fish swim away with the pull of the water to a place that she could only dream about. She stood and straightened out her worn and faded dress. The material had become snug on her figure as she changed and curved. She liked her new shape; it reminded her of her mother's beautiful form. She always adored how her mother moved like an elegant dance that never ended.

Lorelei's bare feet met the soft ground soundlessly as she skipped through the trees, her long hair floating behind her, clinging to the breeze. She had run through these grounds countless times. She would sometimes close her eyes and let her memory guide her through the obstacles that stood as familiar friends. Birds sang a new melody from the trees, and she listened and committed the tune to memory as she hummed along with it. Nature was always singing to her, and when she listened, she could find the most beautiful music. The branches of the trees reached out to her as she passed, beckoned by her song. She reached up and brushed the soft leaves as she passed. Lorelei grinned as a small rabbit followed close on her heels.

When she broke free of the tree line, their small house came into view. It blended in with the surroundings; the walls were constructed of logs, with the bark still adorning the surface. Smoke gently escaped the crumbling stone chimney, and over the years it had come to look like the earth was slowly swallowing it as nature flourished around it and the structure aged. Lorelei stopped to grab the basket of ripe vegetables that she had gathered from the garden before continuing toward the house.

"Here, little one." She reached into her basket, pulled out a carrot, and placed it in front of the almond-colored rabbit. It nuzzled her hand before gathering her offering and retreating back into the cover of the trees. "Take care."

The wooden front door complained loudly as she pushed it open. Her mother's face smiled brightly at her arrival. "There you are... I always worry that something will happen to you when you are gone for so long, especially when you insist on wandering down to the river." A relieved smile brightened her face.

Lorelei smiled reassuringly. "You worry too much, Mother. How can something so beautiful be dangerous?"

Her mother's smile fell. "Beautiful things are the most dangerous, my sweet Lorelei."

"You are beautiful, and there is nothing dangerous about you." Lorelei smiled as she placed her basket upon the table. Her mother managed a weak smile in return, but it did not carry to her eyes. She seemed lost in thought.

"You should come with me tomorrow. It might make you feel better to get out of the house," Lorelei said encouragingly.

"You have no idea how wonderful that sounds, darling, but I must stay here. I am not well enough to venture outside these walls." Her mother gently pushed her rocking chair. It was a constant rhythm that Lorelei had grown accustomed to hear echoing through the small wooden house.

"You have been unwell for so long. Maybe it's time to try something else, like lying in the sun or dipping your feet in the cool water. It might help?" Lorelei suggested with concern. Her mother had been unable to leave the house for as long as she could remember, but she had always looked so beautiful. She didn't understand what ailed her mother, robbing her of the pleasures of life. Her mother's hair was as blond as Lorelei's and fell in soft waves to her waist. Her fair skin was flawless, and her eyes were a bright, vibrant blue like the clearest waters, but she was haunted by something Lorelei could not understand. It saddened Lorelei beyond measure that her mother suffered and she was powerless to help.

Lorelei had never seen her own reflection other than the distorted image on the surface of the water, but her mother had told her she had one green eye and one blue — one like her mother and one like her father. Lorelei had never met her father; he had only been in her mother's life for a short time, and it had left a hole in her mother's heart so deep that Lorelei could still see the sadness lingering in her eyes. When Lorelei asked about him, she could see her mother's condition worsen as her heartache grew anew. Eventually Lorelei stopped asking, because she hated seeing her mother suffer.

"Don't worry, Lorelei, I will be fine. I am not going to leave you, if that is what you worry about. I will be here for as long as you need me." Her mother stopped rocking and looked at her.

"Then I need you forever."

"Come here." Her mother reached out toward Lorelei, who closed the distance between them, dropping to her knees and laying her head in her mother's lap. Her mother softly stroked her hair. She always had a gentle touch that brought immeasurable comfort.

"The rain is coming. I can feel it," Lorelei whispered.

"You are right." Her mother ran her fingers through Lorelei's long hair and began to hum. Lorelei loved her mother's magical voice. The sound was as soothing as the sun on a warm afternoon, or a cold glass of water to quench thirst. Lorelei listened to her mother's song as the day faded into night. When the first drops of rain began to fall, Lorelei lifted her head and met her mother's eyes. Heavy drops fell upon the roof like tiny footsteps, calling to them.

Lorelei jumped up from the floor and pushed open the wooden window, throwing her arms out into the rain. "Hello, rain!" she called out into dark. She skipped out the front door to meet the open sky. Her mother's laughter floated out the window as Lorelei threw out her arms and spun around in the rain. She couldn't stop the eruption of laughter that escaped her as she danced in the raindrops. She loved the feel of it upon her skin, the strength that seemed to collect at her core with every drop that touched her.

Lorelei looked up at her mother leaning on the windowsill with her head on her arms. She watched Lorelei dance, her beautiful blue eyes following lovingly. "Is there anything better than the rain, Mother?" Lorelei called out happily.

"Only you." Her mother smiled warmly at her, causing her beautiful eyes to shine.

Chapter 2

EDWARD

Twenty years ago...

A young man walked down the riverbank, his bare feet tracing its edge as he walked along its length. He loved the feel of the cool mud upon the soles of his feet. He wasn't sure how long he walked, but his strides did not stop, and he followed where they led. He traveled through the trees, listening to the peaceful songs of the birds high in the branches. It was quiet, and he welcomed the sound of the breeze rustling the leaves and the water rushing over the earth on its journey.

Every tree, every plant whispered its secrets to him as he passed, and he listened to their silent language and took comfort in their company. He reveled in the lush greenery that surrounded him. Bending down, he ran his fingers over the soil, sinking his fingers into the giving earth. The feel of it beneath him and the sounds around him acted as his guides. He had lacked the sense of sight since his birth and relied on his other senses to lead him. He hated being dependant on others, but out here in the forest, where it was quiet, with the river to direct him, he could enjoy his independence; his freedom. He knew that he would never lose his way surrounded by the lavish green of the forest, a place he felt at home.

The river was warm from the summer sun, and the earth was moist from the heavy thundershowers of the night before. The sun was reaching its highest perch and was already drying the wetness that saturated the ground. Soon the earth would be dry and thirsty again from the greedy sun.

An alluring song carried to him from a distance. It was the most beautiful sound he had ever heard. He followed it; the captivating voice drew him in. His pursuit took him away from the river. He moved deeper into the forest than he had ever ventured before. He gripped his walking stick, even though amid the trees he was always sure on his feet; it was a comfort he had grown accustomed to. All of the sounds that he had listened to as he had started his journey through the forest quieted as if listening, like him, to the lovely song. He knew that he should be cautious; the silence was a warning to him, but he could not bring his feet to stay. When he drew closer, he noticed the song had given way to tears. Gentle sobs had found him, a whisper on the breeze.

The weeping stopped suddenly, indicating that his presence had been detected by the owner of the beautiful voice. "Are you alright?" he questioned his now silent surroundings. He didn't move to approach further; instead he lingered at the tree line. He could feel the openness before him, the break in the forest from where the song had originated.

"I am now. What is your name?" The woman's voice was so delicate and playful. A smile came unbidden, and his heart raced with excitement. He could not see this woman, but he knew without a doubt that she was just as beautiful as the voice she presented. He could sense her as he could the warm sun on his skin. She had an enthralling energy about her that he could not ignore — she was bewitching.

"My name is Edward. I was just walking along the river when I heard you."

"Come closer, dear Edward," she responded smoothly.

Edward took a deep breath and stepped out into the clearing, despite the dangers that he could sense. He was not afraid, and he welcomed what lay before him.

Chapter 3
LORELEI

Lorelei woke early the next morning. The sun beaming through her window covered her like a warm blanket. The birds called to her from the sky, energizing her to rouse from the comfort of her bed. The shuffle of her feet was the only sound in the house as she made her way over the wooden floorboards that creaked under her step. "Mother?" Lorelei called when she didn't notice her presence in their small home. She looked around, calling out to her again, but was only met by an eerie silence.

Panic swelled in Lorelei's chest as she stood before the door to a room that she had never entered. She had looked everywhere else, and her mother was nowhere to be found. The door had always been locked, and her mother insisted on keeping it that way, but Lorelei didn't know where else to look. When she was a small girl, she had asked her mother why she kept the door locked, and her mother only replied that it held too many memories. She reached for the knob and tried to turn it, but the lock was still firm. She knocked with a sense of building urgency. "Mother? Are you in there?" Lorelei leaned down and peered through the keyhole but could only see shadows in the darkened room. A shadow shifted in the room, causing Lorelei's breath to catch. "Mother?" She was met again by silence.

The front door slammed, causing her to jump. Her nerves were wound tight with her mother's strange absence. She could feel that something was not right; strangeness settled in the air around her. She was worried that her mother's condition had worsened, and she was in need of help. Lorelei just needed to find her first.

Lorelei walked over to the front door that led out to the covered porch. The locks on the doors were all secure, and Lorelei ran her fingers over them curiously before she released them and pushed. It was wedged closed, and Lorelei had to throw her body weight against the door to jar it. She walked out into the early heat of the new day. She turned around, scanning her surroundings that led to the thick trees circling the house. The forest was unusually quiet; the birds did not welcome her as she approached the trees. Not even the breeze rustled the leaves. It was as if everything could sense what she could: the change in the air.

Lorelei kept walking, at a loss as to where her mother could be. She arrived before the rushing water of the stream, and the cool liquid embraced her as she stepped into it. She spun in a circle, taking in her surroundings, but she was only enclosed by more unsettling silence. "Mother," Lorelei called, hesitant to raise her voice as she continued downstream with the flow of the water.

"Go back."

Lorelei spun around, searching for the origin of her mother's voice. It was carried through the air, and she could not focus on a direction. "Where are you?"

A flock of birds erupted from the trees in the near distance, alerting Lorelei. Before she could form a thought, her feet were propelling her in that direction, darting through the trees. The passing trees blurred as she moved purposely. The air took on a strange taste as she swallowed it in deep breaths. Bringing her feet to a sudden halt, she tried to quiet her heavy breathing. Everything around her gave warning of danger, the heavy air, the desperate silence of the creatures — even the trees trembled.

"Lorelei!" Her mother's voice rang out urgently in her ears. It was then that she realized it was not her mother that she gave chase to. It was only her mother's warning of danger that was with her, echoing in her mind. Lorelei remained perfectly still, but she knew that she could not blend in with her surroundings; her hair glowed against the endless green that surrounded her. She tried to steady her breath, concentrating on stilling herself. If she was lucky, whatever stalked the forest would pass her by if she did not draw attention to herself.

The sound of a dry branch snapping screamed out in the silence, causing her to turn with a gasp. Panic seized her as her eyes fell upon an unexpected intruder. Lorelei had lived in isolation from other people her entire life because of the dangers her mother spoke of, as well as the illness her mother suffered that left her unable to leave their home. Now she stood before someone that was larger than she thought possible. He towered over her, causing her to stumble backward. His hair was as dark as the rich soil of the earth and reached his broad shoulders. His eyes were dark and piercing as he studied her under his scowling brow. Lorelei felt her heart race at a frenzied pace, as though it was rising in her throat.

Lorelei looked up at the impossibly large man, trying to keep her legs from trembling. His jaw was square and covered in shadow; he looked hard and coarse everywhere that she was soft and smooth. His chest and stomach were covered with a hard metal shell carved into a pattern that was nothing like her own lines. His arms were bare and bulged in a strange but captivating way that spoke of power and danger. He radiated dominance that both terrified her and intrigued her. She was overwhelmed, having no ability to mask her panic. She had no idea what his intentions would be, and she feared she could not outrun him.

"Who are you?" His voice was deep and vibrated through his heavy chest. Lorelei's eyes widened, and her breath faltered in a strangled gasp when he moved to approach. He waited for a response, but only a whimper escaped her lips. He began to circle her as she stood silently trying to concentrate on drawing breath. "What are you?" he asked when he came to stand in front of her again, this time so close, she had to lean back to look up into his dark, imposing eyes.

"I asked you a question." He leaned in toward her, and she took a step back. "*What* are you?" he commanded with narrowed, accusing eyes.

"I don't understand what you mean." Lorelei surprised herself when she was able to formulate her words. She tried to hold her shoulders back and exude some mock confidence, but her body shook when she tried to command it.

"Are you a sorceress?" he asked tightly, tilting his head to the side. The movement made his hair fall forward, brushing against his cheek. Lorelei found herself momentarily distracted by the strange thought of what his hair would feel like. Would it be soft, despite his outwardly indelicate nature?

"No." Lorelei swallowed, her voice but a whisper. His eyes remained darkly set on her. His strong jaw clenched, his gaze refusing to waver. She could only stare back at him as he seemed to be deep in thought, an inner battle that she could not even begin to figure out.

"Then what are you?" He continued to study her, raking his eyes up and down her body.

Lorelei's flight response reeled. She turned quickly, pushing off at a hurried pace, attempting to gain as much distance as she could. She could feel the man behind her; no matter how fast she willed her feet to move, weaving through the trees, he was on her tail without faltering. His large hand slipped around her waist, and he pulled her back, lifting her from the ground as he held her against him. Lorelei's scream rang out as she struggled against him. He wrapped his arms around her, restricting her arms so she couldn't fight him.

"If you stop moving and promise not to run again, I will let you stand." His breath was hot against her ear. Lorelei tried to ignore the heat that spread across her skin with the caress of his words. The feeling was completely at odds with the fear that fueled her blood. This man was too strong; her struggles were useless against his powerful hold. She was exhausting herself needlessly, and she realized she should be conserving her energy for a more opportune time.

Lorelei stopped moving, nodding but remaining silent. She knew that she was no match for him, regardless of his intentions. "I don't want to hurt you, but if you force my hand I have no choice." He slipped his hand from around her waist quickly, like it pained him to touch her, though he remained close. Once her feet were firmly upon the ground, she turned around, facing him and stepping back slightly.

"What are you doing here?" He waved at their surroundings. "Wandering in these woods?"

"I live here." Lorelei's voice was pitiful to her own ears. She took a deep breath and tried to gather strength.

"What do we have here?" Lorelei turned at the arrival of a new man, a chill assaulting her when her eyes fell upon him. As large and imposing as the first man was, this one was beyond terrifying. He had a dark energy that caused the small hairs upon her skin to rise. Though he was not as tall as the first, he was no less imposing. His dark eyes whispered evil intent as they drank her in. His hair hung straight and lifeless around his sharp, hollowed face, shadowed with a dark patch of growth upon his chin. Lorelei shrank back from his approaching form.

"Not so fast." Her founder reached out and grabbed her arm, stopping her retreat.

"What did you find, Ajax?" The new man drew out his words like a slithering snake. He reached out for her with a sinister smile. All of her mother's warnings about men flooded her mind. She wasn't prepared for this; she wished desperately that she had asked her mother more questions about how to defend herself. She had no clue what these men could be capable of, or how to stop them. She stood defenseless before them. "She's spectacular." He studied her face with a devious glint in his eye.

"Let go of me!" Lorelei struggled against Ajax's hold. He refused to give her any slack to retreat from the dark man surveying her.

"She's a fighter, too." He stood too close before her. "This must be my lucky day." The unsettling stranger reached up and touched her hair curiously, then his fingers began trailing down the length of her neck to her chest, grazed the opening of her dress before pulling the fabric down to reveal more flesh.

"Don't touch me!" Lorelei reached up to knock his hand away at the same time as Ajax stepped between her and the man's unwanted touch.

"That's enough, Marcus!" Ajax commanded, forcing Lorelei behind him, his hand still firm upon her arm. The two men confronted each other with loaded gazes before Marcus stepped away, his arms raised in surrender despite his sneer.

"You want a turn first?" Marcus raised a brow. "Go ahead… but I will have mine," he added with heavy warning.

"No. We are taking her back to camp." Ajax's tone left no room for negotiation. Lorelei feared her fate should things become physical between the two men.

"You cannot take me anywhere." Lorelei tried to pull away, but Ajax's hold on her tightened. No amount of struggling seemed to lessen it. A silent agreement came to pass between the two men, causing the tension in the air to discharge noticeably.

"Sorry, sweetheart. You are coming with us." Marcus stepped forward with a cloth he pulled from his belt and pulled it down over her head. The last thing she saw before the cloth blinded her was Marcus's sinister smirk. "I make no promises for your well-being." He chuckled close to her. His nearness made a cold chill spread over her skin, despite the heat of the sun.

"Please, don't." Lorelei tried to resist. Rough hands grabbed her wrists and began tying her hands behind her back. She knew it was

Marcus by the way he leaned in close to her so she could hear his disturbing breathing. His touch was harsh and invasive as he bound her and guided her feet to an unknown destination. He insisted on nudging her with excessive force, causing her to stumble.

"Marcus," Ajax warned.

The next time someone placed their hands on her was only when necessary to guide her steps. His touch was gentle and never strayed from her shoulder. She knew it was Ajax. She could smell him, his woodsy musk that somehow was more appealing than blooming flowers on a spring day. "Please let me go. I will disappear, and you will never see me again," Lorelei whispered desperately beneath the stifling cloth.

"You will no longer be able to hide in this forest." Ajax spoke low. "You cannot be forgotten."

"What do you plan to do with me?" Lorelei asked, her voice laced with panic, but she was awarded with no answer, only the encouragement to continue moving.

Chapter 4
ARTHUR

Arthur sat in his chamber, leaning back in the exquisite armchair he had commissioned from the finest furniture maker in the land. He ran his fingers over the plush fabric of the armrests; it was lush and the stitching flawless. He had to pay a small fortune for it, like most of the possessions he cherished that now occupied his chambers. The fabricator of this very piece stood before him, awaiting his approval. Leofrick Chaucer had a reputation for excellence in his ability to create the finest furniture, but even with his acclaimed skill the man practically shook before the prince. A glistening sheen of sweat covered his skin as he awaited Arthur's comments. Arthur revelled in his power and how he could wield it over others. He enjoyed the man's discomfort, the way his hands nervously gripped each other.

The chair was worthy of praise, but Arthur would not give it. Not even hint of his satisfaction would be let known of Chaucer's work. He was above making others feel good; after all, even with Chaucer's fame among the people for his craftsmanship, he was inferior to Arthur and always would be.

"It will do," Arthur breathed nonchalantly. He reached into the breast pocket of his vest and presented a leather pouch of coin. Chaucer accepted it with trembling hands. He opened the pouch and a slight scowl presented upon his features.

"Excuse me, Your Highness, but I thought we had agreed on the amount…" Chaucer's voice faded and his sudden rise of confidence left him as soon as the words passed his lips.

Arthur tilted his head with an irritated expression. "You were commissioned by the royal family and bestowed a great honor, and yet you find words to complain?"

"No, Your Highness, I am honored." He bowed

"You are dismissed." With much relief, Chaucer's feet were quick to guide him from the room.

Servants awaited outside Arthur's door to assist him. The shadow upon his chin grew quickly of late. His youthful face had made the transition. It was not the only changes that were brought about by the arrival of his manhood. He craved supremacy like he craved the pleasures of a woman. It was an appetite he could not satisfy, a duty he had been molded for since he was a child. He was the heir to the throne.

Mera, a curvaceous brunette, sauntered into the room carrying a tray of grooming products. "Your Highness." She awaited his nod of approval before she continued her approach. A petite redhead followed closely on Mera's heels. She was a new servant added to his staff, and Arthur had yet to appreciate her upon closer view. He was pleased that she was accompanying Mera this morning, and he could now see what she had to offer. The redhead's eyes stayed lowered in obedience, but an innocent smile graced her lips. He could feel she was captivated by him, feel her awe at being in the presence of royalty. Women were drawn to his power, position, and wealth, always so willing to please him. He smirked as he observed her figure under her plain gown. Her skin was pale and smooth, and it was something he appreciated.

The redhead stepped forward with the cream, awaiting permission to apply it to his face. He nodded, setting her in motion while Mera waited with a sharpened blade. Her small, unsure hands shook nervously as she applied the lather. Her lashes fluttered, meeting Arthur's eyes briefly before they skirted down. A vibrant pink colored her cheeks. His eyes stayed trained on the redhead's petite physique as Mera slid the blade along his chin. The shy girl stood aside, her eyes downcast as she twisted her fingers in the material of her skirt. Arthur felt he rightfully deserved what he wanted, and right now he craved flesh anew.

"Come closer." He waved at the redhead. "What is your name?"

"Anne, Your Highness," she offered with a sweetness that made his groin respond. He appraised her with a lingering look.

"Take off your dress, Anne," he asked as casually as he would for a cup of tea. He basked in her surprise as her bright green eyes widened and flickered up toward his for a moment.

Mera set the blade down, attending the back of Anne's dress without delay. Anne's hands shook as she reached up to grasp the material that slackened around her neck. Mera had been in Arthur's personal service for a little over a year now, and she was used to his requests, undaunted by his hunger for flesh. Being a servant to the royal family brought one's family great honour, and Arthur had learned early that this meant they were very willing to please, while remaining tight-lipped about the goings-on in the castle to secure their positions. Mera had always been a favorite of his; she had curves that could bring a man to tears, and she could work her body like a seasoned whore. Although it did not stop his wandering eye from seeking out all available pleasures, like the fair beauty that now stood before him. He would not deny himself.

The fabric fell from Anne's shoulders, revealing more of her lovely pale flesh. His eyes took in the swell of her breasts and the curve of her hips. He enjoyed gazing upon raw female beauty, making his body react with need. "Tell me, Anne. Have you known a man?" The subtle gasp that escaped her lips excited Arthur, increasing his appetite.

"No… no, Your Highness," she stuttered.

"Then it is about time you have." He smiled. "On your knees, and please me until I tell you to stop." He watched Anne with an impatient glare as she fought through her hesitation.

"Is there a problem?" He raised his brows.

"No, Your Highness." Anne slowly lowered in front of him.

"Shall I finish your shave, Your Highness?" Mera asked in her usual sultry, sensual voice.

"Very well." Arthur leaned back and unbuckled his pants in front of the trembling Anne, who awaited him with an unsure expression. Mera moved the blade in sure, even strokes across his chin. "All done, Your Highness." Mera smiled, wiping the remaining cream from his face with a cloth.

Arthur grew impatient with Anne's tentative touch. He reached out, threading his fingers through her tightly braided hair, pulling her down harder upon him until she gagged around his pulsing erection. "I am a man who does not like a gentle touch." He pulled Anne's head back and looked into her eyes. She gasped from the pain of his grip. "Mera." Arthur called for the brunette's attention while his eyes bore into Anne's.

"Yes, Your Highness?" Mera wiped the blade and set it upon the tray before she turned to him.

"Show our innocent Anne how to please me." He released Anne with a rough hand, causing her to whimper and lean back on her heels.

Mera dropped to her knees beside Anne, and taking the girl's hands, she instructed her how to touch him in the way that Mera had learned he preferred long ago. He throbbed with pleasure, seeing their small feminine hands on him; it took all his energy not to thrust his hips against their workings. Mera confidently showed Anne how to grip him, how to stroke him. Arthur took notice of the redness that took over Anne's face, stretching down her chest to her full, exposed breasts. How it excited him to see such color on her pale skin. It was the color of lust, pain, and rage, all of the emotions that he embraced. He was aroused, and his appetite clawed from his insides. His hands grasped the arms of his chair until the wood groaned in protest.

An abrupt knock on the door caused a growl of frustration to erupt from him. He had every intention of ignoring the request, but the door swung open regardless. The lack of protest from his guards made it clear who entered without allowance. His mother promenaded into his room with her usual air of power, expecting all the pieces to fall how she demanded.

The girls tending to him shrank back with lowered heads. "Your Majesty," the girls proclaimed in unison, unable to mask their surprise and unease at how they were discovered by their gracious queen.

A look of disgust marred his mother's perfect face. "Arthur, dear, why must you consort as such with the servants?" Her voice was lacking emotion as her eyes took in the two girls kneeling before him.

"Mother." He returned her cold, watery tone. "You will get wrinkles if you scowl so much."

His mother smoothed her features and took a slow, deep breath. She was truly exquisite for a woman of her age. The entire kingdom was in wonderment of their ageless queen. Her long golden hair, like his own, hung to her waist. Her eyes were emerald blue, and her skin was flawless. The people loved her purely for her beauty. "There are so many noblewomen vying for your attentions, and you insist on spending time with whores and servants." His mother continued into the room with not a care for her son's current state of undress or the women huddled before him with saliva wet upon their lips.

Arthur waved the girls away. Anne quickly collected her dress as Mera guided her toward the other side of the room. "Those women bore me. They speak of nonsense and will only open their legs if I promise to make them royalty." Arthur buttoned his pants, unashamed that his mother had spied his manhood or the actions through which he sought release.

His mother sighed as she considered his words. "Men are such insatiable creatures." She smiled thoughtfully before brushing hair from his face. Arthur looked like his mother, with the same intense blue eyes. She leaned forward and caressed his cheek with the back of her fingers. "We are hosting the Walthams for dinner this evening. You will do well to be in attendance." She glanced over toward the soundless women. "Finish up, dear, your training awaits." She leaned in and kissed him on the lips before she swept from the room, leaving her scent to fill the air. Her lavender perfume was almost suffocating as it lingered around him, invading his senses.

Arthur stood abruptly. His chair grated against the floor horribly, echoing throughout the room. Anger boiled inside him. His mother thought to control him as she did his father. He would not be her puppet; he would not be a pawn for her to play in her game. He swiped the contents of the table with his arm, causing them to crash to the floor. Water and cream sloshed everywhere, and the bowl clattered loudly, eliciting a gasp from the terrified Anne. In his moment of rage he had forgotten about the women. His appetite came back with vengeance when his eyes fell upon the undressed Anne, grasping her dress tightly to her bosom. Mera, on the other hand, looked hungrily back at him.

Arthur pulled open his shirt, causing the buttons to spray across the wooden floor and roll in every direction. He stalked toward the women. A familiar light flared in Mera's eyes before he claimed her mouth savagely, pulling the dress from her body while pushing her roughly back against the dresser. Her nails pulled at his flesh, leaving angry red trails that excited him. They made him hard with lust. He pulled back from her and watched as she reached up to touch her swollen, smiling lips.

Arthur turned his attention to Anne, looking terrified at the rough display of affection. He reached up and curled his fingers around her neck. Her eyes widened desperately as she whimpered in his hold. She dropped her dress and frantically clawed at his hand that squeezed tightly around her slender neck. "You will please me." He breathed in her face, biting the soft flesh of her cheek. A tear slipped from her eye and over her cheek, red from the assault of his teeth.

With substantial force, he pushed her toward the bed, causing her

to tumble; she steadied herself with her hands as Arthur came up behind her, pinning her to the bed with his weight. "I want to hear your
screams, Anne." He breathed hotly against the back of her neck.

Mera unfastened his pants and pulled them from his hips, freeing
him. She climbed upon the bed completely naked, leaning back on
the pillows, exposing herself and letting her fingers explore her own
flesh. Arthur forced Anne's hands behind her back, causing her to sob
louder as she was forced to lean over the foot of the bed, pinned by his
unrelenting weight. Anne was terrified; he could feel her body trembling beneath his. His eyes remained on Mera as he brought his hand
down forcefully against Anne's round, smooth bottom. The sound of
slapping flesh was thrilling to his ears, as well as Anne's scream that
rang out in the room, her protests continuing as he claimed her without holding back. Raw and savage, he took her innocence.

Chapter 5
LORELEI

The cloth was pulled from Lorelei's eyes. It had been hours breathing through the stuffy fabric. The sudden brightness assaulted her, despite the late hour; the sun was fading. They had walked for hours through the forest, far beyond the farthest reaches of where she had ever dared venture. She was in unfamiliar land, her bearings were off, and everything was strange and unsettling. A shadow fell over her. When she looked up, she flinched at the face that stared down at her.

"Hello, little dove. Miss me?" Marcus gave her a cringe-worthy smile. He grabbed her shoulders and forced her down against a tree. The bark scratched at her skin, but she refused to cry out. She tried to evade his touch, but he was so much stronger than her. Lorelei noticed a long red gash down his neck and dried blood that still coated the wound. She couldn't help the satisfaction that enveloped her, because she had caused the injury earlier when he tried to manhandle her. He had grown tired of her slow pace during their travel and decided he would carry her. When he threw her over his shoulder and cupped backside too eagerly, she raked him with her nails. He was not pleased, and it earned her an unceremonious drop to the ground, but it was worth it.

Marcus proceeded to tie her to the tree he had pushed her up against. "Don't want you to try running off again." His breath was sickly upon her cheek. Lorelei pulled away but his hand forced her close, squeezing her chin painfully. It was true that numerous times through that day, when she felt the opportunity, she had tried to make a run for it, despite the cover over her face and her bound hands.

Unfortunately, it was always Marcus retrieving her, and he would take the opportunity to grope her in some demeaning way as they returned to the others.

Lorelei had counted at least six individual voices as they traveled. They all spoke little and walked with exceptional endurance as they moved on foot for the entire day, stopping only when Lorelei could not go on without rest. She refused to be carried, and when they had tried, she made it exceedingly difficult for any of them, especially Marcus.

She did not know their current location, but trees surrounded them in a secluded area. Lorelei could see many men around them. They were all dressed in similar attire, as if they were ready to go to battle. Stone buildings blended into the thick, treed landscape, trees that were no longer familiar to her. A large opening before the buildings showed a well-used field. A few men sparred in the distance, and wooden structures in the crude shapes of men were erected along the tree line that looked as if they received much abuse from various weapons.

All the men's attention was in some degree focused on her presence. She noticed that not one of them was a female, and a chill racked her as fear climbed across her skin and settled in her heart. Her eyes fell on Ajax, and the strange feelings he stirred within her flared, causing her heart to race. It was a mixture of fear and fascination that she found confusing. Her attention always seemed attuned to him above all others. Ajax was conversing with a gray-haired man; they threw a quick glance in her direction before they disappeared into one of the buildings.

Lorelei was tied and at the mercy of these men who eyed her like she was dinner. Luckily, no one had approached since Marcus tied her. She could take the stares as long as they kept their distance. Lorelei tried to remain strong, but thoughts of her mother and her home soon brought tears to her eyes. She watched the tears fall upon her dress.

Night fell, and the men disappeared into the buildings. She shivered against the tight ropes that bit into her skin, until exhaustion claimed her, despite her discomfort. Not even fear could keep her awake, or the hollow ache of hunger in her stomach after the arduous day of being pushed to her limits.

Lorelei was roused from her sleep when rough hands grabbed her. "What are you doing?" she gasped as she opened her eyes to Marcus.

"Moving you." He dripped menace.

"I'm not going anywhere with you!" Lorelei fought his attempt to untie the ropes from the tree. Fear forced unnatural strength in her as she struggled against him. She landed a blow with her knee that caused him to recoil with a strained breath. Lorelei watched him closely as he recovered. His eyes narrowed on her, bringing himself up to his intimidating full stance. She tried to move away from him, but the ropes only reminded her that she was at his mercy.

Marcus raised his hand quicker than she could register before the sting of the impact burned her eyes and caused her to cry out. "Have it your way, *witch*. You can spend the night tied to this tree." He turned and stalked away from her. Even though her face throbbed with pain and she shivered against the cold, hungry and completely helpless, she still felt relief at being distanced from Marcus. Lorelei tried to stay awake in fear of his return, but eventually, as the night went on, she drifted to sleep again.

Fear jolted her awake the next morning. She wrestled quickly from the hold of her dreams at the first notice of consciousness. When she opened her eyes, her body was alert now that fatigue no longer claimed her. She was grateful that she was alone as she took in her surroundings. Sometime during the night someone had laid a blanket over her. She was puzzled by the gesture, because she thought these men only wanted to do her harm. She was grateful for the cover; her bare legs would no longer be on display to all the prying eyes.

Someone rounded the corner of the nearest building. He tried to avoid making eye contact with her but couldn't resist quick, curious glances. He busied himself collecting water from of one of numerous barrels that lined the side of the building. He was considerably younger than most of the others. His youth still gave him the full cheeks of a boy, but his body was fast approaching the height of a man, though his limbs had yet to broaden with thick, muscled strength.

The sound of the splashing water called to her thirsty body. She craved the soothing liquid upon her dry tongue. "Please..." The boy's attention quickly turned to her plea. "Water?" Her words were as dry as her throat.

He stared back uncertainly before he looked around to see who else was within sight. When he determined they were alone, he picked up his bucket and ladle and walked slowly toward her. She could tell he was nervous as he neared.

"Oliver!" someone called out to him in a demanding tone. The boy was startled by the approaching man and set the water bucket down quickly, causing water to slosh over the side and quickly begin seeping into the dry earth. "Don't go near her," the man called in warning.

"No..." Lorelei whimpered, seeing the water dissipate before her. She tried to reach out toward the wet soil, despite her hands being securely bound behind her. The boy stared in amazement as the water was pulled out of the soil and moved as if running downhill toward Lorelei's outstretched fingers. When the water reached her fingers, she sighed with relief as the water seeped into her welcoming flesh. It did not provide as much respite as it would upon her lips, but it was enough. When she opened her eyes, she looked into the terrified face of the wide-eyed boy, Oliver. His chestnut hair was in disarray, and his eyes matched it almost perfectly in color.

"You *are* a witch." Oliver spoke barely above a whisper, dropping the ladle into the bucket. Even though he spoke the words, he did not have an accusation in his eyes. He seemed more curious than anything.

"No... no." Lorelei defended herself. "Please. I just want to go home." She had always been what she was and never questioned it. Until now she had thought herself like everyone else, but the look on the boy's face told otherwise. Her mother had read her books that told of witches, but they were evil and menacing. She was nothing like the stories her mother had told her, but then she was beginning to question everything. All her mother had ever told her was that she was a miracle and special. Now, tied to the tree under the accusing eyes of her captors, she felt anything but. "Please help me. If you untie me, I will run away, and you will never see me again." She pleaded. If anyone here would have the heart to hear her out, it would be this boy, still untainted by the hardness of life. The innocence and trust of his youth still lingered in his eyes.

"What's going on here?" The man who had been calling to Oliver peered over his shoulder. He had dark eyes, almost black, his skin tanned and scarred from what looked like a violent past. A long beard covered his chin, and his ebony hair was pulled back in a tie, exposing his thick, muscled neck.

"I... I... she was thirsty," Oliver stuttered. He was obviously still shocked by what Lorelei had done.

"Leave her for Crewe to deal with. You have chores, and Crewe is looking for you." The man dismissed Oliver with a wave.

Oliver shot Lorelei a quick look before taking off hurriedly. The man looked down at her before he grunted and turned away, stalking off but grabbing the bucket in the process.

Lorelei didn't know when she drifted off to sleep again; the warm sun had lulled her with a false sense of security. She awoke suddenly when someone touched her leg. She could feel the exploring touch as it pulled her from sleep. When she opened her eyes, two men were crouched in front of her. "Hey, beautiful," one of them cooed when he noticed her eyes open. "We were curious if you felt as good as you looked."

Lorelei tried to scramble to a sitting position, kicking his hand away from her in the process. The other man grabbed her foot and held it tight against the ground. The blanket fell away completely from her legs in the struggle, causing a hunger to fire up in their ravenous eyes. "Leave me alone," she cried out.

"Stand down." Both men stilled when Ajax's voice bellowed from behind them. They pulled back immediately.

One of them defended their actions. "We were just having a little fun. We were not going to hurt the girl."

"I believe you have things to do. I suggest you do them." Ajax avoided looking at Lorelei as he addressed the men. It was obvious he had great sway over these men; they looked ashamed as they listened respectfully to him. At Ajax's dismissal, the men turned on their heels and left without another word. Ajax was powerful; she could feel it in the energy around him. The others listened to him. Even though she knew she should fear this man, it did not stop the yearning to be near him. The desire to drink in his features overrode her logic. It was as if a part of her that was buried deep was awakening and was drawn to him.

Ajax pulled a knife from the sheath in his belt. Lorelei cringed from him as he leaned down. "Please don't kill me… I just want to go home." She pulled against the ropes, her skin already raw and sore. He leaned down closer to her; she could smell his spicy musk, but now with a hint of soap. Lorelei could not stop herself from pulling his scent deep into her, savoring her newfound appreciation for the smell of this intriguing man. She cursed herself for the strange thought when she should be concentrating on the fact that he was a threat to her life. He had taken her from her home, from her mother.

He stilled before looking up at her. The breath died on Lorelei's lips as she looked into his eyes. She instantly became lost in their mesmerizing blue, and the vibrant white ring that encompassed his pupils was uniquely breathtaking. Ajax moved the hand holding the knife, drawing it closer to her. A whimper escaped her lips as she sobered from her once again drifting thoughts.

"I'm not a witch. If I were, I would be a horrible one anyway. I cannot cast any spells or make potions, so I would be no harm to anyone. If you let me go I will just run away. You will never see me again. I will promise you. No curses or spells… or whatever you think I will do." A tear escaped from Lorelei's eye as she pleaded with him.

His eyes searched hers for a brief moment. He was so close that if her hands weren't bound she would have a hard time keeping them from reaching out and running her fingers through the thick chestnut hair that framed his chiselled face. Fear of what he intended with the knife was mixed with appreciation of the heat that enveloped her with his nearness. Thoughts were becoming hard to process as her gaze fell upon his lips. She felt like she would burst from the conflicting emotions that struggled within her. With one look from this man, she was rendered breathless.

A swift motion with Ajax's hand sliced away the ropes that angrily gripped her flesh; Lorelei barely had time to register the movement. The relief was immediate when the ropes fell away. She instinctively brought her wrists up to examine the aggravated red marks.

Ajax reached up and gently took hold of her arm. He examined her injured skin. His touch was gentle, and the contact caused her skin to heat. She could feel color bloom across her cheeks. She lost sight of all logic when she fell under his strange temptation. Lorelei found it overwhelming that a simple touch could send her body into overdrive. She wondered if he enjoyed the contact as much as she. A sigh of appreciation passed her lips as she took pleasure in his explorative caress. His eyes flashed to hers before he abruptly dropped her hand. "They're only shallow abrasions. You will live." His voice was curt. She felt a twinge of disappointment. Maybe he was not affected after all.

"Are you letting me go?" Lorelei looked up with hopeful eyes.

"No." He stood up and pulled her up with him onto her feet. His grip was firm on her upper arm as he guided her to move with him, toward the largest of the buildings. His quick change of demeanor confused her. For a moment he looked at her with what she could only describe as need. She felt the strange desire heating her own core, but now he was as cold as a winter's night.

"What are you going to do with me?" Lorelei tried to dig her feet into the earth to gain leverage from his hold. He was too strong and her struggles gained her no ground, but she continued to fight regardless. "You can't do this... Let me go... You're an evil... evil man... preying on an innocent girl!" Lorelei yelled.

He pulled her close, leaning down into her. "*Innocent?*" His eyes narrowed. "Hardly," he scoffed and continued pulling her along.

"What is that supposed to mean!" Lorelei kicked him in the back of the knee. For a brief second she thought she might have gained the upper hand, but his recovery was swift and his dark eyes were humorless when they turned upon her. He practically growled at her, and she shrank back away as far as she could.

"You would be wise not to piss me off!" Ajax said, his face drawing close to hers.

"I told you I'm not a witch. Let me go home." She tried to twist her arm free.

"You're bloody difficult is what you are. If you want to live to see another day, hold your tongue." Ajax continued to pull her along with his steps.

"*Difficult!* *You* kidnapped me, brought me to this horrible place, and tied me to a tree for men to feel free to help themselves to. I think I am acting like any normal person would. As far as I know, you are the *witch.*"

"You are out of line." Stopping, he turned on her again.

"Likewise." Lorelei elbowed Ajax in the side. The impact didn't even register on his features as he looked down his nose at her. His eyes were dark under the shadow of his scowl. He was a man trained to be a weapon, like all the other men here who fashioned their bodies into hard flesh ready for battle. Looking into his eyes now, she realized it probably wasn't a good idea to aggravate someone who could literally break her in half. They were locked in a staring match, and she refused to look away. She would not let him see her fear, because she needed to hold it deep inside. She was not ready for this world and didn't know how to protect herself from men like Ajax, but she knew that if they knew she was afraid, they would use it against her.

A throat cleared; Lorelei looked up to see many eyes on her. She hadn't noticed anyone else, and suddenly her determined step faltered. Ajax wrapped his hand around her upper arm and directed her through a doorway that the other men had disappeared through, leading her into an open room. They stood before a group of men all as dangerously cut as the rest of them.

Lorelei mindlessly grabbed hold of Ajax's hand, squeezing in search of comfort, surprising both Ajax and herself. She quickly drew her hand back when she realized what she had done, silently cursing her action. Ajax's dark eyes cast an intense look upon her, rubbing the hand she had touched across his stomach as if trying to wipe away the memory of it. The reality caused her chest to constrict painfully. She did not want Ajax to know that despite his hatred for her, he gave her a strange sense of comfort amidst the chaos. It was as if her body did not agree that he was a real threat to her, even though her mind thought better of it. His nearness, although it caused her emotions to erupt in turmoil, still caused a thrilling heat to brew deep within her soul. Ajax stepped aside to put distance between them, abandoning her in front of the panel of men. She now stood completely exposed before judging eyes. She was terrified but refused to let these men break her. She would not cry, standing tall before them.

A man whose hair was peppered white and skin tanned from many years of work underneath the relentless sun sat at the table before her. He was surrounded by the group of men silently assessing her. The only other man she recognized was Marcus, whose eyes she avoided meeting. The older man seemed to be deep in consideration as the other men looked to him for counsel, running his hands over his coarse face and then rubbing his chin thoughtfully. He demanded the respect the others bestowed him; it was reflected in the way they awaited his lead.

"Tell me what you were doing in the Black Forest of Verlas." His voice was as deep and imposing as his appearance.

"The Black Forest?" Lorelei found herself repeating the words. They felt strange in her mouth and did not suit the home that she grew up in.

"We should just burn her now. Why the questions?" said one of the men, who had long black hair tied back from his face to reveal a narrow jaw and sharp nose.

"I agree. She's obviously a witch. Look at her!" another shouted. His face was fuller, with sun-bleached hair cut short. "We don't need any more proof."

"Enough!" The gray-haired man responded to his men's outburst before turning his attention back to her. "My men tell me they found

you in those woods, and I would like to know why you were there."
His eyes narrowed.

"I don't know it by that name, but it's my home."

"No one goes in that forest, let alone lives there. Let's try this again,
shall we? What were you doing in those woods?" His voice took on a
threatening note, and Lorelei knew that conclusions had already been
determined. She could see it in everyone's eyes.

"*Your* men were there," Lorelei pointed out; she couldn't help the
defiance that slipped into her voice.

"My men are not like *most* men." The gray-haired man raised his
brows with an arrogant tilt of his head.

"Then I guess I'm not like *most* women," Lorelei retorted, curling
her fingers into fists at her sides.

"Precisely my point." The man stood up, his chair scraping pierc-
ingly along the floor.

"No. No. *No*, you will not make the assumption like everyone else
that I'm some witch you found in the middle of the woods, because
I will tell you one thing true, if I were a witch I would have already
cursed every single one of you." Lorelei looked around the room at
everyone, driving her point. "Especially *you*!" She pointed at Marcus,
making eye contact with him for the first time since she entered the
room. "And Scowlface too." She pointed at Ajax, who stood off to the
side with his arms crossed. "And you too, Gray!"

Lorelei retracted her finger that she waved in the older man's face.
He was obviously the leader of the bunch of seasoned men that stood
before her. Her confidence wavered again as she took in all the men
staring at her with blank faces, as if she had suddenly turned blue
and sprouted wings. She realized she hadn't just crossed the line; she'd
leapt over it, and she wondered what punishment would befall her for
her outburst. "I apologize. That was rude." Lorelei ran her hands down
the front of her dress. "It is just that … I was taken from my home
forcefully, and all I was doing was minding my own business."

Then something happened that Lorelei did not expect. The man
she had named Gray started laughing. "Well, you certainly act like you
were raised in a forest." The others in the room seemed to fall at ease
as well. All of their stoic faces fell into tranquil grins except for Ajax's;
he stood just as rigid, with his jaw clenched and his eyes narrowed in
suspicion.

"Gray, huh?" The man ran his fingers through his untrimmed gray hair. "I like it." His smile suddenly softened his features, brightening his eyes. Lorelei could see a hint of his handsome youth shine through, now that his grave expression had melted away.

"Crewe?" Ajax stepped forward, addressing the man she had labeled Gray.

"Jax?" Crewe answered, a smile still gracing his features.

"She has cast a spell on you." Ajax set his accusing eyes on Lorelei. "She cannot be trusted."

Before Lorelei could put her thoughts to words, Crewe spoke. "The girl has assured us that she is not a witch." He turned toward the other men in the room. "Until we can prove otherwise, there is no need to act further on this matter." He arose from his chair and rounded the table to approach Lorelei.

"I must admit I do feel a little bewitched…" Crewe ran his hand through his hair like a nervous youth. It seemed so out of character for a man of his stature. "It has been awhile since I have set eyes on a woman, and I must admit, never upon one of such beauty." He presented his arm for her to take. "You must be hungry, dear."

Lorelei looked up at Ajax's glare; his teeth were clenched against words he struggled to hold back. She could tell he was at odds with trying to be respectful of Crewe's position and voicing his concerns on the matter. She wondered what Ajax's handsome features looked like if they were relaxed, with a smile upon his full lips. She wanted him to look at her pleasantly, like all the other men suddenly were, instead of this harsh, accusing look. Her eyes were drawn to Ajax's mouth, where she lingered, and curiosity at what he would taste like filled her. Ajax reached up and ran his hand over his mouth, breaking her trance. Lorelei tried to ignore all the thoughts that had taken over and turned her focus back toward Crewe, who awaited her.

"Yes, thank you." A blush stole over her skin from her wandering thoughts of Ajax; she only hoped that no one could notice.

Lorelei was so overwhelmed by relief that she had suddenly been pardoned of her accused crime she didn't question everyone's strange behavior, although it didn't escape her mind. She hoped desperately that they didn't change their minds again. She was assaulted by uncertainty; the only thing that felt real was Ajax's condemning glare.

Chapter 6
CLARA

The sun was nearing its peak in the clear blue sky as midday approached. There was not a cloud to be seen, and not even an occasional bird was brave enough to pass through the unusually hot air.

"Clara!" She looked up at her father's call. She was rubbing the soft underbelly of a small chocolate-colored puppy that had been sniffing around the wheels of their carriage. The people who had gathered for the Sunday service had long since left and were going about their day, causing the crowds in the streets to thin considerably in the amount of time it took for her father to unload their carriage. He had to make a delivery to the bakery across the street from the church, which was the reason they were lingering in town longer than usual. Her baby brother had grown restless in her mother's arms, and she was no longer able to settle his cries.

"We are leaving." Her father motioned for her to return to her seat, wiping his brow with his handkerchief. They were all suffering from this heat that refused to break. "We need to get your brother home to bed before he brings us all to tears." His familiar warm laugh rang out. He always found a reason to be cheerful, even when things were at their darkest. It was one of the things Clara loved best about her father.

Clara whispered goodbye to the tiny puppy before she pulled herself up into the carriage beside her mother and fussy brother. Her father walked up to the horses to untie them from the hitching post. "Bryce!" Mr. Ingleby, the baker, pushed through the front door and called her father's attention back to their business. Clara had seen the man many times when she went on deliveries with her father. Every time she saw him he looked rounder than the last, if it was even possible. He was the largest man Clara had ever seen. His wide face was always unshaven and dusted in flour, but he had a laugh that always brought a smile to her face. He made the best cookies Clara had ever tasted, and he often let her sample them. She noticed that he passed a small, familiar package to her father, and her mouth watered in anticipation.

"Clara dear? Do you see your brother's bonnet?" Her mother shuffled around on the seat, looking for it. Everyone always said she looked just like her mother, the same brown eyes and hair that fell in tight curls down their backs. Lately, her mother had always looked tired, with dark shadows beneath her beautiful eyes. Her new brother hardly slept, and it was taking its toll on her. "No… maybe we left if in the church. I will go check," Clara offered helpfully, and she climbed out of the carriage.

Clara did everything she could to be helpful to her mother. Her father had entrusted her with that duty, and she tried her best to make him proud. She was becoming the age where people were starting to see her as a young lady and not a little girl anymore, and she was eager to prove what she could do.

Clara hurried across the street and up the stone steps of the grand stone church that stood taller than the other buildings around it. She pushed open the large wooden door to reveal the quiet stillness of the empty altar. It was the first time she had been in the church without a crowd all around her.

Clara could see the particles of dust dancing in the colored light that shone in from the stained glass windows; it was magical and brought a smile to her face as she reached up to gaze upon the colors cast over her skin. The windows were truly remarkable, stretching as tall as the walls, reaching up to the roof. In the stillness she could truly appreciate the art upon the ceiling, depictions from the Bible that were breathtaking in their scope. Running her hands over the ends of the pews, she came to the place they had sat in for Mass. A small white piece of cloth on the floor caught her eye, and she smiled brightly. "There you are." Clara collected the bonnet. She and her mother had spent hours making it in preparation for her brother's birth. Clara's mother had taught her to sew and embroider, and it was a skill they both enjoyed.

A sound pulled Clara's attention to the front of the church. She stilled to listen but was only met by silence. As she turned to leave, the sound of a muffled cry met her again, and this time she knew that it was not her imagination. Her feet led her to the sound, past the altar and toward a hallway that she had not ventured down before. Her heart raced, but she knew she couldn't walk away if someone needed help. "Hello." She couldn't make her voice rise above a whisper; she didn't even know if it really left her lips. She ran her fingers over the wall as she continued down the narrow hall. She came to a door that was left ajar and leaned down to peek into the room. What she saw terrified her, and she gasped, falling into the door.

Two faces darted toward Clara as she tried to gain her footing in the darkened room. The priest who had given the sermon was disrobed, with a woman sprawled out upon his desk. Her naked body was pressed against the wooden surface. Clara had initially thought the woman was being hurt, but the look in her eyes was not that of a victim. Clara recognized the woman immediately as Lady Mansforth. She always sat at the front of the church on Sundays with her husband in their expensive clothes. She had overheard her mother gush over this very woman. Her fine clothes and fancy perfumes were apparently a source of envy for other woman in the community, but Clara had never paid much attention to her. It was always their son that had drawn Clara's eye. He was a few years older, and she had always thought him handsome. He sat with his parents and his sister every Sunday, and just that morning, when she passed him, she noticed he was watching her and held her eye longer than necessary. She had barely been able to contain the butterflies throughout the service. Any remnants of that feeling were now obliterated by the fear that stilled her blood.

"I thought you locked the door," Lady Mansforth seethed. She grabbed for the clothes that she had discarded on the floor. Clara started to back away, but the priest ordered her to stop. He pulled on his robe and made for Clara. Tears fell from Clara's eyes as she tried to move her feet, but fear had rooted her to the floor. When his hand closed around her arm, she gasped at the pressure. He pulled Clara down the hallway, out toward the altar. Clara didn't completely understand what she'd walked in on, but she knew that she had every right to fear the consequences.

The priest lowered his gaze to Clara. His eyes were fierce as his fingers dug into her skin. "Do not breathe a word of this to anyone, do you understand?" A sob escaped Clara's lips in response. "Swear it to God on this altar that you will not."

The front door opened and an unfamiliar man in a tan suit walked in, followed by two women who froze at the sight of the priest and Clara. "What's going on here?" the man asked with an alert tone.

"Witch!" Lady Mansforth screamed out in a panic. "She's a witch. We saw her chanting on the altar in her devil tongue."

Both of the women with the man gasped in horror as their eyes fell on Clara. "Is this true, Reverend?" the man asked.

The priest paused for a moment, and Clara's eyes pleaded with him not to confirm the woman's lies. "I fear it is. This child has been swayed by the devil." The priest nearly choked on his lies. He let go of Clara's arm and proceeded to mark the sign of the cross with words of prayer.

Clara's tears fell freely. "See... she is pained by the words of the Lord," Lady Mansforth cried out, waving at Clara.

"No, please..." Clara cried. "I'm not a witch... They were..."

"Enough! Do not listen to her, she tells the devil's lies," Lady Mansforth cried out. Both of the women fled the church. Clara looked back at Lady Mansforth and wondered why her mother had ever envied this horrid woman. The priest looked pale as he stared back at Clara. She wondered if it was regret that shone through his troubled eyes, or fear of getting caught.

The door of the church reopened almost immediately after the woman left, and numerous men walked in. "Is it true?" A deep voice thundered through the church from the man leading the others. They were looking at Clara as if she were a criminal.

"Yes. Clara Barwicke is guilty of witchcraft," Lady Mansforth declared. "Reverend Benedict and I both witnessed the display of the devil's work here in our very chapel." Her voice took on a steely tone as she brought her hand to her chest. It was the first time Lady Mansforth had uttered Clara's name. Until this moment Clara didn't realize that the noblewoman even knew who she was, but now she wanted to snatch it from the woman's lips. She never wanted to hear her family's name come from her filthy, evil mouth.

"You will come with us." The man grabbed Clara's shoulder and shoved her down the steps toward the aisle. Clara barely kept her feet beneath her as the reality of the situation closed in on her. She knew what happened to people accused of witchcraft. Her parents didn't speak of it much, but children from school whispered of girls being hung or burned. These men would not hear her out as they directed her out of the church, ignoring her protests. She obeyed their order because she did not know what else to do. A man held open the door with his narrowed eyes upon her; no one had ever looked at her like that before. Her legs trembled as she descended the stairs toward the street.

"What is the meaning of this?" Clara's father's voice called out severely, cutting through all the other noise. Clara looked up as he was stalking toward them with an expression he had never worn before.

"Father!" Clara called. Relief washed over her, and she moved toward him, but something hit her hard on the back of her shoulders, and the force of it caused her to fall to the ground. Clara gasped from the pain that radiated through her body. She choked on the dirt that her face was pressed against as she struggled for breath. When she was roughly pulled from the ground, she could see her father struggling against numerous men who held him. A deafening high-pitched sound assaulted her before finally the voices and sounds around her slowly came back into focus; her father's voice screaming for her and for the men to release her. She could hear her mother's screams above all else. She wanted to go to them, but she would not be released.

"Your daughter has been found guilty of witchcraft and will be sentenced." Clara didn't know who spoke. She could only see her father as he received the words and watched his face fall with realization. He struggled harder against the men, even when blood poured from his face and his eye began to swell shut, but it was no use. He couldn't get to her as they forced Clara into the back of an enclosed carriage, shutting the door on her and leaving her in darkness except for the tiny rays that leaked in from the seams. Her own cries echoed in the shell around her, and the uproar outside the dark carriage filled her head.

Chapter 7
BROM

King Brom Floros sat at the head of the grand dining table that ran the expanse of the lavish room. His wife Peronell, the queen, had spent a vast amount of his treasury to turn this room into a piece of art to be adored and envied by the people who had the luxury of dining with the royal family. He did not share her taste in finery, but he had learned long ago that he would pay gravely if he did not entertain her wishes. She was a woman who demanded the best, and as a king he could provide just that; she reminded him of that frequently.

Looking at her now, by his side conversing with their dinner guests, he wondered when he had become unmoved by her appeal. He could see what the people praised her for, her timeless beauty that enraptured everyone who laid eyes upon her. Though when he looked into her eyes he saw what no one else even dared admit: she was heartless and as cruel as she was beautiful. He couldn't remember the last time he had bedded his wife, couldn't remember the last quiet moment they shared together as a couple, and wasn't even sure when their marriage became the façade it was now. He tried to remember a time when she occupied his thoughts in a way that did not stir anger, when she would be the only one that called to his body, but those days were but a memory in another life, long forgotten.

"My lord?" Peronell batted her eyes gracefully, a demonstration that was lost on him. He much preferred the heavy lids of the whores that had occupied his bed of late. He brought his focus back to the conversation before him. He hadn't realized his thoughts wandered so far from the words that were being exchanged in front of him.

Brom noticed everyone's attention was focused on him. "My apologies, Lord Mansforth, Lady Mansforth." King Brom ran his hand over his bearded face. "My mind betrays me; it refuses to let an old man rest from matters of the kingdom."

"No apologies necessary, Your Majesty. We understand the weight that you carry, especially in these times with the witch hunt creating such a stir amid the people," Lord Henry Mansforth assured him.

"Please call me Brom. We are among friends here, are we not?" Brom slapped the table playfully. "Let us escape our titles for the benefit of this meal, shall we?" His smile broadened as he noticed Peronell's shoulders tighten. He knew how she preferred to hold people's titles over them. The Mansforths were luminaries among the people. Their family had held title for many years as one of the largest landowners in the kingdom and dedicated members of the church. As of late, Lord Mansforth had also held an important position in the political force driving the eradication of witches from the kingdom.

Peronell had her sights set on their daughter since she had come of age. The young Lady Mariam would be well received by the people as a match for Prince Arthur; she was young and meek and could be moulded well to perform her duties to the kingdom. Young Mariam would be another puppet for Peronell to manipulate to create her illusion of perfection for the people to worship. Brom did, however, have to appreciate how well his wife played the game; she was a master of deception and manipulation.

Mariam sat quietly at the table, with only occasional glances at Arthur, who sat across from the young beauty with a bored expression. Beside Mariam sat her brother, an aspiring member of the community shadowing his father in the path of politics. He was young but already showed an interest and intellect in the field. He was on the path to earning the title he would one day hold.

"If you promise to do the same." Henry Mansforth's shoulders relaxed as he took comfort in the dismissal of formalities. The women, on the other hand, were reluctant to follow suit.

"Tell me, Henry, how are the trial preparations proceeding here in Falls Landing? I am sure you have heard of the uproar in Bedford with the riots that have been breaking out." Brom leaned back in his chair as dinner was served. "They are using the trials as an excuse to drive a thorn in my side."

"As you know, we have had the few minor instances, especially with Teller and his followers still at large, but other than that, things are remaining orderly to date. Trials have been proceeding as scheduled, and I feel that we are making good progress."

"That is good to hear." Brom leaned in, and the aroma of the food called to his empty stomach. He pushed on, fully aware that no one could begin to eat without his lead. "Teller's influence among the people has certainly caused its difficulties, but measures are being implemented to remedy the issue. As you know, I have been increasing our numbers here in Falls Landing to prevent similar disturbances and outbreaks that have occurred in Bedford. The threat holds that we might have a battle in our very near future, and I need to assure we have the numbers. Teller's resistance grows. We cannot lose order, and steps need to be taken to ensure this. Of course, we need land to house all these additional men and train them; we have currently surpassed our limits."

Henry was an intelligent man, and realization dawned on his features. Not that Brom believed Henry would refuse his request. "Done. The land will be provided for as long as necessary to the kingdom," Henry offered graciously. They both knew well that when it came down to it, he could not refuse the king, especially with the promise of his daughter's position hovering in the balance.

"Waltham will be in touch to make arrangements this very evening." Brom's attention was drawn to the food, now that he had accomplished his objective of the meeting. "Let us eat."

"Yes, enough business. Let's enjoy our meal." Peronell smiled brightly as she reached over to cover Brom's hand with hers in a loving gesture. To the guests she was every bit the loving wife she portrayed, but Brom knew differently. Without the eyes of the guests, she would never bring herself to touch him. It was for show, and she did it well. Brom flipped his hand and grabbed hold of her fingers, discreetly squeezing with more force than necessary.

"Yes, I agree. Please, dear, enlighten us with a conversation fitting of this good meal," Brom encouraged. Peronell pulled her hand gracefully from his.

"Certainly." She smiled sweetly toward her guests. "The time draws near when Arthur is expected to take a wife, and the date has been set when this will take place. We will be hosting a ball to announce Arthur's betrothal. In light of the recent events, we believe it will give the people something to look forward to in these dark times."

Brom took note of Arthur's body language, his rigid shoulders and clenched fists. He could comfortably draw the conclusion that like him, this is the first that his son had heard of these plans for a ball. "I am to take my position leading the men that are to take order against the revolt, Mother. The timing—"

"Could not be more perfect," Peronell interjected. "There is no reason that you cannot make your appearance with the royal army as well as attend your duties as the heir of this kingdom."

"Make an appearance?" Arthur dared to use an insolent tone toward his mother.

"Your mother is right, Arthur. People will be expecting your betrothal to be announced, and in these times especially, we must retain the order of things." Brom reluctantly agreed with his wife. She might be a lot of things, but she was effectual in her position as queen above all. She was born to wield the power she held.

"Excuse me. I find I no longer have an appetite." Arthur stood, his breath forcibly controlled. He obviously did not like the recent turn of events.

"Very well, you are excused." Brom dismissed him with a wave.

Arthur's steps faded into the distance of the hallway before anyone spoke. "Please forgive my son. He is so passionate about rectifying the current disorder of our people."

"Something we can all appreciate." Henry smiled understandingly.

"Under the circumstances of the current situation, I would like to extend the invitation to have your daughter stay in the castle under the watchful eye of our guards. She would receive the best of care, I assure you. With you so kindly offering your land, it's the least we can do in return." Peronell's offer brightened the faces of the Mansforths. The look Henry gave his wife, Rose, was not missed by Brom and the queen. It was the news they were hoping for. Even Mariam's face had with a blush of excitement as she remained obediently poised. Peronell had unofficially announced Mariam as the preferred choice for Arthur's betrothal. Having her stay in the castle would give the people indication of the news to come.

Rose expressed her gratitude. "It would be an honor."

"I am so pleased to hear." Peronell leaned back in her chair, her meal almost completely untouched. She raised her glass of red wine. Brom watched the smile curve her full red lips. "To the good future of our kingdom." Everyone else followed suit in the toast.

A servant approached the table. "Excuse me, Your Majesty. Forgive my interruption. Commander Waltham requests your attention and says the matter is urgent." King Brom turned his attention from his dinner to address the development. Before he could inquire further, Commander Fredrick Waltham appeared at the entrance of the dining room.

"Your Majesty, I would not have interrupted if the matter was not urgent." Commander Waltham was dressed in his full armor, having just left his duties in the field. His height and powerful presence, not to mention celebrated skill with the blade, made him the exceptional soldier he was. He awaited the king's attention with his helmet tucked under his arm.

"Pardon me, duties call." Brom stood and excused himself, leaving Peronell to entertain their guests. He and Waltham went toward the king's private study.

The large wooden doors of Brom's private conference room closed, giving them privacy to speak freely. Unlike the rest of the castle, the room was unadorned, bare, and crude. A large wooden table filled the center of the floor, covered in scrolls and books, tools used for battle strategies. It was a room that he did not let Peronell mark with her design. It was his private room, and it was in this state of undress that he preferred it, bare of all unessential things. The only indulgence upon the wall was the head of the first stag he ever shot when he was a mere boy. It was a prized trophy that marked his love of hunting. Brom turned to his commander-in-chief. "What news?"

"A girl was accused of witchery earlier today here in Falls Landing, a young girl by the name of Clara Barwicke."

"Barwicke?" Brom questioned the familiarity of the name.

"Bryce Barwicke's daughter, Your Majesty."

The recognition was immediate. He was one of the largest grain farmers in Falls Landing. He held no official title, but he was well respected among the people and held considerable sway among the commoners.

"What were the circumstances?"

"It was actually Lady Mansforth who made the accusation. Her Grace and Reverend Benedict witnessed the act."

"Bloody hell. Is there no end to this?" Brom raked his hands over his bearded face. "What of it. Tell me all."

"There is commotion in the streets. There had been a few isolated instances that we have been able to contain until recently. Barwicke has many supporters who feel that the girl is innocent." Waltham paused before continuing. "One of the soldiers was found dead in the town square this evening with the words 'Free Clara' carved into his chest."

Brom let the information sink in for a moment before he angrily swiped his hand across his table, sending the contents soaring to the floor in disarray. "By Satan's hairy arse," Brom exploded. He took a moment as he braced himself on the table. The witch hunt that was sweeping through his kingdom was a splinter he could not remove.

"Was Bryce Barwicke taken into custody?"

"We have yet to locate him. He has not returned to his home. I have men stationed there. Though we know he is not acting alone, so we are questioning anyone who knows the Barwickes."

"Any leads?" Brom pushed his weight off the table, bringing himself back to his full height. He was taller than average in his own right, but his commander still towered over him.

"Nothing is confirmed, Your Majesty. We can only work with what we have. I fear we might not be able to make any progress until they make their next move."

Brom hit the table with his fist. "*Bloody hell.* More traitors, and on my doorstep no less. I do not need this right now."

The door swung open, drawing their attention. "My queen." Waltham bowed with the arrival of Queen Peronell.

Brom shot her an irritated glance to show he was not amused by her presence. Peronell sauntered in the room, turning her nose up at the mess that was now scattered upon the stone floor. She ran her slender finger along the table's surface, noting the unkempt state the room.

"I wish a few moments of the commander's time to go over some security concerns I have." Her sing-song voice was buttered for the commander's benefit.

The commander looked to the king for direction. "What of our guests?" Brom inquired with irritation toward Peronell.

"They left," she answered shortly.

Brom turned back to his commander. "Keep me posted."

"Yes, Your Majesty." The commander nodded respectfully before he left to attend to the queen's request.

Chapter 8
LORELEI

A large fire licked at the thick, tarry sky. The stars were hidden as the night covered them like dark, murky waters. The heat from the open pit kept the chill of the evening at bay as Lorelei sat on a wooden bench, keeping her eyes on the flames instead of meeting the many eyes on her. Crewe had been called away, leaving her alone in a sea of men who were unsure of what to make of her presence. The few times she dared to let her eyes wander, they immediately fell upon Ajax, whose gaze followed her like a predator observes its prey. She could not ignore his presence, and it was a struggle to keep her attention focused elsewhere. She glanced at the forest, wondering how much of a head start she could get before she was pursued, if at all, but the look on Ajax's face indicated he was on to her plan. It didn't matter, anyway; Lorelei had no idea where she was. She didn't know in what direction home lay.

She turned when someone sat beside her. She found herself looking into Oliver's youthful brown eyes and was awash with relief. Lorelei felt a strange connection with Oliver; he held information that would turn everyone against her again, and yet he remained quiet. She could tell he was nervous by the way he fidgeted with his plate. Lorelei looked down at her own plate, untouched. Her stomach was knotted, and she tried to coax herself to bring the food to her mouth; she needed her strength now more than ever, but she could not. She still found herself questioning the sudden change of heart toward her from Crewe and the other men. They had been eager to sacrifice her to the flames, and now she found herself enjoying the fire with the comfort of a meal. It was surreal, and she expected Crewe to have a change of heart at any moment and come storming back, sword in hand.

"Thank you for earlier," Lorelei whispered to Oliver. He smiled. Being around him made everything more bearable.

"All I did was spill water, very clumsy of me." Oliver shrugged.

"You were the first to show me kindness. Thank you." Lorelei found herself matching his easy smile. It felt natural in his presence, and she started to release some of the fear that she held on to so tightly.

"Oliver." He officially offered his name as he stretched out his legs, getting comfortable. Lorelei laid her hand on his, and he brought it to his lips in a friendly kiss.

"Lorelei." She offered with a smile. "Why were you going to help me when you thought I was a..." She trailed off when she thought it would probably not be wise not to say that word with so many ears around them.

"Whatever or whoever you are, Lorelei, you don't seem evil to me... I have seen others killed because someone pointed a finger and claimed they were a witch, when they had done nothing wrong. They were no more witches than I am, and even if they were they didn't deserve to be killed. Let's just say I believe that people should not be condemned simply because of who they are." Lorelei noticed the pained look upon Oliver's face; something about their conversation seemed to stir painful memories.

One of the other men sat down on the other side of Oliver, grabbing the bread from his plate while Oliver was distracted. "Hey! That's mine," Oliver complained as he watched the older man devour his bread. Unlike Oliver's smooth, clean features, this man had a crooked nose and dark eyes, giving him a dangerous look.

"Exactly." The man smiled over his full mouth. "What are you going to do about it?" he taunted playfully, but Oliver did not appreciate the man's humor.

Lorelei picked up the bread from her own plate and placed it on Oliver's.

"I cannot take your food." Oliver raised his hands.

"Please. I am not hungry," Lorelei said reassuringly.

"Well... If you insist." Oliver smiled with gratitude. He couldn't have made the bread disappear any faster if he had used magic. He definitely had an appetite that rivaled the rest of the full-grown men.

"You do not seem so evil yourself. In fact, I can say with certainty that you are my favorite person here."

Oliver's face lit up. "Did you hear that?" He raised his voice, turning to the men nearby. "She likes me best." His grin was refreshing and contagious, and it made her think of her mother. She must be out of her mind with worry not knowing where Lorelei was. Wherever this road led her, she would do everything in her power to make it back home. She knew one thing for sure: she wouldn't let her emotions get the best of her. She needed to stay focused, a thought that seemed reasonable until she looked over and locked gazes with Ajax. Her stomach tightened as she took in his looming presence. When it came to Ajax, focus might truly be impossible.

"Am I still a prisoner?" Lorelei questioned, pulling her eyes from Ajax.

Oliver looked at her, his smile falling from his face. "Of a sort." He shrugged. "People are not supposed to know about this camp. They won't let you just walk out of here on your own, with the knowledge of how to find it."

"*He* definitely looks like he has no intention of letting me walk out of here." Lorelei nodded toward Ajax, watching them from the other side of the fire. "I think he is still on the side of burning me at the stake."

Oliver thoughtfully looked over at Ajax. "He's cautious... You scare him."

"*Scare* him? Not likely. He hates me passionately is more precise." Lorelei sighed, pulling tighter the oversized shirt that was wrapped around her shoulders. One of the men had offered it to her earlier when she shivered against with the cool of the setting sun. She was grateful for the cover.

"I do not think anyone could ever hate you, Lorelei."

"Tell that to the room of men that practically beheaded me earlier with their condemning glares."

Oliver kicked at the dirt. "You confused them is all. You are unexpected and..."

"And what?" Lorelei encouraged when Oliver paused.

"Unnaturally beautiful," Oliver offered hesitantly, raising his shoulders.

"Unnaturally beautiful? I don't even know what that even means."

"You must know what you look like, and you have the most unusual eyes I have ever seen." Oliver's eyebrows raised in surprise when

Lorelei shook her head. "Come on? You never looked in a mirror?" he asked sceptically.

"I have seen my reflection in the water, but it was always moving and never very clear." Lorelei looked down at her hands, examining her fair flesh. It was nothing like the sun-darkened skin of the men around her; hers was pale and shimmered in the light. She had never noticed that before, but then again, she never had anything to compare it to. "I have always hoped I looked like my mother."

Oliver looked over at Ajax. Something unspoken passed between Oliver and Ajax when their eyes met. Oliver lowered his voice so only Lorelei could hear him. "Ajax does not hate you, Lorelei, but he is the best at what he does, and it is his nature to be suspicious. I have never seen him act like this before. Do you know he stayed up all night watching over you after Marcus left you? He will not admit it, but he has a strange fascination with you. It confuses him. I could tell he was angry with himself that he left you vulnerable to Marcus. He even punished the men who bothered you this morning. I overheard his heated words. I have never seen him that angry before."

"Do you know Ajax well?" Lorelei looked at Oliver's warm features, trying to ignore the illogical excitement that bubbled within her at the possibility that Ajax felt something for her other than hatred.

There was nothing similar between Oliver and Ajax. Everywhere Oliver was warm and open, Ajax was cold and mysterious. Oliver was the youngest of any that she had seen in the encampment. She hoped that he would always stay as untainted and open as he was now. She already missed his company, thinking of the time when they would part ways.

"I know him better than most. He is the best fighter any of us has ever seen, even better than Crewe, and that man has fought many battles in his lifetime. Ajax is like a shadow that comes and goes. He is actually the reason I am here. Without him there is no way I would even know this place exists, let alone have the opportunity to be here."

"Does he work for Crewe?" Lorelei thirsted for knowledge, anything that could paint a clearer picture of Ajax.

"Ajax? No." Oliver laughed.

"What is this place, anyway?" Lorelei scanned their surroundings.

"If you want to leave this place, then the less information you know, the better," Oliver warned her.

"Noted." She let all of her questions die on her tongue.

"Do you really live in the Black Forest?" Oliver asked with raised brows. She could tell that he too doubted the validity of the fact.

"Yes, I guess so. Until now it was the only place I had ever known. It was just me and my mother." Lorelei picked thoughtfully at the material of her dress. "Why does it seem so—"

"Unbelievable? Because it is. Everyone knows that the Black Forest is haunted. No one goes near it, well, except for Ajax and a few others. He fears nothing, or at least he did. The men travel through it because they know they will not be followed. Countless men have disappeared without a trace." Oliver's expression led her to believe that he too believed the tales of the forest being haunted.

"Guess it is good that I am not a man." Lorelei tried to lighten the conversation.

Oliver laughed and leaned over the bench, reaching for something tucked underneath. He pulled out a strange wooden box, carved smooth and round, with a handle and strings running the length of its body. Lorelei was drawn to the object as she watched Oliver handle it with care, caressing the strings with his fingertips. The others still lingering by the fire settled, knowing what to expect as she waited with anticipation. She thought she had seen something like it in a book.

"Is that a guitar?" Lorelei couldn't resist asking.

"It's a lute. Very similar, though." Oliver ran his fingers over the strings. "How does a girl that grows up in a forest know so much?

"My mother had books about everything, the world, and people. She loved to learn. When I was old enough, my mother and I read them together more times than we could count. It was our only connection to the outside world."

"Why did you stay?" Oliver frowned in question.

"My mother has always been ill and unable to travel for as long as I can remember. She feared many things and believed we were protected as long as we stayed in the safety of the forest." Lorelei reached out tentatively and gently touched the smooth wood. "I always hoped she was wrong about the world," she added sadly.

Oliver didn't push for more information. Instead he closed his eyes as he stroked the strings with his fingers. A beautiful, harmonious sound flowed from the movement on the strings. Oliver began to sing words to complement the tune, and Lorelei found herself leaning toward him, trying to discover the magic he was creating.

"In the land across the sea,

They speak about sailors true,
In the days of mystery,
When earth was a different place,
And you still will hear the tale,
They tell of their strength,
In their hour of destiny,
They followed the song to cast fate..."

Oliver opened his eyes and smiled at Lorelei's obvious interest in his song as he continued on.

"Beware the siren song,
Close your ears,
Make sure the ropes hold,
Focus your sights,
Beware the siren song,
A song of great beauty and desire,

Guide your ship on the right course... Sing with me," Oliver encouraged Lorelei.

"It's beautiful. Did you write it?" Lorelei asked with wonderment. The music soothed her soul as she listened to the beautiful melody.

"No." Oliver chuckled. "Ajax taught me a long time ago. It's kind of a traditional song or something from his family." He nodded toward Ajax.

"I would love to sing with you." Lorelei smiled brightly.

Oliver proceeded to sing the chorus again, and Lorelei couldn't resist. She loved music, and it readily flowed from her. She flawlessly followed along, even though she had only heard it once a moment before. When she sang, it energized her and enlightened her otherwise bleak mood. She welcomed it and found herself smiling back at Oliver through the words.

"Enough." Ajax was before them with his hand around the neck of Oliver's instrument. Lorelei was taken by surprise by his sudden appearance. He had moved faster than she thought possible. She shrank back on the bench in response to his fierce look.

Lorelei looked around at the slackened faces of the onlookers as they slowly regained their focus, their clouded expressions clearing as if waking up from a daydream. Looking over at Oliver, she noticed that he wore the same blank look as everyone else.

"Leave, Oliver," Ajax commanded.

"I..." Oliver snapped into focus, trying to find his words.

"Now!" Ajax commanded.

Lorelei's attention was pulled toward the sound of clapping. "Simply marvellous," Crewe praised as he approached. "Such a voice." Murmurs of agreement followed. Lorelei took the opportunity to slip away from Ajax's looming form. There was a look in his eye that was nothing short of terrifying. Lorelei could feel both Oliver and Ajax gaze upon her back as she approached Crewe.

"Was the food to your liking?" Crewe asked as Lorelei stopped before him.

"Yes, very much so, thank you. I fear I grow weary of this day," Lorelei lied, desperate to escape the enraged Ajax.

"Yes, of course. Let me show you to a bed so you can rest," Crewe offered pleasantly. Crewe's new behavior toward her was unsettling at best, but she still preferred it to what Ajax was offering. She feared it was only a matter of time before he made his move, and apparently she was building a case against herself. Ajax obviously thought she was at fault for the state of the men by the fire, and truthfully she had no idea what the cause was. She remembered the power that seemed to course through her, as if all the tension in her body was released and she was able to relax. She had lost herself in the song, but did she have anything to do with the men's stunned expressions? She had so many questions for her mother, and no way to ask them.

* * *

Lorelei awoke in the middle of the night when something cool pressed against her neck. She gasped in surprise, but her mouth was quickly covered before a sound could escape. "Not a sound." Ajax's deep voice found her in the darkness. As her eyes adjusted, she could make out his dark shape before her, his addicting scent engulfing her as he leaned down. A sob tightened her chest as the blade dug into her soft flesh. When she regained control of her breath, she nodded against his hand. Ajax seemed to have decided he was going to kill her after all. He removed his hand. "You make a sound and it will be your last," he rasped. Lorelei nodded again, not knowing if he could see her, but she was too terrified to make any sound.

Ajax grabbed her arm and led her out into the hall. Instead of heading toward the front of the building, he led her to the back. Lorelei stumbled in the darkness while Ajax moved with sure steps, as if his eyes were not hampered by the dark. The night air was cool as Ajax pulled her outside. They were faced by a thick forest that Ajax immediately began weaving through without a pause for breath.

"Please," Lorelei whispered. "You are hurting me." She tried not to let her voice falter as she clenched her teeth at the pain of his grip.

Ajax spun in a quick motion, pinning her to a tree as he leaned in. "I should just kill you right now and be done with it." His breath was hot upon her cheek, and Lorelei fought the whimper that crawled up her throat. He pressed his body against hers, and her fear bloomed into something altogether different. Ajax leaned into the curve of her neck; she could hear his slow drawing of breath, as if he was relishing her scent. Lorelei instinctively leaned her head to the side to give him more access. His hand found her waist, holding on to her with a desperation she didn't understand. His cheek caressed hers. The rough feel of him against her softness made her head reel. Her breath became deep and exaggerated as she melted in his hold. She didn't question anything as she reached up and grabbed hold of his shirt, pulling him closer. She gasped when she felt his teeth scraping her chin.

Reaching up, Lorelei ran her fingers through his hair. It was better than she had imagined it would be, relishing the feel of the silky strands. Lorelei was at the mercy of her desires as she let instinct take over and sought the pleasure offered. Her fear became a distant thought as this new need consumed her senses completely. Her skin felt aflame under Ajax's touch. His hands cupped her face, and he stilled before her, holding her still while he gathered control. His eyes searched hers in the dark for answers to questions he never spoke.

The sound of a branch breaking caught Ajax's attention. Ajax raked a hand down his face. "*Bloody hell...* go back, Oliver." Ajax dropped his hands and stepped away from her.

"No, Jax. I won't let you hurt her." Oliver stepped forward. A bow was in his grip, though lowered at his side.

"You can't stop me," Ajax growled. "Go back before someone notices you're gone."

Oliver raised his bow in a defiant response. Lorelei barely saw him draw an arrow, his movements were so swift. He now stood before Ajax with his arrow aimed.

"You are not going to shoot me," Ajax said irritably. The silence stretched on between them before Oliver dropped his aim.

"Where are you taking her?" Oliver demanded. In this moment he seemed so much older than the youthful young man she had come to know.

"*Go back*," Ajax hissed.

"I'm coming with you." Oliver rehoused his arrow and stepped forward, closing the distance between them.

"Do *not* get in my way," Ajax snapped before grabbing hold of Lorelei's arm and pulling her forward through the trees. He no longer touched her with the beautiful intimacy they had shared only moments before. His now-rigid pace and cold glare spoke nothing of the man that had almost kissed her. The heat he had stirred in her dissipated as she struggled to keep pace, though his grip was not as fierce as it had been when he pulled her from her bed.

Lorelei stole glances behind her and could to see Oliver was still close on their heels. His presence brought her some comfort. He seemed to disagree with Ajax's plan, and she could only hope that gave her some kind of fighting chance to survive the night.

Lorelei's bare feet grew sore from their endless venture through the woods; she stumbled with her unsteady pace on the moonless night. Every time Oliver moved to help her, Ajax would warn him away. "I can't walk anymore... You are practically pulling my arm off." Lorelei dropped to the ground. "Whatever you are going to do to me, just do it already," she said, defeated. She was exhausted; it had been days since she had eaten anything substantial, and her body screamed in protest now that the adrenaline was leaching from her blood. She regretted not taking advantage of the food offered to her earlier.

Ajax moved to stand directly over her. Oliver crashed into him, knocking him back. "Leave her," Oliver roared.

"She's one of them, I know it!" Ajax struggled with Oliver's advance. Ajax's size and strength gave him the advantage. Oliver was no match for Ajax's skill, and they both knew it, but it did not stop Oliver from trying.

"You do not know that for sure." Oliver stumbled backward, moving protectively against Lorelei. "She's done nothing to warrant this."

"She doesn't have to." Ajax was a compelling man. His voice growled with undisputable power.

Oliver crouched protectively before Lorelei, ready to fight again, but Ajax did not engage him. Oliver's shoulders relaxed noticeably; he seemed relieved not to have to fight Ajax again. Oliver was breathless in front of Lorelei, and Ajax stood as still as the trees before them cast in shadow on the windless night.

"I saw what she did," Ajax argued with a controlled tone. "I shouldn't even need to have this conversation with you."

"I don't see it your way. She's nothing like you told me. I have seen enough innocent people die. I will not let you do this," Oliver said firmly.

Ajax stood silent, considering Oliver's words. The silence stretched on before he finally spoke. "I am leaving with her. Come if you must, but day is at our heels, and Crewe will discover the girl missing. We need to move."

"Where are you taking her?" Oliver was seemingly content that Ajax was no longer a threat to either of them.

"Letholdus." Ajax ran his hand through his hair.

"Are you sure that's wise?" Oliver asked, but Ajax didn't answer.

"The witch thing again?" Lorelei asked in disbelief.

"Something like that." Oliver smiled apologetically, holding out his hand to help her off the ground, which she gratefully accepted. Oliver didn't let go of her hand as he led her after Ajax, who continued on without waiting for them.

"Thank you for saving me," Lorelei said, brushing dirt from her dress.

"Don't mention it," Oliver continued, taking care to keep a slower pace for her, which she much appreciated. When they finally walked into a clearing, the sun was rising and the earth was brightening. Ajax waited with two readied horses. His eyes immediately fell to their joined hands and his glower deepened. Oliver ignored him, keeping his hold on Lorelei. She was grateful, since it was the only reason she was still able to stand.

"Why two horses, Jax?" Oliver's words were suspicious. "You did not know I was coming, and I highly doubt you planned on giving Lorelei the luxury of her own horse."

"Of course I knew your stupid arse would follow!"

Oliver smirked as he swung himself up onto the horse, reaching down to help Lorelei up. She pulled her attention away from Ajax's impressive form, already upon his own horse. Watching him in the soft morning light reminded her of when she had first set eyes upon him in her forest, and even though Ajax had terrified her, part of her awoke at the sight of him. She didn't understand her fascination with him; his hot and cold intentions toward her were confusing. As much as she tried, Lorelei couldn't make herself dislike him. Instead all she could think about was what would have happened if Oliver had not interrupted them.

"I have never been on a horse before," Lorelei admitted nervously.

"Nothing to it." Oliver flashed his familiar smile, and she slid her hand into his. She cried out when she was grabbed from behind. Ajax hooked his arm around her and pulled her up onto his horse. She found herself enclosed in his arms before she had time to register what was happening.

"She rides with me," Ajax declared impassively "I do not trust her with you."

Lorelei looked at Oliver, who shrugged apologetically. She pulled down on her dress, which rode up dangerously high up her legs in her current position, but to little avail. The material was ripped, and she had never felt as exposed as she did right now. Ajax's body heat enclosed her, and she could feel his breath upon her neck as he reached for the reins. She felt light-headed being so close to him, pressed against his body. Her lips tingled from the memory of having his so close to hers.

When Ajax motioned for the horse to move, it startled her and she grabbed hold of his arms to steady herself. He did not complain about her hold on him, so she found herself able to relax slightly. "Get your hair out of my face before I cut it off," Ajax protested, flipping her long hair away from him in a display of annoyance. Lorelei pulled it over her shoulder and braided it loosely off to the side. Her bare shoulders were now exposed, every movement of the horse causing her skin to brush against him, and she missed the barrier her hair provided. She wondered how the man that had ravaged her body with animalistic hunger only moments before now rejected her so easily. How could he want her one moment and hate her the next.

Lorelei tried to remain alert as they traveled, but the warm morning sun was comforting, and she couldn't stop her heavy eyes from closing, no matter how hard she fought. She tried to keep herself propped forward to avoid unnecessarily touching Ajax, whose body language was nowhere near welcoming, despite the fact that she wanted nothing more than to be in his arms again. It was a battle she quickly lost as she felt herself relaxing into his hard body that remained as rigid as stone.

Chapter 9
BRYCE

The sound of footsteps had become constant background noise as Bryce paced back and forth before a group of men. Most of them were familiar faces he had known for years. Their appearances represented countless memories from his lifetime, but now, as he stood before them, the usual light-hearted banter was not exchanged. Food sat upon the table, hardly touched in the dimly lit room. Everyone was on alert, listening for anyone approaching the small stone house, one of many that lined the street. His wife sat in the corner, still overwhelmed with tears for their daughter as someone else tended their infant son in another room. Bryce could not let himself weep for fear of Clara's future. He needed to act, and he needed to save his daughter.

Bryce had vowed when he was being pushed to the ground, held against his will by guards as his daughter was taken from him, that he would save her from this fate. The memory of watching his only daughter accused of a crime she had played no part in, taken away to be locked in a place that he could dare not think about, constantly tormented his thoughts. He would rise up against his king, the ruler he had pledged to follow and embrace. He would take back what was wrongfully taken from him, and he would not stop until he accomplished this. Even if it meant his life, he would free his Clara.

Everyone in this room was willing to fight for his daughter, and he needed them all.

Peter, the owner of the property, sat to his right. Peter worked metals with Drake, Bryce's long-time friend. Their forge supplied the majority of the royal army with its armour. Peter had offered his home to gather and discuss how they would proceed. They knew they needed to remain hidden now that they had begun to act. Their first drastic act was orchestrated without a plan in place. Though it was not his own hand that had committed the murder of one of the king's guards, he was just as guilty of the crime because he did not prevent it. Anger fuelled them when no one would hear their plea that Clara was innocent. The word of a priest and Lady Mansforth far outweighed any of their own. They had been cornered, and action was taken.

Bryce knew that he could not take his wife and son back to their farmland. The moment they took his daughter away from him, he became a traitor to the king; it was only a matter of time before it was realized. He would not follow any king who would allow innocent children to be sacrificed. The king would want someone to take the blame for the crime committed, and who better than the father of the accused? He was the person who had initiated the retaliation that very day. It wouldn't be long before there was a bounty on his head, if not already. He had to take action now while he still had a family to save.

Their small group of men had gathered to discuss strategy, to think through their actions now that they were wanted men and had to keep a low profile. Simon sat at the back of the table, his features stony and the knife upon his person still fresh with the guard's blood. His face was unshaven and his eyes dark, a look he had taken after his own wife was committed for the same crime only months before. He was out for revenge, and they needed a man like him on their side, someone that would stop at nothing until justice had been served. It was his wife's own sister who had fuelled the accusation, in a state of jealousy. Simon's wife, Gloriana, could grow anything from the earth. Her way with plants was exceptional and praised by all. Their house was surrounded by a garden fit for a queen, and she was as beautiful as the flowers she grew within it. It was for this very gift that her life was taken from him. His wife did not even receive a trial; she, as well as their unborn child, was burned on their own land while he was away. All it took was one person's hateful declaration, and everyone believed it to be true.

"We should wait until the trial. She will be out in the open. There will be a crowd to hide among, to give us cover." Drake had made the suggestion. Growing up, Bryce and Drake were commonly mistaken for brothers. They had similar features that to this day were comparable and confused people who did not know them well.

Bryce stopped walking and turned abruptly toward Drake. "That could be weeks, months. Who knows how long they will draw this out while my daughter sits in whatever dark cell they have locked her in? Remember the state of the women from the last trials. They could barely stand on their own. They were starved and beaten." Bryce's words cracked with emotion. His words caused fresh expressions of anguish from his wife. Peter's wife, Thea, quickly guided her from the room. Bryce's shoulders dropped as he watched his grief-stricken wife disappear from view.

"I agree with Drake." Donald leaned on the table, running his hands through thick red hair that fell to his shoulders. "I think our chances are better if we approach this on familiar ground. Do you honestly think we have a chance storming the bloody castle? They have guards everywhere that won't hesitate to kill us on sight." Donald owned the land next to Bryce. He had four daughters, all with red hair like him. Donald was here now with them knowing that if he did not help take a stand, one of his girls could next be accused of witchcraft. Clara and his daughters had known each other their entire lives. What was stopping someone from turning their finger toward his girls, so close to Clara?

All of the men in this room were here because they would not stand by and let others condemn the women in their lives of witchcraft and have no way to object to the accusation. Donald had already sent his wife and girls away to stay with family, far from the influence of the city, in a place they would be safe.

Bryce didn't know if any one of the men standing with him would make it out of this with their lives. Sitting with them now, he held his shoulders back and his head high. He would gladly accept his fate on the path that now led. He was a loyal man, like the rest of his company. They were all men who had worked their whole lives to provide for their families. They needed to stand together now more than ever to ensure their futures.

"Peter and I have more orders than we can handle with the increase in guards just in the castle alone. They are already making moves to ensure they are not infiltrated since Bedford was attacked. They are trained to fight and kill, and what are we? Farmers, blacksmiths, shopkeepers." He waved his hands around at the men sitting at the table. "We have to be smart about this, Bryce."

"They have Clara, Drake!" Bryce slammed his hands on the table, disturbing the food.

"Yes, they do, but getting ourselves killed in a fool's plan to get her back will not help her."

"I'll do it," Simon cut in, making all of the men turn toward him. "I will get into the castle. Chances of going unnoticed are better if I am alone. If I fail, you have the option of the courtyard when they bring her out for the trial."

"We should wait. I have already heard news that Teller and his men are coming to Falls Landing. He has trained men that are better able to help us," Peter cut it. "It is ridiculous for Simon to break into the castle. It's suicide."

"There is no way to know that Teller is coming here. We have no proof. He is a wanted man. This would be the last place he wants to be seen, and even if he does, how can we be sure he will help us?" Bryce's frustration was obvious.

"Teller is on his own mission of revenge against the king. He will come here because this is where he can make the most impact," Peter argued. "He and his men being here might be enough of a distraction to the king for us to make our move."

"Who is to say this Teller can even make it past the front gates? Why put your faith in a man that is only whispered about behind closed doors? We know nothing about him other than the fact that he is responsible for a rebellion in the outlying towns." Alston rubbed his hands over his thighs. It was the first time he had spoken since they sat down at the table. He was a cousin to Drake. Bryce had known him since they were small boys. Sweat had broken out across Alston's brow, and a nervous energy was heavy upon him. "And breaking into the castle is impossible."

"We do not know anything for certain." Bryce stared at Alston with determined eyes. "Except for the fact I will do everything in my power to free my daughter."

"We are not soldiers! What can we possibly accomplish?" Alston stood up abruptly, knocking his chair backward with a deafening crack against the floor. "This is madness!"

"No one is forcing you to be here, Alston," Bryce said evenly with a penetrating glare.

"You are going to get everyone killed." Alston rounded the table, stopping before Bryce. Bryce did not deny this claim. "You know I am right," Alston declared before he turned abruptly on his heel and stalked from the room, slamming the door behind him.

Silence claimed the room for a moment before Bryce found his words. "I will not ask any of you to give your lives. You know where the door is."

"You do not have to ask," Drake responded. "I would gladly give mine for Clara."

"Aye." The other men responded in kind, raising their glasses.

Bryce looked into the men's eyes before him and nodded his appreciation. He did not have words to express his deep gratitude, but he found words were not needed. They knew how deep his gratitude ran.

"I will be the one to go," Bryce declared. "I won't ask any of you to take that risk. I will steal into the castle walls…"

"No." Simon swung his knife down with enough force to embed the blade in the table. "I said I will go."

"Clara is my daughter. It should be me."

"Gloriana was my wife, and I did not get the opportunity to save her. I will do this. I *need* to do this." Simon stood, pulling his knife from the table with little effort. He looked dangerous, and that was exactly what he was now, a man with nothing to lose.

"Let him do this, Bryce." Drake was by his side with a hand on his shoulder. "We will plan our actions if it comes to having to make our move at the trial. Simon knows what he is doing. He has the best chance of any of us to get inside the castle. Let us make plans to get out of the city. It is not safe for our families to stay here."

"It could be a death sentence." Bryce spoke gravely as he looked up at Simon. He had known Simon before his wife and unborn child were taken from him; that was a different man than the one that stood before him now. This man could never escape the demons that haunted him. Bryce knew he was looking at his future if he didn't get his Clara back.

"Be ready to act," Simon said before he slipped out the front door into the black night. The men were silent as the reality of the situation settled over them. It could be the last time they set eyes upon their friend. The world would never know the sacrifice he made, but none of them would ever forget.

Chapter 10
LORELEI

Lorelei felt herself rousing. The world beyond her eyelids was bright and urging her to see what it was offering. Taking a deep breath, she was awash in an intoxicating smell that stirred her stomach with a warm sensation. A sigh escaped her lips as she leaned against the source of comfort that she took pleasure in. A soft caress moved across the bare skin of her thigh, traveling up her body and across her waist. A moan sounded from her throat before her lucidity and momentary bliss were abruptly cut short. Reality came crashing down on her, and she propelled herself forward. Ajax's arm tightened around her waist, steadying her upon the horse. "Let go of me," Lorelei gasped, his touch suddenly too hot upon her skin.

"If you insist." He released her. Lorelei realized it was the only thing keeping her on the horse, and she tumbled toward the ground. The world was a blur until she crashed on the unforgiving earth. Lorelei could only whimper as her body objected to the rude awakening from a peaceful sleep.

"You dropped me!" Lorelei panted when her lungs could fuel her words.

"You said to let go." Ajax did not show any sign of remorse as he looked down at her with an obnoxious smirk.

"Where is Oliver?" Lorelei looked around in a panic when she realized they were alone. Ajax urged his horse closer to her, casting a shadow down upon her.

"Rode ahead. My horse cannot keep pace with all the extra weight."

"If I didn't think you would chop my hand off, I would smack you across your face right now." Lorelei huffed as she pulled her body off the ground, gritting her teeth against the pain.

She thought she saw amusement flash across his features before the return of his scowl. "I would advise against it, if you want to live."

"Yes, yes." Lorelei rolled her eyes and tried to wipe the dirt from her ruined dress. It had received so much abuse over the last few days that she feared it would soon fall off. The strap over her shoulder had let go with her fall. She attempted to tie it back in place. She looked up and caught Ajax still watching her. It made her skin ignite. She was angry that he continued to toy with her as if she were a plaything. She turned with an exaggerated sigh and started walking away from him.

"Where do you think you are going?" Ajax called after her coolly.

"To find Oliver. He is better company; actually, anyone is better than you," Lorelei snapped, but he looked completely unaffected by her words, and it irritated her further. "Even Marcus," she spat, not really meaning it. "I cannot begin to process your hot and cold moods. It is exhausting. I think it would be best if we kept our interactions to a limited basis."

"You will not find Oliver that way." Ajax looked at her with an arrogant expression that Lorelei wanted to hit off his face.

"I do not need you to tell me where to go." Lorelei turned on her heel and changed course without even a backward glance. She could hear his horse following her as her anger fueled her steps. Lorelei had no idea where she was or in what direction she should be traveling, but she assumed that since Ajax was remaining silent, she was on the right path. An overstated sigh left her lips as continued her pace. She did not even realize she was that obvious until it initiated a response from Ajax.

"Did I hurt your feelings, Lorelei? You seem bitter that your plan to seduce me did not work?" He continued to pester her. "I am immune to your charms."

Lorelei fumed at his callous words. "You cannot hurt my feelings, because it would mean that I cared about your opinion, which, for your information, I don't." She spun around to face him. "And I didn't try to seduce you. It was you who made the first move. I am the victim here, and you will do well to remember that." Lorelei spun around and stalked further ahead. "I would prefer that you just let me go home."

Voices just ahead of her grabbed her attention. She could hear men conversing just before they appeared in front of her. They rounded the trees and stopped when they took notice of her standing in front of them. Their eyes raked over her entire form before they flashed unnerving smiles. Lorelei spun around, looking for Ajax, but when she turned, she found herself alone to face these men. Her heart rate exploded in a frenzy, knowing she was in danger. The look in their eyes reminded her of Marcus. The men's clothes and skin looked soiled, as if they had finished working crops after a day in the sun, but Lorelei knew these men were not farmers. They were armed and did not look like honest men that grew food to provide nourishment.

"Who might you be, little one?" The first man's voice was sickeningly sweet. The sound of it practically slithered through the air before crawling on her skin.

Lorelei's feet started retreating before she was even aware. "I'm… I'm no one."

"Well, if you are no one, then you will not be missed." The other man's smile carved deeply into his hardened, sinister face.

Lorelei felt her eyes widen in panic; she could see how her reaction excited them. "I'm with someone," she said in a rush. "He's right behind me. He knows how to fight. You should leave now before he comes." Her voice sounded pathetic, and she didn't even convince herself.

"I don't see anyone." He reached out toward Lorelei, grabbing her arm. His hand dug into her flesh, promising the pain to come as she struggled against him. "I'm going to enjoy this," he sneered. Lorelei watched the man before her suddenly still. His skin blanched before her eyes, and his cold black eyes clouded. He lifted his arm in front of his face, but his hand was no longer attached to his wrist. Instead it was a bloody stump erupting with blood. A scream exploded from Lorelei's throat as she frantically tried to remove his dismembered hand that still gripped her arm.

The man collapsed to his knees, blood bubbling from his mouth with a strange, wet, gurgling sound. Then he collapsed face first on the ground before her feet. A blade was protruding from his back.

"*Bloody hell!*" The other man was backing away from her. He pulled his sword from his sheath, frantically spinning around and looking for the threat. The blade shook in his grip as his eyes darted around like those of a frightened animal, scanning for something he could not see.

Lorelei couldn't move. Her scream had already died upon her lips as she took in the horrific display of blood and violence. The surviving man tried to retreat, but Ajax appeared before him. "She *said* she was not alone," Ajax growled, excitement flaring in his eyes. He looked deadlier than she ever imagined a man could look. The man moved to swing his blade, but it fell from his grasp. He was already dead, the blood pooling around his feet. Lorelei turned away, squeezing her eyes closed when his body crumpled to the ground.

Lorelei could feel Ajax approach her, sensing his shadow. When she hesitantly opened her eyes, Ajax was looking down at her. "Why didn't you sing?" His eyes were narrowed, as if trying to solve a troubling problem. She knew she should be scared of Ajax, given what he was capable of, but it was not truly fear that he stirred within her. She was relieved that he had saved her and thankful, despite the fact that two men had lost their lives.

"*Sing*?" Lorelei gasped when she discovered her voice. She didn't like the accusation in his eyes. "Are you mad? Why would I sing when someone is attacking me? What next? Are you going to ask me why I did not dance too?" She leaned toward him to emphasize her point as she fumed, the residual emotion from the attack twisting into anger. Her finger was planted against his chest, and she could feel the heat of his breath. She didn't realize how close she was to him until she stopped talking and everything started to come back in focus. Her hand was splayed out on his hard, unyielding chest. The need to touch him overrode her anger. His heartbeat accelerated beneath her hand. Emotion flared over Ajax's features. Lorelei wondered if he felt the strange pull between them. Did he become intoxicated in her presence, as she did in his?

"Everything alright? Why did you guys veer so far off course?" Oliver took notice of the dead bodies. "Looks like I missed some excitement." He tilted his head curiously as he studied Lorelei and Ajax.

"Oliver." Lorelei welcomed him with an embarrassed flush upon her cheeks before she narrowed her eyes at Ajax. He had allowed her to wander aimlessly right into the path of those dangerous men. With that thought, her attention turned toward those very men that now lay dead before her, and she swayed on her feet. It was the first time she had seen the death of men, and it was overwhelming now that she could register what had unfolded.

"Are you alright, Lorelei?" Oliver dismounted as she felt Ajax's hand grip her upper arm.

"I think I am going to be sick," Lorelei gasped, covering her mouth as she pulled away from Ajax's grasp, retreating into the cover of the trees to expel the contents of her stomach. She could hear Oliver and Ajax's voices, but she could not distinguish any clear words, except when she heard her name. She stood up and took a deep breath before she returned. They were standing close, and Oliver stepped back when he saw her. He smiled for her benefit, but it did not reflect in his eyes. Lorelei was worried that they were keeping something from her.

"I got this for you." He held up a package tied in twine. "We are heading into town, and it would be best if you were dressed more appropriately." He smiled, suddenly bashful.

Lorelei looked down at her torn dress that was now spattered with the blood of her attacker before accepting the package. She untied the string and revealed a long-sleeved dress made of substantial fabric. It was long and looked like it would cover her legs. The material was a warm beige that reminded her of the pale bark of a young tree. "Thank you," she managed weakly.

"I know the color is not very nice, but we don't want you to stand out. If we can make it through town without drawing anyone's eye, the better for us."

"It's lovely, thank you." Lorelei attempted a smile, but it felt wrong on her face. "I should go wash up." She turned and walked toward the water she could sense was nearby. She always knew where to find water; it called to her wherever she was, and right now she needed more than anything to feel its comfort.

"Lorelei?" Oliver called after her.

"I don't plan to run off and get attacked by anyone else. I think I've enough of that for one day. I just need to find some privacy to change and water to wash up," she assured him before she turned to leave. She heard Oliver say something else, but his voice quickly faded into the background. Lorelei wasn't sure how long she walked. Her body moved of its own accord until she finally stepped out from the cover of the trees before a small lake. She laid down the dress that Oliver had gotten her and stepped closer to the water. A sigh escaped her lips as the cool water embraced her feet, folding around her like a blanket of reassurance. She immediately felt relief; the water energized her weary body. Quickly scanning her surroundings to confirm she was alone, she pulled off her blood-covered dress and discarded it before walking further into the water.

Lorelei immersed herself, listening to the water whisper soothing words into her ears. She could sense all the life around her, the creatures swimming in their watery tranquility. She turned off all of her thoughts and lost herself into the peaceful swaying of the water. She missed the familiarity and comfort of her river from her home, but it did not compare to being completely enveloped, with nothing holding her to the earth. She felt truly free as she closed her eyes.

She knew immediately when someone entered the water; his presence was undeniable. She could almost feel him herself, as if she was connected to every molecule of water. With his presence came an overwhelming desire that she could not deny. He continued to approach until she could feel his hand reach into the water, wrap his fingers around her waist, and pull her against him. He instantly stilled when her body brushed up against his. The contact with the solid heat of his body caused the familiar rush that only Ajax seemed to be able to ignite within her. Lorelei lifted her head from the water and focused on him. The water circled his chest. "Lorelei... You were out here for a while. I had to check on you." For the first time she could see actual concern on his features.

She reached out and ran her fingers down the hard flesh of his chest, dipping into every indentation that delightfully carved the shape of his muscles beneath the surface of his skin. Her touch continued down his stomach, immersed in the water, until it lingered on the waistline of his pants. She didn't know what possessed her to touch him, but she wanted to, she needed to, with a desperation that continued to grow. She did not understand the obsession she had with her capture. None of these feelings made sense, but to deny them was a battle she knew she would not win. He looked back at her with a hooded gaze, his chest rising and falling heavily as he watched her.

"What does this mean?" Lorelei reached back up to trace the intricate design upon his chest. The tattoo was masterfully scrolled upon a large part of his torso. It was almost as stunning as the man who wore it.

"A part of my history," Ajax answered tightly. "We have to go." He grew restless before her, his eyes suddenly evading hers.

"It is lovely." Lorelei slowly stood up. Ajax's eyes swung back to her, lowering to her shoulders and then the swell of her breasts visible above the surface of the water. His breathing became exaggerated again as he took in her exposed skin.

"Your eyes are glowing." His voice was barely a whisper. His eyes darkened to a deep navy. The beautiful white ring was captivating, standing out in stark contrast.

"Oh…" Lorelei looked away from his penetrating eyes, but he reached up and tilted her face back up to meet him. "They are beautiful… You are beautiful." His jaw clenched as he looked down at her. He was fighting the same urges as her. "I should be immune to this."

"To what?" Lorelei reached up and ran her fingers over Ajax's full lips, ones she now viciously hungered for. Closing the distance between them, she ran her hands along his firm lines, over the curve of his shoulders, until she clasped her hands behind his neck. Ajax closed his eyes briefly, taking a deep breath. When she pulled against him, he gave in immediately, grabbing hold of her waist, crashing their bodies together. Lorelei wrapped her legs around his narrow waist. She could feel his need straining against his pants as it brushed against her center. His breath mingled with hers as they looked into each other's eyes. He was so close, so deliciously close. The thought of this man wanting her delighted her beyond belief. She had no idea what she was doing. Her body moved of its own accord, rubbing against his, seeking all the pleasure he had to offer. Heat pooled between her legs, and her breasts became overly sensitive as they grazed his hard, muscled chest.

"You." Ajax's breath rasped. The world fell away around them as Ajax's lips met hers ravenously, desperate to claim her. He did not seem to mind her innocence when it came to the art of kissing. She let her need drive her as they devoured one another. His tongue sought entrance, and she opened to him, letting him explore her mouth. A feral growl erupted from him, and she drank it in, pushing her pleasure to new heights. The sensations that assaulted her were overwhelming. Her head spun and her skin savored him as she moulded her body to his.

Ajax pulled back with a sharp breath. "Oliver is coming." His voice was broken. "We cannot do this… It is wrong. You have to know this is wrong."

Lorelei's thoughts cleared. "Why?" she gasped in disbelief.

"Because this is not how it is supposed to be." Ajax breathed out painfully. "This." He motioned between them. "This is not how it works. This is not how any of it is supposed to be. I cannot want you like this."

"Why not?" Lorelei stepped back from him, pushing water between them.

"Because I am supposed to hate you." Ajax reached up and wiped his lips. The action made her stomach twist in pain.

"And do you?" Lorelei waited for his answer, but his hesitation spoke loud and clear. She looked at him for a moment in disbelief, but he avoided her gaze. Turning, she retreated from the water. Lorelei wanted to scream out in frustration. She had made a complete fool of herself. How many times was she going to fall under his spell, only to be rejected again? She had to remember that this man was her capturer, and nothing more would come of it. She didn't try to be modest as she left the cover of the water, retrieving the dress that was awaiting her.

"Lorelei? Are you alright?" Oliver broke free of the tree line, his face aflame as he tried to avoid laying eyes on her. She didn't answer; she was too embarrassed and fled into the cover of the trees.

*   *   *

When Lorelei was dressed and had gathered the courage to present herself, she walked out before Ajax and Oliver. The bodies of the men Ajax had killed were gone, with no sign that they had stained the earth with their spilled blood. She was impressed with how well Ajax and Oliver had covered their tracks. Ajax wore dry clothes, but his hair was still wet and glistened in the sun. He still avoided Lorelei. More than anything, she wished he would just give her his usual scowl so they could pretend that what happened in the lake was just her imagination. Oliver looked concerned but still smiled at the sight of her.

"You look lovely, Lorelei. Although I do not think we will get you through town without drawing attention. Here..." Oliver grabbed a piece of fabric the size of a small blanket and brought it over to her. He wrapped it around her shoulders, covering her white-blonde hair. "Try to keep your face covered as much as you can." He winked at her. "You do not pass for a commoner, and we are trying to keep a low profile."

"What if I decide not to cooperate anymore?" Lorelei adjusted the wrap around her shoulders and looked up at the two sets of eyes on her.

"You do not have that option," Ajax said bluntly. She noticed that his eyes were distant, almost sad.

"No one has even told me where we are going." Lorelei pulled the material close to her chest.

"You will know when we get there." Ajax continued to be reticent, and Lorelei knew she would not get anything from him.

She sighed. "Well then, what are we waiting for?" As much as she wanted to return to her mother and the forest she loved, a part of her needed to know where this journey was taking her. She wanted to experience the world she had been sheltered from her entire life. People were much more complex than she could possibly have imagined, the world more beautiful and dangerous than she thought conceivable. A part of her felt like she was always meant to face the world, and for better or worse, she wanted to see it through.

Then there was Ajax. She did not understand his struggle to deny his attraction for her. When he had touched her, devoured her like a starving man, she knew despite his words that he felt something for her. That piece of knowledge was enough to make her want to stay in his company to discover what the future had in store for them. If they parted ways now, she knew that the possibility would haunt her until the end of days, and her heart would always mourn him.

*   *   *

The town was only a half day's travel, and they arrived before nightfall. Lorelei was relieved that she was able to ride with Oliver. Ajax did not argue when Oliver made the suggestion. She held on tight to Oliver's narrow frame as they approached the commotion. "Welcome to Falls Landing." Oliver waved toward the towering walls of the city as they entered the gates. Lorelei had never seen so many people; they lined the narrow streets. So many voices ran together, creating a cloud of noise that hung over their heads. The stone buildings huddled together, creating only narrow alleys where people lingered in the darkness. Small children with dirty faces clung to the legs of people that paid them no mind.

"We leave the horses here." Ajax slid from his horse in a flawless motion, like a well-rehearsed dance. He never even seemed to blink without being in control of the action. Lorelei tried to mimic his smooth movement, but she almost tumbled to the ground. Oliver caught her arm and lowered her slowly.

"Thank you." She breathed in relief when her feet touched the ground. Ajax secured the horses, giving a man that hovered close by a coin that made his eyes light up despite the grime that coated his face.

Lorelei found herself positioned protectively between Ajax, who led them through the crowd, and Oliver, who stayed close on her heels. With all the distractions, she found herself getting lost in the upheaval. She was absolutely entranced by all the people's faces. A firm grip halted her step as she passed carts with people shouting to the crowd.

Lorelei gasped as she spun around to an old woman staring back at her. "Jewelry, dear? This would look lovely on you." She held up a necklace to Lorelei's hooded face. Lorelei's initial fear melted away as she took in the details of the necklace. It was strung with small white shells similar to the shell that her mother wore around her neck. Lorelei reached out to touch their smooth surface; they pulsed beneath her fingers.

"Do you like them?" Oliver asked from over her shoulder.

The old woman grabbed Lorelei's hand with surprising agility for someone her age. She held tightly to Lorelei's hand as she examined the iridescence of the fingernails. Lorelei tried to pull her hand free, but the woman's hold was unbreakable.

"Release her." Oliver's voice was demanding, but the woman ignored him. She reached up and pulled the hood off Lorelei's head. The old woman gasped, along with a few other bystanders. "I said let her go." Oliver now had a knife to the wrist of the hand that held Lorelei. "Do you want to keep your hand?"

The woman pulled back, putting space between them, a surprised look marring her wrinkled features. "Who are you?"

Lorelei looked around frantically at all the eyes staring at her. Oliver was in front of her, pulling up her hood. "Time to move." Lorelei turned and collided with Ajax's chest, which felt like a wall of stone when she made contact. Murmurs of curiosity erupted behind her as Ajax's arm enclosed around her and pulled her through the people pressing forward to see the commotion. His hand sought hers, intertwining their fingers, and he led her through the crowd. The sensation of having his hand within embraced with hers sent rousing tingles up the length of her arm. Lorelei tried to suppress the smile that was trying to force its way onto her face. His sentiment was evidence against his proclaimed hatred of her.

Lorelei could barely keep up with Ajax's pace as he guided them down the streets. He didn't slow until they were in front of a building that looked as unsettling as some of the dark back streets they had passed. Men that looked as if they were part of the shadows leaned against the stone walls, watching them approach.

Ajax released her hand as they walked through the doors. She instantly missed the warmth and comfort of his touch as she took in the gloomy interior. A large wooden bar extended almost the entire length of the room, and the rest was crowded with tables of every size and shape. The eyes of the men were upon them when they entered. Lorelei pulled her hood down further to hide from their stares. Women with figure-hugging dresses, revealing far too much flesh, sauntered around the room with seductive smiles.

"Holton." Ajax acknowledged the bartender by name.

"Letholdus is not here," the bartender responded without pleasantries, clearly knowing who Ajax was searching for. Holton had a long beard that concealed most of his face. His dark eyes regarded Ajax with the weary expression of a man that had seen too much to bother trying to smile at his customers. Men of all sorts leaned against the bar, their fingers holding tight to their drinks as if they held the answers they were seeking. The energy in the room was dark and depressing and unsettling. Ajax scanned the room, ignoring the man's words and seeking his own confirmation.

"That is his handiwork." Holton nodded toward a pile of broken wood that looked as if it once was a table, and possibly a few chairs. "He is no longer welcome here."

"Where can I find him?" Ajax asked, moving toward him, his tone making the bartender step back. Other men that had been watching went back to staring into their drinks. Someone walked in behind them and headed straight to the bar, a small and almost sickly-looking man with sunken cheeks and eyes. He leaned over the bar and spoke to the bartender before backing away from the commotion. Both men turned to look at Lorelei, and she found herself stepping back to find shelter behind Oliver, who was close to her side.

"Who is the girl?" Holton inclined his head toward Lorelei.

"None of your concern." Ajax's words were clipped and irritated.

"You seek information, do you not? So do I. Seems she has a lot of people talking outside." Holton's face broke into a smile barely recognizable through the shadow of his beard.

"Not interested in trading stories. The information I want I will gladly cut from you." Ajax moved closer and leaned against the bar, shoving a man that sat watching upon a stool. The man toppled to the floor, sprawling in an awkward display. He slowly collected himself off the ground without complaint and slunk off to another location. The bartender moved to reach for something, but Ajax jumped over the wooden divider and cut off his movement. A knife was pressed against the shaking man's throat as Ajax forced him against the display of glass bottles. Some toppled and crashed to the floor.

"Hold on now. There is no need for this, Ajax." Holton raised his hands in surrender.

"Jax?" Oliver called hesitantly. Both Oliver and Lorelei were faced with blades from a few men that had approached them from the shadows. They were surrounded by the armed men before they could make a move.

Ajax swung his gaze back toward Holton with a narrowed gaze. "They are not my men," Holton assured him.

"Letholdus owes us. We know that you run with him, and we want our money all the same." One of the men that held a blade toward Lorelei spoke up. The man's teeth were gray as he sneered at Ajax through a mop of unruly brown hair hanging in his face. He turned toward Lorelei, wrenching the hood from her head. The man appreciatively raked his gaze down her body. "Why don't ya hand over the girl, and we can call it even." His company agreed as their hungry eyes fell upon her.

Ajax sighed and released Holton, turning his attention toward the six men now threatening Lorelei and Oliver. The sinister man who had handled Lorelei suddenly dropped to the floor at Lorelei's feet, a throwing knife planted deep in his chest. Lorelei's eyes widened as she watched the man die at her feet but kept her feet planted firmly.

"Why don't the rest of you just walk away with your lives, and we can call it even," Ajax said. Three of the men backed away and retreated through the door without another word. Two others followed quickly when Oliver spun around with his own blade in hand.

Ajax attention was back on Holton, who was now visibly disturbed. His hands were still up in surrender. "Last I heard he was staying just outside town… not a mile… by the creek."

"Now, was that so hard?" Ajax grabbed a bottle of whiskey from the shelf behind Holton and tucked coins into his pocket before jumping back over the bar and stalking toward Lorelei.

"Do me a favor and don't come back," Holton called out after him. "I'm tired of scrubbing blood off my bar."

Ajax dismissed Holton, pulling Lorelei's hood up over her head, and pushed her toward the door. Lorelei didn't need much convincing; she wanted to escape all of the prying eyes and practically ran outside.

"Do you kill everyone that gets in your way?" she gasped as she spun around to make sure no one was following them.

"Yes," Ajax answered bluntly.

Chapter 11
WALTHAM

Commander Waltham looked down at the large map of the kingdom. Every location where Teller's men had been sighted in the past few weeks was marked out before him. He had looked at it so long, the lines were starting to blur together. The positions were random and sporadic, and no sense of plan or formation was making itself known to him, but his intuition told him otherwise. The pieces were there, but he just couldn't put them together. Teller's previous attacks in Bedford, one of the outlying towns, spoke of tactical skill and training. Waltham knew this man had strategy and was out for blood. Waltham could not rest until he stopped him. He ran his hands over his face as he blew out his breath in frustration.

"Commander?"

Waltham turned his attention toward John Blackburn, who stood waiting.

"Come in, Blackburn." Waltham waved him into the tent, his temporary quarters on the Mansforths' property, outfitted that morning. He was pleased with the number of men they were able to recruit for the cause, and the high elevation of the land gave them visual advantage. Waltham was confident they would outnumber Teller's men considerably, even though the amount of Teller's followers was still undetermined. Waltham believed that not even Teller, as cunning as he was proving to be, would be able to convince an army of people to rise against the king. It was a death sentence for any that were discovered.

Blackburn came to stand on the other side of the table. "Progress is being rapidly made, Commander. The rest of the supplies should arrive by day's end. Most of the tents have been pitched, and the barriers are being secured as we speak... Commander?"

"Huh... good. Good." Waltham's attention turned up from the map to Blackburn's concern.

"You are bleeding, Commander." Blackburn pointed to Waltham's neck.

Waltham reached up and ran his fingers along the neckline of his chest plate, and when he pulled his fingers away they had traces of dried blood upon them. He frowned at the discovery. "Must have cut myself shaving." He dismissed the discovery, grabbing a cloth from the side table and wiping away the blood. Blackburn looked unconvinced but dropped the subject. "Any news on the whereabouts of Bryce Barwicke?"

"No, Commander. No sign of him in town, and he hasn't returned to his farm. I have men positioned there. If he steps anywhere on his property, we will know."

"Good. The faster we get Barwicke secured, the faster we can focus on Teller. The last thing we need is another rogue plotting against the king. I need you to send a group of men to Westfort. See if anyone has any news for us." Waltham pointed on the large map before him at the small farming town settled between Bedford and Falls Landing. "I want to know anything. Even if someone thinks they heard someone whisper Teller's name. No matter how insignificant it might seem."

"Westfort remains quiet." Blackburn frowned. "All recent sightings have been in the direction of Rutton and Jeddore, and even further." Blackburn pointed in the direction of the other two towns north of Bedford.

"Exactly. Every lead we get in Rutton or Jeddore ends up a dead end, while Westfort remains untouched. It does not sit well with me. It is too quiet. Send the men and get them to stir things up. Someone is bound to talk. Someone has to know where Teller and his men are."

"Yes, Commander. The Mansforth girl is ready to be transported to the castle."

"Very well. Send word of any developments that need my attention. I should be back before nightfall."

"Yes, Commander." Blackburn saluted him before he left to carry out his orders. Waltham pushed himself off the table and marched from his tent. Things had proceeded as swiftly as Blackburn had indicated. The camp had taken form around him as he lost himself in trying to decipher Teller's next move. New faces surrounded him as he watched the men move about the camp like ants. He could tell that most of the new recruits were laborers and farmers just by observing the way they carried themselves. Most of these men did not know how to wield the weapon they had been given. Though they were being trained in the basics, the skills they needed could not be forged in the short amount of time they would have before they needed to take action. He put the thoughts from mind; he needed to remind himself he could not see these men as individuals, but as numbers necessary to win should they engage in battle. That would be their greatest advantage.

A royal carriage awaited him with an entourage of armed soldiers. The men saluted him upon his arrival, and he gave them their orders before he climbed into the carriage. The young Lady Mariam met him with bright eyes when he sat across from her in the plush interior. He would much rather lead the convoy upon his horse, but the king had requested he ride within the carriage to ensure the girl was under his watchful eye. The king did not want to take any chances with the young lady's life, especially since her father was being so generous with his land.

The girl looked barely out of childhood. Her large eyes stared back at him with excitement and hunger. "Commander Waltham."

"My lady." Waltham nodded with a tight smile. He was not a man to make small talk and preferred to stay focused. Distractions led to death.

"Thank you for seeing to my safe transport to the castle." Mariam's poised words reflected the exemplary young woman she was raised to be, like many other girls born to noble families. The possibility of improving position by marrying their daughter into royalty was now within grasp for the Mansforth family. Waltham avoided the politics of royalty. He was a soldier, commander of the royal army, and his focus never swayed, the very reason he had the highest rank and took orders directly from his king. He was respected among the people, a position he did not take for granted.

"Of course, my lady." Waltham evaded Mariam's attempt at conversation as the carriage moved over the uneven roads. He didn't know which was worse, the incessant chatter of the young woman or the restlessness of being confined to the interior of the carriage without eyes on road.

When the carriage jolted and then suddenly halted, Waltham cut off Mariam's words with much satisfaction. "Stay here and be quiet," he ordered. He opened the door hesitantly to lean out and see the driver.

"Why have we stopped?" Waltham called out. When he was met with silence, he stepped out into the road. He sensed the danger and unsheathed his sword. When his driver came into view, Waltham called to him again, but was met with no response. "Answer me, Charles. Why have you stopped the carriage?" Waltham walked around to look into the face of the unnervingly still driver upon his perch. He stared unblinkingly ahead with unseeing eyes.

The men escorting them on horseback were nowhere to be seen. Only an empty road stretching off into the distance on both sides met his eyes. Waltham climbed up onto the driver's bench, placing his hand on the man's shoulder. The driver slumped forward lifelessly, blood pooling at his feet.

"Commander Waltham?" Mariam's voice rang out.

"Stay in the carriage," Waltham demanded harshly.

"Whatever is going on?" Mariam rounded the carriage. "Where are my escorts?" she asked, noticing the lack of riders. When her eyes fell on Waltham and the dead driver, she let out a shrill, echoing scream.

Waltham jumped down to silence the frantic girl. Picking her up off her feet, he forced her back to the carriage. "If you want to survive, you need to bloody well be quiet. Do you hear me?" He shoved her with a little more force than necessary into the carriage before slamming the door and throwing the lock. Waltham threw the dead man from the carriage and grabbed hold of the reins before sending the horses in a determined stride toward the castle.

Waltham's unceremonious approach toward the city gates alerted the soldiers, and he was met by readied men. "We were ambushed," Waltham informed his men. "Lady Mansforth is unharmed, the driver dead, but the rest of the men vanished. When I exited the carriage, there was no sign of them."

"Who led the attack?" asked Josef Eldrine, one of Waltham's most trusted men and long-time friend. Josef climbed up onto the carriage, took the reins for Waltham, and continued to drive the carriage toward the castle.

"I think it is safe to assume that Teller has arrived in Falls Landing," Waltham said grimly.

Chapter 12
LORELEI

Lorelei took Oliver's hand, helping her down from the horse. They had stopped when they came upon a recently extinguished fire pit with tendrils of smoke curling into the air. Supplies lay scattered upon the ground. Ajax walked around the fire pit, surveying the site. It was nestled amongst the trees, providing good cover from anyone passing by. Lorelei was surprised that he even knew it was here, finding the location as if he had known exactly where to go.

"How long ago was he here?" Oliver asked as he picked up a wooden stick whittled into a stake from the ground and examined it.

"He's still here," Ajax answered with a neutral expression. He reached down and ran his fingers through the dirt, curling his hand around a rock. He rolled it around in his hand before he threw it up into the trees. A blur of movement caught Lorelei's attention as someone dropped to the ground. Ajax rolled away before coming to his feet with his blade in hand. Ajax was now standing before another man as impressive in stature as himself. The man looked like an older version of Ajax, with the same strong jaw and chiseled features. Gray streaks wound through his short-cropped hair and beard, and dark circles lined his tired eyes. They stood with blades to each other's throats, sizing each other competitively. "You have to be quicker than that, *old man*."

"Next time," the man mumbled before retracting his weapon. The older man turned to survey his company, and his eyes narrowed when they landed on Lorelei. He threw his knife, and it struck a tree a few feet from her. She screamed before darting behind Oliver

"Consorting with the enemy now, are we?" His voice was calm, but it held anger bound tight under the surface. "Now I know the reason the curse was not broken."

"That's why we are here." Ajax sheathed his sword and approached Oliver and Lorelei. "Something has changed."

"Letholdus." Oliver extended his hand. "It's been a long time."

"Yes it has, boy." Letholdus looked him over. "You look just like your father."

"Yeah." Oliver looked down at his feet. Lorelei didn't miss the reaction, and the question of who his father was piqued her curiosity.

Letholdus reached around Oliver and grabbed Lorelei by the neck. "Tell me, Ajax, why did you let it live?" She gasped from the pressure before his tightening grasp failed to let sound past her lips. "Please do not tell me you have grown soft," he growled. Letholdus's eyes were dark and menacing as they looked at Lorelei with utter hatred. She noticed the same white ring around his pupils as Ajax, as if white silver swirled around his deep blue eyes. Sharp pain tore through her throat, and black spots riddled her vision.

"Stop! You're hurting her." Oliver tried to pull Letholdus's hold from Lorelei, but the old man had immense strength, and nothing he did made a difference. "Jax, stop him! He is going to kill her."

"Let go, Letholdus. She hasn't taken a soul." Ajax wrapped his arm around Letholdus's neck and wrenched him free of Lorelei. She collapsed, struggling to catch her breath. Oliver grabbed for her, pulling her away from the two struggling men.

"What *goddamn* difference does that make?" Letholdus barked as he broke free and backed away from Ajax. "Killing her will free us."

"You told me that they have to take souls to live. It changes everything. I am not going to kill an innocent girl," Ajax argued. "She does not even know what she is. I brought her here because I thought you might have some insight, but I should have known better." Ajax waved his hand toward Lorelei. Letholdus turned his gaze on her again. His eyes were dark and calculating as he contemplated what Ajax had told him.

"It doesn't change anything that she knows not what she is. It is not for us to question." Letholdus's words were cold and cut deep. He spat on the ground in Lorelei's direction. "She has made you weak. You should be ashamed. If you cannot, then I will. You know it has to be done." Lorelei trembled at his words. She quickly scanned the perimeter with every intention of fleeing.

"No." Ajax stopped him. "I came here to seek your counsel. Find out if you knew of any others like her that walk among us." He placed himself as a barrier between Letholdus and Lorelei. "She is mine to deal with."

"If I knew of any others, I would have killed them. I do not let my cock get in the way of my duty," Letholdus barked.

Lorelei looked down and realized she was leaving marks on Oliver's arms from squeezing so tight. "Sorry," she whispered but was met with only a smile. Oliver didn't seem bothered by Letholdus's threats; she hoped that meant he was confident Ajax would stop him should he try to end her life like he was threatening to do.

"We should get comfortable; this could go on for a while." Oliver led Lorelei to a place where they could sit down and gain some distance from the heated words the other two were exchanging.

"Who is this Letholdus?" Lorelei whispered. She was too curious not to ask.

"Ajax's father." Oliver raised his brows. The answer didn't surprise Lorelei in the slightest. She could have guessed as much herself.

"That would explain the mutual dislike of me upon first sight." Lorelei sighed.

"They are not a typical family..." Oliver looked over at the two men. "They are soldiers; all they know is how to fight."

"What of Ajax's mother?" Lorelei asked thoughtfully. She tried to picture what type of woman would be in the mix of these two as they exchanged words Lorelei thought were only used for enemies.

"She died during childbirth." Oliver smiled sadly.

"Oh... that's horrible." Lorelei's hand instinctively covered her heart with the painful truth.

"Letholdus never got over it."

"Oliver, can you tell me what they think I am... why they think I need to die? Why Ajax believes he needs to hate me?" She bit her lip and looked expectantly up at Oliver. She wanted to know, but at the same time it terrified her.

Oliver stared into the trees, deep in thought, before he began to speak quietly. "Jax found me when I was a small boy. I had no one. He took care of me, brought me food, things I needed, and found me places to stay for years. He was all that I had. I remember when his father found out about me ... he beat Jax so bad, he could not walk for days. I was there, I saw the whole thing."

"Oh my," Lorelei gasped but quickly quieted herself.

They both looked over at Ajax and Letholdus to make sure they were not listening. "I stopped asking questions a long time ago. When Letholdus turned a blind eye to my presence throughout the years, I gave up seeking answers. I was just grateful that I could stay with Jax. He is the only family I have. I have always looked up to him. I wanted to fight like him, train with him, but I now know that it does not matter how much I train. It is not possible to know the skill that he has. Ajax is more than a mere man. I have picked up on things through the years, and some things I have only parts of the whole truth, but I do know that if Ajax truly wanted you dead, you would already be." Oliver reached over and placed his hand over Lorelei's. "I give you my word. I will do what I can to protect you, but the answers you seek should come from him."

Letholdus and Ajax stopped arguing and fell silent. They turned their attention toward the horizon before moving toward Lorelei and Oliver.

"What is it?" Oliver questioned.

Ajax put a finger to his mouth, signaling them to be quiet. "Men approaching." Minutes seemed to pass as everything remained quiet. Lorelei could feel the change in the energy around the trees, as if they were whispering in her ear of the coming danger. She knew the direction from which the men were coming, and her eyes fell on the tree line as well. She pointed, and Oliver's eyes followed.

"Come out, Marcus!" Ajax suddenly hollered. "I know you are out there."

A few minutes passed, and then movement could be detected through the trees. Marcus's form soon emerged, along with several others who were riding with him. Marcus's chilling laugh met them. "You never cease to amaze me, Ajax. How did you know?"

"You are the loudest breather I know. Why are you following me?"

Ajax watched as Marcus nodded toward Lorelei. "Give me the girl."

"Turn around and go home." Ajax waved him off dismissively.

"Crewe was not happy to wake up and see his little prize gone, and then to find out you were behind it. Let her go, and no one will get hurt." Marcus urged his men forward, closing the distance as they filtered from the trees.

"Tell me, Marcus, does anyone ever believe the bullshit that falls from your lying mouth?" Ajax responded in a bored tone, despite the threat at hand. Ajax and Letholdus armed themselves, bringing their swords up. A smile formed upon Marcus's lips. "Men." Marcus ordered his men to advance. Five men, as seedy-looking as their leader, dismounted and pulled their blades from their sheaths. Their smiles revealed teeth as dark as their unwashed hair, and they were tainted with an energy that made Lorelei's skin crawl. These men looked as if they had crawled from the darkest shadows.

"Get her back," Ajax ordered Oliver. "We are being surrounded. Watch your back." Oliver was already shuffling Lorelei away from the unfolding commotion. She could hear the clash of swords.

Lorelei looked back to see Ajax and Letholdus down the men before they could properly engage them. It was chaos as the men descended upon them with no fear of death. One man jumped down from his horse, aiming the downswing of his sword at Ajax, who blocked the blow, jabbing his sword into the man's stomach, spraying blood in Lorelei's direction. She gasped and shuffled backward. The man's eyes glazed over before he met the ground with a sickening thud.

Oliver drew his own sword, tossing it from hand to hand, loosening his shoulders before advancing on more men that seemed to materialize from the trees. Someone grabbed Lorelei from behind, but when she turned she was staring into a dark, expressionless face. Ajax sliced his blade along the back of the man's legs before bringing his elbow up into his neck, knocking the man away from Lorelei. He drove his sword into the belly of the man, still splayed upon the ground. "Try not to get yourself killed." Ajax withdrew his sword, and blood puddled on the man's stomach as his lungs expelled the last of his breath.

"So you actually do care," Lorelei stated mockingly, trying to ignore the death at her feet.

"Hardly..." Ajax turned back toward her after he cut down another man. He wielded his weapon as if it was an extension of his own body. He was as beautiful as he was destructive, the way he commanded his body in a lethal dance. "I do not want to have to watch Oliver sulk."

Lorelei jumped back as moving bodies veered in her direction. She stumbled to avoid getting in the path of swinging weapons. Oliver turned toward her, momentarily distracted, allowing his opponent an opening.

The blood drained from Lorelei's face as she watched Oliver sustain an injury. She thought it was serious by the way the man's sword carved into him. Much to Lorelei's relief, Oliver continued fighting. He quickly managed to regain the upper hand, and the man was soon brought to his knees.

Lorelei noticed a knife lodged in the body of a dead man sprawled out before her. She scrambled over. Grasping the hilt, she wiggled it loose from the man's neck. She swallowed her panic as the sticky blood coated her hands. When the blade was released, blood ran freely from the wound, saturating the earth. Lorelei swallowed the bile that rose in her throat and pushed down the panic that buzzed through her body. Her blood pulsed in her ears, drowning out the noise around her.

Lorelei took a deep, calming breath. She did not want to rely on others to keep her safe. She needed to defend herself. She held the knife firm, observing the action around her as she backed away.

"Have you ever used one of those before?" Lorelei jumped when Marcus appeared next to her. She looked down and saw her hand shaking, and she clamped the other hand around it, trying to steady her hold.

"Yes, of course," Lorelei gasped. "Do not get too close, if you value your life." Her voice cracked, and she cringed at her sad effort to display confidence. Marcus laughed and moved to advance on her. She let instinct take over and swung the blade at him, catching his arm. Marcus withdrew his forearm, looking at the shallow cut she had carved into his arm through the fabric of his shirt.

Ajax appeared before Marcus, a knife to pressed taut against his throat before either she or Marcus could register his arrival. "Seems you underestimated me," Ajax growled in Marcus's ear.

"Apparently so." Marcus looked around at all his men dead upon the ground, as if just realizing that he had to admit defeat.

Oliver appeared beside Lorelei and pulled her against him, wrapping his arm protectively around her. She felt herself relax into his hold.

"I will not kill you this time, Marcus, because you are a Raven, and I respect Crewe, but do not test me again, because I *will* kill you. Now get on your horse and leave. You will not have her, now or ever."

"See you soon." Marcus winked at Lorelei before turning to approach his horse. "Ajax," Marcus said with a cold glare before he turned his horse toward the trees, unfazed by the slaughter of the men he had led.

Lorelei noticed that Oliver was beginning to lean his weight on her. A warm sensation spread across her side. She looked down to see blood seeping into her dress, but it was not hers. Her wide eyes turned toward Oliver, who was disturbingly pale. He tried to smile at her, but his knees gave out and he fell, grunting with the jolt to his body.

"Oliver!" Lorelei cried as she fell to her knees, pulling his hand into her own. Blood saturated his shirt as he bled heavily from an open gash in his stomach. "No… Oliver," Lorelei whimpered. "I'm so sorry."

"It's not your fault," Oliver said weakly. Lorelei ripped material from the front of her dress and pressed it against his side. Ajax was beside her, pressing his hands on Oliver's wound.

"Stay with me, Oliver." Ajax leaned in and took Oliver's face in his hand. "You stay with me," he ordered. "Bring the horse!" Ajax hollered to Letholdus behind them.

"Ajax." Oliver grabbed Ajax's hand. "Please." There was no color left in his skin. It was white, and all the brightness that Oliver normally gave out was draining from him before their eyes. They all knew he was dying.

"Oliver," Lorelei cried as she leaned in and pressed a kiss to his forehead. She couldn't see through her tears.

Letholdus appeared beside them with the liquor bottle Ajax had taken from the bar and poured it on Oliver's side before bringing it to his mouth and downing the liquid. Oliver screamed out at the pain, and Ajax reapplied the pressure. Oliver reached up weakly and grabbed Ajax's hand in a last attempt to speak before his breath died on his lips.

"No." Ajax reached up and shook Oliver's lifeless shoulders. "Oliver!" When he let go, he collapsed back on the ground, his hands covered in Oliver's blood, staring at them in a trance. The look of devastation pulled at his features. She knew in that moment how much Oliver meant to Ajax.

Lorelei placed her hands over the wound. She couldn't lose the only friend she had ever known. She could feel her own pleas, as if she was listening to someone else in the distance. She began to feel a strange sense of detachment as instinct took over. Energy pulsed from the very earth beneath her. Her body was overwhelmed as she let the energy flow into her, causing a growing heat deep within her core as it passed through her fingers into Oliver's body. She could barely hold on to it — the energy felt as if it would pull her apart.

"Bloody hell!" Letholdus snapped. "What is she doing?"

"Lorelei? Lorelei?" Lorelei could hear Ajax calling her, and then his hand was clamped almost painfully on her shoulders until he abruptly pulled away, as if it hurt to touch her. Lorelei thought she could hear Ajax scream for her, but she couldn't understand what he was saying.

His words were garbled and strange. She focused on Oliver, trying to register what she was seeing, but the world around her was blurred and distorted.

The world suddenly snapped back into focus, and Lorelei took pulled a deep breath into her famished lungs despite the tightness in her chest. She looked down at Oliver. "Oliver..." Lorelei whispered, barely legible. She could see the ground in a large circular perimeter around them withered and drained of life. Even the trees within the circle looked as if they would fall to ash in the slightest breeze. Oliver's sudden breath drew all their attention. He gasped as if starved of oxygen. She lifted her hands from Oliver's wound to reveal flawless skin. The only evidence of his fatal wound was the blood that still covered him. He looked up into Lorelei's eyes, awestruck. Dark spots filled her vision until she was overcome by blackness. She was completely drained and could not hold up her body as she let herself fall back. She was not sure if she imagined falling into Ajax's arms or if she was so far gone that it was but a dream.

*   *   *

When Lorelei came to, she could feel that the deep of the evening was upon them. Her cheek was pressed against something soft, and she could feel the warmth of a blanket over her shoulders. She couldn't bring herself to open her eyes; they were too heavy. Voices conversed not far from her, Ajax and Letholdus speaking in hushed tones.

"...I do not know. I have never heard of a Siren doing that." Letholdus sighed. "But it does not matter, because she is one. I can feel it as sure as day and night. I know you can too."

"No... maybe it is because she hasn't taken a soul. I think this means something."

"Why are you looking for reasons to save her?" Letholdus's tone was bordering on accusative. "*Bloody hell*, Jax. What are you *thinking*?"

"It's not what you think. She just saved Oliver. Does that not count for something?" Ajax argued.

There was a long stretch of silence before Letholdus spoke again. "You are not fooling me any... I know the real reason she is not dead already."

"I told you..." Ajax started defensively.

"This Marcus, tell me about him." Letholdus cut off Ajax's words.

"He's still out there, he's ruthless, and I trained the bastard. I know his moves. He will not stop."

"What now?" Letholdus took a deep breath.

"I'm going to kill him," Ajax said matter-of-factly.

Letholdus grunted. "That is one thing we agree on."

Lorelei heard shuffling directly in front of her. "Lorelei?" Oliver whispered close to her. "Are you awake?" She forced her eyes open, revealing Oliver's smiling face. He was lying down beside her. He propped his head on his hand and looked down at her with wide eyes.

"How do you feel?" Lorelei's voice was raw in her throat, and she was still drowsy from sleep.

"You saved me... look, good as new." Oliver lifted his shirt and looked at his stomach in disbelief.

A shadow fell over them from the light of the fire, and they both looked up to see Ajax looming over them. He looked them both over and sighed. "Oliver, could you give me a moment with Lorelei?"

"Yeah, boy, come help me find us some dinner." Letholdus held up a bow.

"But it is night," Oliver protested. "I will not be able to see to walk, let alone hunt."

"Nonsense. It is the best time." Letholdus stalked off into the trees.

"For you, maybe." Oliver shook his head, hesitant to follow. He looked between Lorelei and Ajax, trying to decide if it would be safe to leave them alone together.

"It's fine, Oliver. Go," Ajax assured him. Oliver gave one last glance toward Lorelei, as if to apologize for leaving her alone with Ajax.

"I will be fine," Lorelei insisted, even if it did not feel like the truth.

Oliver reluctantly turned and left. Ajax watched him disappear into the trees before he turned back toward Lorelei.

"What is a Siren?" she asked, catching Ajax off-guard.

"You heard us." Ajax sighed and ran his hand over his face. "A Siren is a creature of the sea that preys on sailors." He sat down next to Lorelei, who was sitting up watching the fire burning in front of them.

"Preys on sailors... as in kills them? You think that is what I am?" Lorelei could feel her brows pull together in confusion.

"Yes, and I know you are." Ajax's tone was terse.

"I have never been to the sea," Lorelei argued with a shake of her head. This conversation seemed beyond logic.

"Maybe that is why you are different." Ajax's eyes were intense. He was serious in every sense of the word.

"How do you know I am a Siren?"

"I know."

Lorelei didn't bother asking anything else. She only stared into the flames, and Ajax remained quiet for a few moments.

"I cannot hate you, Lorelei." When Ajax spoke, she immediately thought back to earlier, in the lake. Heat burned her cheeks. "I do not even think I could kill you if I tried. You are in my head, and I cannot think straight." Ajax ran his fingers through his hair. "I feel like I am searching for answers I will never find."

"I do not have the answers. I know that for certain." Lorelei pulled her eyes from the flames and settled on him. Shadows danced across his face from the fire, and his expression told of his torment.

"You make me question everything." Ajax picked up a piece of wood from the ground and threw it into the fire, knocking over the burning logs and sending the flames higher into the darkening night.

"I don't know anything about being this Siren you speak of. My mother never told me I was one. I know for a fact she is not this evil thing you speak of that preys on sailors. My mother is beautiful and kind and would never hurt anyone. In fact, she does not like water at all. Though she would never admit to it, I think she's scared of it. There is also the fact that I never had the urge to kill anyone. Doesn't that mean anything?" Lorelei found her tone was almost desperate. She laid her hand on the ground next to Ajax's, touching slightly.

"You might. It might be only a matter of time." Ajax retracted his hand, pulling it into his lap. Away from hers.

Lorelei could feel the sting of tears, but she refused to cry. "Have you killed anyone?"

"What? Yes, of course I have, you have seen me do so." Ajax scowled.

"Exactly. What gives you the right to judge, when you have killed yourself?" Lorelei wiped her face with her hands.

"That is different." Ajax narrowed his eyes, turning his body toward hers.

"How?" Lorelei matched his defensive tone.

"The people I killed deserved it."

"If I am this Siren creature you say I am, then what does that make you?" Lorelei dug her fingers in the ground beneath her; the cool soil brought a slight distraction from her emotions.

"What do you mean?" Ajax reached down, grabbing her hand. The gesture surprised her, and a gasp escaped. His skin felt charged against hers. A rushing heat ran up her arm and warmed her belly. His touch was gentle, explorative... testing.

"You are too fast, too strong. You fight like no one else..." Lorelei found herself leaning in toward him. She looked up at his eyes. "I keep thinking about what happened between us earlier..." Her thoughts clouded from her nearness to him. His intoxicating scent captured her, and she wanted to drink him in.

Ajax moved quickly, too quickly for her to react, before he crushed his lips against hers in a demanding kiss. Lorelei panted against his mouth but immediately melted into him, meeting him with the same vigor and passion. Her body exploded with sensations. Ajax was beyond anything she could have imagined; he was addicting in ways she could not even have fathomed before he opened her eyes to this new world. The surroundings faded from her senses as she lost herself in the feel of him against her mouth. The way his hands roamed her body stirred an unnatural heat. Ajax pulled away, leaning his forehead against hers.

Lorelei clung to him, knowing that this candle that flamed between them was too bright, too hot. It was only a matter of time before there was nothing left to burn. "I cannot think of anything else... only you, and it terrifies me." Ajax's confession caused a flood of emotion to wash over her already heightened state. She knew that his declaration was difficult for him to admit. She could see the anguish of his internal battle.

A branch cracked, and they both turned toward Oliver, who was standing just at the tree line. She had been so lost in Ajax that she could not determine how much time had actually passed. "I cannot see a bloody thing," Oliver complained. "If Letholdus wants to wander through the dark, he can do it on his own. I am pretty certain that he shot an arrow by my head. He is insane."

"Watch her," Ajax ordered. He raked his hands through his hair before backing away. "I need to speak to Letholdus." He gave Lorelei a loaded look, reflecting the words that he wished to speak, but instead he turned and walked away. Oliver was quiet as he sat down next to Lorelei, trying to read the emotion passing between them.

"Are you alright?" Oliver reached over and gently rubbed her shoulder.

"Just tired." Lorelei managed a smile.

"Lie down. The hour is late, we should rest."

Lorelei lay down and closed her eyes, but sleep would not come. Letholdus and Ajax did not return before Oliver's breath became deep and rhythmic in his peaceful slumber. So many things pulled at her: the kiss, her mother, Ajax proposing that she was a Siren, Oliver almost dying, and the conversation that she had overheard between Ajax and Letholdus about Marcus still being out there. If she stayed, someone else could get hurt because of her. What if next time she couldn't heal them? She was a distraction to Ajax; she could see him fighting his very nature because of his feelings for her. The only solution she could think of that was best for everyone was to leave, despite the fact that it would break her. She just needed to leave while everyone was preoccupied. She just hoped she could get enough of a head start before someone noticed she was missing.

Lorelei leaned in and placed a gentle kiss on Oliver's forehead. She didn't like leaving him without saying goodbye. She owed him greatly. Standing up on shaky legs, she started walking away as fast as she could. The longer she walked, the more her body became willing, and soon she was moving swiftly through the trees, putting distance between herself and the others.

She walked through the dark forest, breaking free of the cover when she thought it was safe to walk in the open. She could see Falls Landing in the distance as she continued on her path. The reality of being on alone in this unfamiliar land bloomed fear within her. She quickened her steps; she needed to remain out of sight if she was going to survive. She knew the direction of her home; the sun would guide her in the light of the new day. It might take her awhile, but she was determined to make it home to her mother. But it was not long before something stopped her in her tracks. Lorelei felt as if someone was watching her. She spun around to find that no one was behind her, but it did not put her mind at ease.

"Are you looking for me?" Marcus stepped out of the shadows. "You made this too easy. I am almost disappointed, but I can live with it." He chuckled. Lorelei tried to make a run for it, but she was not fast enough on her tired legs. Marcus had his hands on her before she could even get her momentum. "I would not do that, love. Don't try to scream, either. I don't want to hurt you, but if you push me I will have to, and I will enjoy every moment of it. I would even like to have a reason to see just how sweet you are under that dress of yours." Marcus breathed hotly against her neck, and she relaxed her struggle.

Reaching into her pocket, she tried to retrieve the knife she had hidden there, but Marcus was too quick and disarmed her before she could even grasp the hilt. His hands on her made her nauseous, and she wanted nothing more than for him to let go.

Marcus pulled twine from his pocket and proceeded to bind her wrists. Once she was tied, he pushed her up onto his horse before he swung his own leg over and settled close against her. Lorelei said nothing as he rode them directly toward Falls Landing. It was quiet in the dark of night as they approached, and Lorelei could barely make out the large castle that was positioned in the heart of the city. It stretched up into the night sky over the height of the wall that closed in its borders. They approached a group of guards at the entrance, all taking defensive positions at their approach.

"Who goes there?" One of them stepped forward, his hand on the grip of his blade.

"I have the girl," Marcus called out, pulling a poster from his person. Lorelei looked at the parchment that Marcus held up and could not recognize it as her own face.

"Bring her closer." Marcus slid from the horse before reaching up and grasping Lorelei's arm and pulling her down. Lorelei stumbled into his side.

"I do not understand this. Where are you taking me?" Lorelei couldn't keep the panic from her words. She had assumed he was taking her back to Crewe.

The guard stepped closer and reached out to tilt Lorelei's face toward him, examining her features. He turned back toward his men. "It's her." The guard reached for Lorelei's arm, but Marcus stepped in.

"The reward," he insisted.

"Come with us." The guard waved as the others opened the large gate. "His Royal Highness will want words."

Chapter 13
OLIVER
Twelve years before...

The music of plucked strings rang out through a small cottage where a large, warm fire burned, casting comforting heat through the room. Small fingers ran clumsily over the strings, playing a song the small boy had practiced all day but still couldn't master. The encouraging smile of his mother urged him on until he finished the entire piece. She had helped him prepare to show his father what he could create with the instrument he had been given only days before.

When he finished the song, he looked up at his father's face and was met with a smile. His father began clapping, and the small boy danced with excitement. His father's laughter echoed through their small home. "Come here, Oliver, and give your father a hug. I have missed you." Oliver jumped into his father's awaiting arms. He always looked forward to his father's visits. When he was gone for days at a time and Oliver would ask his mother when he would be back, she always reminded him that his father had a very important job, and he couldn't always be with them.

"Are you hungry, Brom, dear?" Oliver's mother leaned in and placed a kiss on his father's head before doing the same to Oliver.

"No, I am afraid I cannot stay long. I have to get back." Standing up, Brom ran his fingers through his son's hair. "Take care of your mother while I am gone."

"I will. Can you stay longer next time?" Oliver said before heading over to the table, where his mother began spooning food into his favorite bowl.

"I will try, my son. Go eat. I need you to grow bigger and stronger than me."

Oliver ran over to the table and climbed up on his chair. "Mother says I already eat a lot." His mother walked over to the door, where his father was readying to leave. They spoke quietly, and Oliver tried to stay silent so he could overhear. Sometimes when his father left, his mother would cry long after Oliver went to bed at night. She always tried to hide it, but he knew. He always tried to make her feel better, even when he missed his father just as much as she did. Oliver knew that his father was a man of great significance, with his shiny armor and sword that was unlike any other that he had seen before. He wanted to shout out to the world who his father was and didn't understand why he had to keep it a secret.

"I do not know when I will be able to return. It is getting more difficult lately to get away unnoticed." Brom reached up and caressed his mother's cheek.

"I know." His mother kissed the palm of his hand before wrapping her arms around his neck. "I knew this would not be easy, Brom."

"Here, take this." His father pulled out a small pouch and placed it in her hand.

"It is not necessary. I made good money these last few days with my weaving." She tried to return it to him.

"I would feel better if you took it," Brom insisted. "Buy the boy some new clothes." He leaned toward her, taking her face in his hands and kissing her deeply before pulling away. "Is Durham treating you well?"

"Yes, of course, always." His mother took a deep, shaky breath. Oliver knew there would be tears tonight.

"Good." He kissed her one more time before he looked over to Oliver. "I will be back as soon as I can, Oliver." His father turned, and pulling open the door, he disappeared into the darkness. Oliver hopped off his chair and ran over to the window, pulling the curtain aside. His father was talking to Durham. Oliver liked Durham; he was always close and protective of him and his mother. He helped them whenever they needed anything, and he even took Oliver fishing on occasion. His mother had told him that his father had Durham stay with them to make sure they were safe when he was not able to. Oliver did feel better knowing that Durham was always close.

"Alright, Oliver, to the table now." His mother called him away from the window.

Oliver let go of the curtain and walked back to the table. They were quiet as they ate. His mother had that distant look she always got when her husband left them, like the weight of the world had settled on her slim shoulders. "He will be back." Oliver smiled as brightly as he could.

She looked up at Oliver, and her eyes shone as she smiled back at him. "Yes, he will, and we will be waiting for him." She wiped her face with her slender fingers. He always thought his mother to be the most beautiful woman he had ever seen, with her long brown hair that she kept down so it flowed around her. Her green eyes were always so bright when she looked at him. It always made him feel like the most special person in the world.

An abrupt bang rattled the door, and both Oliver and his mother jumped in alarm. She turned toward him with fearful eyes. "Hide, Oliver, now. Don't come out, no matter what happens."

"But…" Oliver argued.

"No matter what. Promise me. No matter what."

"I promise."

"Good." She frantically shuffled him toward the hiding place that they had prepared if ever there was an emergency, a secret hideaway that Durham had constructed to conceal them. Oliver had used it a few times to play, and his mother was never happy when she discovered what he was using it for. She reminded him that it needed to remain a secret, because one day it could save their lives.

Oliver huddled inside, and his mother waited at the door until she knew he was out of sight. When she opened the door, Durham practically fell into her arms. Oliver watched from the small opening inside his hiding place. He wanted to crawl out more than anything and go to his mother, he was so terrified, but she made him promise to stay.

"I… sorry, Sybbyl. I could not stop them," Durham gasped. His shirt was completely saturated in blood as he struggled for breath. "Run," he gasped. They door banged open, and his mother was thrown across the floor. Large men poured into the room, all dressed for battle with their weapons in hand.

"Sybbyl Featherston?" one of the guards asked gruffly.

"Yes?" His mother tried to regain her footing and stand before the men. "What is the meaning of this?" She always found her bravery in the face of danger. His father once told him that was one of the many reasons he had fallen in love with her.

"You have been accused of witchcraft."

"By whom?" his mother demanded. "I have committed no such crime."

"By Her Majesty the Queen." The man grabbed hold of his mother as she struggled to free herself. Other men rummaged through their home, throwing around furniture and their belongings. Oliver listened to the sound of men destroying their home. He didn't understand what was happening.

"No sign of the boy," one of them declared.

"Where is he?" the man holding his mother demanded as he shook her.

"You cannot have him." She spat in the man's face and clawed at his hold, to no avail; he would not relinquish her.

The man holding her turned toward the others. "Burn it. Burn it all."

Oliver watched the men toss their furniture into the fireplace, causing it to unleash its flames into the room. The curtains were pulled from the windows and set ablaze before they tossed them around to spread the fire. Through the open front door he could see them drag his mother outside and slide a rope over her struggling frame before they tied it to a horse. He could not hear anything through the sound of the growing fire that began to consume their home, but he did see when the man swung at his horse, causing it to buck and take off at a gallop. He could do nothing as his mother was dragged behind with the rope pulled tight around her neck. His tears were hot upon his face as the fire raged around him. He waited until he could no longer breathe before escaping through the small opening in the back wall.

Oliver ran into the woods in the pitch darkness of the night and fell into the cool soil of the forest floor, where he cried until sleep took him just before dawn. His mother was gone, Durham was gone, and he had no idea where his father was. He was alone in the world his mother had tried to shelter him from.

Chapter 14
PERONELL

Peronell sat next to the king where he perched upon his throne before the small audience of men that had been called for the consultation. The massive throne room displayed the artwork of the most celebrated artists; they had collectively fused their efforts over the years to create the masterpiece that was the magnificent room. The ceilings reached an impressive height, with stained glass windows displaying historic victories of the kingdom that Brom's family had reigned over for the last six generations. Despite its grandeur, Peronell barely noted the details anymore; they faded into the background.

"I want these trials dealt with before Arthur's ball. I want nothing to darken the event," Peronell demanded of the king. Brom only sighed in response to her challenging tone before he turned back toward Reverend Benedict. Peronell hated the way he liked to dismiss her, especially when they were with a respectable audience. Brom's history with his people ran deep, and it had been a hurdle for Peronell in her undertaking to win their favor. When her wishes did not directly align with the king's, she had to be resourceful to get what she wanted.

"Tell me of the Barwicke girl," Brom requested of the priest. "I felt the need to follow up on this particular case, especially since Lord Mansforth's wife is involved, and Barwicke has become a traitor to the crown since the accusation. This is a matter I need resolved quickly." This man was a familiar face in the church of Falls Landing and a staple of the kingdom's religious faith, not to mention the fact that he was very accommodating toward Peronell when she requested it of him.

The man held no true faith in his heart — the perfect kind of man, in her opinion, because he could be controlled easily. "I was informed it was you that made the accusation against the girl," Brom continued.

Peronell tightened her fists at her sides until she could feel the sting of her nails cutting through her skin. Brom's infuriating search for the truth made her skin crawl. The man had power dripping from him, but he refused to utilize it to make people carry out his every wish. Peronell liked to make people bend, to control them and master them. She did not deem it necessary to waste time searching for justice, a fool's errand in her opinion.

"Yes, Your Majesty, as well as Lady Mansforth." The priest glanced toward Peronell for approval, and it was not missed by Brom. His suspicions of her intentions had grown deeper through the years. His vigilant eye was wearing on her. "The girl exhibited signs of the devil in our very church. She has been claimed by witchcraft, I am sure. It has stirred fear among the people, and they are turning toward God more than ever now to help them through this time."

Peronell wanted the king to drop the subject. Her plans to have Arthur marry the Mansforth girl would not be interfered with. The Mansforth family would bring substantial wealth with the union, a wealth that their treasury needed. Even the king questioning the allegation was enough to give people doubt, and she didn't want the reputation of Lady Mansforth or the priest to be questioned in any way. It would cause people to talk, and that could be a dangerous thing.

"Yes, that is very convenient," Brom said suspiciously before he took a deep, thoughtful breath. "The Barwickes have been upstanding pillars of this kingdom for generations. I need your word that these allegations are true before we act on this crime. Bryce's father served my father loyally for years."

"She spoke in tongue, Your Majesty. I speak the truth." The priest looked to all the men he taken confessions from, trying to sell his story.

"And what of the levitation?"

"Levitation, Your Majesty?" The priest's brow furrowed. "I do not understand. What does levitation have to do with this?"

"Seems you and Lady Mansforth should have gotten your story straight before you decided to condemn that girl and send my bloody kingdom into uproar." Brom was losing his patience. "Lady Mansforth claimed the girl levitated at the altar."

"Oh yes… Yes, she is correct. The whole encounter was over-whelming, Your Majesty. Forgive my moment of forgetfulness." Sweat broke out upon the priest's face, his confident demeanor diminishing before their eyes.

"Forgetfulness, *my hairy arse!*" Brom exploded.

"Your Majesty, I am a man of God…"

The bishop stepped forward in defence of the priest. "Your Majesty, if I may. Reverence Benedict has an outstanding reputation with the people. Such an accusation of falsely accusing a young girl for personal gain would cause irreparable damage to the church. The people need their faith to remain strong. We must remember what is important for the people." The bishop was the eldest of the men in the room, and his heavy cloak weighed on his frail shoulders. Brom knew the old man grew weary of late. The old man had little willingness to deal with anything that would question the integrity of the church. He swept things under the rug in hopes that others would not see the dirt that was beginning to pile high within his sacred walls.

"And what of the young Barwicke girl, Bishop? Do I allow an innocent girl to die to hide the skeletons of the church?"

"The sacrifice of few can benefit the whole," the bishop said without remorse. "Not that I am admitting Reverence Benedict's guilt. I am simply stating facts."

"I don't want to hear this *shite!* Men of God? Start acting like it." Brom was losing his temper.

Peronell stepped in. "This is nonsense. The girl has been found guilty by our good priest, of all people. His word is the word of God and as such should not be questioned. We waste time on a truth that has already been found. Hang the girl and move on with it."

"*Hold your tongue, woman.* I will question who and what I please, especially when it comes to these witch hunts. The allegations are getting out of hand. Every bloody person with a chip on their shoulder can point a finger. These are my people, and I am the bloody king, for Christ's sake." Brom slammed his fist against the arm of his throne. "You would do well to attend to other matters, like the whereabouts of your son, who has been noticeably absent as of late."

Peronell narrowed her gaze on the king. His maddening strength of character had got in her way for far too long. He could not be swayed as easily as others; he refused to bend to her will, and she found it draining trying to apply control over him that faded too quickly. The darkness within her began to unfurl, and she could feel it fueling her. Brom reached up and clenched his chest. His face contorted in pain. She pictured her hand wrapped around his beating heart, squeezing the life from his body. An act that she craved with all her being, but unfortunately she still needed him. The king's part in her plan was not complete, and therefore she would bear his presence until she could act on her desires. Shoving them into his mind, she released her dark hold on him.

"Your Majesty." Terrowin stepped forward. The man had been a constant in Brom's reign and his father's before. The old man had a lifetime of history to guide the choices of the future, and Brom infuriatingly valued his opinion on all things, especially over her own. Terrowin was not a fan of Peronell's in return. It was this very man that she began to suspect poisoned Brom with distrust of her intentions.

"I am fine." Brom waved off the concern as the pain faded from his chest. "We will proceed with the current trials. The priest's accusation will not be questioned further." He spoke without conviction, as if a passing thought had escaped his lips without notice.

"Your Majesty?" Terrowin questioned Brom's sudden change of heart. Brom was a passionate man, and the change of heart that Peronell had pressed on him to drop the subject was not fooling those who knew him well. She knew she had to be more careful where and when she interfered, especially now that she was so close to achieving what she had worked so hard for, but she couldn't have him ruining her plans. Using her sway on Brom was always taxing, and she was weakened.

"My decision stands." Brom refused to entertain it further, but his eyes did not convince Terrowin. Brom turned toward the bishop, who looked relieved that his priest was no longer under fire. "Make sure your priest does not find his way into my questioning again."

"Yes, Your Majesty. You have made a wise decision." The bishop took his leave with the priest on his heels.

Terrowin looked up at Peronell, and she gave the old man a cold smile. The defiance she saw in the Terrowin's eyes was all she needed to convince herself that any reason she had for allowing him to live this long was now obsolete; his usefulness had passed. He was another that she would take pleasure in destroying sooner rather than later.

The throne room doors swung open, and Commander Waltham barreled in with his broad, demanding stance. The Mansforth girl, along with a handful of castle guards, filed in behind him. The girl was noticeably shaken, tears streaming down her pale cheeks.

"What news do you bring me, Commander?" King Brom stood as Waltham continued to approach.

"We were ambushed on the road."

Mariam erupted in a fit of sobs as Waltham went into detail. "Escort young Lady Mansforth to her room," Peronell interrupted as she ordered one of the guards to accompany the distraught girl from the throne room.

"Yes, Your Majesty." One of the guards bowed before carrying out the order.

Waltham waited until the girl was removed and her sobs faded into the distance before he continued to relay the details of the attack. "Our men were already missing and the driver dead by the time I noticed anything amiss, Your Majesty."

"Teller and his men," Brom muttered.

Charles Oxon spoke up for the first time this evening. "We do not know this for certain, Your Majesty. We should confirm it is not just another act from Barwicke and his followers before we jump to the conclusion that Teller has come to Falls Landing." He was another member of the king's advisory council. He had bought his way into the royal graces years ago; his political sensibility was impressive, and Peronell could appreciate the man's hunger for power, but his faults lay in his weakness for women. The man could never keep his mind when a woman swayed her hips in his direction. Even now Peronell could feel his eyes upon her, remembering her flesh beneath the material. Charles had an insatiable hunger that made him easy to manipulate.

"If you would, Your Majesty, Barwicke is only a farmer, and his men are but commoners with not the training to administer such an ambush. His attack earlier today with the guard was brutal and spoke of their desperation. Their attack on us now was precise, planned, and implemented with skill." Waltham spoke with a certainty that Peronell knew would convince the king.

"I agree. Alert every available soldier and have them armed and ready. If Teller and his men have made it to Falls Landing, we have to be ready for them. I want extra guards on the castle perimeter. I would not put it against him to make such a bold move as to try and penetrate the castle walls."

"Yes, Your Majesty. I have already sent guards to alert the camp and to increase patrols. I wish to send a scout to call back the men stationed in the bordering towns. I think our resources are best concentrated here at this time."

"Very well. Alert the castle guards of the news and then join us in the council room." Brom dismissed his commander. "Shall we?" he said to his advisors before he stood and they followed him to his private room.

Peronell took the opportunity to remove herself from the king's side and pursue Commander Waltham as he left the throne room. When she neared him, he was speaking with a few of his guards by the main doors of the castle.

"Commander," Peronell called, and every man turned and gave her proper bow as she neared them. "I would like your speak with you on an important matter."

"Of course, Your Majesty." Waltham turned toward the men. "You have your orders. Inform the others." He returned his attention to Peronell and she led him a more private location. He followed her into the grand library. Peronell quickly scanned the room to make sure it was free of prying eyes. Closing the door and setting the lock behind them, Peronell turned her sights on Waltham. There was no need for formalities and secrets now that they were behind closed doors.

"I have missed you," Peronell purred as she neared him. She reached out and ran her finger down his plated chest.

"Your Majesty. Maybe now is not the time to…"

"You and your silly little conscience." Peronell ran her fingers along his cheek, and a darkness swirled in his eyes until his mouth curved into a seductive smile as he gave in to her power. "That's better." She smiled. "Now let's try this again, shall we? I have missed you."

"Not as much as I have missed you." Waltham reached up, unfastened his armor, pulled it off, and dropped it upon the floor before he reached for Peronell and pressed her tight against him, claiming her mouth hungrily. Peronell bit his lip hard enough to draw blood, and then she pulled away from his demanding kiss. He didn't complain as the blood dripped from his swollen lip, running down his chin. Peronell leaned in and ran her tongue along the length of the scarlet red line and sucked the blood from the wound she had inflicted. Waltham groaned in pleasure before he grabbed Peronell by the throat and pushed her against the wall of books that lined the entire enormous library. A few books toppled loose from the force of the impact. Peronell gasped from the blow, a sinful smile curving upon her lips. "I do love when you get rough with me, Commander." Her voice was heavy with lust.

A primal growl erupted from Waltham's throat as he ran his hands down her curves before reaching up and ripping open the front of her dress, revealing her full, round breasts. The material didn't stand a chance against his strength as he forced it back to give him complete access. Waltham pulled at her soft, feminine flesh with his teeth, leaving red marks on her pale skin. The act excited Peronell as her arousal escaped her throat in moans. She writhed under his hold. She ran her hands along his hardened flesh until she curled her fingers into his thick hair, pulling his head back. He was breathless.

"Claim me now." She released him just as roughly. Waltham grabbed her by the waist and turned her as though she was weightless as he pushed her against a large wooden table; he kicked a chair away, causing it to topple to the floor with a crash. Waltham grabbed the material of Peronell's skirting and pulled it up, revealing her bare backside. He groaned in pleasure before he released himself to enter her. He grabbed her hair and forcefully pulled the long strands as he entered her with a violent thrust, causing Peronell to cry out. He pulled her back against him and muffled her cries with his hand as he continued to drive his need into her over and over until she bit his hand and screamed out in release.

Peronell pulled herself from his pulsing need and turned around. She reached up and grabbed his hair, pulling him down toward her, tilting his head to the side and exposing his neck. She ran her tongue the length of his neck before plunging her now elongated, sharp teeth into him. She guided his manhood back into her wet entrance as she continued to drink from his neck. He pushed himself into her until he found his own release. Waltham supported himself against the edge of the table as he leaned into her, spent from orgasm and blood loss. "You are mine," Peronell droned in his ear.

"I am yours," Waltham repeated almost mechanically as he pushed himself from the table. He began dressing. Peronell ran her fingers over the material of her dress, and the fabric began to weave itself back together, repairing the damage as if it had never occurred. Waltham refastened his armored chest plate before turning back to Peronell. She was smoothing her hair to regain her polished appearance before they presented themselves back to the commotion of the castle. Her control over him faded, leaving Waltham confused and looking questioningly at her.

"That will be all for now, Commander Waltham." Peronell tilted her chin.

"Yes, of course, Your Majesty." Waltham nodded respectfully.

Peronell wiped any evidence of blood from her lips before she opened the door. Waltham followed her out into the hall. A small sound pulled Peronell's attention as she looked back into the library, scanning the room for the origin, but Terrowin's voice distracted her.

"Commander?" Terrowin questioned with narrow eyes when he witnessed Waltham and Peronell exit the library together.

Peronell dismissed the old man's question and quickly interrupted. "Thank you for your time, Commander. I know you are a busy man, especially now." Several guards were within range of overhearing their conversation. She was cool and formal as she spoke.

"I am always at your disposal, Your Majesty, to address any of your concerns," Waltham said with a bow before he turned and acknowledged Terrowin as well. He headed toward the king's private council room to join the others to discuss the matters at hand.

"My queen," Terrowin said in farewell, but he did not hide the accusatory look in his eyes before he turned to leave.

"Terrowin?" Peronell called after him. He turned his gaze back to her. "You do not look well, old man. In fact, you look like death." Her words were full of menace.

Terrowin only turned and walked away.

Chapter 15
PERONELL

As a small girl, Peronell had discovered she was different, that she had abilities like no other. When her emotions ran high, strange things would happen. Small objects would move, glass would shatter, or she could change a thought in someone's mind when it suited her.

After a time she confided in her twin sister, who told her that she too was blessed with such gifts, but it was important not to share this knowledge, or to use them against anyone. They kept the secret close, not sharing it out of fear of what others would think. They would slip away into the woods, free of anyone who might witness their actions, and would test their limits. In the beginning they practiced moving things with only a thought, a small stone or leaves. They would stir the wind around them to ruffle their hair or cause the clouds above to release rain so they could dance under the showers. The girls would laugh and dance for hours, enjoying their secret world. It was not long before unease grew within Peronell; passing thoughts became consuming and undeniable as she was pulled toward darkness. Peronell and her sister no longer saw things in the same light. Something powerful began to grow between them.

One day Peronell decided to explore new ways to use her powers. She had grown restless with her sister's complacency and wanted to see how far she could push herself. She left her sister sitting in a flowery meadow next to their house, watching the clouds pass by as Peronell ventured into the forest. It was not long before she came across a deer. The creature stood still on its graceful legs, watching Peronell approach. "Stay," she commanded as she locked eyes with the creature.

She stood before the trembling animal that could not move, despite its instinct to flee. She smiled wickedly before she narrowed her eyes and concentrated on exploring new possibilities. The deer let out a shrill noise before blood began to drip from its eyes. To this day she could still remember the pleasure while she watched the animal suffer as she exercised her control over it.

Her sister found her with the dead animal completely drained of its blood. Peronell did not even remember deciding to act on the impulse, but the thrill of it was still thick within her. The look of horror on her sister's face made her realize the difference between them was very real, despite their identical appearance. Her sister turned and fled from her without a word.

Her father discovered her surrounded by dead animals and high in a state of euphoria from exercising her newfound ability to take life. She was completely intoxicated by the power it gave her. Her sister had run to him and told him of her actions. She felt betrayed by the one person who should have stood by her side. Like her sister, her father did not see her potential; instead he was disgusted with her actions. He had never reacted to her in such a way, like she was the devil himself standing before him. She tried to explain, but he would not hear her. That was the first time he raised a hand against her. He beat her so badly, she could not walk home until days later. She lay upon the earth, unable to move from the pain that her father had inflicted. When she was finally able, she made her way back home. She remembered the look of disgust on her mother's face when she walked in the front door as she ushered her sister from the room. She could hear her sister's tears long after she left. Her father sat at the table and looked at her with a clenched jaw. That was when she realized that he had thought he had beaten her to death. He had never expected her to return.

"You have shamed our family by welcoming the devil into your heart." His cold eyes stared her down. "You are no longer welcome in this house. You are nothing to us. *Nothing*. Leave." Peronell could feel no emotion in his words, she was already lost to the people she had called family. She had never felt so powerless as she did in that very moment, when her family turned her away for something she did not understand.

That was the beginning of the darkest time in her life. She was turned out on her own as a girl, too young to understand the world. She barely survived and was subjected to the darkest moments that she ever endured before she became a woman. Men greedily took her young flesh and discarded her without keeping promises they made. She refrained from using her powers, no matter how hard things became, trying to earn back her family's love and acceptance. She wanted to prove she was not evil like they claimed. She stole food only when she had to, and she learned to defend herself from the predators that sought to do her harm. She became hardened. The girl she once was that used to laugh and run through the fields catching butterflies had died when her family abandoned her, and she mourned herself as much as she did them.

It wasn't until years later that she encountered her parents in the street. Their eyes fell upon her, but they did not acknowledge the shade of a person she had become. Their denial when she was clearly in need caused the wound of rejection to reopen. The pain was too much to bear. It was then that she realized they were just as guilty of the evil she was being punished for. In that moment, she realized something she wanted even more than the family she sought to be reunited with: revenge.

That night she returned to the small cottage where her family still lived, warm and comfortable, away from the hardships she was subjected to everyday. She released the energy that she had held on to so tightly since her father had nearly beaten her to death, and it roared to life within her. A trail of fire flickered before her, growing in intensity as it gathered strength on a path toward the home. The familiar house that now seemed like a place in a distant dream ignited, burning with the same ferocity as her broken heart. She wanted them all to burn; her sister for betraying her, her father for disowning and beating her, and her mother for doing nothing. She could hear their screams as they tried to open the door that would not release and the windows that would not break to allow them to escape. Peronell watched the flames consume the cottage until they suddenly dissipated, leaving no sign that they had ever roared to life. Her sister stood before her on the lawn.

"You will not do this." Her sister was beautiful and full of life, everything that Peronell could never be again.

"You cannot stop me," Peronell seethed.

"I will always stop you."

"Why do you defend the people that would beat and disown their own daughter? Why have you forsaken me? We are the same, sister." Peronell narrowed her eyes accusingly.

"We were never the same. Look at you." Her sister's tone was not condemning but desolate. "You have always played the victim when you have in fact been the wolf among sheep."

Peronell looked down at herself to see dried blood staining her dress. As hard as she tried, she could not remember whose it was. She knew it was not her own, for no injury afflicted her. "You are my sister. How could you betray me?" she said despondently. Her perception of reality was suddenly becoming unstable.

"The moment you allowed evil to enter your heart, you were no longer my sister. It is you who are tainted. You are the one that betrayed us. You cannot even see the truth before your own eyes. Do you truly not see the lies you have spun to justify this hatred within you, the evil that you inflict upon others? You are not the victim; you have never been the victim."

"But our parents—"

"Are dead because of you." Her sister cut her off. "This house, this land, is all that I have left of my family. I will protect it from you." She waved toward the side of the property, where three headstones stood together.

"Dead?" Peronell walked over to the graves. Three stones stared back at her. Her parents' names as well as her own marked their surface.

"Stop pretending you are the one wronged and see through your own web of lies. Face what you have become."

With a touch of her sister's hand, flashes of reality pierced Peronell's consciousness. Memories played before her eyes. The day that her sister found her in the woods covered in blood and the lifeless body of the deer beneath her.

"*Peronell … what have you done?*" Her sister was terrified as she looked down upon her.

"*I want to make them bleed. I want to make them all bleed. I want them to fear me,*" Peronell heard her young voice say. "*I want to see their fear as they look into my eyes and know what I can do.*"

Her sister fled from her, running away and leaving her with only the trees surrounding her. The sun began to fade when her father approached. She looked up from the blood staining her hands. She did not know how much time had passed, but she knew that his color was wrong. His normally tanned skin was white as he looked down at her. There was fear in his eyes, and it made her stomach growl with hunger.

"*Peronell? Darling? I do not understand. Why did you do this?*"

"*Daddy,*" Peronell whispered. "*Help me.*" A tear escaped her eye and trailed through the blood upon her face.

Her father approached, leaning down on his knee. He reached out his hand to her. "Come. *Let us go home. We can talk about this later after we get you washed up.*"

Peronell stared at his hand for a moment before reaching out to accept it. She pulled it against her before pulling a sharp rock across his wrist. She wanted to spill more blood. The idea of it made her heart race. She could hear her father's cries as he tried to pull away from her, but it made his blood flow faster as he struggled with her. Then he began trying to free her hold on him. He hit her with his free hand, but she did not feel any pain of contact. She was consumed with the high of knowing the pain she could inflict on others, the power she could wield over them. When she finally released her father's hand, he pulled it close to his body. His wide, searching eyes landed on her.

Peronell locked her eyes with his, trying to make him bleed out like she did the animals, but the defence of his mind was stronger. Instead she lunged at him, using the rock as a weapon, stabbing him over and over as he tried to flee from her. Every strike caused euphoria to pump within her. She felt completely detached from herself, having given in to the dark need that had been building within her for so long. It was not until long after his struggles ceased that her mind regained some clarity, but the reality of the situation still evaded her, and her own injuries began to register as the numbness wore off and pain began to assault her. Peronell curled up into the side of her father's still body and took comfort in his nearness. His eyes, gray and lifeless, stared up into the sky, and she wondered why he looked so strange.

"*Daddy?*" she whispered. "*Hold me.*"

When Peronell found the strength to move, she crawled from the forest. Her mind was still a haze of confusion. She remembered her father hurting her, and then being alone and cold as the trees swallowed her in darkness. She could hear whispers carried upon the wind. She spun around on her unsure feet to discover the source of the words but was left with nothing. The ground spun and twisted, and she tried to retain her balance as she stumbled through the trees. She tried to focus her blurred vision but tripped over the uneven ground. Upon closer inspection she noticed that there were dead animals all around her. All covered in blood, body after body lining the forest floor, their dead eyes staring back at her.

Peronell was relieved when she reached the field of tall grass that led to her home.

When she opened the door to her home, her mother's wide eyes met her. "*Peronell! What happened?*" Dried blood soaked Peronell's clothing. A sob escaped her mother's lips as she took in her daughter's condition. "*Where is your father?*" Her mother grabbed a blanket and wrapped it around her shoulders. She sat Peronell down and leaned in front of her. "*Darling?*"

"*I am nothing to you,*" Peronell whispered. "*You hate me because I am not like her.*" She pointed at her sister, hatred coating her words.

"*What? Do not be foolish, Peronell. You know that is not true.*" Her mother wiped her face with a cloth. "*I love you both.*"

Peronell looked up, and the blurred image of her father appeared before her. "*You have shamed our family by welcoming the devil into your heart.*" His cold eyes stared her down. "*You are no longer welcome in this house. You are nothing to us. Nothing. Leave.*"

Peronell grabbed a knife and slid it across her mother's throat. Her mother's eyes widened in horror when she realized what her daughter had done. She grasped at her neck, trying to draw in a breath that she no longer could before she collapsed upon the floor.

Her sister's scream tore through the air, pulling Peronell from her clouded thoughts.

"*Sister.*" Peronell stood to approach her.

"*What have you done!*" her terrified sister screamed. "*Leave!*" Before Peronell could move, her body was thrown by an unseen force from the house, the door slamming behind her. No matter how hard she tried to open the door, it would not comply. Her sister's cries echoed in the air behind her as she walked away from the only home she had ever known.

She had been living in a reality that she created to explain the events that had occurred. She had killed her parents that day; they had been dead this entire time. When she accepted her dark gift, it distorted her reality; it made her thirst for power. When she had seen them pass her by without any acknowledgement, it was because they no longer existed. They were but ghosts to this world, memories stirred to life.

Now, Peronell looked up into her sister's sad eyes, and she laughed a heartless, hollow laugh.

"This whole time I lived every moment trying to win back their favor, and they were already dead." She continued to laugh. "The things I have done … for what?"

"As long as I am alive I will make sure that you cannot inflict your wrath upon others."

"Thank you for the enlightenment, sister. Things get a little twisted in my head, but now that I know the truth, I can focus on what is most important. I will become more powerful than anyone, and nothing will stand in my way. See you soon, dear sister." With those words, Peronell turned and left.

Chapter 16
AJAX

The hour was late when Ajax returned to the camp and approached the dying embers of the fire. He could see Oliver's form and the rhythmic rise and fall of his chest, indicating he was deep in sleep. Lorelei was not there, and he could not hear any sound of her moving around nearby. She was gone. His stomach fell with the realization. He kicked Oliver with more force than necessary, abruptly jolting him from sleep. An inaudible protest escaped Oliver before he raised his head, taking in Ajax's stern face and Lorelei's vacant space. "Where is Lorelei?" Oliver became alert instantly, panicked as he scanned the perimeter.

"I was going to ask you the same thing. You were supposed to be watching her." Ajax fumed as he scanned the area, looking for any signs of a struggle, but could find none. She had left of her own accord. "She left." Ajax kicked at the dirt, spraying it upon the hot coals that sizzled hungrily. Claws of dread closed around him, restricting his chest. "*Bloody hell*," he spat out. He knew with certainty that he needed to find her now. Marcus was out there. He would not hesitate to hurt Lorelei, and it made Ajax's blood run cold.

"We have to find her." Oliver rose purposefully to his feet. Ajax knew Oliver well enough to discern that he was heartbroken with the realization that Lorelei had left, though he tried to hide it behind his determined brow.

"*We* are not doing anything. You will stay here and wait for Letholdus to return. *I* am going to find her." Ajax cut off Oliver's protests with a cold stare.

Ajax readied his horse as Oliver looked on. He did not want him present when he confronted Marcus again, and he knew that he would. Lorelei wouldn't have gotten far without Marcus catching her trail. He was an exceptional tracker, but Ajax was better, and he would find her. He would not accept defeat. Ajax mounted his horse, grabbing the reins. He gave a shrill whistle that pierced the air. When he was younger, his father had taught him a series of calls to communicate from a distance. It was a system they had used often in his youth when he still traveled with his father. With his whistle echoing through the trees, he knew that Letholdus would soon return to the camp. "Letholdus is on his way." Ajax turned and left before Oliver could complain.

His horse wove through the trees before they broke free of the tree line and continued in the open terrain. He could still scent Lorelei on the wind, knowing that she had taken the same path. The sky was still black, but he didn't need light to follow her trail. He could find anything once he had its scent, a skill he had perfected long ago and one of the things that made him the best at what he did. He would always know Lorelei's scent; it called to him like none other. He knew the precise moment she was intercepted by Marcus, and he turned his sights on Falls Landing. He urged his horse into a canter. Marcus would pay with his life.

Ajax was halted at the entrance of Falls Landing by the guards positioned at the gates. "What is your business at this late hour?" The guard approached him with reservation. The number of men positioned at the gate had increased considerably. The men were all alert, with their hands upon the hilts of their swords.

Ajax raised his hands to show his compliance. "I am in need of drink, gentlemen." He presented a casual smile as he relaxed his shoulders, seemingly a man bent on escape from his responsibilities.

"Aren't we all," the guard said without humor. "No one passes tonight, king's orders."

Ajax's horse stepped forward, and the guards drew their weapons. "Now, now, do not be so hasty. Are you going to deny a man the pleasure of a drink after his bitter wife kicked him from his bed?" Ajax took note of the guards' demeanor, the way their eyes surveyed him and danced around, trying to note anything suspicious about his arrival. Some of the guards looked young and inexperienced. The king was increasing the size of his force using commoners to prepare for a threat; he could see how terrified some of them were, standing armed without experience to guide their hand should they need to wield their blades.

"Turn and leave before you force us to act." The guard raised his sword. Ajax didn't press for entrance into the city; he knew that if he pushed, they would only push back, and that would raise alarms. There were other ways for him to enter the city unnoticed. "Or would you like to spend the night in the dungeon?"

Ajax wanted to retrieve Lorelei as quickly as possible; he needed to. The thought of something happening to her made him see red. He needed to find her and put distance between them and Falls Landing before the chaos about to unfold before the king's doorstep. He had noted the arrival of men traveling with discretion and purpose toward the city these past weeks. Men posing as merchants, farmers, even beggars under the noses of the king's men. These men were precise and their actions planned. Normally Ajax would stick around for the fight that was promised. The opportunity to brandish his skills, to stretch his muscles. A good fight always warmed his blood, but with Oliver and Lorelei in his care, he could not afford to indulge in the glory of battle.

He couldn't explain his motivation to protect Lorelei; he just knew that he would give his life to do so. He wasn't sure when his feelings had changed from the primal need to kill her mixed with an odd fascination to the now burning drive that ran hot to protect her and keep her close, making him question his beliefs. His body desired her like nothing else, his mind constantly trying to make sense of his need to possess her, take her as his own, and his heart's need to love her like no other. At first he gave into the physical need, thinking it would satisfy his captivation, but it only whetted his appetite. At one point Ajax even tried to convince himself that he was doing this for Oliver, but he knew he would be on the same road if the boy were not involved. He felt his prized control, invaluable to him as a warrior, unravel in her presence. He should have never given into his need; he cursed himself for his weakness. Though deep down he knew that his feelings for Lorelei were unavoidable. He was destined to give his heart and his sanity to one woman. He was hers.

"Very well. Good night, gentlemen." Ajax turned his horse away from the city. Once he was far from sight, he tied up his horse and then circled back on foot toward the walls of the city. He watched the men patroling from the crown of the wall as he slipped through their blind spots and pressed himself against the cool stone face of the wall. Ajax ran his fingers over stone that did not provide much in the way of traction for climbing. He removed the blades hidden in his boots and wedged them between the tightly packed rocks. He ascended as he worked his blades into the small openings, pausing just at the crest, waiting for the guard approaching his position to pass. When Ajax knew the coast was clear, he rose up enough to get a clear view while still remaining concealed from watchful eyes.

A guard was leaning against the stone with his back toward Ajax, who shimmied down the wall so the guard was within his reach. He raised himself up to confirm that no other guards were within view before he reached over the wall, grabbing the unsuspecting guard by the throat, and hauled him over the wall. Ajax crushed his throat before he was able to cry out and then released his hold, allowing the man to fall to the unforgiving earth. He heard the thud of the guard's body meeting the ground before he swung over the wall and ducked into the nearest cover of shadows.

Ajax knew that the guard's absence would eventually be noticed, and although his body would not be discovered until the morning light, Ajax planned to be long gone by then. He moved quickly in the shadows, silent and unnoticed as he fled from the wall into the heart of the city. A poster that littered the streets caught his attention; he picked up the piece of parchment to reveal an uncanny resemblance to Lorelei staring back at him. Their presence in town earlier that day had obviously drawn more attention than he hoped. The poster had the royal seal on it, meaning that his mission had just become much more challenging than he had originally planned.

The reward declared on the parchment was all Ajax needed to confirm what Marcus had planned. Marcus wanted the girl for his own benefit. He was not chasing her down to return her to Crewe, as he had tried to lead them to believe. Marcus's lack of loyalty was the reason Ajax had refused to continue training him, much to Crewe's dismay. Crewe believed Marcus to be his most promising assassin, but Ajax knew that Marcus would turn on his own mother if the purse was heavy enough, and that was not the type of man he wanted to help make into a deadly weapon. If Crewe only knew that his favored student was not the man he thought him to be.

Ajax knew that Marcus would have conducted the business

without delay; the call of coin was too strong for him to ignore, and in this very moment would be enjoying the spoils of his business. Ajax knew exactly where Marcus would be, and he moved purposefully through the streets, keeping out of sight of any patroling guards until the tavern came into view.

As he swung the door open, his presence did not go unnoticed. He knew that he looked deadly. His size and mere presence instilled fear in lesser men, rightfully so, since he was as dangerous as they feared. Holton opened his mouth to protest Ajax's entrance, but Ajax sent him a warning look that made the words die on his tongue.

Ajax took in the surroundings. In this late hour it reeked of despair, sex, and liquor. Dark, tired eyes of soulless men surveyed him curiously over the rims of their glasses. Ajax's eyes fell upon Marcus's form sitting at a table at the back. He was one of the few that didn't openly acknowledge his entrance, but Ajax noticed the subtle tensing of Marcus's shoulders. The shrill laughter died upon the whore's mouth, and she sank further into Marcus's lap, seeking protection. Her breasts were exposed to the room without care. Her hollow eyes took in his stalking presence and widened with fear.

Ajax approached Marcus, slamming the wanted poster upon the table, and he embedded his knife through the parchment. The men within Marcus's company readied themselves to defend their leader. Ajax noticed their full glasses and interest in Marcus and knew that Marcus had bought himself some protection with his newfound wealth; that was the reason for his false sense of security at Ajax's arrival.

"So you do have a heart," Marcus sneered. "Are you angry because it was I who got the girl after all?"

"If Crewe could see you now," Ajax seethed. The questionable characters that Marcus had paid for all crowded around, hungry for violence. Little did they know that Ajax was more than willing to offer it, and they would be on the receiving end.

"Ajax, I assure you that his hatred of you for betraying him overshadows all else. As you can see, I no longer have the girl. Once I got what I wanted, I no longer had use for her." Marcus's lips curled into a derisive smile as he fondled the woman upon his lap. She tried to force a smile onto her face, but her lips trembled with fear. She clearly wanted nothing more than to flee, but Marcus kept a firm grip upon her. Ajax's entire body was rigid with hot, restrained anger, and Marcus had just lit his fuse.

A scantily clad woman climbed to her feet from a kneeling position upon the floor. The man that she had just serviced stood fastening his pants, his attention now focused on Ajax. She smiled seductively as she wiped her face with the back of her hand. "Who is your handsome friend, Marcus?" She sauntered over to Ajax. She stumbled on unsteady feet, oblivious to the tension that riddled the air or the fact that Ajax was anything but friendly. Her dark, stringy hair was in disarray, and the rouge on her lips smeared her chin as she smiled lazily with the intention of seducing him. She had youth, but that was her only appealing quality, and her breath reeked of ale.

"She's on me, Ajax, enjoy," Marcus sneered as he lifted his drink to his lips. The woman pulled the strings of her dress, untying her bodice to display her heavy breasts.

"Do you like what you see?" she purred in a raspy, tired voice. Ajax pushed her hand away irritably when she grabbed for his pants, causing her to misstep. She fell into Marcus, knocking the bottom of his glass that was raised to his lips. The amber liquid splashed into his face and over his clothes, as well as onto the other woman on his lap. Marcus looked down at his saturated clothes and narrowed his eyes before giving a subtle nod to one of his men.

"Look what I get for trying to be nice." Marcus tried to sound casual, but his voice could not hide his anger. A man approached Ajax from behind, but his advance was cut short as Ajax brought his elbow up and drove it into his attacker's face before he turned around, snapping the man's neck. The man fell to the ground, and silence settled over all of the bystanders.

"Who's next?" Ajax questioned the men. The shady men, so eager to protect Marcus only moments before, backed away. "I see your men are as loyal as you are, Marcus." Ajax kicked out a chair and sat down next to Marcus. He could see a nervous sheen break out across Marcus's forehead. "You do not deserve to wear the mark of the Raven." Marcus swiftly grabbed for a blade concealed in his vest, but Ajax intercepted his move, grabbing Marcus's wrist and twisting the weapon from his grasp before driving it into the table next to his own blade. The woman sitting in Marcus's lap screamed and tried to flee. Marcus shoved the struggling woman into Ajax before making a grab for another of his hidden blades.

Ajax stepped easily out of the woman's path as she tumbled to the ground. "Looking for this?" he said. Marcus's fingers searched for the blade that was no longer on his person.

Ajax spun Marcus's second blade around in his hand in a showy manner, similar to Marcus's own flashy blade work, a display that Marcus liked to use to impress others. Without warning, Ajax made his move, bringing the blade down through Marcus's tattoo of a raven on his wrist and into his thigh, pinning his arm to his leg. The mark of the raven was the initiation into Crewe's league of men, trained to be disciplined soldiers for hire.

Ajax had known Crewe for years. He was a good man, and Ajax supported his endeavor to train an elite group of men. The king himself had used the Raven's services many times when he needed something taken care of discreetly. They were disciplined, precise, and most were loyal to a fault, with a few exceptions, Marcus being one of them. Their price was steep, and they were a last resort, but when they were called upon they were always victorious.

A groan of pain exploded from Marcus's mouth in a rush of breath as he grasped at the handle of the blade pinning his arm against his leg. "Bloody shite!" he gasped. Ajax stayed Marcus's hand that now tried to pull the knife free.

"If you pull it out, I will just shove it in somewhere else," Ajax threatened.

"*What did I bloody pay you for!*" Marcus yelled at the men surrounding them before turning his attention back to Ajax.

"Apparently they don't think you are worth saving," Ajax scoffed, leaning back in his chair.

"You cannot kill me. It goes against the Raven's code." Marcus gritted his teeth through the pain. Blood dripped down unto the floor beneath him, pooling under his chair, and sweat ran down his temples.

Ajax tilted his head. "Oh, did you not know? I am not officially a Raven. I do not adhere to any code but my own." He pulled back his sleeves to reveal he did not in fact that bear the mark. The realization dawned on Marcus's features, and fear drained the color from his face.

"There must be some kind of agreement we can come to. Name your price." Marcus reached for his breast pocket, the sound of coins clanging as he retrieved the hefty reward he had collected for turning in Lorelei. Ajax felt the air shift behind him, and grabbed his blade from the table, turning toward the man trying to attack. Ajax drove his blade into his attacker's eye, staying him midstride before he dropped to the floor. The smell of spilled blood was pungent in the dank, stagnant air. Ajax turned his attention back toward Marcus when he felt the sharp sting of a blade piercing his side. He met Marcus's satisfied sneer as he twisted the blade with his good hand and drove it in to the hilt.

The smile fell from Marcus's face when he noticed that Ajax was not yielding to the injury. Instead, Ajax reached down and pulled the blade from his flesh. It was an injury that might have been fatal had he been made of the same flesh as any of the men here. Instead he pulled his shirt up to reveal the already healing wound. Marcus, along with all the other men, stared in amazement as his skin returned to its original state.

Marcus was talented with his blades; his skill was remarkable. It was the reason why Crewe turned a blind eye to his nature and continued to invest in him as a prized soldier, even when Ajax pleaded against it. Marcus's very soul was poisoned by greed and lust.

Ajax flipped back the chair Marcus sat upon. When Marcus hit the ground, his own blade was embedded through his throat into the floor beneath him, pinning him to the ground with Ajax's hand still firm upon the hilt. Marcus's eyes widened in panic as he convulsed, fighting for air.

"Unlike you, I cannot be bought." Ajax leaned in close so that Marcus's fading senses could see his face clearly as he left this world. Marcus grabbed hold of Ajax's shirt, ripping it open to reveal markings that clearly startled him. Marcus tried to speak, but only blood sprayed from his mouth. Ajax looked down, noting that Marcus had seen the intricate design that was tattooed upon his chest, a mark that was thought to be only legend. He was no ordinary man, and now Marcus knew how very wrong he had been to cross him.

Ajax watched in satisfaction as Marcus's eyes glazed over and death claimed him. He reached into Marcus's breast pocket and retrieved the hefty reward that Marcus had collected. Readjusting his shirt before he stood, he noticed the shaken faces of all those who had witnessed the brutal killing. Ajax opened the purse, reached in, and proceeded to scatter the coins upon the floor. "For your silence." The stunned onlookers stood frozen in fear. Ajax turned on his heel, leaving them behind, and tossed the remaining coin to Holton, who was scowling from behind his bar.

As Ajax neared the door, men began diving onto the floor behind him in an attempt to retrieve the money. Ajax pushed through the doors, leaving the chaos behind. He knew where he would find Lorelei. He needed to find a way into the castle.

Chapter 17
LORELEI

Lorelei sat upon the cold, wet stone floor. Her clothes did nothing to quell the chill that radiated from the shadows. The only sounds were the cries of others that shared the same fate, trapped behind the unforgiving bars. After Marcus had delivered her to the castle, she was brought directly down into the dungeons and locked away, with no answers to the countless questions that paraded through her thoughts. The guards said nothing to her as they locked the door, leaving her in darkness. Despair was the only company kept by the bodies huddled in each cell, and Lorelei feared it would not be long until she welcomed it as well.

She leaned against the bars, trying to see down the long corridor lined with cells. It seemed to stretch on endlessly, and she wondered how many people were locked away in the stone walls, praying for freedom.

"Are you scared?" A small voice brought Lorelei's gaze directly across the hall. A young girl on the verge of becoming a woman leaned against the bars; her eyes were haunted in the dim torchlight. She looked so small and fragile leaning against the iron bars.

"Yes," Lorelei answered truthfully. "Are you?"

"I tried to be brave... My father always told me to face things with two feet firm on the ground." The girl looked down at her pale hand, resting against the cold black metal of the bars. "But the guards told me I will never be able to go home. I will never see my family again." A sob escaped her lips as she trembled. Her small frame folded into herself as she dropped her shoulders, shrinking her even further. She closed her eyes and took a deep breath, and when she opened them she wiped her face, smearing dirt across her wet cheeks. Lorelei could tell the girl was desperately trying to hold herself together.

"What is your name?" Lorelei sought to distract her from her sorrow. The dress the girl wore, although now soiled from the dirtied stone floor, looked as if it was a beautiful shade of blue. This girl was loved and missed by someone beyond these walls. She could see the loss the girl suffered in her sad eyes.

"Clara," she whispered softly.

"Clara, my name is Lorelei. We cannot give up hope. Your family needs you to stay strong." Lorelei smiled, despite her own misery. In the darkness it was hard to hold on to something bright. "Tell me about your family."

Clara sat up taller, pulling away from the wall. She grasped the bars with her hands and pulled herself up. "I have a baby brother." She almost smiled. She became lost in her thoughts, and her big eyes flashed with the brightness they had once possessed as she revisited her memories.

"What is your brother's name?" Lorelei encouraged.

"Beval. He is still really small and cries a lot, but he always smiles for me. Mother said it is because he likes me best. Do you have a brother or sister?"

"No, it has always just been my mother and me. I miss her like you miss your family." Lorelei smiled sadly. The truth of missing her mother and her home caused a twist of pain within her chest. She placed her hand over her heart. At times she could almost feel her mother close to her, like she was watching over her. Lorelei hoped with all her being that her mother was well. "There is also someone else…" she found herself admitting. Lorelei wondered how she could have ever thought she would be able to cut her ties with Ajax. "His name is Ajax."

"Is he someone you love?" Lorelei could detect the curiosity in the young girl's voice.

"I don't know. At least… I'm not sure how I feel. Maybe."

"I always wondered what it would be like to fall in love. I bet he misses you. Maybe he will rescue you?" Clara sighed dreamily.

"No. I left him. I thought it was best to leave because being together was too hard." Lorelei watched her hands twist around the bars.

"Oh… but maybe hard is better than nothing," Clara said hopefully.

Lorelei smiled. "Maybe you are right, Clara."

"Do you miss him?" Clara sat up on her knees, trying to draw herself closer to Lorelei.

"With all my heart," Lorelei confessed, leaning her forehead against the bars. She had made a complete disaster of everything.

"That sounds like love to me," Clara said, youthful hope shining through her words. Lorelei smiled thoughtfully in response. Clara dropped her hands from the bars. "They think I am a witch. That's what they keep calling me, but I did not do what they claim." She looked down the corridor as they heard footsteps. She shrank fearfully back into her cell. Clara was swallowed by the darkness, and Lorelei could only make out a shadow. She stayed quiet for a moment until the sound faded away in the distance, and Clara leaned back into the dim light.

"I believe you. I think I am here for the same reason," Lorelei whispered.

"What are they going to do with us?" Clara asked with wide eyes.

"I don't know." Lorelei truthfully didn't know what was in store for them, but she had the feeling that was probably for the best.

"I am so hungry," Clara breathed as she leaned back against the wall.

"We are all hungry, *little girl*," a hollow male voice barked distastefully from a few cells down. "Do you think they care if we starve? They want us all to rot. Now stop your incessant chatter."

"Look at me, Clara," Lorelei said. "Do not listen to him."

*   *   *

The darkness that enclosed them made it impossible to tell the passage of time. Lorelei shifted her weight upon the hard stone that did nothing to provide comfort to her exhausted body. She refused to move from the front of her cell, where she could keep an eye on Clara. The girl's slight form was lying upon the floor, pressed against the bars. The constant rise and fall of her breathing gave Lorelei comfort. Clara had talked to Lorelei until she grew too tired to keep her eyes open. Lorelei sat in the heavy stillness that hung around her. Her eyes watered from the sting of fatigue, and her bones ached, but she feared giving in. The occasional whimper or cry from another prisoner had kept her alert enough to avoid the call of sleep thus far, but she didn't know how long that would last.

A sudden stir of voices roused Lorelei's attention. She sat up taller and leaned against the bars to see what was causing the commotion. She caught sight of a dark form moving soundlessly from cell to cell. The only indication that someone was there was the voices of the prisoners who were questioning the strange presence.

"Clara?" The voice, though quiet, was deep and matched the man's large physique. He stopped at a cell further down, trying to see into the darkness. A thrill of hope exhilarated Lorelei.

"She's here," Lorelei whispered as loud as she dared. The figure turned at the sound of her voice and remained still. Clara reached out between the bars and pointed to the cell across from her. The man moved down until he took in Clara's sleeping body upon the cell floor. He reached in the bars and gently shook her shoulder.

"Clara?" She stirred and lifted her head. "Your father sent me. I need you to remain quiet and come with me." Clara only nodded and sat up and the man moved his attention to the lock. He pulled tools from his pocket and began working on opening the door. Lorelei remained soundless as she watched. Clara climbed to her feet and dusted off her dress, her shoulders higher and her demeanor hopeful. When the lock clicked, Lorelei had to stifle her gasp of relief. The man ushered Clara from the cell. "We have to free Lorelei too." Clara stayed her feet and pointed toward Lorelei.

"No ... no," Lorelei whispered. "Just go." She waved for them to keep moving.

"Free *me*." The loud man that had frightened Clara earlier called toward them. "Take me with you. I can help you." The man spoke too loudly in the quiet surroundings, and soon others were taking notice of the escape.

"Just go, please. There is no time," Lorelei whispered frantically when the man who had freed Clara took a step toward her cell. He seemed to be mesmerized by Lorelei as Clara clung to his arm. "Leave now, before the guards come." Lorelei's words suddenly sobered him. "Clara, you have to go. Think of your brother and your parents," Lorelei reminded her as Clara reached for her through the bars. Lorelei pushed her hand back through and motioned her away as she heard Clara's quiet sobs. "I will be fine. Go."

"Let me out!" the loud male prisoner called again. He made a grab for Clara as she passed, grabbing her dress. Clara's savior pulled her closer, breaking the man's hold.

"Quiet, before I cut your head off," Clara's rescuer whispered harshly before he shoved the prisoner back through the bars of his cell. He wrapped his arm around Clara protectively as they continued quickly down the hall.

"Guards!" the prisoner bellowed angrily. "The witch is escaping!" It wasn't long before the sound of footsteps rumbled toward them. Lorelei grasped the bars so tightly that her fingers ached. The sounds of the guard's voices echoed down the long corridor. Lorelei closed her eyes, hoping they had made their escape. Clara deserved to be free — she *needed* to be free. Then the devastating sound of Clara's scream cut through the commotion, and Lorelei fell to her knees. She could hear a struggle, and Clara's cries carried through the air.

*   *   *

Lorelei lay on the ground, staring up at the dark ceiling that loomed over her, long after Clara's cries faded. The sounds of tortured flesh lingered much longer as the guards punished the man that had broken into their walls and almost freed one of their prisoners. Lorelei wiped away the tears that continued to flow as she listened to the man endure more than she thought someone could withstand. Clara was not returned to the cell across from Lorelei, and she couldn't stand not knowing if she was alright. She desperately hoped that the guards did not raise a hand toward her.

The sound of heavy footsteps that came to a stop before her cell caused Lorelei to rouse and climb to her feet. The guard opened the lock and swung the door open. "Come with us." The guards stood rigid before her, dressed in their metal attire.

"Where are you taking me?" Lorelei questioned whether she should go quietly or fight for what could be the last few moments of her life.

"The prince requests your presence. You are to be taken to be prepared," he responded mechanically.

"Prepared for what?" Lorelei moved to step back when the guard reached out for her, but his hold was firm upon her arm, and he escorted her from the cell. As much as she could not stand the confinement of the dark, cold cell, she didn't know if what awaited her was worse as she forced one foot in front of the other.

Lorelei followed the men leading her of her own accord. She relaxed slightly and felt it a good sign that they did not restrain her. A small voice called to her as she passed a cell. "Lorelei." It was Clara. Lorelei stopped and leaned down to peer between the bars. Clara lay on the floor of the cell with a bloodied, tear-stained face. It immediately made Lorelei's eyes water.

"Clara!" she gasped. The guard was already reaching for her, but she shrugged off his hold until he impatiently forced her to her feet and pulled her away from the cell. "Be strong, Clara!" Lorelei called out. She had so much to say to the young girl, but she couldn't risk it in front of the guards.

Chapter 18

MARY

The streets were dark since the moon cast no light. Burning torches lined the streets, throwing minimal light upon their surroundings. The narrow houses cast looming shadows that swallowed the small figure weaving in and out of their cover. Soldiers patrolled, and fear of being caught fueled her hurried steps. She knew the streets well, having lived within the city walls her entire life. She did not need light to guide her path. When she approached the house she sought, she spun around, checking her surroundings before ascending the stairs. Her knock was only loud enough for her presence to be registered by the inhabitants as she slouched down against the wall, trying to calm her breath.

When the lock released, relief washed over her. Peter Bolton slowly opened the door, wary of who might be calling at this late hour. His surprise at the young girl's presence was evident. "Come in." He ushered her quickly inside. Mary slipped into the dark interior of the house.

"Were you seen? How did you get out of the castle?" Peter gazed out through a narrow opening in the curtains of front window, alert for signs of the soldiers.

"No one saw me. I slipped out when a delivery was made to the kitchen. I hid until it was dark enough for me to come unnoticed." Mary tried to calm the nervousness in her words, but they could barely squeeze past the lump in her throat and fell unevenly from her tongue.

"What news do you bring? Is this about Clara?" Bryce asked, appearing behind Peter. Mary looked up as they were joined by other men. She had expected them and was relieved to know that she had come to the right place.

"I think the better question would be how she knew how to find us. Who sent you?" Drake narrowed his eyes suspiciously at her, still wearing her uniform marking her as a servant of the royal family.

"No one sent me. I overheard other servants talking about Clara and how you were planning to rise against the king's ruling. I recognized Peter's name among those who were suspected to be involved. That is why I came here. I did not know where else to turn." Mary's voice was small and unsure as she took in all of the questioning gazes. Tears started anew, and she could not stop them from falling despite the audience in front of her.

"How can we trust her?" Donald said. "She could have led the guards to our door."

"I knew her father. She can be trusted," Peter confirmed confidently. "He was a good man."

"If she found us, it will not be long before the guards are upon our doorstep. We have to leave," Drake cut in.

"Why have you come, child?" Bryce could not turn to other thought with the hope of news of his daughter. "Do you have word of Clara?"

"No. All I know is that they are keeping her in the dungeon. I came because I saw something... Something horrible, and I do not know who to tell."

"Come, out with it then," Peter encouraged.

"Sometimes I sneak into the library when my work is done. I am drawn to the written word, and it is seldom that anyone enters, so my presence goes unnoticed. Last time I was there the queen came in with Commander Waltham. I hid so no one could see me, but what I saw I will never be able to forget. She put the commander under some kind of spell..." Mary tried to speak between her sobs. She took the handkerchief that was passed to her and wiped her face. "She drank his blood and she did unnatural things... I have never seen a real witch, but how can she not be one?"

"Bloody Christ," Peter said in disbelief. "The queen."

"How can this be?" Bryce was shocked.

"Peter, Darling?" Thea called as she entered the room. "We are ready to leave. The baby is asleep." Thea's attention was immediately drawn to the small girl. "Mary?"

Mary moved toward Thea, who awaited her with outstretched

arms. Mary's small frame was swallowed by Thea's embrace as she looked questioningly up at Peter. Mary took solace in Thea's embrace and cried in her arms.

"She will be leaving as well. She cannot return to the castle," Peter informed Thea, who nodded.

"Come, child." Thea smiled warmly at the girl.

* * *

Bryce

All eyes suddenly turned toward an abrupt knock at the door. Thea quickly led Mary out of the room, and the men drew their weapons before Peter neared the door. He peered through the window and waved for the men to lower their weapons. He opened the door, and a man in full royal armor slipped through.

"Alston," Peter acknowledged.

"You were named as possible suspect and will be questioned. You do not have long before they will be at your door. What of Thea and the others?" Alston's words were filled with urgency.

"Your sister is ready to leave, along with the others," Peter assured him.

"They must go now, Peter. She cannot be caught up in this. Dawson is waiting in the carriage, but he must leave soon. I will not be posted at the gate for much longer. Even now I must get back before my absence is noted. Merek will not cover for me for long. This is their only chance."

"Donald, take the women out the back," Peter said. The plan was to lead the women and children out to the awaiting carriage. They were all at a loss for words. It might be the last time they saw their loved ones.

"What of you? Where will you go?" Alston questioned. "You cannot stay here."

"We have a place," Drake said. "We are leaving now."

"Good." Alston turned to leave.

"Alston?" Peter stopped him. "What of Simon?"

Alston's shoulders dropped before shaking his head. "He will be executed. The trial will be announced tomorrow."

"No," Bryce cried out, raking his hands through his hair.

"Leave now, Peter. I cannot help you once you are discovered. You will meet the same fate as Simon. You all will." Alston's words sobered them from their grief as he turned to leave. "I can play no more part in this once my sister is free of Falls Landing."

"Understood."

* * *

Drake led the men through the back entrance of the tavern in the middle of town; it was their new safe house, a place that would allow them to remain in Falls Landing without being discovered by the guards. Bryce and the others had deep roots in this town where all of them were born and raised. They were grateful to the others who were sympathetic to their cause. These people were willing to allow them to carry out their mission, even though it meant they too were committing treason against the king merely by knowing the rebels' location and intentions.

Men came and went at all hours from the tavern, providing good cover for them, and they would not draw attention. The hour was late when they arrived, but the commotion in the main part of the building was at its peak. The back door was seldom used and well hidden away from prying eyes that were lingering in the front of the building. Holton's tavern was always crawling with men seeking drink and flesh. Parts of the building were cut off from the public through secret doorways built with the intention to hide matters from the law, should it choose to investigate the premises.

Holton was waiting when they entered the building. "This way." He motioned for them to follow. "No need to keep your voices down. You will not be heard over the antics from the bar. I already had to drag one dead body out tonight." He led the men to a wall and removed a picture, revealing the handle of a door that blended flawlessly into the wood paneling. They proceeded up a dark, narrow staircase that opened to a room. "Should you need a fast exit, these windows lead up to the roof."

"Thank you for housing us, Holton." Drake patted Holton on the shoulder.

"It is the least I can do." The bearded man shook Drake's hand before he left the men to their business. "I will send one of the girls up in the morning with drinks and refreshments. They will not speak of your presence." Holton stopped in front of Bryce. "Sorry to hear about your daughter, Bryce. We are all holding hope that she will be returned to you." They shared a look of understanding before Holton turned to leave.

Bryce looked around at their small group. Although they had grown slightly in number, they were still only a few compared to the king's army.

Rulf was a quiet man but skilled with his sword. Bryce had known of the man most of his life, but they had never spoken until now. His wife had recently died during childbirth, and he wanted something to fight for to give him purpose. He said little as the men made their plans, but his brow remained focused. Leo and Cedric were Drake's younger brothers. They, like their brother, were as loyal as they came to those they called family and friends. The family resemblance was uncanny, and those who did not know the brothers often confused them.

"We should try to get a couple of hours sleep before the sun rises." Drake sat down beside Bryce. They all had dark thoughts weighing heavily on their minds. "Simon knew what he was getting himself into. We all knew the risks." Though the words were true, it did not ease anyone's heartache.

* * *

The next morning, light filtered through the small windows within the room. They were all staring intently at the plans before them. Parchment, coins, and objects collected around the room all symbolized the setting of town square, the venue where the girls accused of witchcraft would be punished before the crowds that would gather to witness. This was where their plan would unfold, and it had to be carried out with outmost precision if they were to be successful. The small group had been planning action, but thoughts of Simon's execution weighed heavily on them. Footsteps on the staircase drew them all from their somber thoughts. Holton opened the door with a determined look. "Teller is here," he stated, moving immediately toward the window. "A horse just arrived at the gate with the heads of the soldiers that disappeared from Lady Mariam's escort. It has to be him. The horse is spooked, and they are still trying to calm it. The people are frantic seeing the king's soldiers in such a state."

"He will be here for the execution." Peter was still gazing out the window.

"Who? Teller? How could we possibly know that?" Bryce said as he went back to staring at their plans, hoping something would suddenly present itself. A solution they had yet to discover.

"I agree. Think of all the stories that we have heard. He makes bold moves and mocks the king. A man like that would not hide in the shadows. He would want to witness the chaos he is creating. He will walk around under the king's nose and plan his next move," Cedric offered with an approving look from Leo, who seemed to share his opinion.

"I will not put my faith in a man I do not know." Bryce shook his head.

"Do you honestly think we can pull this off on our own? We have been staring at that bloody map all morning, and we still have yet to figure out a way to survive this. We need help. There are too few of us to carry out any plan with success," Peter pleaded.

"Why would he help us?" Bryce sat back, looking up at his friend. He knew that Peter was right. Even with Drake and his brothers' impressive skill with swords and intimate knowledge of the city, their chances were undeniably slim.

"We have to hope that he is sympathetic to our cause," Drake said.

Bryce took a deep breath, coming to an unspoken conclusion. He looked down upon the candlestick that represented the hanging platform in the middle of town square. "We will need some cloaks, Holton." He reached up and knocked over the candlestick. The sound was piercing in the otherwise silent room.

Chapter 19
LORELEI

Lorelei awoke at the sound of a door opening. She had been taken to a lavish room the night before, after they had escorted her from the cell. She was surprised when the guards led her to this room, thinking they must have been mistaken to drag her from the cold depths of the dungeon to here. A woman had immediately appeared and insisted on dressing her in a sleeping gown, providing a cloth to clean her hands and face, but refused to answer any of Lorelei's questions. Now that same woman approached her bed once again. "I trust you slept well, my lady. I must ready you for your meeting with the prince."

"What does he want with me?" Lorelei rubbed her tired eyes as she tried to rouse her body. As exhausted as she had been the night before, she had spent hours staring at the ceiling long after the woman left, waiting for the guards to charge in on her when they realized their mistake, until sleep finally claimed her.

"That is not for me to know, my lady." The woman pulled back the blankets indifferently before moving to a wardrobe on the other side of the room, shuffling through the garments hung within. A couple of women who looked much younger than the gray-haired woman who had wakened Lorelei began to carry out certain tasks. More women began entering the room, carrying pitchers of water that they began pouring into the large tub in the far corner. Lorelei could see the steam slowly rise into the air from the water. She crawled from bed and moved toward the tub.

Two women immediately started dressing her bed once her feet touched the floor, and Lorelei was surprised by the commotion around her. The call of the water made her skin tingle with anticipation. She reached in and touched the heat of the soothing liquid. She had never felt water warmed to such a temperature. Different smelling liquids were poured into the water, making the room smell like blooming flowers, and Lorelei breathed in deeply.

"I will help you undress, my lady." A young brunette with large brown eyes reached for her gown.

"May I have some privacy, please? I am not used to so much… help." Lorelei backed away. All of the eyes in the room seemed to be on her. "Please. I would like to be alone." Lorelei smiled at the gray-haired woman to whom the others were suddenly looking at for direction.

"Very well. We will return to dress you." She nodded and led the others from the room.

Lorelei breathed a sigh of relief when the door closed behind them, and she slipped from her gown before stepping into the tub and completely submerging herself in the heat of the water. She preferred the refreshing cool temperatures of the water that ran over the earth, but after lying on the cell floor and having the chilling dark seep into her, she couldn't complain. She could feel her body thrum with energy, as it always did when she was connected with water.

Before long the gray-haired woman was at her door, asking if she was done with her bath. "Just a moment, please," Lorelei requested.

The woman gasped with a wide-eyed expression. "Your eyes… they are glowing."

Lorelei turned away from the woman, bringing her hands up to rub her eyes. "Must be a trick of the light." She smiled awkwardly. "I am almost finished, please give me a moment." She wasn't sure if the woman accepted her explanation, but relief washed over her as she left once again.

Lorelei slipped reluctantly from the water before pulling on a large, soft coat that had been laid out for her. She walked over to the dresser, noticing the reflection of the room around her. She knew what a mirror was, but she had never looked upon one. As she approached, she found herself looking at someone she had never seen before but felt she had always known. It was strange to set eyes upon her own person, and she was pleased to see that she did indeed bear a resemblance to her mother. She ran her fingers along her pronounced cheekbones and deep, full, red lips. She focused on her eyes, something she had tried to envision her entire life. They were still glowing, like the woman had mentioned. Lorelei closed her eyes, trying to calm the energy flowing through her, breathing slow and deep to relax her racing heart. When she looked upon herself again, they had faded back to a normal color, much to her relief. She studied them, one blue like her mother's and one green like her father's. A reminder that she was the best part of both her parents was what her mother always told her.

"I trust your bath was to your liking?" The woman was back with her entourage behind her, and Lorelei could only sigh in defeat. The woman searched Lorelei's face for a moment and seemed to accept that it must have been the light that caused her eyes to appear to glow. The women were determined to dress her and ready her for the prince, and she had no choice in the matter. The women set to combing her hair and smoothing lotion upon her skin. It smelled like they had captured summer in the very bottles. Before long Lorelei was dressed in a gown so intricate and exquisite, she was afraid to move, her hair curled and braided into a style fitting for a queen. Looking in the mirror, she felt as if she were gazing upon a stranger.

A lavish tray of food was placed upon the table near the window, and her mouth watered at the sight of the delicious display. "Is that for me?" Lorelei gasped.

"Yes, my lady." The older woman encouraged her forward with a wave of her hand.

Lorelei walked closer to the food as hunger assaulted her. She picked up a piece of bread and bit into the soft texture. It melted in her mouth, and she could not help the groan of satisfaction that escaped her. Lorelei opened her eyes and saw the women watching her.

"My apologies, I am just so famished. Would you like some?" Lorelei offered.

"No, my lady," the older woman assured her quickly, despite the looks on the faces of the young women in the room.

One of the girls went to the door to retrieve a guard. He entered and directed his attention to the woman in charge. "Alert the prince that the girl is ready for him." The guard nodded before leaving.

Lorelei reached out to the older woman, whom the others referred to as Ayleth. "Please," Lorelei pleaded softly. "Does he wish to kill me? Is that why I am here?"

Ayleth looked down at Lorelei's hand upon her forearm. She began to withdraw it out of fear she had offended the woman by placing her hand on her, but Ayleth's hand came up to reassure her. Ayleth wore the brow of a hard, determined woman, but her features softened with Lorelei's plea. "I have worked within these walls for all my life, my dear child. I have seen both virtuous times and dark, but never has the air tasted so bitter. I do fear what is to come, but I can offer you some words to ease your mind. If it were the Royal Prince's wish to do you harm, you would not have been seen to as you have been, though I truly do not know if the outcome will be any more desirable, I am afraid." Ayleth squeezed her hand in a soothing gesture before she gathered the girls to leave the room. "Do not trust easily, my dear." Ayleth offered a small smile before she turned to leave Lorelei alone in the large room.

Lorelei grabbed a napkin from the tabletop and wrapped some of the food in it, tucking it into the folds of her dress. Where the fabric bunched, pockets formed that easily concealed the food within. She jumped when the door swung open again almost immediately after Ayleth left.

"I am to escort you to the prince, my lady." A man stood before her dressed with chainmail and the rich colors of the royal family that Lorelei had noticed on the other castle guards.

"Very well." Lorelei sighed as she moved to follow the man. She had no time to mentally prepare herself for the meeting. She pushed on with the hope that this would not be as bad as her imagination had conjured.

The stone corridors were long and seemed endless as they walked through the castle. They took many turns down halls that looked an exact replica of the one before. Lorelei tried to keep track of their location in relation to the room they had just left but was finding it exceedingly difficult. Small, narrow windows cast minimal light within the stale walls. After many turns, Lorelei was pleased to see the halls begin to widen, though the pictures hung on the walls only made these new areas slightly more welcoming than the last. The somber faces in the paintings stared back at her in a way that made her skin crawl. Light cast by the many torches mounted on the walls made visibility better, and Lorelei was also relieved to know that the castle was not an endless maze.

The guard stopped before a large set of double wooden doors, carved with intricate details of trees in a beautiful display of a forest that reminded her of home. She wanted to run her fingers along the lines, but they swung open before she could entertain the idea. The interior was a large, open room with a ceiling so high that Lorelei had to look up to see its peak. A large stone fireplace moulded into the wall was before her and roared hungrily with a large fire. Paintings of breathtaking scenes adorned the walls, some serene, others violent as they told a story that unfolded throughout the pieces.

Three people stood in the center of the room. Their conversation ceased when they noticed her arrival. Lorelei's feet were frozen to the ground as she squirmed under their studying gaze.

"Come closer." The younger of the men spoke to her. The scroll that he had been reviewing before her arrival was discarded as he passed it to the gentleman beside him. Lorelei was too nervous to call a smile to her face as she compelled her feet to move toward them. All three men were dressed in fine clothing, matching the extravagance of her own apparel. The youngest of the men seemed to hold the power in the room by the way he carried himself and the way that the others responded to him. "Exquisite." The young man's eyes appraised her as if she was a meal to eat, and he was starving. Lorelei attempted to read him, trying to determine if he was a threat to her. He had sharp features that worked together to create a distinguished face with a cold beauty. His eyes were blue but had a strange darkness within them, causing chills to break out upon the surface of her skin. Something dark lurked beneath the exterior of this man, and it terrified her. This was the prince standing before her. She had no doubt after Ayleth's words.

"I have never seen such beauty, Your Highness," the man to his right proclaimed with an awed expression. He was older and had many lines creasing his pale eyes, and his hair was peppered with gray. Lorelei was uncomfortable, as if she was being critiqued like a piece of art, and wanted nothing more than escape their penetrating gaze. The third man stood quietly, silently studying her. His broad shoulders and thick arms looked more like a warrior's than the slimmer build of the others. His eyes were clear and focused, and she could tell by his tense posture that he was trying to read her as well, but not for the same reasons as the others. His eyes were not appraising, but calculating. That was when Lorelei noticed something that caused her heart to race. This man before her had a white ring around the pupil of his eyes, something that Lorelei had only ever seen in the eyes of two other men, Ajax and his father. The feature stood out so abruptly in their similar dark blue eyes. If this man had the same initial reaction to her as Ajax did, she feared he might pull a weapon on her.

Lorelei quickly turned her focus back to the young man in the center when he asked for her name. "Lorelei, Your Highness." Lorelei tried to force a smile when she addressed the prince. She suddenly felt barbaric in this world of titles and finery she now found herself in and did not want to offend someone that held so much power over her.

"I must apologize for your treatment last evening. There was a misunderstanding with my guards as to the reason for you being brought to the castle. I can assure you that it will not happen again." The prince's words did not bring her comfort; his tone implied punishment was dealt to those had brought her to the cell last night, and this only brought her sadness.

"If I may ask Your Highness, why am I here?" Lorelei forced her voice to project in the large room.

His smile was one of amusement. "Your presence in Falls Landing caused quite a stir with the people. Maybe we can start with what house you belong to?"

"House?" Lorelei asked, unsure.

"Your family's name." His tilted his head as he studied her. "Surely someone so lovely comes from noble blood."

Lorelei forced her chin to stay up and to show no weakness to the men before her. "I only have the name of Lorelei, and my only family is my mother."

"Well now, are you not a very well-packaged mystery?" The prince stood from his chair and began to circle Lorelei, who remained still. "Charles, see to it that Lord Caunter is given refreshment as he awaits my father. And send word to Commander Walton."

"Of course, Your Highness." Charles turned toward Lord Caunter. "Follow me, my lord." Lord Caunter followed Charles from the room after he bowed his head and exchanged pleasantries with the prince. His eyes took in Lorelei once more before he left.

When they were alone in the room, the prince stood in front of Lorelei, gazing down at her. Lorelei lowered her gaze, uncomfortable in his presence. The prince lifted his hand to her face and ran his fingers along her cheek in a very slow display before gently closing his hand around her chin, tilting her face up toward him. "Where did you come from?"

"Would you believe me if I told you I do not know?" Lorelei gasped out of fear, but the prince seemed to read it as something entirely different. Excitement flashed in his eyes.

"Tell me, Lorelei with no name and no home, why have you come to Falls Landing?"

"I was visiting," Lorelei answered pathetically. She did not know what to tell this man. She knew that she did not trust him with any truths.

"You will stay here as my guest," the prince proclaimed.

"Why... for how long?" The questions fell from her lips before she gave them any thought.

"For as long as I say." The prince turned his attention toward the door, dropping his hand from Lorelei's face. "Mother," he acknowledged without conviction. Lorelei had not heard anyone enter the room but turned her head to see a very regal woman dressed in a full-bodied gown. It looked as if it must weigh heavily upon her, with all the lush fabrics woven together. Her hair was twisted into an elaborate style, presenting a stunning face that seemed much younger than the maturity she carried herself with. Power hummed in the very air around her as she moved. There was no question that this woman was the queen.

"Arthur dear, whatever are you up to now?" The queen moved toward them with utmost grace. The woman's eyes instantly narrowed as she neared Lorelei. "And this is?"

"Green does not suit you, Mother," Arthur snickered.

The queen turned a sharp look upon her son, causing his laughter to die upon his lips but the humor to remain in his eyes. "When you are done playing with your toys, you will join us for dinner this evening. It is Lady Mariam's first evening with us."

"Of course. I would not miss it," the prince answered in a bored tone. The queen reached down and took Lorelei's hand. Lorelei tried not to pull away from the cold, unnerving feel of the queen's skin upon hers. She ran her jewel-endowed finger down the palm of Lorelei's upturned hand. The tip of her finger was capped with a claw-like ring that ran sharply along Lorelei's flesh until it drew blood. Lorelei gasped in pain before trying to retract her hand, but the queen held true. "I will see you at dinner, Arthur." The queen dropped Lorelei's hand. "Make sure you put your toys away first." Then she turned to leave, as quickly as she had come. Lorelei clenched her fist against the lingering sting of pain.

"Come, I will show you the gardens." Arthur offered his arm; he was not fazed in the slightest by his mother's odd behavior. Lorelei was grateful for the distraction and quickly accepted. The prospect of viewing flowers after being within these damp stone walls made a thrill of excitement course through her.

The sun was warm as they stepped out of a large stone archway that framed the beginning of a vast array of colors. A sigh of appreciation escaped her as she took in the magnificent garden that was groomed to perfection.

"It is quite beautiful." Arthur looked around before his eyes came back to Lorelei, watching her take in the surroundings.

"Why did you bring me here? I do not understand." Lorelei met Arthur's eyes; every time she did she was reminded that he was not to be trusted. Every part of her was repelled by this man. His cold beauty unsettled her to the very core. His eyes held no light, no reflection of the beauty around him.

"I thought you would appreciate the garden." He raised a brow as he studied her face.

"No, I meant, now that I have told you who I am, why must I stay?" Lorelei tried to ask without offending him.

"Because I want to keep you," he answered bluntly.

"People are not possessions." Lorelei tried to make her demeanor seemed relaxed.

Arthur smiled down at her like she was a silly child. They had rounded a corner to reveal a large mural on the walls, a backdrop to a large rose garden with deep red blooms that reminded Lorelei of the blood smeared across her hand. Any further words that had formed upon her lips fell away when she took in the details of the painting.

"It is a depiction of a story about the gods, one of my favorites, actually. There are many different ones throughout the garden."

"What, may I ask, is the story?" Lorelei could not pull her eyes away from the piece.

Arthur pointed toward the portrayal of a beautiful woman; she was formed from the very water that embraced her as she rose above the surface of the sea. She was painfully striking; her face looked lovingly upon many beautiful women within the water before her in a display of worship. These women were portrayed with tails of fish as they encircled a large ship that sailed upon the water.

"The story begins with the sea and the goddess that ruled its vast depths and bountiful reach over the earth. Amphitrite was a beautiful goddess that throve on the stories of the pirates that sailed her waters.

They whispered her name in fear of her wrath, for as their ships sailed her waters, they were at her mercy. She had been known to swallow ships into the darkness of the watery depths, never to be seen again, for merely painting her image in a less than perfect impression.

"When the sailors' numbers grew upon her watery territory and her name became whispered less and less, she retaliated against their insolence. She created beautiful feminine creatures that would be irresistible to men, setting them free into the sea to regain the respect she desired. She wanted power over the men that sailed her sea. She wanted them to fear and desire her above all else.

"These beautiful creatures created by Amphitrite became known as Sirens, entrancing sailors, enticing them with irresistible beauty and song, luring them into the sea and devouring their souls before casting their bodies to the murky depths below. They were as beautiful and deadly as the sea itself. The sailors feared the disappearance of their fellow men. Amphitrite basked in the flood of worship that followed. She was once again the most feared goddess and gained back the respect she craved.

"Amphitrite nurtured her Sirens as children of her own flesh, her pride swelling as wide as the waters in which they resided, but when one of her beloved Sirens unknowingly preyed upon a sailor that had captured Amphitrite's heart, she turned on them. In her grief she granted his surviving sons the gift to destroy her Sirens, bestowing upon them a desire to hunt down every one of them until her waters were free of her own children. The firstborn son of every generation of these three sons was to carry this same gift, until her daughters were no more. These soldiers were called Men of Savas. They were said to be men of impossible strength and speed. They were unstoppable and immune to the lure of the Sirens."

Lorelei was surprised at how familiar he was with the story. She watched the hungry look within Arthur's eyes. He yearned for such power, and Lorelei feared what Arthur would be like if he were unstoppable, like the men he admired. "Why do you look so worried? It is a mere story told to our children." Arthur waved as if to dismiss the story. Lorelei couldn't find words. She could only think of Ajax and what he believed her to be. She felt nauseous. The painting had lost all appeal now that she knew the story behind it.

"You look pale," Arthur observed.

"I fear I am tired and unwell." Lorelei did not even attempt a smile.

She felt drained and wanted nothing more than to return to the privacy of her room and allow herself time to think.

"Jarin, return Lorelei to her chambers," Arthur ordered a man standing at attention nearby.

"Yes, Your Highness." Jarin turned toward Lorelei. "This way, Lady Lorelei."

Arthur raised Lorelei's hand to his mouth, bestowing a gentle kiss. "Until later." He smiled. Lorelei only nodded in response, her throat too constricted to let words pass.

Lorelei followed the guard into the castle. She immediately missed the warmth of the sun, but solitude was more desirable at this moment. "What is that way?" Lorelei asked of a hallway leading down a darker area. It was wider than the other corridors but was dismal and lacked in any finishing touches.

"It leads to the dungeons, my lady."

This was an opportunity to see Clara, and she needed to take advantage. "I lost something important to me when I was in the cell. May I go retrieve it?"

"I will have someone look for it and bring it to you." Jarin did not slow his step.

"But I…" Lorelei tried to object.

Jarin turned and faced her. "I have strict orders to escort you to your chambers, and that is where I will deliver you."

"Very well," Lorelei sighed. Jarin turned to lead on, but Lorelei's did not move to follow. Instead she turned swiftly and moved down the darkened hall on soundless feet. It was an ability she had developed long ago when she wanted to move through the forest without disturbing the timid creatures that lived there. She hoped that she would have enough of a head start before Jarin noticed she was not following him. She came to a familiar door, one that she had been led through when she was taken from the dungeon the night before. Lorelei pulled open the heavy wooden door and slipped through. It led to a dark, narrow staircase with only a few torches to light the way as she descended. When she reached the bottom of the stairs, two guards were stationed at the entrance. They looked at her in obvious confusion as she approached.

"Prince Arthur allowed me to come down here to retrieve something I lost while I was kept here," she said with as much confidence as she could gather.

"Excuse my questioning, my lady, but it seems unlikely the prince would allow you down here, especially unescorted."

"It will be but a moment. I dropped it on the way out. I only have to retrace my steps," Lorelei insisted.

The men looked at each other. Lorelei slipped by quickly. "I will be right back." She moved hurriedly before they could stop her.

Lorelei scanned each cell in the dim light, looking for Clara. She found her curled up in the corner of the cell she had seen her last. "Clara?" Lorelei whispered urgently. The small girl raised her head. A weak smile graced her dry lips. She could hear the guards talking and knew her time was short. She pulled the food she had wrapped and thrust it through the bars. "Take this." The girl reached out and took the package. "Hide it," Lorelei ordered. "I will try to bring you more when I can."

"Thank you," Clara's frail voice responded.

Footsteps neared, and Lorelei knew she had run out of time. "I will be back, Clara. Be strong." She moved quickly away from Clara's cell and pretended to search the floor as Jarin rounded the corner with a very displeased look.

"Found it," Lorelei announced, tucked a stone she found upon the floor in her pocket, and patted it with a smile.

"Let us get you to your chambers." Jarin was unamused and did not take his eyes from her as he led her out of the dungeon. He only spoke to her when necessary and made certain that she went directly to her room before giving the two guards stationed at her door orders to see that she stayed within.

Lorelei was only in her room a few moments before the door opened and a woman entered carrying a tray. She observed Lorelei with a narrowed gaze. She was a brunette with eyes that matched perfectly the color of her hair. She was taller than Lorelei, with full curves that announced themselves through her full skirt. "I was sent to help you undress," the woman snapped as if wanting to be anywhere but in this room.

"Thank you." Lorelei was grateful for the help. Her dress was tied intricately along the length of her back, and she could not reach the ties.

The woman used more force than necessary as she loosened her dress, but Lorelei held her tongue; she needed the help and would not be able to manage on her own. When the woman pulled down the heavy fabric of the dress, Lorelei stepped out and felt immediate relief from the restricting form. She was brought a nightgown before the woman poured her wine to drink from the tray she had brought in when she arrived. "To help you sleep. Do you need anything further?"

"No, thank you..." Lorelei trailed off. The woman was already retreating through the door before she had spoken her answer. "Nice meeting you, too," Lorelei breathed sarcastically. She brought the glass to her lips and breathed in the sweet aroma of the wine. It smelled delicious and made her mouth water in anticipation. The thick fluid was as delectable as its aroma as Lorelei let the velvety smooth texture flow into her mouth. A comforting heat radiated from her stomach.

Lorelei noticed movement from the corner of her eye. She turned to see a dark figure of a man. She barely had time to react before he was upon her. His hand closed around her throat as she struggled against his hold. She had never seen this man before, with dark, unfeeling eyes as haunting as his brutal, scarred features. The pressure upon her throat caused darkness to spot her vision as she clawed at his grip. She managed to land a blow with her knee that jarred his hold enough to break free.

Scrambling to the other side of the bed, her feet barely grazed the floor before she was hauled backward. His hands found her neck again, this time pinning her down so she was immobile. No sound could pass her lips as she tried to call for help. She was no match for his strength. She could feel her body weaken without breath. A burning sting tore across her neck as his hand suddenly released her. She tried to draw much-needed breath, but her body would not cooperate. Panic seized her as the man loomed over her. His cold, emotionless eyes were the last thing she saw before only darkness.

Chapter 20
BROM

King Brom leaned back in his chair, hearing it groan in protest at his substantial weight. His body no longer held the form of a soldier from his youth but reflected his life of indulgence. His private sleeping quarters were only decorated with his favored weapons, swords he had wielded in battles, and armor from his numerous triumphs. His most treasured prize of all was the first bow his father had given him. He had shot his first deer with that very bow, and it was the start of a lifelong love of the sport of hunting. Basic furniture and a bed occupied the room, with no unnecessary decor. It was simple, far from Peronell's ornate styling of the rest of the castle. Peronell had not shared a bedroom with him since the birth of their son, another preference of his. His hatred for his wife was almost tangible, and he knew that it was returned in kind. Over the years they had found a way to coexist, fulfilling their duties as king and queen.

Brom tried quieting his mind to concentrate on the woman before him, but he had found himself lacking in control as of late. He wound his fingers through the young woman's long brown hair, reeling in the softness of it. Sadness washed over him as he was overcome with memories. "Sybbyl…" he breathed.

The girl pulled away from his lap, looking up at him. "My name is Maria, Your Majesty." Her swollen lips smiled nervously.

"Your name is what I say it is, child." He spoke more harshly than he intended, but he did not feel guilty. He did not feel much of anything lately but the anger and darkness that seemed to be festering within him, something he could not escape. He knew that his heart was poisoned, slowly changing him into a stranger. He was now only a shadow of the man he once had been. Brom brought his wine glass to his lips and drained the last of the spiced red contents. He had lost count of how much he had consumed today. It was the only thing that he felt he had control over, and it took the edge off his frayed nerves. Brom closed his eyes briefly and relaxed into the blissful numbness that the wine brought to his mind. He tossed his empty cup upon the floor and turned his attention back to the woman tending to him.

She stood up; her long brown hair flowed in long waves over the soft pale skin of her shoulders. "I have missed you, Brom." It was a voice that he had mourned for the last twelve years, no longer the faceless girl that he had called to his chambers to service his needs but the woman he had thought about every day for as long as he could remember.

Brom was speechless as he looked upon Sybbyl. *His Sybbyl*. It had been years since he set eyes upon her beauty. He feared the years would slowly dissolve his memory of her until he could no longer recall her face, but he had been wrong. He forgot nothing. She was the best part of him, and when he lost her he had turned into a man he no longer recognized. A man that was becoming as dark as the evil from which he had tried to protect his kingdom. "How is this possible?" Brom closed his eyes and opened them again, but she was still peering down at him with her clear blue eyes and soft smile.

Sybbyl leaned into him, pressing her naked flesh against his body. His hands eagerly drank her in. "My sweet Sybbyl." He gasped as he returned her affection, kissing her soft lips that sought his.

"Make love to me," she whispered against his ear. She lowered herself onto him, her wetness welcoming him. Brom gasped in pleasure as she rocked her body against his. Sybbyl leaned back, exposing her perfect breasts as she moved like a graceful dance. His sun-weathered hands roamed over her perfect creamy skin, relishing in the feel of her body. A pleasure he never thought to experience again.

When her moans became strangled, Brom froze in place. "Sybbyl?" Her eyes were no longer clear and vibrant but dull and cast in white. An angry red line cut across her throat before blood began seeping from the wound. Brom watched in a state of shock as the thick red fluid flowed over her pale flesh. "Sybbyl!" Brom gasped, desperately clinging to her.

Sybbyl's hand reached up, running her fingers limply down his chest, gasping for a breath she could not seize. A stinging sensation burned over his chest. He looked down in confusion to see the clawed ring of Peronell carving a line in his skin through the fabric of his shirt. When he brought his gaze back up to Sybbyl, it was no longer her but Peronell upon his lap with a twisted smile. "*You* killed her and your bastard child. It is your fault they *suffered*."

He threw Peronell off him, and she landed hard on the stone floor. A whimper of pain escaped her lips as she looked up at him with terrified eyes. The girl that he had originally welcomed to his chambers was sprawled out naked on the floor beneath him, tears threatening to fall from her eyes. Blood dripped from her swollen lips, and her skin was red from abuse. He did not remember striking her, but she lay terrified before him. Brom shut his eyes tight and tried to shake off the chill that was slithering under his skin. "Go!" he ordered the petrified girl.

The girl frantically gathered her clothes, pulling them on before she fled to the door. Brom didn't bother with words of apology for the way he had treated the young girl or seek in any way to comfort her. He couldn't bring himself to grant her that respect. He only could think of pouring himself another drink to slow his frantic heart and clear his mind of the sight of his beloved Sybbyl suffering, and the sorrow that if she really had been here with him now, she would no longer love the man he had become. Brom filled the glass to the brim and downed it as if dying of thirst. It dripped down the front of his shirt as he drank it greedily.

A knock on the door called his attention. "What is it?" he barked abruptly. The door opened, and Josef Eldrine entered.

"Your Majesty, I apologize for my intrusion, but there has been a development. Commander Waltham awaits you in the council room." Josef bowed his head, awaiting a response.

Brom took a deep breath. "Let me change my clothes."

"Would you like me to send someone in to assist you, Your Majesty?" Josef stood respectfully by the door, his hands linked behind his back.

"No. Give me a moment." Brom waved dismissively.

"Very well. I will await you outside your door." Josef bowed, turning to leave.

When Brom walked into his council room, Commander Waltham met him. His arms were crossed and brow furrowed as he looked at the map before him. As the king entered, the men turned to acknowledge his entrance with a proper show of respect. John Blackburn stood to the right of Waltham, and Josef took his position amongst them.

Arthur stood in formal dress, leaning against the table. His son had a natural affinity for strategy when he wasn't chasing the fairer sex, which was far too often for Brom's liking. Charles Oxon stood amongst the group, as well as a few men that Brom did not recognize. "Your Majesty, may I present Lord Cedric Caunter, Marquis of Thetford. He brings urgent news of Teller."

"Lord Caunter, forgive me, but I must question your validity. These are not times when trust can be given easily, as I am sure you are aware of," Brom informed him.

"Of course, Your Majesty. I would expect nothing less," Lord Caunter agreed.

Charles moved around the table, presenting a scroll that he rolled out before the king. The document showing the Caunter family crest and proof of nobility was laid before him. Arthur nodded when the king turned his eyes to his son, indicating that he had already reviewed it for authenticity.

"I know your father." Brom turned his eyes from the scroll back toward Lord Caunter. "Tell me, how is he? I am ashamed to say that it has been a very long time."

Lord Caunter looked down thoughtfully before he brought his gaze back up to the king. "He is no longer with us. It is the reason I am here today. Teller and his men murdered my father."

"I am sorry to hear that. He was a good man I once called a friend." Brom reached down to lean against the table. His head still swam from the wine. His hand slipped slightly, but no one seemed to notice except for Waltham, who was watching him intently. Brom realized long ago that the man missed nothing, and it was one of the reasons he was the best of his soldiers. "Tell me the news of Teller."

"I returned home from a hunting trip to find the town in disarray. They had attacked at dusk before night fell, taking out our defences. So many innocent lives were lost… I found my father. He was barely conscious but was able to tell me what I needed to know. They believed my father dead, and he had managed to overhear them talking about heading toward the castle. They had a head start, and I followed their trail to your doorstep."

"Yes. We already know that they are here. What can you tell us of their numbers?" Waltham asked, eager for the information.

"They are outnumbered by your defenses, having only a small fraction of men compared to your numbers, but they are trained and keep hidden in the shadows. Our soldiers did not see them until they were already upon them. They are made up mostly of thieves and honorless men. I have brought men with me that have fought against them and survived. We wish to offer our help to prepare your men to fight them so we can eliminate them once and for all. Witnesses were able to provide a description of Teller so that I might present a face to place with the name." Charles presented the sketch to Brom. "I am at your service, Your Majesty." Lord Caunter bowed before the king.

"I want this face everywhere in Falls Landing." Brom handed the sketch back to Charles.

"Commander Waltham, see to it that Lord Caunter and his men are cared for, and then I want the men informed. You are all dismissed. I need to speak privately with the commander."

When the door closed behind the others, the commander was the first to speak. "Word has been sent to the Ravens with my fastest informant, Your Majesty. They should arrive within a day's time."

"Good, let us hope they arrive before Teller makes his next move. If the Ravens can deal discreetly with Teller, we can put this mess behind us. Inform me when they arrive. What of Barwicke?"

"We have extra eyes ready for the execution of Simon Cheney. We have it on good authority that he will make an appearance."

"Did Cheney give up any information?" the king asked hopefully.

"No, Your Majesty. As persuasive as we were, he still gave nothing. However, from what the people have told us of Barwicke, he will not hide while one of his men is being executed. We are trying to solve this as quickly as possible. We do not believe they would risk trying to enter the castle again, especially with the measures we have taken to ensure this to be impossible. We will draw them out of hiding."

"And if not?" Brom ran his hand thoughtfully over his beard.

"We still have the girl. They will not sit by silently forever. When is the trial?" Waltham leaned against the table. Lowering his head, he was at eye level with the king.

"A few days' time. Certain measures must be taken with the witch trials. The bishop needs time to ensure things are carried out properly." Brom noticed the dark circles under the commander's eyes. The man refused to rest until current threats were contained.

"Of course, Your Majesty. We will find them before then," Waltham said.

"Make sure that you do. Let me know of any developments immediately," Brom said dismissively.

"Yes, Your Majesty." Waltham bowed before turning to leave.

"Commander, keep your eyes on this Caunter character," Brom insisted. He knew nothing could be overlooked in the current state of affairs.

The commander's eyes swung around to meet Brom's, and he nodded. "Yes, Your Majesty."

Chapter 21
TELLER
Five years ago...

Twilight was upon the earth, and the shadows had merged, slowly dissipating any lingering light from the retreating sun. A man moved on soundless feet as he approached a small cabin tucked deep within the woods. Only the dull light of a fire could be seen within the window. He moved around to the back of the house. A window was left slightly ajar, and sliding his fingers within, he gently lifted up the window panel. His feet landed in the darkness of an unoccupied bedroom. He slipped his hand around the handle of the door and opened it enough to view the main room of the cabin. A woman stood in front of the fire, humming to herself as she stirred the contents of a pot hanging above the flames. Her figure was breathtaking. The fabric of her skirts did nothing to hide her enticing curves, and his heart raced thinking about them. He slipped through the opening while she was preoccupied and moved toward her.

"When are you going to accept the fact that you cannot sneak up on me, William Teller?" Her voice sang out beautifully. Although he could not see her face, he could hear the smile in her words.

"Never!" He grabbed her around the waist, causing her to scream with laughter.

"You brought me flowers!" She took them from his hand. His arm was still firmly wrapped around her waist. "They are beautiful." She turned around and gave Teller a quick kiss on the lips.

"That is all I get after traveling far and wide, braving many dangers to find you the most exquisite flowers in all the land?" Teller raised his brows in mock outrage.

"What did you have in mind?" She raised her eyebrow suggestively.

"Well, since you asked." Teller smiled wickedly, wrapping his arms back around her and pulling her close, nestling his lips against her neck. "It involves a lot less clothing," he whispered against her skin.

"If it were up to you, William, I would never be dressed."

"And what is wrong with that?" Teller reached up and ran his fingers tenderly down her cheek, looking into her clear blue eyes. "Have I ever told you that you are the most beautiful woman in all of creation, Josselyn?"

"Every day." She wrapped her arms around his neck. "Every single day, my love."

"That's not nearly enough," he responded.

"Are you hungry?" Josselyn asked, pulling away to check on the stew.

"Starving." Teller leaned in to smell the delicious food simmering over the fire.

Josselyn reached up and placed a hand upon the mantle to steady her when a wave of dizziness overtook her.

"Josselyn?" Teller was immediately reaching for her. "What's wrong?"

"I am fine, just tired," Josselyn tried to assure him, but Teller's determined face indicated that he did not believe her. She sighed in defeat as he led her to a chair. She knew Teller well enough to know that he would not let it rest until he had the whole truth. "It is my sister. She grows stronger still…"

"There must be something that can be done?" His brow creased in concern. "Tell me what to do."

"There is nothing. She has found a way to tip the scales. She continues to gain strength, despite my best efforts. I am only growing weaker, and now…" Josselyn's words died away. Her body stilled and her usual crystal blue eyes took on a white sheen. Teller grabbed hold of her hands, rubbing them to comfort himself more than her, because in this state she was disconnected from her body. He had witnessed her episodes many times, but they never became easier to bear. He knew that she would be drained afterward. She had already looked so pale and tired before that, and he feared she would not weather it well. The knowledge that she gained from her visions always weighed heavily on her. No matter her actions, she could never prevent fate.

Josselyn's heart was the purest he had ever known. She had become his world when he stumbled into her life, and he never looked back. He lived and breathed every day for her, and he wanted to give her everything. The fact that she struggled before him from a threat that he could not defend her from tortured him. He wanted to fight for her, to destroy the very thing that endangered his Josselyn, but he was powerless. She refused to give him the information he needed to protect her, no matter how he pleaded with her. She insisted it was her battle to fight.

As Teller gently held her hands between his, he recalled the first time he laid eyes on her. He had been traveling without a destination, a man without a purpose, moving from one town to the next, fighting every man who was brave enough to challenge him. Then one day on his travels he came upon her small cabin in the woods. He had his weapon drawn, unsure of what he had happened upon so deep within the forest. The nearest town was miles away, and he immediately assumed he would come upon the types of men that could no longer show their face within society. This was the type of person he came across hidden within the trees, far from law and penance.

He broke through the tree line, and his eyes fell upon her small, delicate frame amongst rows of plants in the vast garden. She stood up, even though his steps were without sound, and turned toward him. "It's about time." She smiled as if they were the best of friends.

"Excuse me?" Teller's face was a mask of confusion. He could form no other words as he took in every detail of the woman before him. Her long auburn hair was tied into a braid that fell over her shoulder and down to her narrow waist. His eyes roamed longer than proper on her curves before he brought them back up to her eyes, blue as the sky on a clear, sunny day. She was truly breathtaking to the point that Teller thought she was but a dream, an illusion of a beauty far beyond the world. She wore a knowing smile, as if she knew secrets that he was dying to deliver.

"You must be hungry," she said easily. "I have stew upon the fire. Come."

Teller shook his head to clear the spell. "You do not fear me?" he asked as she turned to lead him toward her house. "I am a stranger. I could mean you harm."

"No, William, I do not fear you." Her eyes lit up as she moved to approach him when he made no move to follow her. She closed the distance between them. "Do you fear me?"

"How do you know my name?" Teller looked into her deep, entrancing eyes.

"I know a lot of things." She giggled, reached up, and laid her hand on his chest. The unexpected motion made Teller tense under her touch. "Your heart races."

"Not from fear," Teller confessed. "What is your name?"

"You should be afraid." She dropped her voice to a whisper. "I am a witch."

"I do not fear beautiful creatures." He found himself breathless, as if he had come from battle. "A name?"

"You should. We are the most dangerous of all." She winked playfully. "My name is Josselyn." She took his hand in hers. Teller looked down at their entwined fingers. The simple touch made his blood warm and head swim. The truth of the matter was that he was terrified of the woman. It was as if she had reached into his black heart, and emotions he didn't know he could feel were now rushing through him. "Come, Teller, I wish to bewitch you." This time he fell into step behind her, his hand still in hers.

"You already have," Teller admitted, and Josselyn responded with a gentle squeeze of his hand as she led him into her cottage.

Josselyn now gasped for air, bringing Teller back from his memories. Her eyes, now clear, stared back at him. The color slowly returned to her skin as her body returned from the stasis that claimed her when she received visions of the future.

Teller grabbed a blanket and laid it over her as her teeth began to chatter from a chill. He pulled her onto his lap, showering kisses on her face.

"Why do you always fuss so much about something that is and cannot be changed?" Josselyn said quietly. "You know that I will be fine." She reached up and lovingly stroked his cheek.

"Because I love you." Teller squeezed her tightly. "Tell me what you saw." He tucked loose strands of her hair behind her ear.

A sad smile graced her lips. "Will you do me a favor?"

"Of course, anything."

"I need you to go to the healer. There are some rare plants I need that he grows." Josselyn moved to stand, and Teller assisted her. "I will need to write it down." She walked toward her table and retrieved her quill and a small piece of parchment. She sat down on the chair and wrote with shaking hands.

"Are you alright?"

"Yes, of course. I will be fine in a moment's time." Her smile was more convincing this time, and it put Teller at ease. Josselyn finished writing and folded the parchment before passing it to him. "I am just glad that the future is something my sister cannot access. At least I have that over her."

"This looks like a lot of ingredients. What is it for?" Teller asked, refolding the parchment and tucking it into his pocket.

"It will make me feel better. Stronger." Josselyn smiled.

"Then I will leave now."

Josselyn reached for Teller's hand. "There is time. You can leave in the morning. Now we must eat so this food does not go to waste, and then I do believe that I owe you for the beautiful flowers you have brought me." Josselyn reached up and ran her fingers through Teller's hair, pulling his smiling lips down upon hers.

Chapter 22
LORELEI

Light began seeping into the darkness that had claimed Lorelei. She was slowly becoming aware of the pain burning in her chest and neck. She didn't have the strength to face it and yearned to return to the unfeeling darkness that she was roused from, but her body would not obey. Clarity began to return as it bled through the haze. A warning of danger pulled at her, forcing her eyes to open. The light she was met with, although dim, stung her sensitive eyes. Her head throbbed as it tried to make sense of her surroundings. Blurred images gained clarity as reality tightened its hold on her.

Stone walls passed by, and it took a moment for her to realize she was being carried. She was held tightly against cool, plated armor in a vise-like grip. Her body did not obey as she tried to force herself to take action, and panic began to rise in her throat. She couldn't lift her gaze to see who carried her or determine where she was being taken. Instead, she felt herself falling away into the darkness again as her eyes closed without permission. Lorelei wanted to scream out in frustration.

She was only conscious for flashes of the journey, glimpses of dim light that told her nothing of where she was or who she was at the mercy of, and then only to feel herself fade again into the pain that consumed her. A moan from her own lips roused her as she was shifted and placed on a hard, unforgiving surface. The sensation of being lain flat caused a sudden rush of pain. She felt someone move her hands, then her feet, before she was able to pry her eyes open.

The figure of a man slowly came into focus standing over her. He was dressed in the full armor of the soldiers throughout the castle. Lorelei tried to move her arm, only to be met with resistance. She managed to turn her head slightly and focus enough to notice that her wrist was strapped beside her. Panic forced its way through the pain, finally giving her the strength to move. Lorelei quickly realized that she was immobile, her wrists and ankles bound. She whimpered in fear as she continued to struggle against the restraints.

The soldier reached up and removed his helmet, looking down at her with black eyes before stepping back and standing mechanically beside her with an unfocused gaze. Though it was not the same man, the look in his eyes reminded her of the man who had attacked her, that same emotionless gaze. "What… what do you want with me?" Lorelei managed through her dry throat. The words felt like sawdust in her mouth, and her throat ached. He remained unresponsive, as if she hadn't spoken. "Does the prince know I am here? I am talking to you!" Lorelei tried to kick out in exasperation at the guard's refusal to even acknowledge her, but the strap held tight.

Lorelei took in the surroundings of the dark room. Jars of all shapes lined every possible surface, filled with substances she could not even fathom. Some she could not bear to see because they looked like parts of what would have once been living things. A large stone fireplace dominated the room and roared hungrily beneath dozens of steaming pots suspended over the flames. There were two windows in the room, but they were blocked by plants.

"What do we have here?" Lorelei turned her head at the sound of the raspy voice. Another figure came into view, and Lorelei shrank away as far as her restraints would allow. The dark gray eyes of an elderly man looked down upon her. He was draped in a black cloak with a long rope tied around his waist that held many tools. "So you are what the queen is so fascinated with."

"Who are you? What do you want?" Lorelei gasped painfully.

The man's features shifted and changed before Lorelei's eyes. "I like her." The man spoke again, but his voice was different, younger. Reaching up, he ran his fingers along her cheek. The man now looked decades younger, a youthful face pressed forward stretching the wrinkled skin of the old man.

Lorelei tried to move away from his touch, but she found herself mesmerized by the features that continued to alter before her eyes, transforming. He aged again, but instead of becoming the old man, he became someone altogether different. His eyes changed from gray blue to a vibrant green and his nose became slightly broader, his brow more pronounced as he studied her with wonder. It was hard to determine the age of this new face; his skin did not tell of his age, but his eyes held the endless knowledge of someone of maturity. They were strangely unfocused, and Lorelei became lost in them. "Yes, she has a wonderful energy about her, an absolutely exquisite creature. What do you think she is?"

The older man's features once again took center stage as his skin sagged and his eyes darkened. "I have no idea, except for the fact that she is clearly not human."

A small wooden bowl was placed beside her, and then she could feel a damp cloth pressed against her neck. Lorelei sighed with pleasure as the liquid soothed her pained skin. "Truly remarkable." As the cloth was lifted from her neck, she could see it was covered in blood, causing her to gasp. "The water healed the remaining wound and left no scarring. It looks as if she was not even cut."

"Interesting." Another voice overrode the old man's and spoke through a mouth that again now seemed years younger.

"Scarring from what?" Lorelei panted at the still visible signs of her blood upon the cloth.

Green eyes looked down at her sympathetically. "Your throat was cut, as well as many lacerations to your chest."

"What?" Lorelei tried to pull herself from the table, to only be pushed back by a hand upon her chest.

"Please do not try to move. You will only hurt yourself," the green-eyed man ordered. Lorelei relaxed back into the table. Something about this version of the man made her want to trust him, against all reason. He reached out gently and touched her hair, as if trying to soothe her. Lorelei studied his movements, slowly becoming lost in thought. "You remind me of... I do not know. I think I can remember someone," he said as he pulled his hand away, saddened by his thoughts. Lorelei watched his mannerisms, the way he never really met her eyes when he spoke to her but rather was more attuned the sounds she made, even the slightest movement. She realized that he was blind in this form.

"I do not understand." Lorelei's words were only a pained whisper as she looked up into his strange, comforting eyes. "Why are you doing this to me?"

"I do not know. I am bound to her... I'm so sorry. If only I could remember." He pulled back abruptly, reaching up as his hands began clawing at his own face. He struggled against an unseen force until his eyes shifted back into the dark color of the old man's. He took a deep breath before collecting himself.

A sharp sting in her arm made Lorelei cry out. "What did you just do?"

"Belladonna."

"Belladonna?" Lorelei questioned with wide eyes.

"It is deadly nightshade; it contains a high level of arsenic as well as other ingredients that will encourage the lethal effects. Truly it is our best concoction. We have been perfecting this particular poison for situations like this. It should bring almost instant death." The old man smiled as he looked down at her while patting her shoulder, as if commending her for doing a good deed, and then stopped with a curious expression as if he was waiting for something to happen.

Lorelei's eyes grew heavy as a constricting feeling tightened her chest. She couldn't resist when her eyes closed and she drifted off. Her body gave in to the sudden exhaustion before she could register what had just occurred.

*   *   *

After an undetermined amount of time, consciousness started a slow trickle of light into Lorelei's dark, numb state. She could hear the commotion around her before she was able to open her eyes. The room was much darker now, and strange shadows were cast around her. She could barely determine who was speaking as she listened to voices drift across the room.

"We should run some more tests. She should not have survived it," the old man said.

"She seems to be able to break down any poisons with a water component."

The youngest of the three men's faces appeared, hovering over her. His hand began to caress her shoulder, moving toward her breast. Lorelei struggled against his advance, but she was helpless to.

"Stop. Please Stop!" Lorelei could barely form the words as she tried to struggle. He leaned down against her and ran his tongue along the side of her face while his rough hands fondled her.

"She tastes delicious." He breathed his hot, rancid breath against her cheek. Lorelei whimpered in response to this invasion of her body. She stilled as he pulled away abruptly and watched his features stretch as if his face was being torn apart, an anguished scream escaping his lips.

Lorelei was mesmerized by the strange incarnation of the man before her. He cried out in agony, grasping at his chest as a large mass began to protrude under his garment. His face stretched, causing his eyes to bulge, his skin pulling taunt. Other features appeared next to his own, forming a new face, dividing from his own as it pulled away. Two personalities strained against each other, trying to gain control of their shared body. Lorelei was relieved to see those green eyes appear on the new face, the least threatening of the three men that presented from his character. He reached up and pulled the weakening partial form of the younger man into himself, absorbing him completely. "Many apologies." He faltered, grabbing for the side of the table. He leaned against it, trying to calm his heavy breathing and regain his strength.

Lorelei did not know how to respond; instead, she only stared at the creature before her. One body housing three different men. Though she would have thought it impossible, here she was lying before it. "Who are you?" she asked in astonishment.

"I…" He bent over in agony before he pulled his body upright, and green eyes were no longer looking upon her.

"That is precisely what we are trying to determine about you." The older man had returned. "Do you care to share with us?" The old man had retrieved a magnifying glass and was examining her fingernails, very interested in their pearlescent glow. He pulled a sharp object from his belt and cut a piece of her nail from her finger before collecting it in a small dish.

"No," Lorelei managed weakly when he released her hand. It felt lifeless and foreign as it landed back on the table.

"I did not think it would be so easy." He frowned thoughtfully at her before turning and leaving her line of vision, although she still could hear him shuffling around the room.

"Why are you doing this?" Lorelei pleaded.

"We do what the queen wishes." She heard the voices of the old and young man mesh together. There was adoration in their tone. "And she wishes you dead."

"Why? I did not do anything." Lorelei felt a tear slip from her eye.

The old man leaned over her. "Her Majesty owns us. She created us, and we shall serve her always." He smiled with misplaced pride. "She does not like things more beautiful and powerful than her. We can feel your power. She can feel it, see it, so you must end. Cease to exist." He pulled his robe aside, and Lorelei noticed the gaping hole in his frail chest where a man's heart would be. "She owns us," he repeated before moving away from the table. Lorelei squeezed her eyes tightly closed, trying to clear her mind and formulate a plan to survive this.

The guard at the foot of the table still stood motionless, eyes focused on nothing. It was as if his mind no longer occupied his body. He did not even seem to be conscious until her captor requested his assistance and he walked out of her line of sight. Both sets of footsteps faded into the distance. Lorelei strained to see where they had gone; neither could be found in her line of sight. The onset of silence led her to believe they had left the room. Her breath was returning to a normal rate, but she was still weak, her body protesting when she tried to move. She found sleep once again calling to her, but she refused to leave herself vulnerable to these men. A low hum of energy that she hadn't noticed before tingled through her fingers, pressed against the wooden table. Her body began to crave it and pull it into her like a glass of cold water to her parched mouth. Although it was not much, it did offer slight relief as she felt soothing heat flow into her body.

Lorelei could feel some of her strength returning and twisted her wrists to see if she could loosen the straps. The wood beneath her groaned quietly in protest before giving way, and her wrist pulled free, along with the strap. She stilled momentarily, hoping neither of the men noticed what she had done. When she was confident had gone unnoticed, she pulled her other wrist free before she discreetly worked on her legs.

Lorelei's eyes moved toward the only door she could see in the cluttered room. She gathered her remaining strength and pushed herself off the table. The wood cracked and gave way under her weight, but she no longer needed its support. As soon as her feet met the floor, she dashed across the littered room. Her fingers grasped the handle of the door and wrenched it open. Her feet halted instantly when she was met by Queen Peronell, an unamused scowl upon her face.

Lorelei backed up into the arms of the soldier, who was now behind her. His armor-clad arms fastened around her, stealing her breath as he held her immobile. Lorelei had no choice but to surrender.

Peronell swept into the room, the scent of her sickeningly sweet perfume suffocating in the already warm and airless area. The room crackled with a strange energy around the queen and felt harsh as it brushed against Lorelei's skin.

"Tell me," Peronell seethed. "Why is our guest still breathing, if you are the very best at what you do?"

Fear radiated from the man, and the features of all three personalities blurred together in a strange ensemble that made it difficult to focus on his face. "My queen." The voices overlapped as they bowed to her. "We gave her very potent elixirs. She should not have survived any of it." The youngest man spoke above the others.

"I do not care about your failures," Peronell spat as she spun around with a narrowed gaze that landed on Lorelei.

"Yes, of course." The elderly man, seemingly the only one present, judging by his features, was studying the table that Lorelei had been secured to. "This is an interesting development." He broke a piece of frail, splintered wood from the table that crumbled in his hand. "She drew the life force from the wood."

"What does that mean?" the queen demanded, spinning to lay her eyes on Lorelei with disgust as she tapped a clawed nail upon her lip.

"We do not know for sure. We would like to study her. Find out what makes her the way she is. It could help us learn." The trio of voices collided together.

"No. I want her gone. Arthur has developed an unhealthy obsession with the girl, and too many others are asking questions," Peronell snapped.

"Yes, of course, my queen. We have just finished something that should work. We have concluded that she heals from anything with a water or living component. We have created something with neither of these that should burn her from the inside, while leaving her looking untouched. She will not survive it." The older man was now at the forefront of the body.

"Go ahead, then. Give it to her," Peronell said impatiently, waving the man to move.

"Yes, Your Majesty." He picked up a metal bowl on the table and made his way over to Lorelei, who began a futile attempt to escape the guard's grasp.

"Do not do this, please," Lorelei pleaded as he neared her. "Please." She could see only a flash of the green eyes she was looking for before they were gone.

The guard pushed her down to her knees, forcing her head back. She was still weak and couldn't resist his iron hold. Lorelei tried to spit out the liquid that was poured in her mouth, but the guard forced it open and she couldn't avoid swallowing some of the putrid liquid. Even though only a small amount slid down her throat, the blaze that erupted inside of her was agonizing. She felt like she had swallowed fire that was now spreading through her.

"Did she swallow enough?" the queen questioned from where she looked on.

"Yes. It is as good as done."

"Very well. Take her back to her room and make sure you are not seen."

Lorelei could no longer hold in the scream that tore from her very soul; it felt as if she was being burned alive. It did not take long for her to succumb to the darkness as she collapsed to the floor.

Chapter 23
ARTHUR

Arthur looked down at the flawless face of his mysterious guest. From the moment he laid eyes on her, she had looked too beautiful to be real. How he craved to own her, to spoil her, and to most of all taste her delicacy and have her submit to him in every way imaginable. She had consumed his thoughts, haunted his dreams, and now anger devoured him in constant waves like a stormy ocean upon the shore. He wanted blood for this.

Lorelei lay lifeless upon the bed. Her perfect features looked restful, as if she slumbered peacefully on the silken sheets, not forever lost to him. Arthur sat down on the edge of the bed, reaching up he traced her features with a gentle caress, memorizing every detail before leaning down and pressing his lips against hers. Reaching for his dagger, he lifted a long strand of her white gold hair, running the blade over the soft, smooth texture before he cut through, releasing a handful that he brought to his face and inhaled deeply.

The door opened, pulling Arthur from his thoughts. He turned to see the young servant Anna walk into the room. Her eyes widened in fear when she found him in the room before bowing her head. "My apologies, Your Majesty. I did not realize you were in here."

Arthur was instantly aroused, filled with need as the girl trembled before him. The girl's fright fueled his desire, and he remembered how her body had quivered beneath him as he crushed her with his weight. When Anna raised her eyes, she observed his hungry gaze and a whimper escaped her lips, making him harden. He remembered her pale skin and the way it reddened beautifully under his forceful hand. He needed release, and she would appease him. "Come," Arthur commanded.

Anna moved on hesitant feet toward the prince, knowing that she could not disobey him, and he smiled sinfully at the thought. "I want this room filled with flowers, and I want her dressed in the finest gown. No detail left untended."

"Yes, Your Majesty." Anna bowed.

Arthur advanced upon Anna, taking hold of her. She could not stop the gasp of fear that escaped her as his fingers pulled tightly on her hair. He held her head back, forcefully staring down at her with eyes so menacing, they did not reflect the light within the room. "I want you in my quarters when I return from breakfast."

"Yes, Your Majesty." A tear slipped from Anna's eye and slid down her cheek. Arthur watched its descent down her pale skin until it disappeared under the collar of her dress. He could see the frantic beat of her pulse in her neck, and it made his mouth water. He released her suddenly, causing her to tumble backward to the floor. She sobbed and covered her face with her hands to quiet herself. Arthur temporarily dismissed the distressed girl from his thoughts until he appeased his mother's latest request. He was required to attend breakfast, hosting his future bride.

*   *   *

"Good morning, Mother." Arthur leaned down to press a kiss to his mother's cool cheek. Only Peronell and Lady Mansforth were present in the dining hall when he arrived. His mother seemed displeased with his late arrival, but she did not voice it.

"Good morning, dear." His mother smiled as she patted his hand. "So glad you could join us this morning."

"Will Father be joining us?" Arthur asked curiously. His father's absence for family affairs as of late had not gone unnoticed.

"No. Unfortunately, the king has already left to oversee the execution of the prisoners."

"I should be with him," Arthur announced. He would much rather bury himself in the duties of the kingdom and strategies of war than the forced pleasantries of polite company; also, the viewing of an execution always managed to excite him to no end. His mother knew this well.

"There is plenty of time, and I assure you your father does not need your assistance at this time. Besides, your presence is needed with the women in your life." Peronell tightened her lips and raised her chin. Arthur knew the signs that she wanted him to drop the subject and be a dutiful son, but he was restless and could not stomach any food. "We need to finalize the plans for the ball and how you will announce your engagement to Mariam."

"Yes, of course." Arthur tried to sound sincere. He greeted young Mariam with a kiss on her hand before he took his seat beside her, ignoring her innocent flirtations and stolen glances. He gave the young girl the occasional smile and even listened to her constant jabbering to appease his mother. He leaned against the table and moved his food around his plate with his fork. His appetite waned dramatically as he breathed in the aroma of the food. His mother kept up the flow of conversation with Mariam. They spoke of every imaginable detail for the coming ball, and all he could do was sigh in response. His mother's eyes darted to him occasionally in warning, but she did not force him to join their conversation, and for that he was grateful. He looked over at Mariam, his future bride. At first glance she was a pretty girl, but upon closer inspection Arthur could not help but think that her features were boring. She lacked the curves of a woman's body, despite her age. She looked like she was all angles beneath the folds of her skirt. Her body did not call to him, and he found it rather hard to pretend that he was attracted to her.

He was supposed to be listening to the women's incessant chatter; instead his mind wandered to things much less innocent. A dark hunger grew within him, he felt consumed by it. He did not know how to satisfy this craving for power, desire... blood. He wanted to relish the pain of others. It had started off as fleeting thoughts when he consorted with the servants and whores. The hunger would rise in him until he started inflicting pain on those who allowed it and then eventually on those who did not. Now his sexual desires were homogenous with those dark thoughts. He could no longer separate the two or appease them, especially now that he felt cheated of his most desired prize, the late Lorelei. He wanted blood spilled — he needed it. He yearned to know who had deceived him. The guards were being questioned as to who was in Lorelei's quarters when she was poisoned, but he was not a patient man.

"Any word, Mother?" he interrupted. He did not have to clarify the subject of which he spoke. He stilled his bouncing knee under his mother's glare. She knew he spoke of Lorelei. She would not take kindly of his mentioning Lorelei's name in Mariam's presence, and he could see her displeasure at his even discreetly bringing the subject up. It was already brought to his attention that Mariam had questioned why Lorelei was in the castle, fearing what it meant for her position. He rubbed the back of his neck before raking his hand down his face.

His mother's measured gaze did not leave him. "I assure you, darling, all necessary steps are being taken, but you must remember we are not currently in a state of leisure. Such matters are not high priority."

"Of course, Mother," he responded curtly.

"Are you alright, Arthur?" Mariam questioned, reaching out to place her hand upon his.

"Yes, of course." Arthur pulled his hand away before contact. His gaze fell to Mariam's exposed neck. Her heartbeat was loud enough for him to hear, and he could envision the dark red blood that flowed just below the surface of her skin. Arthur stood, knowing he had to leave immediately. "Ladies, if you will excuse me. I have matters to attend to." He nodded at the two sets of eyes on him before he excused himself without another word, ignoring his mother's voice as he left the dining hall.

Leaving the room allowed him to collect himself and regain some semblance of control. When he entered the main hall, the guards were audience to a fellow soldier who recently joined them with urgent news. Arthur's presence was immediately acknowledged as he approached.

"Your Highness." The soldier bowed respectfully. "Lord Terrowin's body was just found below his chamber window."

"Show me," Arthur demanded.

*   *   *

Arthur found himself staring down at the unnaturally contorted body of Lord Terrowin. His mouth was frozen open in a silent scream, blood seeping from his eyes and ears, and his skin a sickly white. Arthur looked up at the window high above carved into the stone wall of the looming castle. It was a fall no one could survive. "Any witnesses?"

"No, Your Majesty."

"Seems to be a theme of late," Arthur responded, unamused. He leaned down over the body, observing the final moment that was carved into the dead man's features... utter terror. "Tell me your secret, Terrowin," Arthur whispered. Terrowin's lips moved so slightly that Arthur would have missed it had he not been watching closely.

"...the queen."

"Sorry, Your Majesty, did you say something?" Josef Eldrine said from behind him. Arthur hadn't noticed his presence among the nameless others. He looked over at the soldier and all the other clueless faces that had not witnessed what had just occurred. This dark energy within him seemed to have affected him in more ways than he realized. He could feel the influence he had held over Terrowin's deceased form. It was he who had forced the truth from Terrowin's dead body. It was he who now knew that his mother had a secret agenda.

"Yes ... has the king been informed?" He spoke so Josef could hear him clearly.

"Yes, Your Majesty."

"Good." Arthur discreetly wiped a drop of blood from Terrowin's lip, rubbing the viscous liquid between his fingers. With his back to the group of guards, Arthur brought his hand to his mouth and sucked the blood from his finger. He relished the flavor upon his palate. He wanted more. He *needed* more.

* * *

Arthur threw open the door to his chamber, startling the two women inside. The door resounded with a loud blow against the wall. Mera was the first to recover when a sly smile sprang to her seductive lips. She set a tray of wine and grapes upon the table before she made her way over to him. "*Hello*, my prince." She smiled playfully, reaching out for him. When her eyes met his, she faltered, the curve of her lips turning into a slight frown. "Your eyes... they are black." It was the first time the confident Mera had ever wavered since she first came to him. "Are you well?" She stayed her feet, even taking a step away from him.

"Very." He smiled, causing her to relax slightly. He sought Anna across the room as she stumbled back, knocking over a chair. She was terrified; he could feel her fear as thick as a fog reaching out across the room. He stalked toward her, pulling her fear into his lungs, and enjoyed the thought of devouring it. She backed into the corner as he closed her in on her, placing his hands on either side of her torso to prevent her from fleeing.

"Do not do this." Tears fell freely from her eyes as she looked pleadingly up at him.

"One of the benefits of being a prince, dear Anna, is that I do not have to listen to others, especially servants that are supposed to do what I say." Arthur's voice seemed strange to his own ears, but he did not give it any thought. He reached up and pushed her hair back from her face, exposing her neck, before tearing open her bodice to expose her breasts. Arthur reached up, grabbing her flesh in his rough fingers while pushing his weight into her. A sharp sting in his chest caused him to pull back. He looked down to find the hilt of a dagger protruding from his chest. The pain quickly twisted into dark, powerful pleasure as a smile curved his lips.

"Apparently, young Anna…" Arthur pulled the blade from his chest, eyeing his blood coating the metal. "I do not possess a heart." He gave little thought to fact that he should be dead, feeling stronger than ever.

Anna's terrified eyes watched him before a scream tore from her lips and she frantically tried to push him away. Arthur drove the blade into Anna's stomach, ceasing her struggle. A pained gasp escaped her lips as she looked down at her scarlet-soaked stomach. Arthur pulled the blade out of her flesh before raising it to his lips, licking the warm blood from the cool knife. It tasted of sin and pleasure, and he wanted more. Arthur carved the blade across the soft skin of her neck and leaned down to suck the delicious life from her. Her struggle quickly faded and her lifeless body began slipping from his grasp to land upon the floor.

He turned to see Mera watching him with a horrified expression. "Her fiancé was just killed in the ambush by Teller… She was grieving." The words left her lips mechanically as she looked down at Anna's body.

"Then I guess I did the fair Anna a favor." Arthur wiped his mouth with the back of his hand. He was drunk on lust and power. He felt invincible as heat pulsed through him. He was reborn.

Mera stood terrified. She had always hungered for the power he held, wanting to be close to it, to feel it, but now she was petrified. Scared of how powerful he had become. He liked this new side of her, and right now he thought of nothing more than taking what he wanted. He would make sure she never forgot how powerful he was.

"What do you wish of me, my prince?" Mera tried to appear unaffected, but her hands trembled and her voice was not as assured as it normally was. Arthur grabbed her and threw her onto his bed, proceeding to remove the rest of her clothing until she was naked and pinned under his weight. He pushed himself into her, driving his furious lust as far as he could inside her body. The bed groaned in protest as he invaded her. Her screams of distress aroused him and his thrusts became more frantic.

Arthur's roar of release drowned out Mera's cries. He was sated for a moment until thoughts of Lorelei surfaced in his mind. "Leave." He dismissed Mera callously. She slid from the bed without question and retrieved her dress, pain written on her face as she moved. She looked across the room to Anne's lifeless body before taking a deep, shuddering breath and heading slowly toward the door.

The door swung open before Mera was able to reach the handle. The queen, flanked by two guards, stepped into the room, causing Mera to step back and bow. "Your Highness." Her voice shook as she spoke.

The queen's gaze took in the dead girl and the bloody mess that spoiled the room. "Arrest her." The queen pointed a finger at the pale Mera. "She obviously killed the other servant in a fit of jealously, just as she poisoned Lorelei, my son's treasured guest. She must pay for her crimes."

Arthur sat up, unfazed by his nakedness as his mother and the guards set eyes upon him. He had only eyes for Mera. "Is there proof?"

"Of course." Peronell met his searching gaze.

Mera turned a shade of gray as she shook her head. "But... I didn't." She turned toward Arthur. "I would never, my prince. You must believe me."

"Silence," the queen demanded. "Take this girl to the dungeon. She will await her sentencing for the crimes mentioned." The queen looked on with a smile of satisfaction as the guards led the shocked Mera from the room.

"I will have someone come and clean up this mess. Once you have rested and dressed, we will talk." Turning on her heel, the queen left her angered son behind her.

Chapter 24
SIMON

"Move!"

Simon stumbled when the blunt end of something hard and unforgiving met his lower back. He barely managed to compose himself before he fell to the ground, reaching out his chained hands to break his fall. The guard who had hit him snickered, kicking dirt into his face. He was weak from lack of sustenance and his body complained with every movement from the beating the guards bestowed upon him. He was not sure how much time had passed since he was caught trying to smuggle Clara from the dungeon. He had not seen her since the guards took her from him. She had clung so tightly to him, looking to him for safety, but he had let her down. The vision of her sad eyes and frail face haunted him as the guards pulled her from him, beating him senseless, and then he awoke to immobilizing pain. He had tried to call out to Clara to see if she was well, but the guards were always quick to silence him.

"Get up." The guard jabbed him in the shoulder again.

The sun was warm upon Simon's face as he was ushered outside the castle walls, a false sense of security, for he knew where he was being led. He was chained to two other men, both looking down at him as he tried to find the strength to get to his feet. One was thin and malnourished, looking as if he had spent an eternity within the damp walls of the dungeon. The other was tanned from the sun and held substantial weight to his large frame, but his mind seemed untethered. The man also seemed strangely confident for someone who was marching to his death.

The large prisoner's hand clamped around Simon's upper arm and pulled him up to his feet. "Thank you. If we were not walking toward certain death, I would insist on buying you a drink." Simon tried to sound nonchalant as he took a deep breath, trying to find the strength to keep moving.

"I will take you up on that." The man smiled. It seemed strange to see a smile upon the face of a man who looked like he was created to kill.

"Good man, think positive." Simon chuckled despite the circumstances.

"Shut up and keep moving!" the guard threatened as he turned to lead them on.

The large man chained in front of him nodded toward Simon before turning and continuing forward. Simon had woken up in the cell across the dark corridor from the strange warrior-sized man after the guards had beaten him within an inch of his life. The man was there every time he opened his eyes, leaning out through his own cell restraints. "Silent, Simon," the man had called him when he was conscious enough to acknowledge his company.

"How do you know my name?" Simon whispered through his pained throat during their first encounter, lying on the cold, damp earth as his body screamed in protest from the assault.

"I overheard the guards talking about a man by the name of Simon Cheney, idiotic enough to think he could smuggle a prisoner from of the dungeon. They have a sense of false security, Silent Simon. I assure you they will know this soon enough." The man's voice was unusually deep and gravelly, suiting his large physique.

"Why do you call me Silent Simon?" Simon whispered through his pained throat and swollen mouth.

"They beat you until you blacked out, and yet you refused to answer a single question. I respect silent men. Most men crumble under pressure. I have seen too many break. Weak men bring death and destruction to those around them." The man's piercing eyes looked out through his bars down at Simon.

"Who are you?" Simon asked, trying to move his aching body but feeling the pull of slumber.

"Today you can call me the destroyer of false security." The man chuckled mischievously.

Simon could not respond as he drifted off again, welcoming a reprieve from the pain that ravished him. When he awoke, he was once again in the company of man across from him.

"What of the girl?" Simon questioned when he could bring himself to speak. He was fearful of the answer he would receive.

"Alive."

Simon sighed in relief.

"Drink your water. They will come for us. You need your strength." The man nodded toward the small bowl of dank water sitting just inside his cell.

"Why?" Simon asked. The water tasted grimy when he placed it to his lips, but he was desperate and drank it regardless.

"It is the big day tomorrow." The man smiled excitedly as he rubbed his hands together.

Simon needed no further explanation. A public hanging was the king's favorite form of punishment, regardless of any actual guilt.

Now, Simon kept his head down and listened to the sounds of their chains as they made their way toward the center of town. He tried to avoid taking notice of the onlookers that watched them in anticipation of the show. Simon envied their naiveté, the lack of understanding of the injustice that occurred right under their noses.

He felt as if he had walked for miles on his tired legs before the platform came into view and the crowd thickened. They were hungry for the death that would be demonstrated before them so that they could be reminded they were alive.

They were led up a narrow staircase to where the executioner awaited them, his mask in place as he stood a generous height above the other guards upon the stage, his fingers tapping on the handle of his axe as if he could not contain his excitement for the coming kill.

Simon looked around and noticed the king and palace guards standing at a safe distance from the crazed crowd. He scanned the mass of people and stopped when his eyes caught someone in particular whom he had hoped would not be stupid enough to try anything. Bryce Barwicke was standing off to the side of the stage. No one seemed to notice Bryce, who was hooded. Simon knew it was him; he knew the man well enough to pick him out of a crowd, even when he was trying to disguise himself. Simon kept his eyes on Bryce until their gaze connected and Simon subtly shook his head to let Bryce know not to try anything.

A large, round man with his beard waxed to unnatural points shuffled onto the stage. "*Clarke.*" Simon seethed when he recognized the man. Clarke had been one of the influential voices behind his wife's accusation of witchcraft, leading to her violent death. Simon's breathing became exaggerated, drowning out the hum of the crowd as he focused on the large man addressing the crowd.

Chancellor Lief Clarke pulled down on his taut vest. The buttons threatened to release his girth. Simon could not bring himself to listen to the words the man spewed out over the crowd, soaking up the attention they were giving him. He was a man of greed, with no honor. It was known that the man's twelve-year-old wife, barely free of her childhood, had died giving birth while he was out making use of the whorehouse. Now rumor had it he already had another young girl lined up for not three months later. His family's money bought him immunity from judgement.

"No man can escape the penance for his crimes," Simon's warrior friend assured him after taking note of Simon's reaction.

"I hope you are right, my friend."

One of the guards stepped forward to unchain the other sickly-looking prisoner. He had not spoken a word to either of them as they had marched and still remained eerily quiet. He already looked like a shell of a man, his body frail and beaten as he was pulled roughly forward and shoved down on his knees before the block. "You cannot kill a man that is already in hell!" The man's voice was strong despite his slight frame when he broke his silence. "We are all already dead!" The man continued to rant, spit flying from his mouth as he barked at the people.

"Doran Brooker, found guilty of theft and sentenced to death," Chancellor Clarke bellowed to the crowd, his face reddening in exertion.

The executioner stepped forward, raising his axe into the air over the still-screaming prisoner before it was brought down through his neck without resistance. Blood sprayed over the onlookers at the front of the crowd, and they cheered with wild excitement. Doran's head missed the awaiting basket and rolled off the platform, falling to the ground.

"Bit of a chip on his shoulder, that one." The warrior made a joke of the ranting Doran Brooker, who had revealed in his last moment that he had much more to say than they had anticipated.

"I had actually pegged you as the crazy one." Simon could not help but smirk.

"Fair assumption." The warrior's lips turned down in mock humor. The guard approached, unchaining the warrior from Simon. "Do not forget you owe me a drink, Silent Simon."

"What is your name, friend?" Simon requested.

"Mad Margas." Margas smiled wickedly.

"Somehow I am not surprised." Simon shook his head in disbelief.

The guard tried to push the hulking man forward, but Margas shrugged off the guard's attempt with a growl, throwing him a look that made the soldier hesitate and step backward. Mad Margas was intimidating in every way, befitting his warrior's form, and looked the perfect embodiment of health and strength. Strange markings were etched into his exposed arms and disappeared under his tattered shirt. He towered over all the other men, save for the imposing executioner.

Three other guards advanced ensure Margas cooperated, but they did not lay a hand on him as he knelt down without protest in front of the bloodstained block, his hands and feet still chained behind him. The executioner wasted no time readying himself as Chancellor Clarke proceeded to tell the crowd that Margas was a man without a name, a drunk, a wanderer who came into their town and assaulted one of the good guards that were protecting the good people.

The executioner, completely sheathed in black garments, raised his blade. The crowd hushed and all eyes waited in anticipation. When the blade began its descent, it took a moment for the witnesses to realize that the executioner had missed his mark. He spun and the blade sliced through the chains that bound Margas's hands and feet, releasing him. Margas jumped to his feet as the executioner tossed him the axe and then proceeded to unsheathe a sword, taking a stance against the advancing guards.

One of the guards upon the platform advanced toward the executioner, his spear aimed true. The executioner dodged the attacking guard, grabbing hold of the spear in the process. While holding firm, he kicked the guard back with enough force that the man was thrown into the other guards, knocking them down. The executioner reeled back and launched the weapon into the air. The spear soared toward the king with perfect accuracy. At the last moment Commander Waltham threw himself into the path of the oncoming weapon. Waltham absorbed the impact of the spear, piercing deep through his breastplate. The roar of the crowd reached deafening levels.

The king's men quickly drew him and the injured commander into retreat, heading back toward the castle walls and away from the chaos. Guards seemed to advance from every direction, and Simon barely escaped a swinging blade.

"Simon!" Margas called out over the deafening screams of the crowd. "Your chains." Margas freed Simon before returning to the fray. "Get cover now." A guard advanced toward Simon with his sword at the ready. Simon pulled the chain from his metal shackles to defend himself. He twisted it around his hand. Before the man engaged Simon, he dropped abruptly to the ground, an arrow protruding from his neck. Bryce appeared behind the body, grabbing the dead man's sword and tossing it to Simon.

"I should have known you would do something stupid." Simon sighed at his friend.

"We can talk later." Bryce spun around with blade in hand, ready to take on a charging guard. He drove the blade into the torso of another man, who crumpled to the ground.

"Move!" Bryce ordered, shoving pressing bodies aside. The frantic people made it difficult for the guards to regain order. Bryce jumped down into the cover of the crowd, avoiding the soldiers spilling up onto the stage.

Simon began to follow Bryce when he noticed Chancellor Clarke avoiding the battle, looking for a way to retreat from the fighting. In the frantic commotion of the crowd, a woman tripped and fell at his feet, blood seeping from a wound on her head. The woman reached for Clarke, but he simply turned away from the woman's pleas, starting in another direction. The guards were scanning the crowds for the culprits, but the men had dispersed immediately into the cover of the swarming crowd.

Simon kept Clarke in his sights, avoiding unnecessary confrontation with anyone else, because he did not have much strength; his injuries still hindered his movements. When Clarke disappeared around the corner of a building, Simon was quick to follow. He closed the distance between himself and Clarke as the man disappeared behind a doorway. He swung the door open and Clarke turned in surprise, having realized he was being pursued.

"Simon Cheney?" Clarke gasped. The overweight man panted as he leaned against a table for support.

"Surprised?" Simon said sarcastically.

"I…" Clarke ran his hands down his stomach and raised his chin, trying to give the appearance of confidence. "I had nothing to do with your wife's death. You have to believe me when I tell you that when it came down to the accusation and trial, I was only the figurehead. If you want someone to blame…"

"Enough, you pompous shite!" Simon moved so he was within arm's length of the trembling man. "I know who is to blame."

"But her sister, Alianor..." Clarke began.

"She was actually one of the first people I paid a visit to after I buried my wife. Turns out her husband left her and took everything, so she hanged herself. She knew that I would come for her and decided to take the easy way out. Unfortunately for you, Clarke, I know what your involvement was, and you will not get to live without answering for your crimes." Rage pumped through Simon's blood.

"I served justice. Gloriana was guilty of witchcraft."

"Said a jealous sister eager to be rid of the sister that was everything she could never be. You were more than happy to go along with the charade because of your damaged pride, still angered that Gloriana had refused your advances when you were mere children. You are a pitiful man that does not deserve to continue enjoying the pleasures of life, not when you have robbed it from so many others."

"You cannot kill me." Clarke backed away as far as he could manage.

"I do not want to kill you, Chancellor Clarke." Simon narrowed his eyes.

Clarke breathed out in relief. "Well then..."

"But I will make you suffer." Simon smiled as he lifted his blade. Clarke stumbled backward, the scent of urine filling the room along with the anguished screams as Simon delivered justice.

"There you are!" Bryce swung open the door. "We have to leave Simon, *now!*" Bryce looked down at the bloody scene before him. "Finished?"

"Yes." Simon wiped his blade on the unconscious Clarke and sheathed it at his side. The man had squealed and cried, offering promises and money. He proffered anything he could think of until finally blacking out. Simon assumed it was the loss of his manhood that finally made him give up his fight. "Let's go."

Chapter 25
AJAX

A guard outfitted in full armor marched down a long, darkened hallway. The torches did little to illuminate the darkness that was now falling with the evening. Raw determination fueled his steps as he followed the directions he had been given by the previous owner of the armor that he now donned. The man now lay dead within the bushes of the castle's breathtaking garden.

Ajax entered the castle without raising any alarms. No one questioned him. Before he entered the castle walls, he knew who would be waiting within. He felt the familiar presence before he laid eyes on a face that he had not seen in a very long time.

"Lord Caunter, would you do me the honor of joining me in my conference room? We have much to discuss." The king addressed the familiar face as Ajax discreetly looked on, no one the wiser that their fortress had been infiltrated.

"Of course, Your Majesty. I am sorry to hear of Commander Waltham's injuries. Though I have only known him a short time, I know he is a great man and commander."

"Thank you, Lord Caunter. His injuries are being tended to, and we can only hope for the best. Come, let us discuss matters in private." The king led Lord Caunter, along with a few others, toward a conference room closely followed by four guards. The king and his company entered the room, leaving the guards stationed outside the doors. Lord Caunter was the last to enter, his eyes falling on Ajax's concealed face before giving him a subtle nod, an acknowledgement so slight, it was missed by all other eyes around them. Lord Caunter swung the door behind him without latching it closed. Ajax took his position with the others, standing as close to the door as he could manage. With the door slightly ajar, he could catch their words as they spoke.

"Lord Caunter, you have already had the privilege of meeting Josef Eldrine. He is to be standing in as commander."

"Yes, good evening, Commander," Lord Caunter acknowledged. "Sir Blackburn and I have tracked Teller's men after the attack today. His men are well trained and evasive, but their numbers are few. We believe that they have retreated. Men have been seen scattered and fleeing toward outlying towns. I do not believe they were expecting to face such a large force of soldiers."

"Our sources have come to the same conclusion," Commander Eldrine confirmed.

"However, Teller does not seem the type of man to give up so easily. We should remain on high alert. Follow any possible lead that might give us until we confirm his men are not planning any further attacks. I think we should continue our questioning, offering incentives for people to come forward with information."

"Very well, Commander. Send some troops out to try to round up some of these treasonous men. I want them arrested and within my keep. Most important is Teller himself, so keep ears to the ground about his whereabouts. He may have dropped his intentions towards the crown, but I will not fold so easily in making him pay for his crimes. What of the nameless prisoner that escaped? Was he questioned at all while he was here within the dungeon?"

"No, Your Majesty. He was believed to be a mindless drunk when he was arrested. He could not even remember his name."

"*Bloody hell!* We had one of Teller's men in our dungeon, and we let him walk away." A crash resounded inside the room, and the voices quieted. "What of Bryce Barwicke? Was he spotted before Simon Cheney made his escape?"

"One of the guards thought he had seen him, but he was not close enough to give a positive identification."

"Let us hope today ends before anything else can add to all the shite being dumped on us. Lord Terrowin had been advisor to my father before me and a trusted advisor to me all these years. He too is gone from us on this day. I need time to pay my proper respects. I trust other matters will be tended to, and I will be updated with any further information should it arise. I want double the amount of guards on duty at all times."

"Yes, Your Majesty."

The door swung open, and Lord Caunter and a few other men left the room. Ajax watched the men leave with the feeling of unease. He needed to find Lorelei, and quickly. His eyes fell on a cloaked man approaching, led by guards. The new arrival was flanked by two others, all of them discreet with their identities. He knew the men well from their movements alone. Crewe was here. The king had called upon the Ravens, and now Crewe and his men were here to do the king's hired bidding. Ajax needed to get Lorelei as far from this place as possible.

The guard at the front of the advancing men approached the door, alerting the king that his guests had arrived. "If you will excuse me, gentlemen. I will leave the commander to oversee things here and inform me of any further details. I have a matter that needs my immediate attention."

Ajax looked at Crewe, who had no idea that Ajax was in his presence. As much talent as the man possessed, he was still restricted by the limitations of man. The king led Crewe and his company toward another location to conduct their business. The guards proceeded to trail the king's group, but Ajax fell back.

He moved determinedly through the halls, listening for any hint where Lorelei could be located. He passed many guards as he searched the hallways, but he could not question them for danger of rousing suspicion. He turned the corner and noticed a few servant girls carrying large vases of floral arrangements. "Good evening, ladies. May I help you?" Ajax offered, wearing the disguise of flirtatiousness.

The women turned in surprise, either at his arrival or his offer. "Good evening, sir," one acknowledged politely. "Yes, it would be lovely to have a strong set of arms to help us carry all these flowers. There is more in the room we just left. If you would not mind collecting those, we would be in your dept."

"It would be my pleasure." Ajax bowed before the women, causing them to blush at his chivalry. He entered the room they had indicated and grabbed a few of the largest vases, following the women up a staircase and down a long stone hallway.

"Here we are," the gray-haired middle-aged woman announced as she pushed open the door. Ajax stepped in the room behind the women. He was not expecting the sight before him. Lorelei was laid out upon the bed, her body pale and unnaturally still. His heart threatened to stop within his chest at he entered the room and neared the bed.

"Is she not breathtaking?" The younger blond next to him spoke after she had placed her flowers on the already full table. "It is a shame someone so beautiful was taken so soon." She plucked a handful of white flowers from one of the vases and leaned in to begin weaving them through Lorelei's silken hair.

Ajax reached up and pulled his helmet from his head, dropping it to the floor, along with his gloves and then his breastplate. He moved through the thick, suffocating air of the room to stand beside the bed, devastated.

"You are not a guard, are you?" the young servant asked innocently.

"No, I am not." He reached down and took Lorelei's small, cool hand in his, placing a small kiss upon her cool flesh. "I am sorry I failed you," he whispered into Lorelei's hand.

"Was she yours?" the girl asked as she continued arranging the flowers in Lorelei's hair.

"I was hers," he responded dejectedly. "I am hers."

"I am glad she had someone better than Prince Arthur." The girl spoke again, only to be reprimanded by the older woman. "He was not worthy of a girl like this. I only met her for a moment, but she was so lovely and kind to me."

"Hush, Helena. We cannot speak ill of His Highness," the older woman warned.

"Did he do this to her?" Ajax turned toward the younger girl.

"No... We heard it was one of his personal servants, jealous of his intentions with her," Helena said sadly.

"What are *your* intentions here?" The older woman came to stand beside Ajax.

They both turned to the young girl when she inhaled sharply in surprise. The flowers that she had woven into Lorelei's hair had turned to ash, disintegrating under her fingertips. "What is happening?"

Ajax stood up and grabbed handfuls of flowers from the vases, placing them upon Lorelei's skin, and watched as they too collapsed into dust. "Place the flowers on her skin," he ordered the women before he leaned in and placed his hand against her chilled cheek. "Lorelei? Wake up, Lorelei. Come back to me."

A slight, almost nonexistent breath passed Lorelei's lips, all the assurance Ajax needed to know that he could still help her. "She's alive, barely." The flowers continued to turn to dust once in contact with her, and slight color began to return to her pallid flesh. "I need to get her out of the castle."

"What is she?" Helena looked upon her with wonder.

"One of a kind."

"What can I do to help?" Helena said eagerly.

"Do not be foolish, girl. We cannot help, for it would be our lives." The older woman once again stepped in and then turned her attention toward Ajax. "You must leave."

"Ayleth, you once helped me when no one else would, and now I want to do the same for someone else in need." Helena's words seemed to smother the fire in the stubborn woman's eyes, and a small, sentimental smile graced her lips.

"I am not leaving without Lorelei. I must take her with me," Ajax said. "With or without your help."

"Take her down the hall to the right. Take the staircase at the end of the hall, down three flights, and you will come to the kitchens. Take an immediate left, and you will come to a doorway guarded by only two men. It leads directly to the beach. The patrols there are regular, but you may find a way to pass unnoticed at this late hour. I believe it is your only chance to leave with the girl in your possession. Any other way the guards' numbers are too great, and they will stop you before you leave these walls." Helena walked toward the open door and looked nervously down the hallway.

"Thank you." Ajax gathered Lorelei's frail body in his arms.

"I will cause a distraction, but you must hurry." Helena smiled.

"I will guide you." Ayleth sighed in defeat. "Though I must insist you wear your helmet. There are not a lot of guards that look like you. Best try to conceal your identity so you do not get us all killed with your heroics."

With Lorelei cradled in Ajax's arms, the young girl left the room. The older woman cautiously stepped out into the hallway and then signaled Ajax to follow her. They could hear the young girl talking to an approaching guard around the corner, so they hastened to the stairwell. A few servants passed them on the staircase, but with a nod from the woman leading him, they only stared curiously before continuing on.

When they neared the exit Ayleth had spoken of, Ajax laid Lorelei down. He swung the large door open. Two guards flanking the door turned toward him. Ajax did not wait for them to draw a conclusion. "I have a message for you," Ajax announced. Reaching out, he grabbed both men by the neck and smashed their heads together. Neither had time to react before collapsing.

Another guard appeared at the mouth of a pathway leading away from the castle. He immediately advanced with his weapon drawn. Two others followed close on his heels, eager to engage. Ajax unsheathed his sword. Pulling it back, he swung it into the blade of the oncoming soldier; the man's grip faltered, and he lowered his guard. Ajax took the opportunity to pull his sword down the man's unguarded torso. His blade scraped through the layers of the armor, cutting into the soft, buttery flesh. Ajax knew the feeling well; he knew where to hit an opponent to cause the most damage. This man was already dead; he just hadn't realized it yet. The man reached down with his free hand and pressed against his wound.

One of the other guards tried to approach from behind, but Ajax swung his arm back. The hilt of his blade collided with the man's helmet, and the force knocked him back into the stone wall. Blood gushed from a wound, obstructing the guard's view. The first guard dropped to his knees as the life drained from him. The remaining guard faltered, seeing what he was up against. Ajax swung his sword; this guard could not keep up with the pace of Ajax's strokes. Ajax cut him down quickly and then walked over to the remaining guard, still hunched against the wall, unable to see through the blood pooling from his wound. Ajax thrust his sword into the man's neck. His groan was cut off and he slumped to the ground.

Ajax walked back in through the door, after confirming no other guards were approaching. A bow was leaning against the wall, along with a quiver filled with arrows. Ajax threw it over his shoulder in anticipation that it might prove useful. The servant was still standing protectively next to Lorelei with a look of shock. "There are usually only two guards." She had wrapped Lorelei in a dark, coarse blanket to conceal her white dress. "This should help to avoid being seen. Take care of her."

"I will. Thank you." Ajax collected her in his arms.

"Helena was right. We must help those we can. There is only so much light left in this world. We must not let it be extinguished. I believe that girl..." the old woman nodded toward Lorelei "...has a purpose in this world." She patted him on the shoulder. "Go now. Others will soon come." With those last words, the woman turned and left, hurrying up the stairs as quickly as she could manage.

With Lorelei in his arms, Ajax moved within the shadows toward the beach. He could hear the voices of more soldiers before he set eyes

on them. He knew their numbers were too great to expect to pass
undetected. The beach below had heavy surveillance. He laid Lorelei
down in the cover of the trees and made sure the blanket concealed
her before he ventured in for a closer look.

Ajax counted twenty men on the narrow beach meeting the ocean.
They stood relaxed as they conversed and scanned the perimeter.
From this location the ocean was too rough for a port, but the king
did not rule it out as a possible point of access for the enemy. Large
rocks jutted from the frothing water. With the amount of guards, Ajax
would not get by unseen with Lorelei in tow. He would take on every
one of those men if need be. He was not shy of the challenge; usually
it would excite him, if not for the fact that he needed to get Lorelei
somewhere safe to heal.

Ajax moved to a safe distance from Lorelei so she would remain
unnoticed when he drew the guards' attention. Once he took up a position, he aimed his bow and released an arrow into the group. Even
in the darkness of night, Ajax's aim was true. The men reacted with
surprise and confusion when one of them fell, an arrow jutting from
his neck. Ajax moved silently through the cover of the wild growth
until he found another position. A few men were already moving toward his last position while the others drew their weapons and took
up a stance.

"How many are there?" one man called out.

"I cannot see a bloody thing," another called out.

Ajax released another arrow, lodging in the back of another guard.
The man screamed before he dropped to the sand. The other men's
voices raised considerably as they panicked.

"Over there!" one screamed, pointing slightly away from Ajax's
current position. Ajax crouched low and moved swiftly in the cover
of the shadows. Kneeling, he aimed again, taking down the men that
were venturing too far outside the group. His tactic was to keep moving, confusing the men into thinking they were dealing with multiple
attackers. There were a few archers in secluded locations, and those
were his first targets. When these men were eliminated, he concentrated on shaving numbers from the mass of men on the beach. Their
numbers were cut down considerably; each arrow had found its mark.

The attention of all the men was focused on Ajax when he left
his cover. Momentary confusion befell them as they watched him
approach. Ajax was dressed in the same attire as the men he was

approaching. "Who goes there?" one of the men called out. Ajax raised his hands to show he was friendly. His sword was secured to his waist.

"Good evening, men." Ajax reached up and pulled off his helmet when he was close enough to speak.

"Who are you, soldier?" one of the men questioned through narrowed eyes, his sword drawn and pointed toward Ajax.

"I am your worst fear." Ajax smiled wickedly before he drew his sword.

"Kill him!" one of them shouted. Ajax raised his sword, and it clashed against another as one of the men closed in on him. He deflected the blow, kicking the man back to gain some room. Pulling a knife from his breastplate, he plunged it into the neck of another soldier. He swung his sword, carving through their advancements. Men fell at his feet, unable to match his pace. Every man that he cut down was replaced with another, until they began to disperse. Ajax pulled his blade from the torso of one of the faceless men he had slain. Blood dripped from the man's mouth before he landed at Ajax's feet. Ajax wiped the blood from his face, taking note of remaining soldiers closing in.

"There seems to be only one," one of them called out.

The blade of one of the men sliced deep into the exposed flesh of Ajax's shoulder, but it did not slow him. The wound would close quickly; he would not weaken, unlike the men he confronted. Their numbers declined as Ajax made play of their efforts.

"I found a girl," a soldier called out as he walked onto the beach, Lorelei stumbling behind him as he held onto her. The man's face dropped as he noticed how many of his fellow guards had fallen at Ajax's feet. Lorelei was conscious but looked weak, and she staggered. Ajax knew they did not have much time before others came. He cut down the remaining men in a frenzy of blows. When he sank his blade into the last man standing before him, he turned and made for the man holding Lorelei.

"Stay back!" the man called, but as Ajax neared he grew terrified and released Lorelei, backing away while trying to draw his sword with trembling hands. Ajax could hear more men approaching. He reached down and picked Lorelei up in his arms, making a run for the ocean.

"We have to swim, sweetheart," he told her as he neared the water. The water splashed around them as he entered its cold darkness. "Take a deep breath," he ordered before diving down with Lorelei tight within his grasp. He kicked with all his strength as he swam around the rocks and into the depths. Lorelei seemed to have gained strength and pushed away from his hold. He surfaced for air and looked into her glowing eyes. She seemed so alive now compared with when he had found her. He was relieved; though surrounded by water, she looked every bit the Siren he was raised to destroy.

"Ajax…" Lorelei's relief suddenly washed from her face and was replaced by fright. "Ajax?" she whispered as she reached for him, but before he could grab her outstretched hand, she was pulled under. Ajax dove down after her, desperately trying to grab hold of her as the unseen force pulled her away from him. It did not matter how hard he pushed himself, he could not stop her… she was gone.

Chapter 26
TELLER
Five years ago...

William Teller dismounted when he arrived at the small cottage of the healer. It was nestled deep in thick trees. The wild growth of nature provided the perfect camouflage to ensure that only those who sought the place out would be able to find it. The sun was nearing its peak as midday approached, and Teller was anxious to return to Josselyn.

Before he could announce his arrival with a knock upon the door, it swung open and Edward greeted him. Teller had met him a few times since he had come to know Josselyn, but this was their first meeting without her company.

"Is Josselyn not well?" Edward questioned. His green eyes were so vibrant and soulful, it was hard to believe they did not possess the gift of sight.

"No, unfortunately not, I am afraid."

Edward beckoned Teller inside, opening the door wide to allow passage.

The interior was filled with plants that upon closer inspection were unusual in origin. Teller took in the vibrant colors and intricate flowers of the foliage. He had never seen these species in all the lands he traveled. Some even cast a dull glow into the room. Edward was not just a simple healer, like the people believed. His ability to manipulate and use plant life was nothing short of magic. The jars that lined the room were evidence of this fact as they swirled with unknown energies.

"Tell me, healer, how do you keep prying eyes from condemning you for the dark arts?" Teller lifted a jar from the table. The contents swirled and changed from a dull blue to an explosion of bright red that heated the jar in his hand.

"Only those born of magic can see what truly exists before them, Man of Savas."

"Ah... So you have discovered what I am." Teller set the jar back down upon the table. "What shall I call you then... fairy?"

"I have been called worse." Edward shrugged. "At least my people are not cursed."

"As much as I would like to continue this conversation, Josselyn sent me for some things she requires." Teller pulled out the parchment upon which Josselyn had written words in a strange language. He tried to pronounce what was written, but he did not even know how to form the words.

"Apparently the men of Savas do not possess an affinity for the old language. Here." Edward reached out to accept the parchment.

"Are you not blind?" Teller questioned as Edward attempted to retrieve the parchment from him.

"Very." Edward pulled the parchment from Teller's hands before placing it on the table. He picked up a jar of viscous-looking liquid that he poured upon the parchment. It began to turn into vapor and dissipate into the air. Edward ran his fingers through the steamy substance, seeming to absorb the knowledge he sought. "These are not ingredients."

"What are they, then?" Teller asked in confusion. Edward's silence and saddened disposition caused anger to surface. "Tell me now, *healer*."

"I knew a Siren many years ago," Edward said thoughtfully.

"Sirens have been gone for over a hundred years. Killed by my people," Teller said stubbornly.

"Not all, apparently. She was very much alive when I came to know her. I knew what she was before I even came to meet her. I sought her out because I knew that I needed to find her." Edward curled his fingers into a tight fist.

"Did you kill her?" Teller asked, curious where Edward was going with his story.

"Not intentionally, but yes." Edward's words were so full of sorrow that Teller could not shake off the pain that the man radiated. "She believed she was the last, but her death did not break your curse. I can still see it pulsing in your very being. That is why I warned Josselyn about you. That giving you her heart would lead to her death."

"She knew who I was from the beginning. She assured me she was immune to..." Teller shook his head.

"And you *believed* that?" Edward's tone rose slightly.

"Yes," Teller said defensively.

"You are more foolish than I realized. Josselyn has always been a stubborn girl, following her heart beyond reason. It may not have been your curse, but falling for you did weaken her. She allowed her sister to find a loophole while she was blinded by you."

"Blinded?" Teller raised his brows. "Explain to what you are referring." His tone now bordered on irritation.

"Witches are always born in twos. Did Josselyn tell you this?" Edward leaned against the table.

"No, but I know she has a sister, and their struggle for power. She does not like to talk about it often. It causes her too much pain."

"They are born in twos to represent the balance of nature. Josselyn represents life, purity, love, and her strength is her heart. Her sister Peronell represents destruction, hate, greed, and her strength comes from pain. One cannot exist without the other. As long as they both live, balance will be maintained and neither could tip the scales of nature, until recently. I thought that in Josselyn allowing herself to be distracted by you, it diminished her strength against her sister, allowing Peronell to flourish. Even knowing it would bring her death, she still welcomed you. Our Josselyn did not do this in vain; she possessed a gift like no other. She would not be selfish if it meant others would suffer by her hand."

"What!" Red began to color Teller's vision. "What do you speak of? What does the note say?"

"I will tell you, but know that I was wrong to doubt her belief in you. Our Josselyn has always been a keeper of secrets. A burden she had to carry on her own," Edward said sadly, folding the parchment and passing it back to Teller.

* * *

Teller rode home as fast as he could compel his horse. Fear constricted his chest as he pushed the creature to its limits. What Edward had told him caused him to flee to his house, desperate to find Josselyn. Even though Edward had spoken the words, he could hear Josselyn's sweet voice in what she had written.

My dearest William,

I knew your face before I ever laid eyes upon it. I dreamed about you as a small girl, picking flowers upon the field. You owned my heart then, before you knew I even existed, and it will forever be in your possession.

What I did not share with you was the fact that destiny brought you to me. You were always prophesied to finish a battle I could not win. I dreamed of a fate where you and I could be without this great burden over our heads, but it was not meant to be for us. You are the strength that I lacked, you are the light within my darkness, and you will bring end to this unseen war.

Now is my time. I have always known this. You still have a role to play, and it is by far the most important of all.
Forgive me, my love
I will be waiting until we meet again,
Forever yours,
Josselyn

Teller wished he had the ability to move the very earth beneath his feet. He had inhuman strength, agility, speed, healing — all meant to make him unmatched in battle against his enemy, but none of that helped him now. He had never felt as helpless, unable to defeat the mass of land now separating them. He rode on without faltering, noting nothing of his surroundings until he passed the king's soldiers. He had never seen the king's men escorting a royal carriage so far from the castle in this isolated area. There was no one of noble status or royal contacts in this area; there were only scattered farmlands and things to which they paid no mind.

The sight of the royal guards made a heavy weight settle within him. He continued without slowing until he came to a few men herding sheep along the pass. He slowed his horse to speak with the two.

"The royal guards that passed by here — did they come from the mountain or the main road?" The two men looked at each other. By the looks on their faces, he knew the answer before they spoke.

"The mountain," the older man said hesitantly.

Teller urged his horse on a direct path up the mountain toward the sole residence there: Josselyn's. When he approached the property, it was too quiet. The tracks on the ground confirmed his fear that the soldiers had been here. Not even the rustle of wind through the trees could be heard when he dismounted and charged into the house. "Josselyn! Josselyn!" he called as his eyes scanned the dim interior.

Teller's eyes fell to the fire; upon the floor he could see Josselyn's slender hand, the light of the flames flickering over her pale skin.

"Josselyn." Her name tore from his throat. Teller crumpled to the floor at the sight of her body, an empty hole in her chest where her heart should have been. Tears blurred his vision as he looked down upon her face. Her eyes were closed, and she looked so peaceful. She was as brave in death as she was in life.

Edward's words played through his thoughts. *"Josselyn has made sure her sister cannot gain the one thing that will make her unstoppable, because she gave it to you. Her heart."*

Teller held her body tightly, afraid to let go. Josselyn had made him want to live again; she had given him the gift of love, something no other had given him during his long existence. To be Savas was to live a cursed life, born to a mother that would not survive her son's birth, to a father that would blame his son for the death of his beloved. Consumed by the need to eliminate an enemy, they were created to wipe from existence, to crave death and vengeance for a crime they did not witness, but were engineered to avenge.

Teller now had a new vendetta. He would avenge Josselyn's death and in turn bring about the demise of the king. A path he knew would lead him to Josselyn's sister.

Chapter 27
LORELEI

Lorelei opened her eyes. The bright moon stretched far into the depths around her. She was surrounded by the cool embrace of the ocean, swaying with its movements. For a moment she relaxed in the feeling of peace that flowed within her. She no longer felt the effects of the poison burning through her veins, instead only tranquility. Her mind was quiet, numb, until a flash of lucidity roused her from her dreamlike state… Ajax.

The water in front of her began to shift and move, taking on a watery form with an iridescent glow. It transformed into the figure of a woman, blending and moving as if one with the ocean. She was exquisite and otherworldly. Watery hair floated around her elegant face as she studied Lorelei in turn. She reached out and cupped Lorelei's cheek. The sensation was solid, unlike the water she was composed of.

"Born of water and earth." Her lips did not move, but her silvery voice floated to Lorelei's ears. "What are you named?"

Lorelei's hand moved toward her mouth; she could not speak immersed in the water.

"You do not need to speak aloud, Lorelei. I can hear your thoughts. You are an unexpected treasure, Lorelei of two elements. Did you know that most magical beings only draw upon one elemental power?"

Lorelei shook her head. The current shifted, and the woman's body rolled into the passing water, only to appear again in a different location. "I thought my daughters to be all but vanished forever. Hunted by the very beings I enabled. It has been so very long since I have felt them. You, Lorelei, resemble your mother. I remember her well, for she was my favored daughter. She was stronger and more beautiful than the rest, but also the one to betray me." Her words were full of sorrow.

Fear jolted through Lorelei's veins as she realized that this woman might be an adversary. She knew nothing of this entity, and she had been foolish to let her guard down.

"Do not fear, child. I wish you no harm. I am Amphitrite, Goddess of the Sea. A name once worshipped and feared among the men that sailed its vast depths, but I now grow weary of heart. Sailors have forgotten my name, and I tire of reprimanding their insolence." Amphitrite dissipated and reappeared within reach of Lorelei. "You wish to know of your mother? I will grant this for you, but in return I will ask something of you."

Lorelei shook her head nervously. The idea of what this goddess would request was terrifying. She could only imagine what she would want of her. "You cannot refuse a goddess, Lorelei. I only made it seem a request out of courtesy." She waved her hand between them, and Lorelei's eyes blurred out of focus until a scene unfolded before her.

A large ship sailed on the water's surface, a crew of men busily tending to the sails. A tall, imposing figure stood at the wheel of the ship. His square jaw was covered in a few days' growth, hair tied back from the insistent breeze. His dark, piercing eyes demanded respect. Lorelei realized she was looking through the eyes of Amphitrite herself as she observed the ship and captain from afar. A feeling of adoration bloomed within the body she currently observed from. The man explored the waters, seeking treasures and gold. His very presence among his men brought great respect and admiration.

Amphitrite had warned her Siren daughters to stay away from his ship, so he would sail the seas untouched by the troubles that assailed other pirates upon the waters. She favored this man above all others and did not wish him to fear her, but to love and appreciate the gift of safe passage that she bestowed upon him. After a time, Amphitrite began to believe that he did not appreciate her love. He stopped staring into the horizon in the hope of seeing her. He stopped whispering words of affection into the breeze to be carried to her, and he stopped speaking her name.

She requested her most beautiful daughter test his love for her. Aisling was to go to him and ask for his heart. If he denied her, then Amphitrite would know that he still cared for her. Aisling, keen to please

Amphitrite, accepted the request. She sought out the captain, drawing him in with her ethereal beauty to see if his devotion wavered.

When Amphitrite approached the ship, she discovered that Aisling had given the captain the Siren's kiss. When a Siren called upon the soul of a victim with her song, she could steal it from the body with a kiss. The act of separating the soul from the body was fatal, and the captain was no longer. Amphitrite was furious with her beloved daughter.

"How could you!" Amphitrite rose up from the sea. Her anger caused waves to crash against the ship as a heavy storm brewed around them.

Aisling shrank away from the lifeless captain. "I was told that if he proved untrue to you, he must be ended. I thought that is what you wanted." Aisling's regret poured from her defeated posture. "I am sorry, Mother, please forgive me."

The ship swayed dangerously in the rough waters. The crew began frantically trying to secure the sails at the sudden violence of the wind and the stirring of the sea. It was then that they noticed their captain dead upon the deck and two beautiful, deadly women in their presence. They bowed to the goddess when they recognized who stood before them.

"We are sorry to have offended you, Amphitrite." Amphitrite calmed the restless waters, letting the sea settle, as she watched the men beg for her forgiveness. They pleaded with her to spare their lives; the sight of their trusted captain dead caused great sorrow and fear. Her power made them tremble, their screams causing her power to pulse within her.

A cabin door swung open, and a young man not long into manhood joined the men on deck. His eyes fell on the body of the captain before his expression turned horrified. "Father!" he screamed. One of the men held him back from his father's body and the possible wrath of the goddess.

"Stop, boy!" one of the other men ordered with a stern expression as he signaled to the women. "Show your respect to the fair goddess, Amphitrite, who graces us with her presence."

"Your captain was a father?" Amphitrite questioned the older man, struggling to hold the young man at his side.

"Yes, Goddess. He has three sons on board this ship. Please, they mean no harm. They are mere innocent boys, eager to ride your sea by their father's side."

Once again the door swung open, and a man followed by two more boys slightly younger than the captain's first son but nearly identical in appearance joined them. The man who accompanied the boys immediately stopped them. "Go back inside and stay there until I call upon you." The man tried to dismiss the boys, but Amphitrite stepped in.

"Bring the boys forward," she commanded the hesitant sailor. He obeyed out of fear.

Amphitrite studied the young men. "Three boys, all with the likeness of their father. Your hearts will not be swayed so easily. You will love only one, strong and true, with fierceness like none other. You will grow into the strongest of warriors, sentenced to seek revenge for your father's death. This will fall to your first sons until the waters are free of my Sirens who have betrayed me. Only then will your curse be broken, the mothers of your children will no longer suffer, and your sons will finally know your love. You will finally find peace from your endless hunt. This I curse you."

The three young men fell to their knees, grasping at their eyes and grabbing at their chests. Painful cries poured from their mouths until finally the pain appeared to subside. When they opened their eyes, a white ring encircled their pupils.

"Eyes that will see the truth in your enemy and markings that symbolize your curse," Amphitrite announced. The oldest pulled his shirt up to reveal a dark marking etched into his reddened skin. "People will grow to fear the strength I have given you. Serve me well. Avenge your father and myself by ridding the waters of that which I cannot bring myself to do, for until this day they were my treasures. Only then will you find your freedom."

"Mother, please!" Aisling whimpered. "Do not blame my sisters. Let it be me to suffer. It was I who chose to listen to them when they told me to give him the kiss. It was I who did not confirm this with your greatness."

Amphitrite turned her attention once more to her beloved Siren, but pain now colored her vision. "You did not act alone in this. The others were consumed by envy for you, and in that they played their part. I created you to exist without consequences, but I revoke that gift. I will not hear your pleas or come to you in need. You will await your punishment and accept it when it finds you. I release you all."

Lorelei gasped without breath as she was brought out of the memory that she had lived through Amphitrite's eyes.

"Yes, your mother was part of the legend. She brought forth the destruction of the Sirens and the creation of the Men of Savas, and she escaped her punishment. I have felt every one of my precious Sirens die within my sea, each bringing a piece of my heart with them as a Savas delivered the sentence." Lorelei looked at her questioningly. The death of her daughters caused her so much visible pain. "What was done could not be undone, even if I wished it so. Even a goddess must live by certain rules." Amphitrite's voice faded to a sigh as her body dissipated into the water.

Lorelei spun around, searching for the Amphitrite when she did not immediately reappear. "What I ask of you, Lorelei," Amphitrite's voice found her before her body appeared again, "is that you bear my successor." Her watery hands reached out and pressed against Lorelei's flat stomach. "When you come to bear a child, it will be a son, brave and strong. He will have a great appreciation for life and its precious balance. He will accept his crown when he is ready and set foot into my waters. Then, and only then, will he become King of the Sea."

Amphitrite looked up into Lorelei's face. "I choose you because like your mother, your heart is true. A Siren was born to bring wrath upon those who affronted me. I was a spiteful goddess, creating my children with an evil nature. Your mother fought that instinct from the beginning, one of the many things that made her stand out from the others. She found a way to escape the wickedness inside her by creating you, a Siren that does not require the souls of men to survive. She created something that not even a goddess could."

Lorelei placed her hand over Amphitrite's, still resting upon her stomach. "Your mother will know peace, and your son will know love," Amphitrite continued.

Lorelei smiled at the goddess and mouthed silent thanks before Amphitrite faded from sight, flowing into the current of the water and leaving no sign that she was ever there. Lorelei felt an arm wrap around her waist and pull her toward the surface. She stared into the dark water, wondering if the goddess she had just encountered was only a dream. When she broke the surface, she turned into the tight embrace of Ajax, who clung to her in fear that she might be taken from him again.

"Lorelei?" Ajax breathed, unsure of what he was even asking her. "Thank the gods you are alive." He sighed in relief.

Lorelei scanned their surroundings. "Where are we? How did you find me?"

"I have no bloody clue. I have been swimming for hours, trying to find you, and if not for your eyes glowing I would probably still be swimming up and down the shore in search of you. Can you swim?"

"Yes." Lorelei started swimming for the shore alongside Ajax and did not stop until her feet touched the sand. She pulled her heavy body from the water; the sodden weight of her dress was considerable.

The moon was full and cast substantial light upon them as they made their way closer to the trees, giving them shelter from anyone who might be searching for them along the beach.

"Will they find us here?" Lorelei remarked after trying to find her bearings.

"We will be safe. The guards will not travel this far."

Silence fell over them as they stood before each other, drenched and tired.

Ajax was the first to break the silence. "I thought you had died."

Lorelei tried a weak smile. "Thank you for saving me." Looking at Ajax now, the light of the full moon brightening his perfect features, she wondered how she had found the strength to walk away.

"Always." Ajax's smile was relieved, and it made Lorelei melt. "What happened out there?"

"I am not sure. I am still trying to make sense of it myself."

* * *

Lorelei sat by the small fire Ajax had made to warm them. Her dress hung from a tree to dry, leaving her only in a thin white undergarment. After struggling relentlessly to remove the wet dress, she had to ask for Ajax for help. Heat enveloped Lorelei when he approached; her eyes fell upon his defined chest. His pants hung low upon his waist and the lines of his hard flesh looked delicious; it was hard not to reach out and caress him when he neared. She could still feel the lingering sensation of his touch as he loosened the fabric.

Lorelei considered the intensity of her attraction and the depth of her feelings toward Ajax. It was very different from what she felt for Oliver, who she considered a good friend; she always enjoyed his company. She cared for him deeply. With Oliver it was easy and comfortable, but with Ajax everything was intense, terrifying, and explosive, and even still, she yearned for it more and more with each passing moment.

"How is Oliver?" Lorelei asked quietly. They had been sitting in silence ever since Ajax helped remove her dress. She was not sure what was on his mind as he stared at the flames, his intense gaze seeking her out periodically. She watched his jaw clench, and it made her nervous.

"He is well and still with Letholdus. We will find them tomorrow." His words were curt.

"Good." Lorelei breathed relief. "Is he angry with me?"

Ajax looked at her hungrily, causing a fire to erupt within her. He was dangerous and so inviting at the same time, it made her head spin. "No."

"Are you angry with me?" Lorelei questioned innocently. When Ajax did not immediately respond, she continued talking for fear of further silence. "I left because I thought it was the best for everyone. I did not want anyone else getting hurt because of me."

"I am not angry, Lorelei." Ajax sighed, roughly running his fingers through his hair before lying back on the ground. His eyes began searching the sky. "Is that the only reason you left?"

"Yes. My mother always told me that I should follow my heart, that it would never lead me astray." Lorelei sighed.

"That is horrible advice, Lorelei," Ajax responded in a deadpan tone without moving.

"Why do you say that?" Lorelei sat up, trying to look at his features.

"Because that is how people get themselves and others killed."

"I do not believe that. Do you know what my heart is telling me to do right now?" she asked in a more playful tone.

"What?" Ajax turned his head toward her.

"To kiss you." Lorelei smiled nervously.

"Get some sleep, Lorelei. We have a long day tomorrow." Ajax groaned the words, throwing his arm over his face.

"It is all I can think about." Lorelei stood up and walked over to him. He moved his arm and looked up at her as she stepped over his body and sat down, straddling his hips. "Do you think about it too?" Her voice was breathier now that her body was against his.

"I will not be able to stop, Lorelei. If you start this... I want it too much." Ajax sounded pained as he placed his hands upon her hips, attempting to hold her still. The feel of his hands upon her bare thighs was almost too much to bear. His breathing became heavy and labored as he remained as still as stone. "I thought I was too late. I saw you lying there on that bed. I thought you were dead, Lorelei. I do not deserve this."

"If I would have died, it would not have been anyone's fault but my own." Lorelei stroked her fingers along his flat, hard stomach.

"I should have protected you." Ajax pulled his hands away and raked them down his face.

Lorelei laughed. "I believe it was not that long ago that you wanted to see me dead, Ajax. How things have come full circle." His beautiful lips pulled into a smile, and she felt some of the tension leave his body.

"I love your laugh." His confession excited her. It was the first time he had used that word for anything in relation to her.

"Every time I am with you, even when I am not, I think of how you taste, how you feel against me. I wonder if I could ever be close enough to you for this hunger in me to be satisfied." Lorelei placed her hand against her racing heart and took a deep breath. "Is this normal?" She grabbed his reluctant hand and placed it against her chest for him to feel the effect he had on her. The sensation of his hand upon her breast, with only a thin, damp piece of material separating them, caused shivers to assault her. Ajax awoke so many feelings that had been unknown to her before now.

Ajax took her hand in his, placing it on his own heart. It raced under her fingers, bringing a smile to her face.

"I am normal."

"No, Lorelei. You are not normal. You can never be normal. Nor can I. Do not ask more of me, for I am cursed." His removed his hand from hers, letting it fall to his side. He stared up at her sorrowfully. "I cannot give you what you want or take what I want."

"I know who you are, Ajax of the Savas. I know that your family was cursed by a vengeful goddess. We are supposed to be enemies, but against all logic we are here now, and I want nothing more than to give you all of myself. What if this moment is all we have? I will regret it for the rest of my life if I do not follow my heart. Let me love you tonight. Let me love you for as long as I have, however long that is. I will regret nothing if it is with you, I promise you."

"Lorelei…" Ajax started.

Lorelei leaned down and placed her lips against his, staying his words. For a moment he remained still, and Lorelei feared his rejection until his resolve crumbled and his hands found her. His lips responded to her urgently. He sought to bring her closer to him, even though there was no space between their heated bodies.

Lorelei pulled at his bottom lip with her teeth before she pulled back from him, causing him to groan in complaint. Their breathing was both stilted as they looked at each other. Ajax reached out and grabbed the hem of her slip, pulling it up over her head and discarding the material.

"You are so impossibly beautiful," he whispered heatedly.

"I feel the same about you. Ahh..." Lorelei began to giggle when Ajax flipped her onto her back. He leaned over her, brushing her hair from her face as he smiled down upon her.

"If this is possibly the only moment we have, then I will make the most of it." Ajax proceeded to shower kisses along her neck. Lorelei's laughter died away as his lips made their way to her sensitized breasts. Her head spun with pleasure, her body ignited with his touch. It was moment she knew would be impossible to ever forget or regret, for in this moment he was hers and it felt overwhelmingly right.

His body pressed against hers made hers come alive with overpowering sensations. A current of pleasure rushed through her body, heating her core. She could feel her heartbeat everywhere, her hands, face, and groin as it pulsed with excitement. His touch was the greatest indulgence, his lips the sweetest treat, his bite against her skin stimulating beyond all reason.

Ajax explored her body like she was the greatest treasure, like she was all the answers he sought. Lorelei's hands fisted his hair as his mouth met hers. His taste was addictive, his tongue masterful. She discovered the lines of his hard, sinewy body, every dip and curve her fingers sought, appreciating everything it offered her. They were oblivious to the passing of time as they were lost in the moment. The light of the fire danced across their skin, setting the perfect ambience under the light of the full moon. When he entered her, she was overcome by the feeling of knowing it was written in the stars that they should be together. This moment was fated to happen, and her heart was always meant to be his. This was where she belonged, in Ajax's arms.

Chapter 28
BRYCE

Bryce Barwicke stared into the amber liquid in the mug before him as if it would suddenly present the answer he was seeking. The noise around him faded into a constant hum. His thoughts were of his daughter locked away in a dark cell and his inability to free her from unjust punishment. The uncertainty of his family's future weighed heavily upon his shoulders. Bryce had always prided himself on his ability to protect his family, to keep them safe from evil. He never considered that evil to be the very king that he served. He never imagined that one day he would be committing treason, but he harbored no regrets other than he wished he were better prepared to fight this battle. Though he had some training with weapons, most of his time was spent tending his fields.

Bryce ran his hands over his rough beard; it was a recent addition. Bryce was partial to the new look; it made him less recognizable, and that worked to his benefit. Holton had assured Bryce and the others that they would be safe within the bar. He knew how to be discreet, especially with so many men in favor of their cause. Those who did not agree were turned away before they entered the premises by the men posted at the entrance. No one would think anything of Holton turning away customers; the man was known to be opinionated and difficult at the best of times.

Though large amounts of the king's men still remained stationed at all their posts around the city, the patrols had died down now that word had spread that Teller's men had retreated. Bryce now sat in the commotion of the bar, no longer fearful that the guards would make an appearance without a heads-up from the lookouts. Many of Teller's men sat around him in this very bar awaiting their next move, unbeknownst to the king and his men.

A large man pulled up a chair across from Bryce. He sported a shaved head, with markings extending from the collar of his shirt up the sides of his neck. Although his eyes were a light shade of blue, the white circles around the pupils of his irises gave them a strange, unnatural look.

"We have not formally met. My name is Margas." The man held out his large hand.

"Bryce Barwicke. I am grateful that we are on the same side." Bryce nodded toward the man's muscled physique. "I would not want to fight the likes of you. I would fear my chances."

Margas leaned back in his chair with a smile. "Yes. I would not want to come to arms against myself either."

Bryce laughed, brought his mug to his lips, and drained the remaining ale. "So I hear you are Teller's right-hand man."

"You could say that," Margas replied. "Teller is family." He shrugged. "And I like a good fight."

Bryce raised an eyebrow at Margas's strange explanation. "Is Teller to join us?"

"He will remain behind the scenes for now," Margas replied easily. "He likes the element of surprise."

Simon appeared before them, setting a full glass of ale in front of Margas. "As promised."

"Good man." Margas smiled and slapped Simon on the shoulder. He stumbled slightly under the force.

"Hey now, I am not built of stone," Simon complained, though his smile revealed he was jesting.

Margas downed his entire glass of ale, wiping his face with the back of his hand, turning his attention back to Bryce. "So your daughter is one of the girls in the dungeon, the tiny one with the brown hair and matching big brown eyes."

"Yes, Clara is her name." Bryce looked into Margas's eyes. "She is not what they accuse her to be."

"I know. Witches are rare creatures. In fact, centuries can pass without a single birth. These witch trials are nothing but a game, cowards pointing fingers at others. These people would not know a witch if she were standing right in front of them." Margas shook his head.

"I will drink to that." Simon held up his glass to meet Bryce's before they both drank.

"Simon tells me that you need a distraction to free your daughter. I believe we can offer just that." Margas smiled deviously as he leaned confidently back in his chair. "You see, we are very good at causing a scene."

"I have noticed." Bryce nodded.

"Listen up," Holton called to the many faces in his bar, hitting a mug against the bar's surface to gain attention. "Fendrel here has an announcement to make. A notice directly from the King's Guard." Holton motioned toward a skinny man beside the bar, with long red hair and a patchy beard. The skittish Fendrel took in the room's attention before rubbing his hands down the front of his worn shirt, taking a deep breath.

"The Witch Trials will take place tomorrow at high noon." Fendrel's voice wavered slightly, but it projected surprisingly well for such a slight, nervous-looking man.

"So soon?" Bryce questioned in disbelief. The voices around the room resumed at levels intolerable to Bryce.

"I suspect they are trying to draw you out while they believe Teller's men have fallen back. They want to regain order quickly before he makes his next move," Margas explained, as if this was expected.

"Margas!" All three of them turned toward the approaching man known as Sadon. Bryce knew his face from those present at the execution but had not personally spoken to him. He was the same height as Bryce but hardened by the trials of war. "You should come quickly." His expression was grim.

Margas stood and followed Sadon through the back exit. Bryce and Simon followed, along with a few other men. Outside in the dark alleyway, Sadon led them to the back of a wagon. He pulled a thick blanket aside to reveal two dead men. "Donald and Henry. We found them like this at their post. Identical wounds, directly piercing their hearts. No sign of a struggle."

Margas cursed under his breath. "I will send word to Teller. Tell the men the Ravens are here."

The other men were visibly upset at this new development. "Who are the Ravens?" Bryce questioned.

"They are assassins, hired by the king. Be ready for my signal tomorrow when the trials begin." Margas grabbed the blanket and covered the corpses of the two men.

"How will we know your signal?" Bryce asked Margas, forcing his eyes away from the wagon.

"You will know."

Chapter 29
LORELEI

"Wake up, sleepyhead." Oliver's voice roused Lorelei. She opened her eyes from a restful sleep to see his smiling face looking down on her. "Finally, I thought you were going to sleep the day away."

An answering smile found her lips as she gazed upon his face, only to fall away when she noticed Ajax's absence. "Where is Ajax?"

"He left to go see someone a few hours ago, said it was important. He told me to let you sleep, but as you can see I am not that patient. Besides, I was worried about you."

Lorelei looked down and realized she was covered in a warm blanket. "He made sure you were comfortable before he left. Who would have thought?" Oliver shrugged. "There is some food if you are hungry."

Lorelei yawned and rubbed her eyes, still heavy with sleep. "I am sorry for leaving you, Oliver. I thought I was doing what was best." She sat up next to him, securing the blanket around her. There was something calming about being in Oliver's company that she took comfort in.

"What is best is if you stay by my side in case someone stabs me again," Oliver joked, coaxing a laugh from her.

"Oh, I missed you so." Lorelei smiled, feeling as if a weight had been lifted from her shoulders.

"Not as much as I missed you." He winked. "Promise you will not run off again."

"Promise. Now turn around so I can dress."

"Here." Oliver passed her a folded piece of fabric. "You cannot wear that dress." She pointed to the intricate gown hanging from a nearby tree branch. "You can't walk around looking like a princess."

"Oliver, did you buy me another dress?" Lorelei appreciatively took the fabric and unfolded it. It was a plain ankle-length dress in a shade of pale blue.

"Actually, I stole this one." He leaned back and crossed his legs in front of him.

"Gone for only a few days, and you have turned into a criminal," Lorelei teased.

"That is why you cannot leave again." His smile widened, and his messy hair fell into his eyes.

"Not if I have a choice." Lorelei leaned in and kissed him on the cheek.

"What was that for?" Oliver's face flushed as he reached up to touch where Lorelei had kissed him.

"For being a good friend." Lorelei reached up and playfully nudged his shoulder.

"I am glad I met you. There is something about you that makes people want to be better than they are. Even Letholdus seems less insane lately."

"I am glad I met you too, Oliver. Is Letholdus here?" Lorelei asked nervously. She was not sure about being in his presence after witnessing his distaste for her and her kind.

"Yes." Oliver gave her a sympathetic look. "He will not harm you; Ajax threatened to skin him alive if he lays a finger on you." He climbed to his feet. "I will leave you to dress."

"Thank you, Oliver."

* * *

Lorelei stood with her toes in the water. Oliver and Letholdus seemed otherwise occupied, so she had taken a moment to enjoy the view of the ocean, to feel the temptation of the water's call. Lorelei closed her eyes and let her mind drift as she breathed in the salty morning air. She listened to the comforting sound of the waves as they pushed and pulled against her skin in a soothing, rhythmic motion. A song stirred in her thoughts, one she had no recollection of ever learning. Lorelei hummed the melody, releasing it into the ocean breeze.

The events of the night before flowed into her mind. Ajax's loving embrace had given her a feeling of utter contentment as she fell asleep in his arms, feeling adored and satisfied. Already she yearned for him again, wanting to be near him.

"Stop!" Lorelei turned when Letholdus's abrupt shout pulled her from her drifting thoughts.

"Letholdus?" Lorelei's eyes fell upon Letholdus, approaching her like a hunter would its prey.

"Stop singing!" he barked again. Lorelei stumbled backward out of fear, bumping into something. She regained her footing before turning to see Oliver standing behind her. He was in some kind of trance. His eyes were glazed, and an eerie glow encased his body. She remembered the strange look in his eyes when she had stayed with Crewe's men at the campfire, but the fluid substance that encircled him caused her heart to race within her chest. It was beautiful and enchanting as it called to her.

"What is happening?" Lorelei's fear slipped into her voice, and then suddenly a wave of hunger washed over her, making her mouth water. "Oliver?" Lorelei reached out for him, but Letholdus grabbed her wrist, stopping her from making contact. His grip upon her arm tightened painfully before he released her. "Do not touch him, *Siren*." He spat out the word as if it were poison.

Lorelei ignored the throbbing pain in her arm as she looked at Oliver. "What is it? What is wrong with him?" she asked meekly, relieved the hunger was subsiding now that she could process rational thought.

"It is his soul." Letholdus's accusing glare seared her. "You called it from within him."

"I do not understand." Lorelei was shocked.

"A Siren's voice can call upon the soul of her victims. You feed off the souls of men that fall under your trance. I have hunted your kind for my entire existence. I was created to kill you, as was my son. It is why we suffer the fate we do, because you exist. I should end this now before you embrace your nature." Letholdus's words were hateful.

"I have never taken a soul… I promise you." Lorelei planted her feet squarely in the sand. She was not sure if he actually intended to harm her, but she knew she would not surrender to this man without a fight. "I did not mean to do this." Lorelei wiped a tear from her eye, and soon more followed as she was powerless to stop the sobs that racked her body. She looked at Oliver, standing motionless before her in his dreamlike trance, and the reality of what she had done terrified her.

"I know," Letholdus admitted, to Lorelei's surprise, stepping back, her display of emotion obviously making him uncomfortable.

Lorelei took a deep breath and turned toward Letholdus. "How?" she managed weakly.

"When we look into the eyes of a Siren, we see every soul that has suffered at her hands. You have none." Letholdus pulled a flask of whiskey from his breast pocket and took a long swallow. "For now," he added harshly.

"May I ask you something?" Lorelei knew she might have been pushing, but there was something on her mind.

Letholdus tipped the flask to his lips again, draining the contents. "I do not feel overly forthcoming at the moment." Though he seemed uncooperative, he remained at her side, his expression tormented.

"The curse... How is it different for you and Ajax?" Lorelei pressed, knowing that Letholdus could possibly become volatile, and Ajax was not here to defuse him. The curiosity was too much to contain.

"It is not." Letholdus lifted his shirt, revealing angry red lines marring his flesh of his stomach. Lorelei gasped when she took in the extent of the raised skin. The wounds had healed, leaving behind extensive scarring. "Every time I have a thought to do harm, had an urge to strike out against Ajax, I take my knife and drive it deep, and I twist and twist until there is nothing left but the pain."

"But you are supposed to heal quickly." Lorelei gasped in disbelief.

"As I age, it has slowed. It normally takes a day for an injury to completely heal." Letholdus dropped his shirt, hiding the evidence of his self-mutilation. Lorelei was awash with new appreciation for the damaged man before her.

"There are so many, they cannot all possibly be from today." Lorelei reached out unconsciously. The urge to give him comfort was overwhelming, but he pulled away from her, as if she had threatened to burn him. His guard reinforced and the cold, detached man she had come to know returned.

He stepped back out of reach. "They are." His words were clipped.

Lorelei could not help but cringe at the sting of his words. She turned her focus back to Oliver. "Will Oliver be alright?"

"Yes." Letholdus's tone was cold. "My son believes that because you can survive without souls, it is a sign that the curse is coming to an end. I will respect his wishes and his feelings for you, for now. I will spare your life, but if at any point I feel that you mean harm to my family or anyone else, I will kill you without question, regardless of what my son says. Do I make myself clear?"

"Very," Lorelei said, shrinking away from him.

"No more singing, or I will cut out your tongue," he added with a growl.

"Lorelei?" They both swung their attention toward Oliver. His hands went up to his head. "I… That was strange." His gaze went back and forth between Lorelei and Letholdus's blank faces. "What is going on? Did something happen?"

Letholdus turned on his heel and left as quickly as he had come, returning to the horses while keeping his eyes trained upon her. Lorelei remained wary for a moment until she was sure Letholdus was not going to change his mind and come after her. "I apparently almost ate your soul," she said in anguished disbelief as she looked up at her closest friend. "You should stay away from me, Oliver." More tears slipped from her eyes.

Oliver placed his hands on her shoulders. "Do not be so hard on yourself. You are just figuring out who you are." He pulled Lorelei into a hug, and she gladly accepted.

"What if Letholdus were not here? I do not know what would have happened." Lorelei pushed against his chest. The reality of the situation caused panic to swell and fuel more tears.

Oliver reached up and brushed a tear from her cheek with his thumb. "I do. You would not have gone through with it."

"You did look pretty tasty." Lorelei smiled through her tears, and a strangled laugh escaped her.

Oliver too laughed at her jest. "I guess you missed out. Come, Letholdus has the horses ready."

"Are we heading back toward town? Is that where Ajax went?" Lorelei asked. Even though she had almost stolen Oliver's soul, he seemed to be back to his usual self.

"Definitely not. We overheard that the witch trials are happening today. That is the last place we should be." Oliver shook his head to emphasize his point.

"Witch trials?" Lorelei's interest was piqued.

"Yes. It is when the people accused of witchcraft are going to be sentenced." Oliver rubbed the back of his neck. The subject seemed to disturb him.

"Sentenced? What does that mean?" Lorelei was unnerved by the word.

"They will be hanged." Oliver's hand dropped to his side like dead weight.

"What if they are innocent?" Lorelei looked up at Oliver, searching for signs of hope. Instead she was met by his grim expression. "Clara. I have to go." She grabbed hold of Oliver's sleeve. "I have to go, Oliver."

"What? No. Teller and his men are crawling all over the city, waiting to strike. The Ravens are hiding in the shadows, and the king's guard is in full force today. We are not going anywhere near there."

"Who are the Ravens, and who is Teller?"

Lorelei could tell he was struggling with what he should share with her. He sighed exaggeratedly before speaking. "The Ravens are Crewe's men. We suspect they are here to eliminate Teller. We spotted them heading toward the castle yesterday. Teller, well, he is like Ajax. So you can see why I cannot let you go into town."

"I have to go. A young girl named Clara is one of the accused. I have to make sure she is safe. I have to make sure she gets back to her family. I made her a promise when we were locked away in the dungeon. I cannot let anything happen to her." Lorelei grabbed hold of Oliver's arm pleadingly.

"Lorelei, Teller is like Ajax and Letholdus. His instinct will be to kill you. Not to mention that if the prince sees you, he is not going to let you go a second time."

Something Oliver said had stood out. "Why did Ajax not know what I was when he first saw me, but Letholdus did without question?"

Oliver sighed. "Letholdus had actually seen and killed your kind. Ajax was born after they believed the Sirens were extinct. He was uncertain. His instinct warned him that you were not what you seemed, though he could not see the evidence in your eyes. He could not see the souls of the men you destroyed. That was why he had originally believed you to be a witch."

"What of Teller?"

"He was born after, like Ajax." Oliver looked narrowly at her, trying to determine where her questions were leading. "His men have been planning attacks on the crown."

"Then he might not pay me any mind. I think he was in the castle when I was there. There was a man with the same eyes, and he dismissed me. As you said, he has other plans that are occupying him. We can be discreet, and I will make sure the prince does not see me."

A hopeful smile flashed across Lorelei's face, but Oliver could only respond with disbelief.

"You do not even realize how ridiculous that statement is, Lorelei. You do not look like a normal girl. Teller might not know what you are when he first lays eyes on you, but he will figure it out, and as for the prince, I am sure he has eyes everywhere."

"Prince Arthur still thinks I am dead. I will take my chances." Lorelei bit her lip in anticipation. She needed to convince Oliver. She knew it was her only chance.

"Lorelei…" Oliver shook his head.

"No, Oliver, you said before that someone you knew had been wrongly accused of witchcraft. What if we can save Clara from that same fate? Should we not at least try?"

"My mother." Oliver let his shoulders fall as his eyes dropped to his feet. Pain was etched all over his face.

"Your mother was accused of being a witch?" Lorelei gasped. Reaching out, she took his hands.

"Yes, I could not save her." Lorelei's heart constricted when Oliver's grief-stricken eyes met hers.

"I am truly sorry about your mother, Oliver. Was it recent?" Lorelei leaned in and embraced Oliver, trying to soothe him.

"No. I was only small, but I remember everything about her." Oliver leaned back to look at Lorelei's face. "Even if we convince Letholdus to let us go back to town, how are we going to save this girl? There will be guards everywhere."

"No one will suspect a simple girl and a young man with such an innocent face could cause trouble. There has to be a way."

"Innocent? I thought I was rugged."

"Of course. That is what I meant to say," Lorelei said, trying to conceal her smile as she patted him playfully on the cheek.

"I am going to be in so much trouble, Lorelei. Ajax is going to cut off my head for letting you do this." Oliver ran his fingers through his hair. Lorelei knew that if anyone would understand, it would be him.

"Thank you, Oliver." She threw her arms around Oliver's neck.

He wrapped his arms around Lorelei's shoulders in turn, giving her a squeeze. "Let me do the talking when it comes to convincing Letholdus. We both know you are not his favorite person."

"I think that is a good idea."

"There are a few conditions you have to agree to first. One, you have to stay out of sight at all times. I do not want anyone knowing you are there. Two, you have to be willing to abort this attempt if either Letholdus or myself deems it too dangerous. And three, most important of all, you have to do everything in your power to convince Jax not to kill me when he finds out."

"I will," Lorelei said hopefully.

* * *

Lorelei waited while Oliver talked privately with Letholdus. Sitting on the beach, she scooped up the sand and watched it pour through her fingers. She could sense Letholdus's approach before his feet came into view.

"I am always primed for a good fight. No one can call me a coward, but something tells me that you have a plan that you are not divulging to Oliver," he said flatly. "I want to know what a tiny thing like you has planned before I agree to anything."

"You are a lot like Ajax," Lorelei said thoughtfully, still watching the way the sand poured from her hands.

"He likes to think otherwise," Letholdus replied indifferently.

"I need to make sure Clara is not prosecuted for being a witch." Lorelei looked up into Letholdus's calculating stare. "I cannot stand by knowing that she will be hanged."

"What makes you think you can make a difference?" Letholdus's tone almost seemed bored.

"I don't. I just know that I need to try. Clara is only a child. She has a mother, father, and brother. She deserves to live her life, and she is not the only one on trial. There are others." Lorelei looked up at Letholdus's hardened features.

"Teller will know what you are." He narrowed his eyes.

Lorelei looked up at Letholdus, holding up her hand to block the intense sun. "Are you concerned for my safety, Letholdus?" She raised her eyebrows, warranting an irritated scowl from him.

"What makes you think that I will follow along with this charade?" Though his tone indicated annoyance, Lorelei could sense that his resistance was waning.

"Like you said yourself, you are always primed for a good fight." He assessed Lorelei quietly for a moment, deep in thoughts she could not even begin to understand.

"*When* Teller finds you, I will not stop him from killing you." Letholdus waited for her reaction.

"I understand. Will you make sure that Clara is returned to her family and Oliver is safe?" Lorelei ran her fingers back and forth thoughtfully through the sand, leaving tracks along its surface.

"And Ajax?" Letholdus said curiously.

"We both know that Ajax will be fine." Lorelei smiled weakly, trying not to think about Ajax. She could not afford to lose focus; thinking of him would make her doubt the actions she planned to take. There was no room for doubt.

"Until recently, I would have agreed with you." Letholdus turned his gaze toward the water's horizon. She did not question his words as she followed his gaze to the seemingly endless sea. "I hope my son is right about you, Lorelei." Letholdus's surprising confession stunned Lorelei. "For all our sakes." Before she could utter a response, he was already gone.

Lorelei stood up, still looking out at the water. Wrapping her arms around herself offered little reprieve from the chill that spread across her skin, despite the warm sun. "Please forgive me, Mother, that I may not return to you. I have to follow my heart, and right now it is telling me to save Clara." Lorelei let the wind carry the words away from her. She wiped her face before taking a deep, calming breath. She cast one last fleeting look over the water before she turned to join Letholdus and Oliver on a path she realized might very well be her last.

Chapter 30
AJAX

"From the whispers, I can tell you already know that the Ravens have arrived." Ajax leaned into an open window to set his eyes upon Margas, sitting before the arsenal of blades he was sharpening and polishing with utmost diligence. Ajax always knew how to find his fellow Savas. When they neared each other, it was like a low hum of energy that guided them toward each other. The same force allowed them to be aware of each other in battle, to know the others' moves before they made them.

"Ajax, you are even prettier than the last time I laid eyes upon you." Margas smiled teasingly. "I am surprised it took you this long to show up. You are usually on the front lines with the promise of a good fight."

"Yes, well, I have been otherwise occupied as of late," Ajax said dismissively.

"Did you finally find someone more attractive than yourself to catch your attention?" Margas mocked with good-intentioned humor. Setting down his blade, he stood up.

"I see that you still have not found a woman who can stand the look of your ugly mug," Ajax retorted in kind.

"There is bound to be one out there somewhere." Margas opened his arms to embrace his old friend. "Good to see you, cousin."

"You as well." Ajax noticed the other men in the room watching him with interest. They were all preparing for battle. "Crewe wants Teller's head."

"Your Raven friends already took out two of our men. Are you going to call off the hounds?" Margas's mood turned serious as he focused on matters at hand.

"I do not think they still consider me a friend. In Crewe's eyes I betrayed him. I took something he considered his property, and I killed his favored apprentice."

Margas studied at him thoughtfully for a moment before a slight smile curved his lips. "Ah… a girl?"

Ajax only gave a slight nod. There was no point in denying the truth. Margas was one for prying it out.

"Well, *shite*. That will do it." Margas shook his head in disbelief.

"Do you and Teller have a plan?" Ajax changed the topic.

"There is a plan, and it is about to unfold before you. Do you wish to join in the fun?" Margas rubbed his hands together eagerly.

"The witch trials." Ajax saw the plan come together in his head. He heard the commoners talk of the event to taking place this very day. The excitement was humming through the streets. "I thought Teller had settled down in pursuit of the quiet life."

"Has is really been that long since you have been in touch?" Margas shook his head. "I did not realize that you did not know."

"Know what?"

"The king's men killed Josselyn, Teller is seeking revenge, and I am simply along for the journey."

"No." Ajax was shocked. He had not had the opportunity to meet the fair Josselyn, but he knew how deeply Teller had fallen for the woman. It was one of the many reasons they had followed different paths. Teller had found a reason to settle down, while Ajax had still yearned for combat. It was in this time that Ajax had fallen into regular dealings with the Ravens.

At that time, Ajax had recently parted from his father because of their difference of opinion regarding Oliver. He had been only a child, terrorized and in need of stability, and Ajax felt a bond with the young boy, a kinship that he had never known before. Ajax's mother had died giving birth to him, and he had been raised by a father who could never forgive. Ajax had only known resentment until Oliver had shown him what true family was.

For a long time Ajax and Oliver lived meal-to-meal, stealing to survive. Ajax would bet the fiercest of warriors that he could defeat them in battle. They would always take the bait, because to them he looked like an overconfident young man that they could easily knock some sense into. Even then Ajax possessed a strength they could not fathom, and he could easily overpower them. Now, full-grown men went out of their way to avoid him, and they would never enter willingly into a fight with him. Memories from that time surfaced. He had been so focused on his own life that he was oblivious to Teller's loss.

The night Ajax met Crewe, he was fleeing a robbery he had committed in the city of Rutton. The wealthiest city outside of Falls Landing, Rutton had a number of treasures to be acquired if one knew where to look. It was midday. Ajax never waited for the cover of darkness, his confidence in his skills unwavering. He and Oliver were exiting a house in which they had pocketed some coin and a few pieces of jewelry, when they were spotted. They were scaling down the outside of the house when one of the city guards noticed them. "Stop!"

"Apparently, stealing is illegal," Oliver said sarcastically.

"Learn something new every day." Ajax jumped the remaining distance to the alley below.

They ran as soon as their feet hit the ground. Oliver lagged behind. "Pick up the pace," Ajax encouraged.

"Trying." Oliver panted heavily as they weaved in and out of the narrow alleyways. Ajax grabbed Oliver's arm and darted to the right, pulling him into a small alcove. The guards were still in pursuit and closing in quickly, their numbers increasing as more men joined the pursuit. Ajax jumped up and grabbed on to a wooden beam on the exterior of a house, pulling himself up and into an open window before reaching down to help Oliver, who was barely able to climb into the window and out of sight before the guards came barreling past them. "That was close." Oliver was still struggling for breath.

The door swung open to the room they were in, and a man and woman shuffled in, embracing. They did not immediately notice the two intruders, consumed as they were by one another. The male was focused on removing the woman's dress, but her eyes searched the room before falling upon Ajax and Oliver. A scream tore through the air as she struggled to cover anything that might be exposed. The man looked up, his features changing immediately. Ajax and Oliver decided to exit before a confrontation could occur. "We were just leaving. Please continue," Oliver blurted.

Ajax jumped through the window, grabbing the ledge while reaching out for Oliver. Oliver jumped, grasping onto Ajax's offered hand before throwing his weight out of the window, swinging up to grab on to the ledge of the roof. Ajax was quick to follow as he pulled himself up behind Oliver.

"Move! The guards can easily spot us up here if they look up," Ajax ordered as they began jumping between the roofs of the closely constructed homes. "Below, left. Guards."

They changed direction and headed to a more concentrated area of stone houses, allowing more places for cover. "Here." Ajax leveraged himself down between two walls as they descended down to street level.

"You made that look so easy," Oliver complained as he set his feet down upon the ground. Scrapes marred his hands and exposed arms.

They headed further into the inner city, where shadows huddled in the corners of the dark, decrepit buildings despite the sun overhead. The dampness in the air was suffocating, and the putrid smell of waste washed over them as they passed through the side streets.

Ajax slowed when they entered a sheltered alleyway. They had lost the guards, and Ajax allowed Oliver to catch his breath and rest for a moment before they found a place to settle for the night. Oliver was doubled over with his hands upon his knees, gasping for breath. Ajax could feel the menacing energy encircle them before his eyes registered the threat. "Stand up, Oliver," he warned.

"You must have something of worth burning a hole in your pocket to justify your quick getaway." A man stepped out of the shadows. He looked at home in the dark shadows of the city. His face was covered in a few days' growth; his hair lay unwashed and limp against his pallid skin. A scar ran from his forehead, through a milky eye into the center of his right cheek.

"Actually, we were out for our daily run, trying to keep fit," Oliver said fearlessly, patting his stomach. Ajax could not help smiling. Oliver never showed fear, even when it was warranted.

More men moved in to circle them, all just as sinister as the first. "Empty your pockets."

"We would rather not." Ajax stood his ground. Oliver, just as stubborn, stood unwavering at his side. The men were armed and waving blades, trying to intimidate them.

"Very well, then we will empty them for you," the scarred man snarled. "Boys." He ordered his men to advance.

Oliver and Ajax dropped into defensive positions, back to back. Only Oliver had a blade, a small knife he kept strapped to his belt that looked pitiful next to the numerous weapons now drawn and aimed at the two of them.

One man advanced toward the unarmed Ajax, who twisted, and

reaching out, grabbed the man's sword by the blade, tugging it from his grasp. Ajax's blood coated the metal, though the wound on his hand had already begun to weave itself together. He continued with his momentum, and spinning, he kicked the man's feet out from under him. Ajax pinned him to the ground, the man's own blade pressed against his throat. The onlookers were momentarily stunned at the realization that Ajax and Oliver were not going to be easy prey. The man at Ajax's mercy made a play for his knife; Ajax thrust the sword into his chest. The man expelled a moan that bubbled from his mouth as thick, viscous blood ran down his cheek and dripped to the earth.

The circle of men closed in on them. Ajax cut down each one as he approached, slashing through their numbers, all the while trying to pay attention to Oliver. Although he had trained Oliver with blades, and the boy showed impressive skill for someone of his age, still a child by every right, he was not like Ajax. He could be seriously injured if he made one wrong move. Ajax noted that Oliver had already replaced his trusted knife with a sword he had pilfered from the scabbard of one of the unsuspecting men. Oliver's strength was speed; since he had a slight built and was smaller than his opponents, he used this skill to his advantage. Ajax disarmed another man and now handled two blades that he swung through the mass.

"Get down!" Ajax hollered to Oliver before he spun around with his blades. Oliver dropped to the ground. Ajax's swords sliced through the throat of one, causing him to sputter and collapse. Another took the blade across his stomach, and his insides slipped from his body despite his effort to hold his wound closed.

"Keep close!" Ajax yelled at Oliver.

"I am trying."

Oliver grabbed a larger blade that had been dropped by one of the dying men and stood to confront the remaining men. He summersaulted away from a descending sword, coming to the feet of another attacker. Oliver raised his blade up to puncture the man's stomach. The man had his arms raised to strike Oliver. He looked down in shock at Oliver's blade buried deep within him, his blood running down the length.

When Ajax dropped the last man standing, he turned toward the scarred man. He sighed impatiently when he noticed that the man had Oliver in his hold, a blade against his throat. "I told you to stay close," Ajax scolded Oliver.

"Give me what I want, or I will kill him," the scarred man demand-ed, without thought of his men dying at his feet. He pressed his blade tightly to Oliver's throat, causing a trickle of blood to escape and drip down his shirt.

"How about you let him go and let us walk out of here with every-thing on our persons, and I will let you live," Ajax countered.

The scarred man sneered, showing off his black teeth. "You are not in the position to make demands."

"Wrong," Ajax retorted. He whipped a knife through the air. The man did not realize the blade was thrown before it pierced his good eye and lodged deep within his head. Oliver's eyes widened as the man dropped with a sickening thud.

"Did you even aim? That was ridiculously close to my head!" Oli-ver complained.

"I did not miss."

"Whatever. I just do not like knives being thrown at my head." Oli-ver rubbed his hands down his face.

"I saved your life, did I not?" Ajax was picking through the weap-ons discarded on the ground, looking for anything worthwhile.

"I could have taken him." Oliver sulked as he grabbed his favored knife off the ground and wiped the blood from the blade.

Ajax only rolled his eyes in response before they both turned at the sound of clapping.

"Impressive." A man approached. He stood out in their dark, dirty surroundings. He was not cut from the same cloth as the men that resided in this part of the city. Instead, this man wore well-tailored clothes. He had distinguished features, with graying hair that was swept back into a tie at the base of his neck.

"Who are you?" Ajax stepped protectively in front of Oliver.

"I mean no harm." The man smiled. "I wish to introduce myself. My name is Crewe Carmichael, and I think we can be of help to each other."

"Is that crazy son of a bitch Letholdus with you?" Margas now brought Ajax back from his thoughts. Of the remaining Men of Sa-vas, Ajax was the only one with a surviving father. Both Margas and Teller had been forced to kill their own. When their mothers died during childbirth, their fathers slowly lost their sanity, submitting to the curse. Overcome by a grief that infected them like a disease, they became filled with hatred for their sons.

Ajax was convinced that the only reason his father never attempted to kill him was because he was always lost in a state of inebriation, too saturated with drink to even form the thought. For as long as Ajax could remember, Letholdus had started and ended his day with a bottle. As great a pain as Letholdus could be, Ajax feared the day he too might have to kill his own father out of self-preservation.

"Not today." Ajax smiled thoughtfully. "I cannot fight with you, as much as it pains me to decline. I have to get Oliver and Lorelei far away from this madness."

"You know it will not end well with the girl, right?" Margas said bluntly.

"Unfortunately, I am well aware. I did everything in my power to prevent it and failed; now I am too deep." Ajax shrugged. He had spent most of his life avoiding women, staying focused on his skills as a fighter; he should have known better to think that he could avoid his fate.

"When all this is over, I am going to find a place in the middle of nowhere and live by myself for the rest of my life to avoid all this cursed shite."

"Good luck. I don't think it will be that easy." Ajax gave Margas a friendly pat on the shoulder. "Give my best to Teller."

"Of course. We are heading out now. Are you sure you are not up for a good fight before you leave? There is promise of blood and glory." Margas tried to sway him.

"Until next time." Ajax held out his hand, and Margas took it in a firm shake.

"Bloody curse gets us all." Margas shook his head. "Until next time then."

Ajax slipped through the window and moved soundlessly through the alleyway. He planned to keep a low profile as he exited the city. The population was now gathering in the town square with the trials set to begin.

A figure darted into Ajax's peripheral vision. Ajax veered off course, tailing the man. This man did not move like a normal civilian; he was trained in stealth. Ajax could smell the scent of a Raven anywhere. Even though he could not see the man's face, he recognized him as Brenner. He had seen the man trail on many occasions, and his movements gave him away. He followed, staying out of view, as Brenner joined four others in a discreet location. Ajax recognized Crewe's form among them.

"We have spotted the girl in town. Should we pursue her?" Brenner questioned Crewe.

"We need to focus on the task the king has given us. Locate Teller. He is the priority. I will deal with Lorelei in time." Crewe was a soldier through and through, always focused in the acts of battle.

Ajax pushed off the stone wall with a quiet curse and moved on swift feet. As much as he wanted to confront Crewe, that matter needed to wait. He needed to get to Lorelei before Teller and Margas spotted her. He was furious that Oliver and Letholdus had disobeyed him, walking straight into the very situation he had tried to avoid.

Chapter 31
LORELEI

Lorelei pulled her cloak tightly around her shoulders, securing the large hood so it concealed her face. She followed Oliver through the large crowd converging in the center of town. Letholdus had disappeared into the many bodies when they arrived, seeking a better vantage point. Since her earlier conversation with Letholdus, he seemed to be more tolerant of her, but not to the point where she would consider him friendly. Still, it was an improvement.

Though Letholdus had agreed to their plan, he did not share the same motivation to save Clara; instead he was excited by anticipation of the potential storm brewing within the city walls. Even though his mindset did benefit their cause, it did not take much convincing to get him to follow along with their plan. It was more or less like waving a bottle of whiskey in his face; he could not decline.

Lorelei paid special attention to keeping a low profile. She was not sure where Ajax was. She remained on alert for his whereabouts. She knew that if Ajax saw her, he would drag her kicking and screaming from the city walls. As much as she wanted to see him, she needed to make sure Clara was freed.

She had asked Oliver why the promise of violence was so enticing to Letholdus. It was part of the curse to seek brutality and destruction. Lorelei was grateful he was not currently directing these tendencies toward her. It was a hunger the Men of Savas could not sate, even when the Sirens were thought to be extinct. They sought reprieve in any type of violence they could find. The only peace they ever knew was in another, a love they found so pure and true that when they lost it, it destroyed them beyond repair, driving them mad.

"So Letholdus lost his love when Ajax was born?"

"Yes, he is only a shell of the man that he once was, from what I have heard. He keeps himself in a state of perpetual drunkenness in fear of what he is capable of." Oliver frowned.

"I suppose it is working, in its twisted way," Lorelei responded sadly. "Why do you suppose he has not killed me, knowing what I am?"

"I truly do not know. There are forces at work that want you alive, because it is truly a miracle that you are."

Lorelei and Oliver now stood in the sea of people. "Let me know when you see her, and I will signal Letholdus. Do you still have the knife I gave you?" Oliver's expression was serious now that their plan was unfolding. There was no room for his usual humor now that lives were at risk. Oliver had seemed unsettled since they left for the city, and she knew it was because he felt guilty for disobeying Ajax. She had put Oliver in a difficult position; he had to betray Ajax's wishes and undertake something that posed great risk to all of them. Lorelei prayed they would be successful.

She patted her side with the concealed weapon under her cloak. "Good." Oliver nodded curtly. "Do not be afraid to use it, Lorelei." She could tell he was nervous about the amount of soldiers that were stationed in the city. They were not taking any chances.

"Oliver?" Lorelei reached out and placed her hand upon his shoulder. She had so much to say to him. She wished there was another way to save Clara without putting him in harm's way. Now that they were amidst the danger, she feared what they had to face. The entire perimeter was thick with patrolling guards. The solidity of their plan seemed to slip through their fingers.

"I will move in and see if there are any openings. As soon as you point her out to me, just hang back in the cover of the crowd and slowly move back, ready to flee. Once we make our move, there will be others that follow suit. Teller and his men are afoot. Every woman on trial has family here; as soon as the opportunity presents itself, it could turn into mayhem. It may be the only way we can make this happen. Be ready," Oliver whispered close to Lorelei and smiled reassuringly. "And if you see Ajax, you might want to make a run for it, because he will not be happy with us."

"Thank you for everything."

"Don't thank me yet." Oliver gave her shoulder a squeeze. "It will be a miracle if we pull this off."

The smile fell from Lorelei's face when the prisoners shuffled into view and the roar of the crowd rose considerably. Her eyes immediately found the sullen face of Clara among the others. "That's her, in the middle." There were at least ten women in total, Clara being the youngest. Lorelei had to stay her feet from trying to move toward the terrified girl. She had to be smart about her moves if they were going to be successful.

Oliver's eyes met Letholdus's across the crowd, making discreet signals before he turned his attention back toward Lorelei. "Move back now," he said warningly. "Any sign of trouble, fall back to our meeting place. I am serious; if anything happens to you, Ajax will kill me." Oliver slipped through the bodies in front of him, leaving Lorelei in the center of the crowd.

Lorelei too moved through the bodies, trying to get a better view of the stage. The women trembled, bound to each other by chains as they huddled close. Their hair was knotted and unkempt, their skin pale, with dark circles under their eyes. These women were starved and terrorized and now faced their death for fictitious crimes.

Two men in front of Lorelei began to shove each other. It upset the crowd around them. The larger of the two men swung his fist, connecting with the other man's face. He dropped to the ground awkwardly, unconscious. Lorelei gasped in disbelief while the rest of the crowd continued as if the scuffle had not occurred. The man on the ground was ignored by everyone standing around him; a few people even tripped over him. When Lorelei tried to push her way through to check on the unconscious man, she was met with resistance as people moved and pushed her further away.

Lorelei continued on, trying to avoid getting tangled up. The people were boisterous, shoving and yelling in anticipation. A man grabbed her by the wrist, swinging her around to face him. "Lost, sweetheart?" He leered down at her.

Lorelei tried to pull her hand free of his grip. "I am looking for someone." She wrenched her arm back.

"I know most everyone in these parts. Try me." Lorelei was confused by the mixed signals this man gave. Her instincts were on alert to danger, but his words seemed genuine.

"Do you know Clara Barwicke's family?" Lorelei straightened her shoulders, making her look more confident.

The man's eyes were lidded with dark thoughts. "No, but I can help you in other ways." A cold smile curved his lips, revealing missing teeth.

Lorelei tried not to react when a chill crept along her skin. "No, thank you." She turned and wove through the bodies, putting distance between her and the disturbing man. When she glanced back to see her progress, the man's cold eyes were still on her retreating form.

Lorelei turned, running into someone before she had time to react. "Why are looking for the Barwickes? What business do you have with them?" Lorelei looked up at the man she had collided with. He was cloaked, a graying beard shadowed his face, and deep brown eyes looked intently back at her. His hands remained at his sides and made no move to touch her. Even though Lorelei did not know the man, she wanted to trust him. His eyes were not cold and tortured like the man before; instead his were that of a sound, determined man.

"I need to find Bryce. It has to do with his daughter." Lorelei spoke quietly, pointing at Clara.

He looked at her thoughtfully for a moment. "Follow me. Pull your hood down over your face."

Lorelei reached up and pulled the material down tightly while following the man. They came to a small group of men standing along the edge of the crowd. "This woman was asking for you by name. She said it's about your daughter."

Lorelei looked into the tired face of the man she was led to. His eyes were sad but determined, like those of the man that brought her here. "I think I can help," Lorelei offered. All the men with him regarded her with narrowed expressions.

"We do not have time for games. My daughter is being tried, and I do not intend to let that happen without a fight."

A voice began addressing the crowd from the platform. Lorelei paid no attention. "I know you do not know me, but I met your daughter when I was kept in the dungeon with her. I want to help bring her back to you. I do not have time to explain what I am going to do, and you may not believe me regardless, but I need you and your men to cover your ears when I sing. I am going to get to the stage, but you must make sure that you cannot hear anything. I should be able to buy you enough time to get to Clara and free her without having to confront all the guards."

"Bryce?" one of the men said in disbelief. "This is ridiculous. Do not waste your time with her. They have already started. We need to get ready."

The men all turned their attention to the stage, where the first woman was brought up and forced to stand at the front of the stage. Her stomach was swollen with child. "Cedany Wade, accused of witchcraft," a voice announced over the hum of the crowd.

"Jesus, they are not wasting time. We have to move." Another man leaned into Bryce.

Lorelei pulled the hood off her head and grabbed hold of his hands. "Please, I can help." She looked Bryce directly in the eyes. She could feel the crackle of energy under her skin, feel it rush over Bryce. The widening of his eyes indicated he felt it, and it was enough to convince him that this was not some mere woman standing before him.

Letholdus appeared next to the men Lorelei was addressing, as if he appeared out of thin air. "You should listen to her. Margas and his men can cause a distraction for you, but there are still enough guards here to cause some serious damage to anyone caught in the crossfire, including your daughter." He stepped out behind the men. "She is surrounded by guards. There is no way to ensure she will not be hurt. This woman is capable of causing a better distraction than what you have planned."

"You are with Margas and the others?" Bryce asked Letholdus — though it was obvious based on his appearance alone. Letholdus, like Ajax, had something undeniably exceptional.

"How do you plea?" The man upon the stage addressed the young pregnant woman.

"Please... I am with child," the woman sobbed. "I am a woman of the church... I am not a witch." A guard positioned behind her slipped a noose around her neck. The woman's cries became desperate.

"Should we make our move, Bryce?" one of the men standing next to Clara's father asked.

"No Donald, we have to wait for Margas's signal."

"They are going to kill that pregnant woman," the dark-haired man beside him said desperately. Lorelei recognized him immediately as the man that tried to break into the dungeon and free Clara.

"We cannot risk it without Margas and his men. We have to wait," Bryce said. "I will not risk it."

A man approached without a hooded cloak like the others. He was not shielding his identity like the other men involved. His brow was furrowed, and he looked troubled as his gaze skimmed their surroundings.

"Holton?" Bryce said. "Why are you here?"

"It's Alston. He is with the king's guards," Holton said nervously.

"Do not move!" Bryce turned to see guards approaching from behind their position, but before they could move he and his men were surrounded by the king's guards, with weapons drawn. They had no option but to admit defeat.

"Alston betrayed us, that backstabbing *shite!*"

Lorelei looked at the approaching guards. Letholdus was gone. "Cover your ears when I sing." Her eyes connected with Bryce's for a moment before she ducked into the crowd. Bryce's men tried to scatter behind her, fleeing into the crowd as the guards began to pursue. Turning around and pulling her hood up, Lorelei pushed her way through the people. It was then that she spotted Oliver across the crowd. He looked at her questioningly before his eyes widened in panic. Lorelei turned away from his pleading gaze. She could not stand the look of pain on his face when he realized what she intended. He was too far away, with too many people in his path, to get to her in time. He could not stop her.

Chapter 32
TELLER

"Glad that you could join us, Lord Caunter. The trials have just begun." King Brom addressed him as he approached, waving toward the stage and the large crowd.

"Yes, well, I go where the action is." Lord Caunter smiled as he bowed in respect to the king.

"I do not believe you have had the pleasure of meeting Peronell, my queen." King Brom waved at the very regal woman at his side. "My dear, this is Lord Caunter, Marquis of Thetford." Peronell was dressed in an exquisite gown made of the finest fabrics. She truly was a sight to behold against the sullen backdrop of the stone city.

"No, I have not. It truly is an honor, my queen." Lord Caunter had not seen the queen in close quarters, and the realization of who she was hit him like a knife to the chest. The pieces fell together, and he could finally see an end to his chase. His outward appearance was as smooth as unsettled water, but inside a storm brewed.

"Excuse me. I do not have the stomach for such things." Peronell abruptly stood, and one of the guards immediately escorted her to her awaiting carriage.

"A royal bitch, that one," King Brom muttered under his breath. "Tell me, Lord Caunter, have you fallen under the spell of a bloody woman?"

"Yes, I did," Lord Caunter admitted.

"Pity, I guess we are all to be damned to the sharp temper of a woman." King Brom chuckled humorlessly while shaking his head.

Their attention was pulled to the stage as the announcer declared the first accused woman's guilt. She stood before the crowd as her sentencing was announced. The panic-stricken woman swayed on her feet, clinging to her rounded stomach. The people grew louder, some jeering while others shouted in outrage.

"What of the unborn child?" Lord Caunter questioned as he watched the woman begging for mercy to save her unborn baby.

"Her husband claims that she slept with the devil, and it is his child that grows within her," Priest Benedict answered. He was standing close to the king's side, fascinated by the horrific scene. "We must end it, along with its devil-loving mother, before it is able to release its wrath upon us."

"If I may, Your Reverence Benedict, how do we know that her husband speaks the truth? What proof is held over this woman to condemn her?" Lord Caunter questioned as he watched the commotion.

"A witch can hide in plain sight. They are masters of disguise. We sometimes have to rely on the noble word of our citizens to point us in the right direction to rid our city of evil. Once the blame is cast, the people will not rest until punishment is carried out."

"And if untruthful blame is cast, what then?" Lord Caunter asked pointedly.

The priest scowled, as if he could not believe that he was being questioned about the possibility of being misled in dealings with witches.

"Spoils of wars, my friend," King Brom laughed. "Where is my bloody drink!" He turned his attention to a nearby servant, who immediately refilled his glass. The king was already noticeably inebriated.

The canopy set up to house the king and nobles was guarded by rows of men, armed and ready for action. The king was not taking any chances after what had happened at the last execution. Lord Caunter recognized most of the noble faces that stood around him. Most of them lived a life too comfortable, making them soft and round. Husbands and wives, although standing dutifully side by side, could not stand the sight of each other as they distracted themselves by indulging in the fine foods being served. Hungry faces from the crowd tried to peer in and dream of such luxuries the king and noblemen were waving in front of them, oblivious to the evil that festered in the hearts of these people.

Lord Caunter's eyes returned to the stage, declining the drink offered to him. The guards were already unchaining another woman.

She had long chocolate hair that glowed shades of auburn in the afternoon sun. A young girl clung to her hand. The striking brunette tried to soothe her before being wrenched away and pulled up the stairs leading to the stage. Caunter had to commend the woman for her fierceness in the face of death. Another of the imprisoned women standing among the others fainted, falling with a sickening thud upon the stony ground.

"Mera!" the young girl screamed out to her, too young to be guilty of any crime.

"What of this woman?" Caunter asked of the beautiful woman being led up on the stage.

"She was Prince Arthur's personal servant. She made an attempt on his life. The queen, thank the heavens, caught her before she was able to carry out her plan. A witch as evil as they come, that one." As the priest spoke, he wiped the perspiration from his brow; even in the shade of the canopy, the sun was merciless.

A guard approached the king, bowing. "Commander Blackburn sent me to notify you that the informant led us right to Bryce Barwicke and his men. We have them surrounded and will deliver them to the dungeon."

"Very well," King Brom said without praise before he drained the last of his glass. "About bloody time." He raised his glass, signalling for a refill.

Lord Caunter turned his gaze to the pregnant woman on the stage. With a nod from the announcer, the guard standing behind her kicked the stool out from under her feet. She grasped frantically at the rope, trying desperately to take a breath. Lord Caunter raised his hand, signalling to those who were secretly awaiting him, unbeknownst to the king and his company. Instantly an arrow flew through the sky and pierced the rope that held the woman suspended. She dropped the few feet to the ground, gasping for breath as she pulled to loosen the rope.

The guards immediately took defensive positions, withdrawing their weapons and preparing for battle. The guard nearest the pregnant woman grabbed her by the hair and wrenched to her feet before he slid the blade across her throat. Blood seeped from her neck as she opened her mouth in a silent scream.

"No!" A lone woman's scream rose up over the roaring crowd, drawing Lord Caunter's eye.

"Your Majesty, we need to get you to safety." A handful of guards appeared before the king. Armed men rose up on the perimeter of the enclosure, redirecting the guard's attention to the immediate threat. The king was forced back into his chair while the guards struggled to keep him safe from the imminent danger. Men poured in from every direction, confronting the guards. The civilians in the crowd panicked, trampling over each other to get to safety, men, women, and children in an all-out panic.

"It's Teller. He's here!" the king hollered. He grabbed the bottle of wine next to his chair and tipped it up to his mouth, draining the remaining contents while mumbling in anger.

Lord Caunter stood in front of the king, seemingly shielding him should one of the attackers break free of the guards. Although Caunter craved violence like no other, he never condoned the killing of innocent women and children. The scene of the woman upon the stage haunted him.

Caunter noted a cloaked woman climbing up on the stage amid the chaos. She scrambled desperately to get to the dying pregnant woman. Throwing herself to her knees, she pressed her hands to the woman's neck. Caunter narrowed his eyes to note that the woman's eyes seemed to glow in the brightness of day. Something about the woman called to him, pulled at something deep inside him. It took great effort to remind himself of what needed to be done. He needed to stay focused. Everything else could wait.

A young man ran up to stand before the girl, standing in a defensive position before her, sword drawn. The boy looked familiar to Lord Caunter as he watched him vying to protect the girl, fighting off the few guards still lingering upon the stage. Her hood had now fallen to her shoulders, and white blond hair fell around her like silk, glistening in the sun. It was the same girl that was in Prince Arthur's company, the one thought to have been murdered. Her impossible beauty and her eyes. "It cannot be..." Lord Caunter said with sharp realization. When he had first laid eyes upon her, he was haunted by a restless nature. Something about her was unusual, but he could not place it until now.

Lord Caunter shook his mind free of the entrancing pull toward the stage. He turned his attention to the king, his blade in hand. The king's shock registered on his face.

"Normally I do not kill unarmed men, but you see, my Josselyn was unarmed when you sentenced her to death, so I will return the favor." Lord Caunter sank his blade into the stomach of the king. King Brom gasped in pain, and words failed him.

The king's eyes widened in shock at this unexpected development; he had believed Lord Caunter to be trustworthy, of the lineage of the Marquis of Thetford that had served the king for generations. "Pity, you would have liked the real Marquis of Thetford. He was a very loyal man to the crown before I ended his life. I am actually known as Teller. Have you heard of me?" Teller laughed as he twisted his blade then withdrew it. He leaned in and spoke with menace and hatred. "I will leave you to watch your kingdom fall. You will not heal from this injury; it will be a slow, painful death." Blood dripped from the king's mouth as he grasped at his wound.

The noblemen that had witnessed the attack on the king huddled fearfully away, no one coming to his aid. Teller took a step in their direction, causing them to scream in fear. A rounded man with a pointed moustache released his bladder, and Teller turned away in disgust. The priest backed away with the other spineless men, mumbling words of prayer. "God does not save men like you," Teller spat. The guards, on the other hand, were too engaged in battle to notice the king's condition.

"The king has been injured!" Teller hollered to the soldiers.

The guards in hearing range moved to close in tighter to the king, trying to provide protection, but they were under so much duress that some began to lose their edge. "Get the king to the castle! Retreat!" Teller ordered.

A couple of guards grabbed for the king, dragging him from his chair in attempt to get him to safety. The king looked at Teller with wide, accusing eyes, trying to find words, but his mouth would not obey through his suffering.

Chapter 33
BROM

"Lord Caunter is Teller," the priest informed Commander Blackburn, who was now at the king's side. Reverence Benedict found his eagerness to talk now that Teller was no longer within striking distance. "He injured the king. Arrest him!"

Commander Blackburn looked up at the priest from his quick assessment of Brom, who was being carried by a couple of soldiers. "Get him on my horse. Take him to the castle," he ordered before telling other soldiers to provide cover.

"Where is Teller?" Commander Blackburn asked, withdrawing his blade. He shoved away a few civilian men that stumbled into his path. Blood was smeared across Blackburn's face, and raw, angry determination poured from him.

The priest turned around and pointed to the canopied area they had retreated from, but Teller was nowhere to be seen. "He was there a moment ago."

King Brom grunted through the pain as the soldiers lifted him upon the horse while fighting off approaching men. Soldiers were facing off with countless faceless men throughout the courtyard. The sounds of clashing blades and screams saturated the air. He could not determine if one side was getting the upper hand, but the amount of men fighting his soldiers was overwhelming. So many souls were willing to go against their king, despite the penalties for such a crime. How could a revolt of this magnitude be constructed beneath him and rise so aggressively while he was naïve to it? He was a good king... He was once a good king, and the realization of that fact washed over him in a sickening realization.

With death calling his name, his thoughts seemed to have a clarity that had been long lost. He had deviated so far from his path, and he was blind to the truth that he had neglected the people he was sworn to protect. Even now he could feel the darkness grasping at him, tainting the very blood that spilled from him, a slow poison that robbed him of his strength and his ability to be the king that his father raised him to be. His father was a monarch held in such high regard that men had given their lives for him; men had stood beside him and trusted him without question. The late king would be disappointed in the state of his kingdom now.

A young man came into his line of vision as he was ushered through the crowd. "No..." A mumbled breath came from Brom's numb lips as he tried to form words. The pain began to fade from thought as he looked at the ghost before him, but he soon discovered the young man was as real as the battle surrounding him. The young man did not notice Brom as he fought among the men, but Brom could notice nothing else — he had the exact likeliness of his Sybbyl. That was how he recognized the young man. His beautiful Sybbyl that was taken from him... The boy's hair was as dark and thick. He could picture Sybbyl laughing and dancing under the sun. He could hear her beautiful sing-song voice even now, as if it was haunting him through the sounds of war. His reality was slowly crumbling. She held so much life, love... eyes so soulful that you could not help but fall into them. Eyes he had dreamed about every night since. "Brom..." He could hear her whisper in his ear.

Brom moved to sit up from his slouched position.

"Your Majesty, stay down, it is not safe." Brom didn't know who spoke; one of his soldiers, perhaps.

"Oliver," the king tried to shout, but it came out strangled. "Oliver!" He managed to project his voice, which rang out over the crowd. The young man turned. The moment their gazes met, he knew that there was no denying the truth. His son had survived. The guards closed in and ushered Brom away from the madness, but he knew that Oliver had recognized him and that all was not lost. He had left a legacy after all, something untainted by evil.

* * *

Brom's vision blurred, and the sounds of the battle faded in and out before he opened his eyes, looking into Arthur's face. "Father? Father?"

Brom tried to take in their surroundings. They were within the castle walls, and the chaos had dimmed around them.

Brom tried to focus as he looked into Arthur's eyes. The same deep, dark evil stared back at him as when he looked into the eyes of Peronell. With death upon his doorstep, her grip on him was loosening. He could see the swirling darkness leaching from him, dripping through his fingers that covered his wounds — or was that blood? Memories came crashing into him like waves upon the shore. Peronell was the true witch among his people. He could hear her devilish words within his head, swirling together like the buzz of a thousand bees. The first time they had met was not the coincidence, he believed; he was always a part of her plan.

Their wedding night unfurled within his mind. Peronell did not lay with him in their marriage bed. What he thought was her love was a spell upon him while she laughed in disgust at the thought of giving him her flesh. Never a loving gesture or caress was exchanged between them, but he was a tool she used to obtain her goal. Their years together were lies as she tore him down into the broken man he was now. Every touch she bestowed upon him, she seeped her dark magic into him, strengthening her hold. She had destroyed the king that he was supposed to be, making him a prisoner of her magic, and he was not strong enough to stop her. Peronell was always so eager to support the cause of the witch hunt and point the finger of blame at innocent people for a crime she was guilty of without remorse; instead, she relished the thought of death.

"You are not my son," the king whispered while pushing Arthur away.

"What?" Arthur gasped in outrage. Arthur's skin lacked natural color, and his eyes were darker than he had ever seen them. The boy he had believed to be his son for all these years was now a stranger before him, an evil only Peronell could spawn. He was not sure that Arthur was fully aware of what he was becoming, but the transformation had begun, and Brom feared what was to become of him.

"Your mother and I never consummated the marriage. It was all a lie. You are not my son... you are not my son." Brom's words tumbled from his lips.

Arthur backed away. "You are injured. You do not know what you are saying," he pleaded, but his posture and the desperation in his voice indicated he was already accepting the words. Already he knew on some level that they were not of the same blood.

"I know... My son's name is Oliver... Oliver." Brom's grasp on reality was slipping. He could feel his mind drifting in different directions.

"Take him to his room and have the doctor tend to him immediately. Now!" Arthur screamed, raking his hands through his hair.

"You!" Arthur pointed at the priest that was cowering in the corner of the room. "Go with him."

"Your Highness." One of the men stepped forward. "The girl, Lorelei, was spotted in the crowd. She is alive."

"How can this be?" Arthur looked into the soldier's eyes.

"We believe she is in the hands of Teller." The soldier looked back at Arthur with desperate eyes. "He is no ordinary man. The men have said he cannot be killed. He heals as our blades cut... it is unnatural. Evil."

"Put all available men on the doors," Arthur demanded. "No one gets into this castle." He stormed off.

Chapter 34
LORELEI

Lorelei looked down determinedly at her blood-covered hands, pressed to the throat of the woman lying before her. The sounds of battled faded to a muted hum as she gazed down at the dying woman staring up at her, the light fading from her eyes. Lorelei screamed out as she felt the rush of heated energy tear through her body, directing it into the woman before her. She could feel how weak the woman had grown; she was slipping away like water running through her fingers. The wooden platform groaned and snapped as Lorelei pulled the life force from it, giving it to the mother and unborn child. Weblike lines spun out through the wood, turning it grey and brittle.

A soldier jumped up on the stage, unaware the structure was compromised. He fell through the weakened wood, the jagged pieces tearing at his flesh and impaled him as he struggled for freedom. New energy flowed into Lorelei as she began siphoning his. The man's movements began to slow, his eyes darkening, and his skin bled of color. Lorelei looked away from him, horrified at what she was doing to the man but relieved that his death gave her the needed energy to finish healing the woman and baby. Their heartbeats echoed louder and stronger through the connection, while the man's grew weaker until his stopped completely. The new energy was different. It had a strange feeling as it traveled through her and left her.

The color returned to the woman's skin before she gasped in new breath. Lorelei could not help but smile. The woman looked upon her with wonder. "How?" She reached up and touched her neck, which, although still covered in blood, was now healed. The woman grabbed

Lorelei's hand and squeezed tightly, whispering words of gratitude.

"Your baby is strong," Lorelei assured her. "Though I do believe her birth is near."

Oliver, who was standing protectively by Lorelei's side, immediately reached for the woman once she began stirring. He lifted her, careful to avoid stepping on the weakened places. "Get her to safety!" Oliver passed her off to another man Lorelei did not recognize. Then he reached down and grabbed Lorelei by the shoulders. "Let's go!"

"Clara!" Lorelei called out as she swayed upon her feet. The chained women were in the middle of the battle, bound and unable to find cover. They huddled close to each other. Clara looked up at Lorelei, and relief flowed into her big brown eyes.

"Lorelei!" Clara gasped. She scrambled to her feet, but the chains would not allow her to move.

Ajax appeared in a blaze of fury, cutting through the soldiers. Blood splattered his face and clothes as he continued to take down all who approached him. He made his way toward Lorelei and Oliver.

"Please free them!" Lorelei called out to him, pointing toward the chained women. Ajax ignored her plea. Coming close, he drew her protectively to his side.

"We need to get out of here now." Ajax grabbed hold of Lorelei's hand, ushering Oliver to follow.

"I won't leave until Clara is freed," Lorelei said, digging her feet into the ground. She pointed to the women huddled together. "Please." Ajax looked into Lorelei's eyes, and his shoulders fell as he gave in to her request.

"Get her out of here, Oliver," Ajax called over his shoulder as he headed toward the women. Sunlight glinted blindingly off his sword as he rained it down on any who stood in his way.

A new wave of the king's men flowed through the crowd, and the fighting intensified. Letholdus made his entrance just as fiercely as Ajax, cutting down men, but the lineup around them seemed endless as the battle stretched on through the streets. Screams of victims rang out over the clashing of swords.

One of the women chained to Clara was impaled by a swinging sword. The women were in immediate danger as the men who tried to come to their rescue were prevented by the unrelenting soldiers. The attempt to free the women seemed an impossible task when so much action was playing out directly in their path.

Lorelei knew it was time to act. She did not know if she would be able to affect so many people, but she had to try. She could not just stand by as people were slaughtered in the streets. She looked up at Oliver, who was pulling on her arm in attempt to get her to follow, while defending them with his blade. She grabbed Oliver, swinging him back to face her. She raised her hands up to cover his ears before she began singing. She was weak, but she pulled from deep within herself to call upon the song. Words she did not realize she remembered until they flowed from her lips like an old memory coming to light.

"Lorelei, no!" she heard Ajax cry out, but she tried to drown out his voice and concentrate on forcing hers to carry as far as she could, squeezing her eyes tight and praying that she had the strength. The sounds around her began to wane and slow. Lorelei felt Oliver's hands grab for her when she swayed, supporting her.

Lorelei opened her eyes to see all the faces of the men in a daze. Their weapons hung from their slackened grip before they dropped to the ground. The effect of her song stretched on for as far as she could see. Haunting white eyes stared back at her as they were surrounded in a fluid energy that instinctively made her mouth water.

The men she had approached earlier, Bryce and the others, weaved through the masses closing in quickly. Some had cloths tied around their heads, while others used their hands. They had listened to her warning.

Lorelei's eyes found Ajax, who was jumping over men in a scramble to get to her. She saw fear in his eyes, something she never thought she would ever see on the warrior's face. A sharp pain in her side stole her breath, and a gasp stole the words from her mouth.

"Nooo…" Ajax cried, spinning frantically in search of their surroundings for something or someone, Lorelei was not sure.

Lorelei looked into the eyes of Oliver, who was pulling her hands from his ears and looking down at her, stricken with panic. Lorelei's eyes followed his to the arrow that was now lodged deep within her side. Her dress was warm and wet as her blood ran. "Lorelei," Oliver gasped, reaching down to lift her up against his chest. Ajax was upon them in a flash, taking her from Oliver and holding her protectively against him.

"Letholdus," he called out to his father, who was close behind him. They nodded in silent communication before Letholdus turned and disappeared in the sea of people.

"Clara… Clara?" Lorelei forced the words through her tightening chest as she tried to fight against his hold. Ajax did not respond; he only pulled her tighter against him as he moved through the crowd. "Please." Lorelei forced her head up to try and see behind them. The men with Clara's father were now escorting the women through the still-dazed crowd. Lorelei's eyes fell upon Clara's tear-soaked face, tucked within her father's embrace.

"Clara is good, Lorelei. She is with her father," Oliver said beside her. The reassurance allowed her to relax against Ajax's hold. Some of the men began to stir as the effects of her song came to an end.

Lorelei looked up at Ajax; she liked to think that even for a brief moment, despite everything between them, he was hers. His features were so perfect, they seemed unreal. She could not see him as an enemy, born and bred to kill her. Even when they first met and she believed him truly capable of the task, she was drawn to him with a force she could not deny, no matter how hard she tried. It was as if they were destined to meet, fated to find each other.

Not until the moment of their meeting did she feel truly alive. It was as if her very being reveled in his nearness, her soul calling out to him, wanting him, desiring him. She needed him like the breath upon her lips, and she feared nothing when she was in his arms. She realized with complete certainty that what she held for him was love, pure and true, and she gave her heart willingly and without expectation. Her feelings for him were as intense as he was physically as a warrior.

Lorelei knew death might come for her. She could hear it whisper to her, though she did not fear it. In this moment, she was only grateful that Clara was returned to her family, and that she was blessed with having experienced a love far beyond what she thought possible. It was a gift that she now knew to be the greatest treasure in life. Lorelei reached up and caressed Ajax's neck. He turned his worried gaze down upon her. "You will be alright. Hold on, Lorelei." He could not hide his fear. She tried to respond with a weak smile, despite her pain.

"Promise me something... please," Lorelei whispered she felt her consciousness fading, darkness clouding her vision.

"Anything."

"Take me home." She did not even know if the words left her lips as she felt herself slip away. Pain was coursing through her body, and she could no longer hang on. She gave in to the blissful numbness that was calling to her.

"I promise." It was the last thing Lorelei heard.

Chapter 35
ARTHUR

Arthur stormed through the castle halls in search of his mother. He wiped the sweat from his brow with the back of his hand. He felt weak and strange, as if his body was not his own. Something dark pulled at him from within with a thirst so great, it could not be satisfied with drink. Arthur tipped the whiskey bottle up to his lips, realizing it was empty. He threw the bottle against the wall, where it shattered with a piercing crack. Arthur grabbed hold of his hair and pulled it in frustration. When he had killed Anna, it was a short-lived moment of complete contentment. Now, his restless, dark nature was tormenting him once again. It was stronger than ever. He seemed to be torn between reality and haunting images. Everyone he looked at seemed to seep blood from their mouths, eyes, ears. He knew it to be an illusion, but it would not cease to plague him. Arthur could feel his grip on reality slipping, and these new desires pulling at him confused him. He was not sure how to appease his own appetite. He was starving, and the liquor only made his composure worse.

Arthur stumbled as he approached the doors of his mother's private chamber. He steadied himself on the frame of the door. The halls were quiet, despite the haunting truth that lay outside the castle walls. The king's guard was losing as his father lay dying from a wound that he would not survive. He knew it was only a matter of time before the castle was breeched.

Arthur pushed the doors open with force that caused them to slam against the walls. A priceless vase crashed upon the floor in his path. The pieces crunched beneath his shoes as he moved about the room. "Mother!" he screamed.

His mother had a love for finery that rivaled his own. The room was masterfully decorated with pieces of art displayed everywhere, making it look more like a showpiece than a bedchamber. His eyes caught a slight opening in the wall behind a tapestry, barely noticeable. When he neared, he could feel a draft through the small crevice. He dug his fingers into the gap, wrenching it open. Stale, humid air met him as he stumbled in toward the dark stone staircase. He could smell his mother's scent hanging in the air like a sickening fog as he entered the narrow stairwell.

A dull light broke through the darkness as he neared the top. The room opened up to reveal a large fireplace and a considerable collection of oddities. Unlike the beautiful ones his mother displayed in her room, these were dark, twisted, and they called to him with a seductive power. The room was aglow with many torches around the room, allowing him to see the secret his mother had kept from him.

He knew his mother could sense him, but she did not immediately acknowledge his arrival. Her hair was disheveled, fallen loose from the sleek twist she had worn earlier. It fell around her shoulders, making her look younger and vulnerable, but he knew she was not.

Commander Waltham's body was laid out on a large wooden altar, his features and pallid skin showing that death had already claimed the injured soldier. A strange, cloaked man drew symbols on Waltham's bare chest with a dark viscous substance that looked black in the dim light. The markings were concentrated around his injury. The cloaked man's features blurred when Arthur looked at him, as if he could not quite focus on his features without them shifting to another face altogether different.

"A war rages outside our walls, your husband is dying, and you are hidden away performing witchery!" Arthur fumed. His sudden outburst made his head spin, and he leaned against the door frame for support.

"You need to drink if you are to keep your strength, my son. Denying yourself will not help. Look at you." His mother looked up from the mortar and pestle she was using to grind strange herbs she had scattered over the table she was working at.

"Drink?" Arthur said in disbelief.

"Blood, my son. Denial will not change what you are, and I find it rather exasperating." Peronell dismissed him with a downcast gaze and continued working on her task. At the mention of blood, Arthur's mouth watered, but he tried to push it from his mind.

"What exactly am I, Mother? Care to enlighten me?" Arthur pushed off the wall and closed the distance between them until he was leaning against the opposite side of her table. "I am tired of your secrets."

"You are my son, Arthur Floros, heir to the throne of Everon, the largest continent in the land," Peronell said with a raised brow, her patience taut.

"Am I the heir? I just came from father. He told me that I am not his son," Arthur spat angrily.

"A mere technicality, inconsequential when he dies." She shrugged indifferently. "I must admit his death is rather convenient, since I no longer need him. You are coming into your power, and you are ready to take on your role. I never cared for that man; in fact, he disgusts me. His righteousness was always enough to gag a mule. You should be thanking me that I saved you the burden of carrying such annoying qualities, standing in the way of your own glory." Peronell wiped her hair from her face with the back of her hand.

"Who is Oliver?" Arthur questioned, anger burning through his veins like the thirst that clawed at him.

"A problem that was dealt with long ago." Peronell turned her attention to her cloaked assistant. "Bring in a girl."

Arthur spun around and watched the silent man shuffle through the door. His mother's strange helper made him uneasy, and he was reluctant to turn his gaze back to his mother until the man removed himself from the room.

"He spoke of him in the present tense. Are you sure this Oliver is no longer a problem?"

"The king has been unraveling for years. I assure you it is madness that has confused him." Peronell seemed certain of this truth, and it was enough to ease Arthur's concern. Peronell picked up a small flask of dark red liquid that looked to be blood. She pulled the cork from the neck of the bottle to reveal the sweetest smell he had taken in. His mouth watered immediately, and need swirled through him. "What is that?"

Peronell smirked. "That, my son, is the blood of a very powerful demon." She recapped the flask and set it down upon the table. Arthur moved to grab for it, but his mother stopped him with a force unseen. Arthur could feel the restraint despite the fact that his mother had not moved to hold him back. "How are you doing this?"

"I merely have to look into someone's eyes, and I can bend them to my will, well, most of the time, anyway. It does seem to be unreliable at times, depending on the individual. Right now, my son, you are an open book, and that makes it easy for me to reach inside you and gain control." A cold smirk curved her blood-red lips.

"The blood…" Arthur said, eyeing the flask.

"It is all there is left. I will not risk it falling into the wrong hands." Peronell slipped the flask into the pocket of her garment.

The cloaked man returned with a whimpering young woman in his clutches. The woman was frail and terrified. His mouth watered as he scented a sweet aroma in the air, not as enticing as the blood within the flask, but it pulled at the hunger gnawing at his insides. "Please let me go." She trembled, causing the scent to thicken in the air.

"It is her fear that you smell. It makes her taste so much more satisfying. Drink, son. You need your strength for the road ahead." Arthur's denial melted away. He was overcome by bloodlust. Every logical thought he desperately tried to hold on to fled from his mind as his instincts took over. Arthur reached for the woman's trembling shoulder and pulled her closer, breathing in her intoxicating aroma. His mother rounded the table with a knife in hand. She ran it along the pale, soft skin of the woman's neck. A scream erupted from her mouth with the sting of the blade. She struggled against his hold with a newfound energy.

Peronell ran her finger over the blade. She examined the red liquid with dark, hungry eyes before she slipped her finger into her mouth, savoring the flavour. "Enjoy, my son." Her voice was a sultry moan. Arthur returned his attention to the blood slowly dripping from the wound. Sinking his teeth into her, he was enveloped by the warm, spicy liquid that flowed into his mouth and warmed his body. He drank until the woman slipped from his grasp, collapsing lifelessly to the floor. Arthur sighed in contentment. He relished the feel of his satisfied body, his torment over.

He turned his heavy-lidded gaze toward his mother, who looked on appraisingly. He wiped his mouth with the back of his hand, smearing the blood across his face. "What. Am. I?"

"You are my greatest creation, my dear boy. I was born a witch, born a twin to a matched power opposite my own. We were destined to stand in each other's way to create balance. When I found a way to tip the scales, so to speak, she bested me. Though in the end I found other ways. There are many sources of power in this world, if you know where to look." Peronell's dark, emotionless eyes met his. He could see his own corruption reflected in his mother.

Peronell pulled he blood-filled flask from her pocket and looked at the substance with respect. "You see my son, demons crawl upon the earth, tempting man to do their bidding. With a simple whisper in a man's ear, a demon can have him doubting his wife's love and fidelity to the point that he takes her life, spilling her innocent blood upon the earth for the demon to feed on. They can convince a woman that her newborn baby is evil and must be drowned. They can convince a man of the cloth to take pleasures in the flesh of youth. They have so much power over mankind. I found a way to tempt the demon to come to me, and a bargain I made in exchange for his blood. Its blood is so potent in dark magic that it can create wondrous things. With this power I have been able to push thoughts into the minds of others."

"This demon you speak of, what did you offer him?" Arthur narrowed his gaze.

His mother threw her head back in a dark, rich laugh. "I offered him my body. A demon craves flesh, to devour and feed its crude sexual desires." Peronell pulled open her robe to display her perfect curves. Her large, full breasts hung heavy over her narrow waist that flared out into hips that called to every man's deepest desires. Arthur could not look away, even knowing the flesh he looked on hungrily was that of his own mother; his mind was still reeling from the power of the blood that flowed through him.

"Look closer, my son." Arthur watched as her perfect skin melted away to reveal mangled flesh, torn and healed into an unnatural texture. Breasts marred beyond recognition and angry red lines carved up the length of her neck and down to the untouched portion of her legs. "I barely survived. If it was not for drinking some of the blood, I would not have. You see, a demon cannot cause physical harm with their own hand to someone without their consent, even though they crave blood and thrive on pain. It is part of the laws that bind them. It gave me newfound power when I drank of it. I became more powerful than I could have ever imagined, and by surviving I was able to carry its child, a son, the next heir to the kingdom. Though I too now lust for blood, a side effect I have found to be very pleasurable."

"Then it is true…" Arthur leaned against the table as the truth settled in his bones. "These cravings… I am a demon?"

"Part demon. Unfortunately, your blood is not as potent, but regardless, a great king you will make." Peronell rounded the table and closed the distance between her and her son. "I made you powerful, able to make people bend to your will. You only need to tap into those powers of persuasion. Make people do what you want..."

"Yes..." he whispered thoughtfully. He could recall more than one moment when he had pushed a thought into someone's mind for his own benefit. It was exhausting, and he did not fully understand it then, but now... the possibilities... "How did I not know this until now?"

"I could not have a half demon child running around the castle, drinking the blood of people. I had to put controls on your mind until you came of age when you could embrace that side of you, to truly understand your power. I could not let Brom see the truth... Unfortunately, he is from a bloodline that was spawned from a goddess of Astraea. The will of justice was strong in his bloodline. The demon blood did not affect him as quickly or as effectively as I would have liked. It took years breaking him down into the pathetic king that he is now, drowning himself in drink and whores."

Peronell reached up and stroked her son's cheek. "Tell me you love me," she whispered close to his ear. "Tell me you love the power that runs through your veins." She took Arthur's hand in hers and placed his hands upon her naked breasts, now returned to their former perfection. "Tell me you love the body that gave you life." He squeezed her flesh harshly, repulsed by his lust for his own mother and the fact that she was offering something that he might not be able to decline. Her invitation to her flesh intrigued him in an immoral way.

"Look at me," his mother ordered, though it was no longer her voice but that of his true desires. Arthur looked up into the eyes of the most captivating woman he had ever seen; lust swam through his body, elation from the blood that still thrummed through him. He knew it was not really Lorelei, but his body reacted so violently to her nearness that he could not deny it. Her perfect body was on display for him to take. He pushed her back against the table, unsettling the objects upon it. She laid back in offering upon the surface of the table, spreading her legs open to him. He could feel the last remnants of his hold on humanity break free as he looked upon the face of evil, the seduction of it, and he was accepting it.

Knowing it was his mother that wore the face of the Lorelei did not stop him from taking pleasure in the illusion. Lorelei was a woman he would destroy to own, devour, and possess completely. Arthur raked his hands down across her breasts and flat stomach, leaving red marks on her flawless skin. The sight excited him further. Cupping her breast, he squeezed her soft flesh in his calloused hands, pinching her nipples tightly between his fingers, making them peak to tight, perfect buds. Her back arched off the table as moans of pleasure escaped her sweet, full lips.

Arthur undid his pants, releasing his erection that he forcefully shoved into her awaiting center, objects falling to the floor and shattering with every vigorous thrust. His mother's screams of pleasure drowned out the noise. Over and over he pounded into her, only seeking his own satisfaction. When he found his release, sobering thoughts crawled into his mind. He withdrew and righted his clothes. He paid no mind to his sated mother still spread upon the table, no more illusion to hide the truth.

Objects on a nearby table caught his attention. The white blond color was so distinctly Lorelei's that it left no question. Arthur walked closer to observe what he suspected it to be. A clump of her silken hair, a small dish of what looked of nail clippings with a pearlescent glow, blood in vials, notes on parchment that he did not have to read to know what they would entail. His suspicions caused anger to burst through the surface, where they were already heated and scraping to escape. "It was you that took her from me. It was never Mera who poisoned her. It was you!"

"She was a distraction," his mother responded without concern as she returned to her feet and tied her robe.

"A distraction? She was mine, and you had no right!" he snapped and hurled the dish across the room, shattering against the stone fireplace.

"You are set to marry Mariam Mansforth. It would not look good for you to be seen with another woman before the proposal is announced at the upcoming ball. The people cannot doubt the unity of your marriage." Peronell's cold, impersonal demeanor unnerved Arthur.

"The *people*... The same people that are fighting our guards this very moment. Do you not understand what is *happening*?"

"We will prevail. We always do. Now is your time to take hold of your duties as king. It is more important now than ever. Mariam's family comes from substantial wealth and connections. We will need them on our side." Her tone was still devoid of emotion.

He moved in closer to his mother. "I do not care what you think,

Mother." He reached up and closed his hand around his mother's throat. "I hate you." He seethed as he squeezed tightly around her neck. "And I will end you." The tighter he squeezed his mother's neck, the less he could draw his own breath. He released suddenly, causing her to stumble backward, both gasping for breath.

The malicious smile that formed on her lips as she looked at him. "You cannot kill me, son." She finally showed signs of humanity when she laughed. "Your life is connected to mine. You cannot live without me. A sort of life insurance plan, so to speak. So by killing me you will kill yourself."

"I will find another way to make you pay for what you have done!" Arthur yelled. The realization of what Commander Waltham must mean to his mother gave him an idea. He stepped back, withdrawing his blade. Turning quickly, he drove it through the eye of Commander Waltham's still body. Arthur upset the table, sending his body crashing to the ground.

"NO..." His mother's scream filled his ears and the room with desperation. He kicked over a couple of the torches that immediately set the room aflame. His mother ran to Waltham's body, and her face fell in horror when she looked upon the damage that Arthur had inflicted.

It wasn't enough; he wanted her to suffer more. He wanted her to pay dearly. Arthur grabbed hold of his mother, reaching into her pocket, and retrieved the vial of blood. He could feel her power reaching out in an attempt to stop him, but he pushed through it. Her attempts to stop him were futile; power coursed through him, and he saw red. Arthur did not stay to see the destruction that he left in his wake. He threw his mother to the ground and stalked from the room. He was determined to show her that she would not wield power over him.

Arthur did not stop until he came before the door of the room in which he knew Mariam to be; the guards positioned at the door did not object to his arrival. Inside, Mariam, along with a few servants, huddled in the far corner. "Do not open these doors under any circumstances until I say," Arthur informed the guards. They obediently heeded his command, closing the door, returning to their post.

"Your Highness." The servants acknowledged his arrival, stepping aside to let him approach Mariam.

"You are scared," he observed as he watched her tremble. Reaching out, he ran his fingers along her exposed neck and down her arm.

"I fear for my family," she said in a small, nervous voice.

"I am sure your family will be fine. They probably took cover the first sign of trouble, running off with the protection of the king's guard. It is yourself you should fear for." He smiled sinfully. Mariam's eyes widened slightly. He could see her racing pulse against her neck.

"Have the rebels breached the castle walls?" Mariam asked.

"No, not yet." Arthur twisted one of her loose curls around his finger. "But if they should, you will already be dead." His words were coolly detached. A whimper escaped Mariam's lips. She tried to step back, but Arthur would not release her hair. She knew the evil that she looked upon; she could see her own doom in the reflection of his eyes. Arthur grabbed hold of more of her hair, wrenching her closer. Tears were streaming down her face as sobs racked her.

"Please…" Her desperation was like the aroma of fine wine.

Arthur grabbed hold of Mariam's chin forcefully. "I do not wish to play my mother's game any longer." Her cry rang out loudly over those of the terrified servants, huddled by the door, pleading for the guards to open it.

Arthur lifted Mariam's small frame into the air and sank his teeth into the soft flesh of her neck. Her fear and struggle against him caused her blood to pump heavily down his throat. He was instantly in the throes of an incredible high. He savagely ripped at her flesh, drawing more and more blood until it no longer flowed from her body. Arthur grabbed hold of Mariam's head, pulling until the rest of her mangled neck gave way to the force, pulling it from her body.

Arthur turned his attention to the servants. One fainted, the other curled against the door covered in her own vomit. Holding Mariam's head, he walked toward the door and requested the guards open it. The door swung open immediately. The guards were shocked when they took in the scene of the room.

"Kill them," Arthur ordered the guards, pointing toward the servants. The one covered in her own sickness scrambled across the room, huddling against the bed.

"Your Highness?" the stunned guard asked, taking in Arthur's appearance, covered in blood and carrying the head of Mariam, the girl in their keeping.

"It's either their lives or yours. You choose," Arthur demanded before he walked from the room.

He heard the woman's scream erupt a moment later, and then it was cut off.

Arthur walked with determined steps, coming to a group of guards escorting his mother. She was now dressed in her usual cold, unapproachable perfection. When her eyes met his, her narrowed gaze took in his appearance. The guards acknowledge him as well, their eyes falling to the severed head in his grasp, dripping blood upon the floor.

"This is what I think of your plans, Mother." He tossed Mariam's head toward his mother's feet. It landed with a sickening thud against the floor, blood spraying onto her pristine gown.

Arthur turned toward the six guards and their shocked expressions. "Everything is as it should be." He pushed into their minds. "I am in charge, and you will listen to me."

"You…" Peronell started, but Arthur cut her off.

"Find me the Ravens. I require their services immediately," Arthur ordered the guard closest to him.

"Right away, Your Highness." The brown-haired soldier, similar in age to Arthur, bowed respectfully before he turned to leave.

"Arthur!" his mother said in a warning tone.

"Arrest her. She is a witch," Arthur spat. "Do not look her in the eye; it will give her power over you. Prepare the men. We are moving to a safer location."

"Yes, Your Highness. What of the king? He cannot be moved in his condition," one of the remaining guards said.

"We will leave some men behind to guard him."

"You cannot do this to the queen, your own *mother*," Peronell cried when the guards seized her.

"I believe I just did," Arthur said in an extremely satisfied tone.

Chapter 36
BROM

King Brom wiped his handkerchief over his brow. He could feel the chills rack his body while perspiration beaded upon his flesh. He felt weak from blood loss, pain radiating through his body and settling in his bones. The physician had just bandaged his wound with a grim expression. Brom did not bother asking the prognosis; he could already feel his body accepting its fate. He took a deep, agonizing breath, making him shudder with the effort.

"Priest?" Brom requested.

"Yes, Your Majesty." Reverence Benedict leaned into Brom's line of vision. The man's full face was pale with fear, and dark circles lung heavily under his eyes.

"I need to… write something…" Brom forced out his words breathlessly.

"Or course, Your Majesty." Brom could hear him shuffling about the room in search of parchment and quill. Brom made an effort to sit up but thought better of it, letting the priest assist him.

Brom forced his eyes to focus as he struggled to write upon the parchment. His fingers were numb, causing him to lose grip on the quill. The priest dutifully collected it every time and placed it back into his feeble fingers. When Brom completed the task, he signed his name at the bottom, verifying the document.

Disruption down the hallway caused all eyes in the room to turn toward the door. Sounds of struggle could be heard outside the walls. The guards in the room armed themselves, standing ready by the entrance to defend the king. When the commotion ceased outside his room, silence fell for a moment before the door swung open. Armed men poured into the room, swords raised and clashing with the handful of guards in the king's company. The king watched his men fall until there was no one left in his defence.

The largest of the intruders Brom recognized as the escaped prisoner stood at the foot of his bed, looking down at him.

"Who… are you?" Brom gasped.

"My name is Margas, and I fight with Teller to right the wrongs that you have made."

"Did… you come… to finish me?" The king did not fear his looming death, because he had already accepted his fate. He could not help but feel appreciation for the strength of the man standing before him. He was skilled in combat, with abilities Brom had not seen surpassed in his lifetime.

"No, Brom Floros of Everon. You are sentenced to watch the downfall of your kingdom, a kingdom that you cast into darkness and suffering through your greed and ignorance. The slow-acting poison that now runs through your blood will be a slow, painful death, stretching on for days, and you will suffer every moment as you have made your people suffer. This is your punishment."

"You may leave." Margas pointed toward the physician cowering at the far side of the room. The man trembled as he gathered his supplies, quickly leaving the room. "You, priest. You will stay and pray for the king's damned soul."

The priest backed against the wall; he could not contain a whimper. He only nodded. Margas turned to leave, but the king's plea took his attention. "Please… give this to the young man named… Oliver… he fights with you…"

Margas narrowed his eyes before grabbing the parchment the king held in his shaking grasp. Unfolding it, he read what it contained. He looked up at Brom's face, taken aback, but giving a nod, he left the king to serve his sentence.

Chapter 37
AJAX

Ajax cradled Lorelei's injured form tightly against his chest. He need-ed to get her outside the city and away from further danger. Oliver stayed close as Ajax moved determinedly, cutting through alleyways. Ajax was angry with Oliver for disobeying his orders, but that matter had to be put on hold for now; they both knew the danger Lorelei was in, and that took precedence.

They left the heart of the battle behind as they moved toward the outer limits of the city. The sounds of the ongoing fight grew in in-tensity behind them. There was no sign of Letholdus, who had disap-peared in the commotion. Ajax knew that he would turn up eventu-ally once he had his fill.

Danger was lurking everywhere, opportunity for evil to present it-self in any form. Ajax could see the occasional face peering out of the narrow windows, both intrigued and terrified of the action. The cow-ards that fled from the real fight were seeking out defenseless bystand-ers to prey on. Any one of these people hiding from the dangers could become a victim. The guards that normally patrolled the streets were distracted, allowing the perfect opportunity for criminals fulfill their dark needs. Ajax could sense menacing energy and their watchful eyes. He could hear the cries of lone victims scattered in the outlying areas.

A woman's scream rang out as they passed a darkened alleyway. Their attention was pulled to a man forcing himself on a young girl, who was struggling to no avail. He laughed menacingly as he tore her clothes away, savoring the power he was wielding over her.

"Oliver!" Ajax said in a forced whisper. Oliver had already changed direction to intercept. Ajax sighed in frustration as he halted; he knew Oliver could not continue while leaving this girl in the man's clutches. All Ajax could think of was getting Lorelei and Oliver to safety; stopping would slow them down considerably. The town was currently full of wrongdoing, and they could not stop it all.

Ajax spun around, his instincts on alert. He could not wield a weapon with Lorelei in his arms, and he feared putting her down. He could feel her warm blood saturating his side, and the urgency of her injuries clawed at him. He could not lose her.

Ajax watched Oliver confront the man; he could not help but feel some pride. Oliver's nature had survived a life that turned most people hateful. When Oliver had come into his care, he insisted that Oliver learn to fight and defend himself. Ajax feared his natural good nature would make him an easy victim. His years of training, even though Oliver was still young, now were reflected in his skilled hand. Oliver possessed a strong sense of morality and obligation unmatched by any. He would become a great man, Ajax was sure of it.

Ajax could sense someone closing in. He turned around to see who was crawling out of the shadows. "Crewe." Crewe was accompanied by some of his men as they spread out in a defensive position. They knew all too well whom they had encountered, and they were not taking any chances, watching Ajax with keen interest and fear.

"Ajax." Crewe's eyes fell on Lorelei in Ajax's hold, and he could see Crewe's subtle tells of anger.

"Do not do this." Ajax brought Crewe's focus back to him; he could see the clenching of his jaw and the anger that radiated through Crewe's stance. "You cannot kill Teller. You will only succeed in getting yourself killed."

"Does your traitorous heart still care for your old friend?" Crewe spat viciously. "I am loyal to my king, Ajax. I know this is not a concept you are familiar with, but it is one that I live by. I will kill Teller, and you cannot stand in my way."

The men with Crewe were on edge, their gazes skirting between Crewe and Ajax. They knew what Ajax was capable of. They had witnessed him in combat first-hand, had been trained by his hand in many instances, and Ajax knew they were smart enough to figure out if they raised arms against him, it would not end well for them.

"I do not need to stand in your way. You cannot defeat him, so heed my warning," Ajax insisted.

"Why is that, Ajax? Is he like you? Well, let me tell you a little secret: everything can die, even you." Crewe spat upon the ground.

"Is that a threat?" Ajax raised a brow.

"It certainly sounds like it, does it not?" Crewe's anger rolled off his rigid shoulders.

"The girl is mine, Crewe," Ajax said stonily when he noticed Crewe's attention fall to Lorelei once again.

"For now." Crewe's words were full of hostile intent.

"There are reasons for what I have done. Betrayal was never my intention." Ajax did sincerely regret that their relationship had taken this turn.

"Nevertheless, here we are." Crewe spread his arms.

The young girl Oliver had saved ran past them, her cries lingering behind her. Oliver returned to Ajax's side, appearing unharmed and ready to help should he be needed. Crewe momentarily focused his attention on Oliver. Ajax knew Crewe's mind was calculating Ajax's weaknesses as he sought revenge.

"If you decide to act against me or anyone I care about, I will stop you before you even formulate a plan."

"Is that a threat?" Crewe threw Ajax's words back at him.

"It certainly sounds like it," Ajax retorted arrogantly. He was tired of this exchange.

The two of them stayed in a locked gaze. Ajax accepted the fact that the wound ran too deep between him and Crewe. Those many years of camaraderie were but a memory now, meaningless. Ajax now had one more enemy to add to his growing list.

"Is there a problem here?" Letholdus made his appearance with a devious grin. His size and appearance did not go unnoticed, as well as the blood that saturated his clothes. He was still armed with his sword, blood dripping from the blade. The similarities between Ajax and his father were obvious.

"Until we meet again," Crewe said. He backed away, and he and his men dispersed.

"Was it something I said?" Letholdus shrugged, sliding his bloodied sword into his scabbard.

"It is about bloody time you showed up," Ajax snapped at his father. "We were just going to leave your arse behind."

"Ha. You need my arse now more than ever. I spoke with Margas. He said you have some explaining to do." Letholdus was enjoying his son being in his current predicament. He took a new flask from his pocket and took a long pull.

"Yes, well, it will have to wait." Ajax continued onward.

"It was Teller's arrow," Letholdus informed him. "I couldn't stop him."

"I know."

When they collected their awaiting horses and put comfortable distance between themselves and the city, Ajax stopped to assess Lorelei. She had started to whimper, and her temperature was high as she faded in and out of a restless slumber.

"How is she now?" Oliver asked as he leaned in to feel her hot skin. Ajax laid her down next to the fire Ajax had insisted Letholdus start. Ajax tore open her dress around the arrowhead still embedded in her side. Dark black lines extended from the wound, stretching out across her pale skin in stark contrast.

Oliver gasped at the sight of it. "What is that?"

"Poison," Ajax cursed. His suspicions were confirmed. He withdrew his blade and turned toward his father. "Give it here." He made a motion.

"I have none left," Letholdus said defensively.

"Give it here, or I will rain the fires of hell down on you!" Ajax barked angrily. Letholdus looked back at him defiantly before finally caving in. Ajax grabbed the flask furiously from his father's extended hand, uncapped it, and poured it on Lorelei's side and on the blade of his knife. She was still only semiconscious; restrained gasps left her lips.

"What kind of poison does that?" Oliver held back the material of her dress, allowing Ajax better access to her wound. The angry black lines could be seen stretching and moving across her skin, leaving the skin a pallid gray.

"The kind that kills Sirens." Ajax looked up to meet Oliver's intense gaze. Fear was etched on his expression. He noticed Oliver's hands tremble; they both knew the severity of the situation, though neither one of them could admit defeat.

"Stop it then, and fix it. There must be a cure," Oliver pleaded. "You know how to fix this, right?"

"I do not." Ajax breathed out in frustration.

"What?" Oliver choked.

"Hold her still." Using his knife, Ajax began to extract the arrowhead lodged in Lorelei's side. Oliver struggled to hold Lorelei still, her screams piercing as she writhed. Oliver tried to soothe her as she strained against the agony. Tears streamed down the sides of her face, her cries raw and crushing. Ajax throat tightened to the point where he found it difficult to breathe, working as quickly as he could.

"All done." Reaching up, he brushed her damp hair from her face.

"It… hurts…" Lorelei cried, trying to move her heavy arms, but they would not obey her command. "What…" She tried to look down at her wound.

"It was a poisoned arrow. I had to remove it," Ajax informed her. Her eyes came up to his; they were filled with unshed tears. Ajax wanted to wipe away her tears, take away her pain and heal her, but he was powerless. He had never felt as helpless.

"Why… do people… insist on poisoning me… it is so… painful." Lorelei's words were breathless and forced.

"Because everyone wants you dead," Letholdus responded matter-of-factly, warranting cold glares from both Ajax and Oliver.

"Heal yourself, Lorelei." Oliver sprang up, releasing her shoulders. "Like you did before."

Lorelei closed her eyes in concentration. Taking a deep, sobering breath, she spread her hands out at her sides, feeling the earth between her fingers. She could feel the energy pulsing just below the surface, but when she tried to draw upon it, she was met by resistance. She could feel a barrier that she had never encountered before.

"She cannot," Ajax said, meeting Lorelei's beautiful wet eyes when they opened and looked up at him. "It is part of the characteristics of the poison. It prevents her from using her powers while it…"

"Stop it," Oliver shouted at Ajax. "Stop this. It's your fault!"

"*My* fault? I was not the one to bring her into town when I specifically told you not to," Ajax roared, causing him to flinch. "You knew who I was meeting; you knew they would act before they asked questions."

"Stop…" Lorelei gasped. Her pained cry was enough to defuse their anger. "I made… my own choice… be mad at me."

"There has to be an antidote." Oliver looked over at Letholdus, who was observing the situation indifferently. "Letholdus, please," he begged. "You must know."

"Why would we create a bloody antidote for a poison we created to destroy our enemy? Do you really think that we thought that one of our own would be stupid enough to fall in love with a bloody Siren?" Letholdus said with annoyance, waving his hand at Ajax before he pulled he tipped his flask to his lips in greedy drink.

Ajax leaned down and placed his lips over her wound. Lorelei gasped at the contact when his mouth met her skin. His thoughts returned to the intimate evening they had shared upon the beach. The beautiful moment they had shared would be forever present in his thoughts. She had so much claim on his heart, he feared what would be left if she departed. She was too beautiful to leave this world. He could not let it happen. Now, with his mouth on her feverish skin, he was hoping he could draw any lingering poison out of her wound. He spat out a mouthful of blood mixed with the overly sweet taste of the poison before continuing the process until he could no longer taste the extract of the poisonous flower.

It was told that Amphitrite's sister, Perse, had shown the Men of Savas the unique flower when she longed to help end her sister's grief. The flower was called a Syrania, a beautiful blue blossom that glows under the light of a full moon. It had once only grown in Perse's own personal garden, until she spread the seed out into a strong breeze, allowing the flower to spread throughout the land. A sweet nectar on the night of a full moon drips from the bloom. It was fatal to Sirens when mixed with their blood. It was one of the means that the Savas had used to wipe out their population so long ago. It was one of the reasons they had prevailed so thoroughly.

Ajax pulled back the material of her dress to look at the dark lines marking her skin, but his attempt had not slowed the effects. Lorelei had once again slipped into unconsciousness. Oliver sat silently, staring helplessly at her feverish form.

The sound of a horse and carriage came from the distance. Letholdus and Ajax stilled, listening. After a moment's hesitation, Ajax pulled his blade from his side and quietly stood. Letholdus did the same, preparing for a confrontation as the carriage drew near.

A lone man atop an open back wagon moved toward them. His carriage came to a stop a short distance from them, and the man raised his hands to show that he was unarmed.

"Be ready," Ajax ordered quietly. He motioned Oliver and Letholdus to stay back as he approached the man. He wanted them at Lorelei's side in case this was a setup, though Ajax could not sense any other men in the surrounding area. All indications led him to believe this man was truly alone, and for some reason unbeknownst to him, the man requested their company.

"Who are you?" Ajax called out as he neared the wagon.

The man wore a dark cloak pulled up over his head; his face was pale, with dark circles under green eyes that seemed to glow, even in the dimming light of the fast approaching evening. Long, unkempt brown hair hung around his face, with lines of gray twisting through it. "I only wish to offer my help."

"Why?" Ajax was highly sceptical.

"It is in my interests to see the girl well." The man's voice was soft, with underlying strength that gave his words full meaning. "I offer a ride and a destination that will have what she needs to cure her."

"Again, I ask why?" Ajax narrowed his eyes suspiciously, even though he felt the need to trust this man in their hopeless situation.

"I mean to write some wrongs that were written in this life. You may keep your suspicions, for they keep a warrior such as yourself sharp and better prepared for what awaits you. I offer help and ask nothing in return. It is a choice you must now make. Time is not on your side," the man said urgently.

"Yes." Oliver answered the man, to Ajax's dismay. "We accept your offer."

Ajax turned an annoyed glare toward Oliver. "Do you ever do anything you are told?"

Oliver shrugged. "Lorelei said we can trust him." Ajax turned around to see Letholdus awkwardly holding Lorelei up in a sitting position. When he noticed Ajax looking at him, he feigned disinterest and let go. Lorelei fell back to the ground. She whimpered in distress and Oliver quickly returned to her side. "You are such an *arsehole*, Letholdus!"

"Why do you think you can help her? She has been poisoned..." Ajax returned his focus to the stranger.

"By the nectar of a Syrania flower." The man finished Ajax's sentence. "There is a cure."

Ajax looked back at Lorelei, and his shoulders fell in defeat; he had no other options. "If you mean us, specifically the girl, any harm I will kill you," Ajax practically growled.

"Fair enough." The older man nodded, seemingly pleased.

* * *

They rode in silence for most of the evening. In the back of the wagon, Lorelei fell into a fitful sleep, her body putting up a good fight against the poison. She was much stronger than she looked — she needed to be if she was going to survive. Ajax remained on alert, scanning their surroundings while he kept an eye on the driver next to him. They headed east from Falls Landing. Their destination was conveniently in the same direction of Lorelei's home, where Ajax had promised to take her. The only information the man would give him was the fact that he knew a healer near the Black Forest who knew an antidote for the rare poison.

Oliver tried to stay awake after securing the horses to the back of the wagon and crawling in next to Lorelei, drifting in and out of sleep by her side. He woke periodically to check on her condition and then drifted back to sleep. Letholdus had no reservations, falling into a deep sleep and snoring loudly after he downed the rest of his flask. The night aged and the dark hung over them like a cold fog.

"You are injured," Ajax observed, finally willing to break the silence between him and the stranger. He could smell the tang of blood in the air. At first he thought it was just Lorelei, but the smell became more potent sitting next to the man. The man turned his gaze from the road, looking in Ajax's direction. "Your robe is saturated in blood, and it is scorched," Ajax continued.

The man looked down at his robe. "Yes. I am injured, but I will survive the journey, if that is what you are concerned about." A wry smile graced his lips.

"I do not believe you are helping her without selfish reasons. I cannot figure it out. Lorelei said that you have helped her before, and she trusts you, but I, on the other hand…" Ajax voice reflected his discomfort with the situation.

"I have heard many tales of your kind, Savas. You are the last companion that I would have thought to aid Lorelei. We have something in common, you and I. We both doubted what we were told to believe. Strength of heart, I would like to trust it is."

"What of you? I know that you are more than you seem." Ajax tried to keep the accusation from his tone.

"What I am, what I was, no longer matters," the man said thoughtfully.

"I cannot lose her," Ajax said flatly after a moment of silence.

"I know, my son." The man patted Ajax on the knee. "I can see it in you. I gave my heart to someone long ago, and when she left this world, she took it with her. All that is left is what you see." Ajax could feel the chill of the man's skin. "I am now but a body, going through the motions." There was something unsettling about this man that Ajax could not place.

"What is your name?"

"Edward Belet." Edward seemed to contemplate his own name.

"The healer?" Edward's name had been well known among people at one time. He was known to have miracle cures, saving countless lives.

"I was at one time, but no more." Edward seemed content not to continue their conversation. "You should get some sleep."

"I'm good," Ajax insisted despite the fact that he immediately grew tired; he felt the heavy pull of sleep calling to him, despite the fact that only a moment ago he was alert and ready to take action.

"Sleep, my son, you need your rest." And that was the last thing Ajax heard as an unnatural sleep pulled him under.

*   *   *

Ajax jolted awake when the movement of the wagon ceased. The morning sun was already casting its glow. He cursed himself for falling asleep and leaving them vulnerable. He spun around to confirm that Lorelei, Oliver, and Letholdus were still with him and safe. Much to his relief, all three were still asleep in the back of the wagon.

Edward was sitting quietly next to him; his skin almost looked translucent in the light of day. He seemed strangely serene, given his injuries. The bench beneath him was stained with his blood, and yet he seemed unconcerned, almost separated from reality.

"Do not be angry with yourself. You needed rest. You still have many more obstacles before you that you cannot face without your strength." Ajax took notice of their surroundings. Trees stood tall, casting shadows down upon them. They seemed to be in the middle of nowhere, away from civilization.

"*You* made me fall asleep," Ajax accused, but he was not given a response. He did not need one to know the truth. Ajax never fell asleep when on guard; he could go days without rest. "Where did you bring us? Oliver!" Ajax reached over the back of his seat and swatted Oliver on the head. "Check on Lorelei." Oliver jerked awake and leaned over to address her.

"Where have you brought us?" Ajax didn't bother to hide his anger. His muscles were tight with restrained energy, ready to take action should he see the signs of danger.

Edward turned toward him. "Where you need to be," he answered. Ajax noticed for the first time that Edward did not look directly at him as he spoke and did not focus on any particular object.

"Are you blind?" Ajax gasped in disbelief.

"Last I checked." Edward gave him a small smile before he moved to dismount from the wagon.

Ajax jumped over the front of the wagon, landing before Edward. "Are telling me you drove us all night, and you could not bloody see where we were going?"

Edward was unaffected by Ajax's outburst. "I do not need to see to find my way." He walked slowly toward the trees. "Besides, would you have come with me had I told you that I could not see?"

"Hell, no!" Ajax snapped.

"I have made my point," Edward said with that sense of peacefulness that was driving Ajax mad.

"You know… I had wondered many times since my Aisling died why I was forced to carry on. Forced to endure when I could not bear it, but it was all because a piece of my heart still existed, and I was needed for this moment. This is what I was waiting for — for when she needed me." Edward continued to walk away, leaving Ajax in confusion.

"What are you talking about? And where do you think you are going?" He grabbed Edward by the shoulder. The material of his rope slipped off his frail shoulder, causing his garment to fall open. Ajax eyes landed on Edward's injuries with shock. Edward looked like he had been torn apart, his body mangled beyond recognition. Blood ran so freely that Ajax was surprised the man was still alive, let alone standing on his feet. "What? How?"

Edward grabbed Ajax by the wrist, jarring him. "Things are not always what they seem." His green eyes suddenly focused for the first time. Ajax looked into Edward's spellbinding gaze, a doorway into his soul. Ajax's senses were overloaded when a surreal sensation washed over him. Even the ground felt as though it fell away from his feet. A lifetime of emotions ran through him, glimpses of memories, feelings. It was beyond anything Ajax had ever experienced. He raked his hand down his face, trying to regain his senses.

"Jax!" Ajax turned toward Oliver's call, still out of sorts. "She's getting worse." The panic in Oliver's words caused Ajax's heart to race, and his focus snapped back with vengeance.

He turned back toward Edward, only to find that the healer no longer stood before him. Ajax spun around, trying to locate him, but it seemed as though he vanished, and the only thing that remained was the blood that had pooled on the ground where he stood.

Ajax looked up to see Letholdus standing beside him. "What did you do with him?" Letholdus looked strangely out of sorts, even for him. "He was here one moment and then gone the next?" Letholdus looked down at the blood staining the ground and the trail of it leading up to the wagon. His father looked like hell, with dark circles under his bloodshot eyes. "*Shite!* I need a drink."

Ajax moved toward the back of the wagon to check on Lorelei, swinging himself up beside her. He could already see the black lines stretching up the pale, delicate skin of her neck and down her slender arms. Panic took hold of him. He had no idea how to save her. Edward had been his one hope to finding a cure, and now he was gone. Oliver looked up at him, hoping for answers, but Ajax had nothing to offer. Ajax leaned down and gently brushed the back of his fingers across Lorelei's cheek. A soft, pained whimper passed her dry lips.

"Lorelei…" Ajax whispered desperately.

The sound of a woman's voice grabbed their attention. They looked to the trees. A mature woman walked out of the forest, basket in hand. She stopped abruptly when she noticed she was no longer alone, observing them from a distance, as they too observed her. Her gray hair was swept back in a loose bun, her dress pulled up and tied at the waist to reveal brown leather boots. She looked small and delicate at first glance, though the stubborn set of her shoulders spoke otherwise.

The woman began walking toward them without hesitation. Clearly she didn't fear these warriors from whom even hardened men cowered. She walked directly to the place from which Edward had disappeared. Closing her eyes and tilting her head back, she took a deep breath and released it with a sigh. "Edward…" She smiled.

Her eyes suddenly snapped open to regard her company. "You know this bastard Edward who brought us out to the middle of nowhere with a sick girl in our care?" Letholdus spat on the ground near her feet. He was the closest to the woman and towered over her small frame.

The woman pulled an exasperated sigh in to her lungs. "Of course I do," she said, as though the man before her was a complete idiot. Ajax immediately liked her. "Let me see the girl." She turned toward the wagon.

Ajax picked up Lorelei and carried her down from the wagon. "Are you a healer too?" Ajax asked hopefully.

She looked up at him with the same green eyes that Edward had, a gentle smile gracing her lips. "Come." She motioned for him to bring Lorelei as she turned on her heel. The woman led them to a small, isolated cottage. Inside the air was humid and warm; the interior was full of flowers and collections of glass jars. It certainly looked like the home of a healer with all the potions that littered the room. Oliver noticed a strange-looking flower with black stripes and unusually shaped petals.

"Do not touch that!" the woman barked at Oliver, causing him to withdraw his hand quickly. "It is a flower that brings death."

"Why would a healer have such a thing?" Oliver's eyes widened in horror; he had almost touched the flower.

"Not everyone wants to be fixed." She gave Oliver a loaded gaze. "Lay the girl here so I can look at her." She cleaned off the nearest table.

The woman peeled back the material of Lorelei's dress to address the wound, taking note of the lines the poison had marked her skin. Her study drifted to Lorelei's face. Reaching up, the woman brushed Lorelei's hair from her face. "Sweet Lorelei... dear child," the woman said with nurturing familiarity, placing her hands on either side of Lorelei's face in a loving caress.

"You know her?" Ajax asked with a furrowed brow.

"Yes, Savas." The woman left Lorelei's side. "It is almost too late. It is a good thing she is only half Siren, or she would already be dead."

"You can save her then?" Ajax allowed himself to grasp at the words of hope she offered. The hand of despair loosened its hold on him.

"Yes," she answered with certainty.

"What of the man that brought us here?" Oliver spoke up, now keeping his distance from everything in the room for fear of bringing about his own demise.

"My son." Her admission only confirmed the suspicion Ajax had when she saw they had the same green eyes. "He was imprisoned by an evil he could not fight. Now he is free of the pain that was forced upon him. I felt his death last night but only knew of the peace he found when you arrived."

"No, he did not die last night. He brought us here," Ajax corrected her. "He was here this morning. Outside, until he disappeared."

The woman looked up from her work; a small smile played upon her lips. "I felt the moment he left his body. The knowledge found me within moments of his passing. He brought you here, yes, but not in the physical form he was born to."

Chapter 38
LORELEI

The world came back to Lorelei in bright flashes. When her eyes opened, they stung with the presence of blinding light after taking comfort in the solace of darkness. She slowly regained awareness of herself, as well as the dull heat that still burned in her side. A tingling sensation embraced her entire body, but thankfully the overwhelming pain was muted to a faint echo.

Looking around, she took in the unfamiliar surroundings. The ceiling was constructed of rough wooden beams. Heavy floral scents assaulted her senses. The air was warm and thick. Lorelei found the strength to move her hand, bringing it to her injured side. It was covered with a thick, viscous paste. Lifting her fingers up, she could see a dark green substance on her fingers. The smell was putrid.

"Try not to move too much." A woman's voice carried from somewhere in the room.

"Where am I?" Lorelei's mouth was dry, and her tongue felt too large for her mouth.

"You need to drink first, questions can wait." The woman's face loomed over her, gray hair swept back from a noble face, enchanting green eyes that reflected the beauty of her youth. Instant recognition pulled at Lorelei's memories. The woman tipped a cup to Lorelei's lips; the cool, refreshing liquid pacified her dry mouth.

"I know you... you are the woman who brought things to our cottage," Lorelei said. A slight frown creased the woman's face. "I know you did not want to be seen, but I know it was you. Sometimes I would hide and watch you. I never understood..."

"I am a lot slower in my old age. I cannot sneak around like I used to, I suppose." There was a slight droop in the woman's shoulders when she spoke.

"Why? Why am I here now? Where are Ajax and Oliver?" Lorelei looked around the room.

"They are outside. I sent them out when they insisted on bickering. They all think they know what is best for you, foolish men. The reason you are here is so I can heal you. You were poisoned and nearly died." The woman busied herself at Lorelei's side. "You really are quite remarkable. Your two heritages play off each other beautifully. Your healing abilities are amplified… and your nature of a Siren is more recessive."

"I am close to home then?" Lorelei interrupted. The realization of this fact just occurred to her. "Have you seen my mother?"

"Yes, you are close, but I have not been back to your cottage since before you left." The woman smoothed Lorelei's hair back from her face.

"Oh…" Lorelei's hope deflated. She wanted assurance that her mother was well. "I need to go to her. She has no idea where I am." She attempted to lift herself from the table, but the old woman pushed back her shoulders with a firm but gentle hand. "Please, I was taken from the woods. My mother does not know what happened to me."

"Not right now, my dear." The woman looked at her warningly. "Now you need to finish healing."

Lorelei submitted. Laying back, she watched the woman fuss over her injury. "What is your name?" she asked of her mysterious savior. She felt peace in this woman's presence, a sense of comfort. She had known of this woman for years. Since Lorelei was a small girl, she looked forward to the packages that were left upon their step. Parcels containing clothes, food, and even toys when she was small. Books, too; her mother used to teach her how to read and about the world. She dreamed about what existed outside the shelter of their forest, but her mother's fear kept her close to her side, her dreams of exploring only a fantasy.

One morning, when Lorelei was still small, she had wakened early and decided to go collect flowers for her mother. It was that day, when she was wandering through the quiet forest, that she noticed a woman walking through the forest toward their home. She was the first person that Lorelei had seen beside her mother, other than the pictures in books. Lorelei was unsure if she should let herself be seen. The woman's nervous disposition made her stay hidden in the tall brush. She had watched the woman set a package on their doorstep and turn to leave without making a sound.

After that day, Lorelei would sometimes feel the woman's familiar presence, even when she could not actually see her. Lorelei felt as if the woman was watching over her and began to take comfort in knowing, despite her mother's warnings, that others could be kind and caring. Once she gained the courage to ask her mother about the woman. She noticed that the news brought her mother distress. "*One can never truly know the intentions of others. Be careful, Lorelei.*" Her mother never admitted to knowing the woman or the reasons for her generosity. Her words of caution caused Lorelei to remain in the shadows, never reaching out to the woman — though she began to doubt her mother's insistence that the world was a place to be feared. She dreamed of all the possibilities that existed outside the enclosure of their trees. Her imagination had no bounds.

The old woman looked thoughtful for a moment, as if deciding whether or not to share this knowledge with her. "Avina," she finally admitted with a small smile.

"The man who brought us here, the one that was working for the queen, where is he?" Lorelei questioned the older woman. She recognized their similar eye color.

"My son, Edward. He is no longer with us." Avina's eyes watered, becoming glossy as she spoke, but tears did not fall. She held her mourning tightly within her, mixed with an obvious sense of relief.

"I could sense he was a good man... the queen had done something to him. I do not understand it..." Lorelei's words faltered, unsure of the realness of her memories.

"Yes. I know," Avina said, taking a deep breath. She looked into Lorelei's eyes as she pondered painful memories. "The queen is a witch of dark, cruel powers. She took my son, cast her evil spell upon him, binding him with two well-known apothecaries of the dark arts. His power was great but too pure, so she bound him to these men, darkening his heart, and made him pliable to her needs."

"That is horrible..." Lorelei could not help the sorrow that washed over her.

"I never told him about you..." Avina stroked her hair in a motherly manner. Her eyes seemed distant as she reminisced.

"I do not understand." Lorelei shook her head in confusion.

"When my son came to me all those years ago and told me what he had done, I was devastated."

Lorelei remained motionless; her eyes remained locked on Avina, completely captivated. "Edward knew she was a Siren before he even sought her out. At the time I believed he was such a fool to risk his life.

"My sweet Edward was denied the gift of sight from the moment of his birth… others saw it as a defect, but he never did. He saw the world differently, with a beauty others could not comprehend.

"When he came upon her in the forest, she was already weak from hunger. It had been months since anyone had gone missing, but still she resisted what he could offer her. I should have realized that it meant something then. A Siren with iron will, to deny herself her very nature, but I was angry and ruled by emotion… It is a funny thing that we have to wait until we are old and gray before we understand life.

"Somehow, against all odds, she had become with child. Maybe it was because she fled the sea and it changed her, or maybe she had always been different. You see, Sirens do not bear children. They take life, unable to give it, but nonetheless she carried you. It was a testament that nature does not always follow its own rules.

"My son came to me while she was in labor. I remember that night as if it were yesterday. It will never fade, never leave me. By the time she was ready to birth, she had grown so weak that she was struggling to hold on to her life. I had never seen my son so terrified. He begged and pleaded with me to help her." It was then that the tears in Avina's eyes were finally set free. She was admitting guilt, a burden that had weighed heavily on her shoulders for many long years.

"It was I who pulled you from your mother's womb, when she was too weak to push. It was I who pushed the poison-coated dagger into her heart, because when I knew what she was, I knew that she had taken many innocent lives, and I believed it was an injustice to let her live another day.

"Even though I knew that you were a part of her when I looked upon you, all I could see was my son. I decided then that I would leave it up to fate to decide what would become of you. I swaddled you and left you in the arms of your dying mother."

"Edward was my father?" Lorelei was shocked. She had felt a connection with the man from the moment she laid eyes on him, but she never imagined it was because he was her flesh and blood. She mourned the opportunity she had to know him, and now it was too late.

"Yes, my child." Avina placed her hand over Lorelei's.

"My mother did not die. She lives," Lorelei sobbed as tears streamed down her face. "She survived it. You do not have to feel guilt for what you have done. She has never spoken ill of you. She does not blame you."

"No, my child, your mother simply defied the laws of death. Her soul stayed and lingered watchfully over you, protecting you, nurturing you." Avina's sad eyes looked down apologetically.

"No, you are wrong…" Lorelei pulled her hand away from Avina's touch.

"Edward thought you died that day too, with your mother. When I came out of the room to his awaiting face, so much hope… I told him you had both died. You were so small, your eyes did not open, and you made no sound. It was easy for him to believe that you were dead. I convinced him to leave the two of you in your home. To let you both rest in peace. He never returned to the forest after that day. It was too painful for him. He was too broken. When I came back weeks later, I could never have imagined what I found upon my return."

Lorelei pushed herself up from the table, against Avina's wishes. "No… no. You are wrong. Why are you saying this? Why?" She was overwhelmed and terrified of what this woman was confessing. She knew her mother was still alive. She had grown up with her mother's constant love and presence — she was physical and real.

Lorelei scrambled off the table, backing away from Avina.

"Lorelei, I am sorry… but please, you need to rest now. I fear that I confessed too much, too soon. I have not felt your mother's presence in the forest since you left. I fear she may not be there when you return. I do not know what you will find… Wait till you are well and strong." But her plea fell upon deaf ears. Lorelei needed to find her mother and confirm that she was indeed home, waiting for her.

Lorelei fled toward the door, pushing it open, ignoring Avina's calls. The pain in her side increased, but it was bearable. Pressing her hand to the wound for comfort, she quickly scanned the area for Ajax or Oliver. Both appeared before her, alarmed by her unceremonious exit from the cottage.

"I need to go home." Lorelei could not rid her expression of the fear and panic that assaulted her. "I need to see my mother." Neither of them responded; they only looked at her in confusion. Lorelei turned around to see Avina in the doorway of her house, regret written on her features. "Thank you for your help, Avina, but I have to go now."

"Maybe you should lie down. You look pale." Ajax seemed surprised by her quick recovery.

"No, I need to go home," Lorelei insisted.

"We cannot take her back to the black forest. That will be the first place the prince looks for her now that he knows she is alive. Crewe is working with him. He knows." Letholdus stepped in.

Ajax turned to him with a surprised expression. Lorelei herself was surprised by the concern Letholdus was expressing for her well-being. "I promised her I would take her home," Ajax said with finality. "We are going."

"I wish you well, Lorelei." Avina placed a gentle caress on Lorelei's shoulder before retreating back into her house, closing the door behind her.

They took the wagon to the edge of the forest before they continued on horse. Ajax, Oliver, and Letholdus remained on guard as Lorelei remained quiet and determined. Oliver only made one attempt to ask her why she was so upset, but her tears made him stop questioning her, returning them all to silence. Lorelei was too overwhelmed to explain what Avina had told her. She was exhausted from her injury, and she struggled to hold herself together with Avina's words cycling through her thoughts. She leaned in against the comfort of Ajax's body, his arm wrapped around her waist, holding her firm.

Lorelei felt a small amount of comfort when the forest became familiar. She had missed her home greatly, and a small amount of joy weaved into the turmoil of her emotions. The trees swayed gently in the breeze and the quiet, serene surroundings were like listening to her favorite song. She could hear Letholdus grumbling his complaints that she was taking them to the middle of nowhere with no place to buy much-needed drink. Since he had run out of liquor, Lorelei had noticed a much darker version of Letholdus taking hold. His sick sense of humor dwindled away to leave only the angry version that she knew she should steer clear of.

A cry of relief was followed by a smile of appreciation; she was home. Never had the small, run-down cottage looked as good as it did in this very moment. Lorelei moved to dismount, but Ajax held firm. "Let me make sure it is safe." He spoke close to her ear. The heat of his breath stirred her already heightened emotions.

Ajax slipped from the horse, closed his eyes, and listened to their surroundings, and then approached the front step of the house. "Good." He nodded.

"Mother!" Lorelei called. Oliver was at her side, gently helping her dismount. He was still apprehensive about her injury. Lorelei ran toward the house and swiftly ascended the front steps, pushing the door open. "Mother?" The house was quiet and untouched. Everything was exactly how it was when she left. Her cup upon the table next to her book, her mother's blanket that she had knocked onto the floor in her search for her before she left the house... "Mother?" Panic made the world seem strange and unnatural.

"Lorelei, there's no sign of your mother outside." Ajax's large frame stepped into her home. It had never seemed particularly small to her; it was always the right size for her and her mother, but having Ajax standing in their kitchen gave her a different perspective. It was strange having him here, the place that she had ever only shared with her mother. Two very different parts of her life were suddenly crashing together.

Lorelei was grateful he was with her now. She could not imagine not having him in her life. She reached out and wrapped her arms around his narrow waist. He immediately engulfed her in his hold, infusing strength into her body. Strength she badly needed.

"Ajax?" Lorelei looked up into his beautiful face. "I need you to open a door for me. It is locked, and I do not have a key."

"Sure." He smiled and leaned down to kiss her gently on the forehead.

Oliver joined them in the house. "Everything alright? Did you find your mother?"

"No." Lorelei managed a small, sad smile.

"Maybe she left to find you?" Oliver offered hopefully.

"No. I can still feel her here," Lorelei said thoughtfully. Taking Ajax's hand, she led them to the locked door. She had never known what her mother kept in the room. As a child, she would always have so many ideas that made her mother laugh, never once confirming or denying any of Lorelei's suggestions.

Ajax wrapped his hand around the handle and snapped it off as if it were a brittle piece of wood. Pushing the door open slightly, he stepped back to allow Lorelei access. "Do you want me to go in first?"

"No." Lorelei took a deep, calming breath before she reached up and pushed the door open. She was met by stale air, smelling faintly of her mother. "Mother?" Lorelei called into the room before she entered hesitantly. She was only met by silence as she ventured further into the small room. It was dark, with heavy curtains blocking the sunlight. Lorelei could make out a form on the bed. "Mother," Lorelei sighed in relief. She reached out and touched her mother's soft hair. She smiled when she heard her mother whisper her name in response. It sounded strange and distant, but Lorelei's relief overrode any concerns.

"You had me worried." Lorelei reached up and drew back the curtains, flooding the room with light. Dust danced wildly around her. A scream tore from her throat when she looked upon her mother.

Ajax and Oliver barreled into the room, stopping short when the saw what lay upon the bed: the corpse of a woman long passed. Her body was mere bones, while long hair that matched Lorelei's fanned out over a white gown that lay over her fragile remains. A dagger like that Avina had spoken of lay beside her on the bed, and in her arms was cradled an empty blanket — the blanket that Lorelei realized had once swaddled her as she was placed in her mother's dying arms.

The room that Lorelei once believed held treasures untold, full of wonder, was her mother's grave. All those years ago, her mother had died, and she had not known the truth. Her mind struggled with the reality of it all. Lorelei sat next to her mother's remains. Reaching up, she ran her fingers through the soft strands of her mother's hair. It felt just like it always did.

Lorelei felt Ajax's hands rest upon her shoulders, pulling her back into his arms. She submitted to his embrace; she needed his comfort as her tears flowed. She buried her face in his chest, letting herself mourn.

When Lorelei collected herself, she took a deep breath. Something on the other side of the room caught her attention. She pulled away from Ajax's hold and walked over to a dresser, She ran her hand over the smooth wood, covered in a thick layer of dust. Upon the dresser sat a few items, but one thing stood out above the rest: a necklace with a beautiful white shell strong upon it, so vibrantly white, with a blueish hue. She knew every detail of it before she even studied it. Her mother always had it around her neck. Lorelei wiped the tears from her face as she turned to Ajax and Oliver's questioning gaze. They seemed unsure, looking at her as if she were about to fall apart before them.

The words tumbled from her lips of what Avina had told her at her cottage as Ajax and Oliver stood silently listening. Words that were hard to form, but they needed to be said. She needed to accept the truth.

"We should give her a proper burial." Ajax broke the silence after Lorelei's words had died away.

"No, I need to take her to the sea." Lorelei smiled. She had a strange, comforting feeling that it was what her mother would truly have wanted. "I need to set her free."

"Ajax! Oliver! We have company!" Letholdus called to them.

Chapter 39
AJAX

Ajax stood before the cottage. The trees stood tall around them as he closed his eyes in concentration. Letholdus's skill of detection was impressive, but nothing matched Ajax's precision in calculating an oncoming threat. He could feel Letholdus and Oliver near him; they too were on alert. "There are a dozen, maybe more, moving in," Ajax informed them. "Lorelei, get back inside."

She only shook her head. She looked terrified and defiant at the same time; under different circumstances he would find it adorable. Now he only wanted her to be out of danger. He shot her a displeased look. He did not have time to argue. Lorelei was a distraction he was not used to dealing with. Oliver had always been capable of holding his own, but Lorelei was a wild card that pulled him in every direction, stirring emotions he never believed himself to be capable of. Ajax motioned toward Letholdus and Oliver, showing the men would leave the forest. They both immediately took a stance to confront the oncoming threat.

Letholdus's excitement showed in his composure, while Oliver, on the other hand, looked pale as he stole quick glances back at Lorelei. He too wanted her out of sight, but she refused to leave. Ajax turned toward the trees. Their trackers were upon them. Ajax was not surprised when Prince Arthur presented himself first upon his midnight steed. He was accompanied by some of his own guards as well as some of Crewe's men as they poured out into the clearing on horseback. Crewe himself was notably absent, leaving Ajax to believe he was still in pursuit of Teller or possibly dead.

Prince Arthur's gaze skimmed over the three men opposing his arrival and fell on Lorelei with a sinister smile. Ajax could see the twisted prince already believed he had won. This man obviously did not know who stood before him; if he did, he would not seem so callous.

"That was certainly a decent trick you pulled, leaving me to believe you were dead." Arthur spoke with dark confidence. Lorelei took a step back, retreating further under the small porch of the cottage, away from Arthur's words. "No matter, you will have plenty of time to make it up to me," Arthur sneered. "And do not try sing again. It will not work. I have figured out what you are." Excitement flared in his eyes.

"You have no claim on her. Leave this place now before I slaughter you where you stand," Ajax said. Arthur's eyes flared with anger. Ajax noted that the four Ravens accompanying Arthur looked odd. He recognized the men's features, although their bulkier frames and darkened eyes set them apart. They exuded a strange energy that caused shadows to hang off them. Fearless, savage expressions pulled at their features. Something sinister lived inside these men.

"She is mine," Arthur said in a deep growl.

"Do you hear that, men?" Ajax spoke to Oliver and Letholdus at his side. "The little shite prince thinks he can take whatever he wants. Shall we give him a dose of reality?"

"Hell, yes!" Letholdus said.

Ajax saw the excitement in Arthur's expression; the proposed violence thrilled him.

"Crewe Carmichael told me that you would not be easily killed. I brought some reinforcements that you shall discover are more than capable now that I made some minor adjustments." Arthur waved to the Ravens. Dismounting, they stood in a defensive line facing Ajax and the others. "You see, I have enhanced their abilities, so to speak. It will be you who receives a dose of reality." Arthur laughed coldly as he waved his men onward. "Bring me their heads."

Ajax crouched as the men marched forward, his eyes keen to discover their weakness. One of the men swung his sword at a tree that stood in his path, cutting it down in one sure stroke. A sharp crack sounded as the twenty-foot tree began to fall. Ajax shifted quickly to avoid its path.

"What the hell!" Oliver gasped as he too avoided the falling tree. Whatever Arthur had done to them made them dark and powerful with lust for blood. There was no sign of humanity left in these damaged men. Ajax growled as he met the first with a forceful clashing of swords. The dark hollowness of the man's eyes showed the evidence of his tainted soul.

A sadistic smile carved the face of a man Ajax had once considered an ally. Roger pushed his blade against Ajax's until they both broke hold, stepping back to engage again. Letholdus was holding his own against his opponent, and Oliver had speed on his side, making him an impossible target. The other man, known as Francis, unfortunately sought the opportunity to collect Lorelei while they were all engaged.

The urgency to protect Lorelei drove Ajax to fight harder, driving his blade toward madness. He could not let them get hold of her; if they did, they would gain the upper hand. These men were now larger and stronger, but they lacked skill. Ajax took advantage of an opening. Roger did not cover his body. Instead the enraged man concentrated on landing blows upon Ajax, without properly defending himself. Roger put too much confidence in his newfound strength, believing himself to be invincible. Every swing the man took, Ajax took notice of his failure to cover his body. Ajax's blade sank into the Roger's side, forcing the blade deep, and blood ran over the hilt of Ajax's sword, soaking his fingers. Ajax kicked Roger backward, releasing his blade. He did not waste time, focusing his attention on the back of Francis, closing in on Lorelei.

Ajax pulled two throwing knives off his person and threw them in quick succession. One lodged deep in the back of Francis's neck, the other in his back. Francis immediately swung around, growling, while reaching behind him to extract the knives. He started to advance on Ajax, anger pouring from him like steam. Ajax let another fly from his grasp, embedding in the man's heart. Francis's eyes widened with shock. He stumbled and then collapsed heavily upon the ground, dark black blood pooling around him.

Ajax's eyes met Lorelei's. So much emotion passed through him as he looked upon her. He refused to let her fall into the clutches of Arthur again. He turned to meet the oncoming Roger, back on his feet. His wound bled freely, and an oily black saturated his stomach.

Ajax and Roger raining untiring blows, their swords clashing and scraping against each other's as they fought. The injury that Ajax had inflicted upon Roger did not slow his onslaught. Ajax twisted out of the way as Roger brought a forceful swing down upon him, but spinning with his momentum, Ajax managed to bring his blade up across

Roger's stomach, still bent forward with the thrust of his strike. The blade had cut deep, and Roger looked down to see his blood and in- nards leaking out of the gaping wound. New rage boiled within the in- jured man as he wielded his blade with new vigor. Ajax was impressed by the force of the man's attack as it radiated down his arms when their swords clashed.

Ajax dodged another blow while swinging out his arm, slicing across Roger's neck; his blade met little resistance as it carved through the flesh. Blood sprayed out. The sound of Roger's body meeting the ground was a very satisfying victory. Ajax looked up into the nar- rowed expression of Arthur, who had watched his reinforcements fall before his eyes.

Letholdus stood behind Ajax, wiping the blood coating his blade on the shirt of his victim. Oliver was withdrawing his knife from the other man, looking a little worse for wear. He did not heal instantly, like they did; his injuries would linger long after. Oliver grabbed his shoulder that was bleeding through his shirt, flinching. His face was beginning to swell, and blood seeped from his lip.

"Good." Oliver waved breathlessly, wiping the sweat from his brow. "Just a scratch."

The rate at which Oliver's blood saturated his shirt told another story. "Protect Lorelei," Ajax ordered him. He turned back toward Ar- thur, who had dismounted. He had watched as the demonic men were cut down, though he did not seem fazed.

Ajax looked on as Arthur grabbed hold of one of the men still standing at his side, sinking his teeth into the man's neck. His cry was short-lived as Arthur greedily drained his blood and dropped the man at his feet.

"What the bloody hell!" Letholdus was taken aback.

Arthur's other soldiers began to retreat in fear. "Stop!" he called out, making the men stay, instantly immobile. "Kill the old man," he ordered. They turned obediently as if they were puppets and zeroed in on Letholdus.

"Old man?" Letholdus complained as he readied himself to engage the onslaught.

Ajax met Arthur's cold stare as he approached him. "I will enjoy this," Arthur seethed with dark satisfaction as he withdrew his sword.

"Not as much as I," Ajax responded before he too advanced, clos- ing the distance between them. The two clashed in intense combat.

Every swing was met in kind as they each tried to gain the upper hand. Unlike the other men that were infected with evil, Arthur seemed to embody it. His confidence and comfort with it made him an effective opponent. Ajax could not help the unnerving feeling that the man radiated; it slithered over Ajax's skin, trying to force its disease upon him. Every time Ajax's blade made contact, Arthur would heal, much like him, though Arthur's wound would blacken and then fade in a matter of moments.

"We have more company," Letholdus called out just as an arrow cut through the trees and pierced Ajax's side. He stumbled backward with a curse. He was unable to extract the arrow while Arthur was raining blow after blow, so the wound could not heal as he remained trained on Arthur. The pain in his side was minimal, but it was soon accompanied by many more as the arrows continued to fly from unseen archers.

"Hold on," Letholdus called out and disappeared into the thick trees. Ajax lost count of the arrows embedded in his skin; he could feel the sharp sting of two in his leg. His side, shoulder, and back were riddled with wounds, but he forced himself onward, continuing to meet blow after blow. Pushing on through the pain, he gained some advantage, forcing Arthur backward, stumbling over the fallen tree. Ajax took advantage of Arthur's vulnerability and jumped in the air, coming down with his blade readied. It sank deep into Arthur's heart.

Arthur gasped, looking at the blade lodged in his body. Then Ajax was stunned to see a smile. Arthur drove his own blade under Ajax's ribcage, deep into his body. He could feel the blade cut through his organs. "Did I forget to mention that I cannot die?" Arthur laughed wickedly, giving the blade a twist.

Ajax struggled to draw breath, blood spewing from his mouth as he grabbed for the hilt of Arthur's sword, though Arthur held it firm, pushing it deeper into Ajax until it exited through the back of his shoulder blade. Ajax's scream of agony rang out through the air, swallowing Lorelei's cries as she realized what Arthur had just done. Letholdus appeared behind Ajax, pulling him off Arthur. Ajax fell to the ground in blinding pain, reaching for the hilt and gathering strength to extract it, but it was slippery from his flowing blood, and he could not grip it. The arrows dug into his flesh as he leaned against the ground. His head swarm with lack of oxygen because he could not draw breath with the sword impaling him.

Oliver appeared before his blackening vision. He could not make out the distorted sounds that he made. Burning pain assaulted him as the blade was withdrawn. His lungs immediately gorged on breath, pulling painful amounts into his damaged chest. He could feel hands on him, shaking him, and suddenly the voices became clear, his focus returning. "Get up!" Oliver yelled in his face. "Now!" Ajax felt the sting of a slap across his cheek.

Ajax jerked upward, gasping for breath, Oliver's devastated gaze upon him. Lorelei screamed out for Letholdus, bringing Ajax's attention to the fight before him. The crushing realization of what was unfolding jolted him into motion. Arthur's blade swung as a strangled cry left Ajax's lips. He could not react fast enough, and Arthur's blade swung across Letholdus's neck, separating it from his body, the only way to kill a Savas, ending his life, and Ajax could not stop it. "No!" His father's body crumpled to the ground.

Chapter 40
TELLER

Teller looked up at the intimidating cliff face that looked down on the enraged ocean. The waves crashed and frothed against the blackened rock, making the surface slippery and hard to grasp. A near impossible climb, but Teller did not fear the fall. He would not meet his death if he fell into the swells of the ocean, pitching his body into the unforgiving rock, breaking every bone. His body would heal in a matter of moments, and the pain would be short-lived. Should he fall, it would only force him to climb anew.

What Teller sought at the top of the cliff, he would submit to that fate a hundred times over. Heavy clouds had blanketed the sky, promising a brewing storm. It would only be a matter of time before the rain assaulted him. The sun was cast aside, leaving no evidence that it remained in its perch, causing an eerie darkness to settle over the land. Teller found footing in the rock face before beginning his ascent.

Teller had tracked the guards ushering the queen from the castle. Teller's own men now stormed through the castle walls, seizing it. Prince Arthur had his mother, Queen Peronell, taken to this perilous location with heavy guard, with the notion that it would make it impossible for someone to gain access to her. Teller would not be outplayed in this game. No location would keep him from his prize; his plan to avenge his Josselyn would not be thwarted, now or ever.

Finding purchase on the sheet of rock was challenging, but Teller was pleased with the progress. When he could hear voices carried from the crest, he slowed his movements. The queen's shrill protests were the most pronounced. She was unhappy with the arrangements for her care; the guards were blatantly ignoring the queen's requests as she continued her outburst. Their loyalties lay with Prince Arthur now that the king lay dying within the captured castle.

Teller listened intently to the sounds above him as he stayed just out of view. He counted three men in Queen Peronell's immediate company. He knew countless others stood guard along the path they used to reach their location to ensure no one got close to the queen.

"Does Arthur plan on leaving his own mother on the clifftop while he runs off after some filthy whore?" Peronell spat at her keepers. "You cannot treat me as such, I am your queen."

"Our orders are to keep you in this disclosed location until order is restored in the castle or another secure location for your safety," one of the guards responded irritably. They had obviously heard more they could stand from the irate queen.

"He could have at least sent me somewhere indoors, where I could be warm and have a proper meal. This is barbaric! I am not a prisoner! I will see to it that you are all punished for my treatment... Look at me when I speak to you!" The clouds clapped loudly overhead before they opened up and poured heavily. Teller adjusted his grip; the water made the rock surface difficult to grasp.

"We are under strict orders not to make eye contact with you under any circumstances," the guard insisted.

"Nonsense, look at me!" Peronell growled in frustration.

When Teller sensed one the guards near the edge, he unsheathed his knife, and with a quick thrust he swung his arm up and impaled the man. Twisting, Teller pulling him over the edge. The man did not even have time to react before he fell to the savage waters below.

"What the hell! Did Morgan just fall?" Wide eyes peered over the edge, searching out their fallen comrade. When they landed on Teller, the guard immediately moved for his weapon. Teller was too fast. Swinging himself up, he kicked out the man's legs and embedded his knife in the man's neck. Teller looked up to see Crewe before him.

"Lord Caunter?" Peronell questioned when she laid eyes upon him.

"I guess you were not there for the big reveal, Your Highness. Let me take this time to formally introduce myself. My name is William Teller." Teller gave a curt nod in her direction, his eyes taking in his surroundings.

"Teller?" The queen was legitimately surprised. "I knew there was something disgusting about you when I first saw you. I just could not put the pieces together." Her eyes locked with his, causing him to smile with amusement.

"Ah… that witch shite does not work on me." Teller turned to lay his eyes on the familiar man that approached him. Crewe, leader of the infamous Ravens, came to stand a short distance from him.

"I have been looking for you, Teller. You are not an easy man to track." Crewe stood rigidly. Crewe's intention was very clear.

"Yes, I have been told I am a sneaky son of a bitch," Teller said teasingly. Crewe's expression darkened. Reaching into his shirt pocket, he withdrew a glass vial filled with a deep red liquid.

"That is mine!" Peronell spoke up determinedly. "I order you to give it to me at once!"

Both men ignored the queen, much to her displeasure. Crewe pulled the cork from the vial and tipped the contents up to his lips, greedily drinking the entire vial.

He doubled over, pulling at his skin. His body distorted before Teller's eyes, his muscles shifting and bunching in unnatural ways, stretching his clothes until the seams gave way to the metamorphosis. His skin took on a translucent gray sheen, with pronounced dark veins mapping his body. He opened his eyes to reveal glowing red irises, ready to tear something apart, a far cry from the well-composed, disciplined man Teller had met before.

"I know who you are, Teller. I know that you are the same as Ajax, and so I had to tip the odds in my favor." Crewe's voice was deep and gravelly as it radiated from his enlarged, mutated chest.

"What was that shite? Did you make a deal with the devil?" Teller asked with raised brows, still a little taken aback.

"Close." Crewe chuckled sinfully. "I drank his blood."

"I think you may have gone overboard. I hate to be the one to enlighten you, but you are now one ugly fellow," Teller said, relishing the anger that he was stirring in Crewe.

Crewe growled in rage. "This is not a game!" He withdrew his sword.

Teller tried to get a read on his opponent. He knew Crewe was an exceptional fighter with notable skills, but he did not know how this transformation would affect the way he fought.

"No? Such a pity." Teller withdrew his own sword. They advanced on one other, their swords commencing a deadly dance. Crewe's strength was great, his newfound power making him a difficult opponent, and his skills as a fighter were evident in the way he handled his sword.

Teller quickly realized that the only way to outmaneuver Crewe was with speed and agility.

Crewe was not used to his bulkier frame, giving him a weakness that Teller moved to exploit.

Normally, Teller would take pleasure battling such a worthy opponent, but he was too close to achieving what he had set out to do years before. He moved with intention of ending the fight as quickly as possible, taking every opening that Crewe gave him, cutting at his thick flesh to release his infected blood.

Two of the king's guards appeared and joined in the fray, but they were easily eliminated, their bodies joining the others over the cliff's edge. Teller's fight was fueled by an intensity that mere men could not withstand, though the distraction allowed Crewe to gain some ground on him. Unfortunately for him, the wounds he inflicted healed before they hindered Teller's performance.

Crewe began concentrating on targeting Teller's neck and chest; he knew that anywhere else was not worth the effort, because Teller healed too quickly.

Teller was not fighting a typical soldier, and he needed to keep his head about him. It was a worthy battle. As he dodged the full impact of Crewe's sword, the tip of the blade cut through Teller's shirt, tracing a line through his flesh. Teller in turn plunged his sword through Crewe's chest, causing him to come to a halt. Shock showed on Teller's features when Crewe stepped backward, pulling his body off Teller's blade, a sinister smile playing on his features.

Teller growled in frustration. He threw himself into direct, accurate swings, cutting into Crewe's flesh at every opportunity. Crewe's strength refused to wane as he pressed on in a frenzy of blows. Rain poured heavily from the sky, making seeing difficult as they continued their fight. Dark, blackened blood ran off of Crewe's body.

Teller launched himself at Crewe's body again when Crewe lifted his arms in a powerful swing. Teller's blade sank deep into Crewe's body. Looking down at the wound, Crewe stumbled to his knees. His chest was now riddled with cuts, and he finally was succumbing to the injuries, to Teller's relief. Teller withdrew his sword, only to sink it in again and again, shredding Crewe's body. When Teller withdrew his blade for the final time, the momentum caused Crewe to slump forward. With a closed fist Teller hit him in the face, forcing Crewe backward with a heavy thud upon the rock, unmoving.

Teller swung around to face the pale Peronell with heavy breath. She had been watching the throes of battle in front of her. She had a clear understanding of what would befall her. He closed the distance between them, cold hatred radiating from him.

"I have waited a long time for this." He grabbed Peronell's face, squeezing relentlessly. Her hands were chained, making this too easy, but he did not find it any less fulfilling. Peronell tried to twist from his grasp, but Teller did not relent.

"I know that you had a sister by the name of Josselyn." His words made Peronell stop struggling. "I know that you had her killed for some sick, self-serving scheme. I am here now to avenge her death. To put an end to the real witch who infects the world with her disease." Teller spat his words in her face.

"It was you that she gave her heart. I can see it in your eyes. My weak sister was so eager to hide among her trees and animals, to give up her potential for what? Love?" Peronell threw her words at him. "Love is for children. For stupid, naive children…" Her words died away as she realized that Teller had pierced her chest with his blade. Looking down, she could see her blood spilling as he slowly pushed it deeper within her, nearing her heart. She tried to cry out, but the pain stopped her, stealing her breath. His grip held her still, despite her struggle.

Teller stilled his blade as he felt burning pain rip through him. A cold smile spread across Peronell's face. Looking down, Teller saw his own body painted with his life force. The tip of Crewe's sword protruded through his stomach. He had let down his guard. The all-encompassing emotion of revenge had caused him to turn his back on his enemy. He had not made sure the threat was eliminated, a weighty mistake that could cost a price he was not willing to pay.

Teller took a deep breath. Swinging around, he knocked Crewe back, releasing his hold on his sword. Crewe's injuries made him slow. Blood poured freely from his multiple lacerations, all of which would have been fatal if he were still a mere man. Teller reached behind him and began pulling the blade out of his body as quickly as he could manage; his organs struggled to mend themselves, his heart laboring under the stress of injury.

Crewe struggled to his feet, pulling a whip from his belt; the end was frayed and strung with sharp metal shards that would tear flesh on contact. Teller spun and kicked Crewe as hard as he could.

The force caused him to stumble toward the edge. Teller advanced quickly, plunging his blade into Crewe's neck, and then kicked him again. Crewe's footing faltered, and he stumbled back, disappearing over the ledge.

Teller spun around toward Peronell, thrusting his hand into her chest, tearing the remaining flesh and grabbing hold of her heart. Pulling it free, he watched Peronell's eyes widen in terror. She looked down at her heart in Teller's grip and surrendered to death.

Teller felt the grip of Crewe's whip grab hold of his neck, and snapping into place, the metal shards lodged deep in his neck, pulling him back toward the cliff edge with a great force. Teller felt his feet leave the ground, and time slowed. He savored the retribution for his sweet Josselyn, numbing the pain of his head being torn from his body. Sailing over the lip of the rock face, he glimpsed Crewe's body. Reaching out, Teller locked his hold on Crewe. He was only met by slight resistance as he pried Crewe loose. Crewe submitted to the fall, giving one last tug on the whip impaling Teller, who felt the last of the metal planted in his neck tear through. His head was separated from his body. He was free of this life, free of his curse, and he was overcome with relief that he would be reunited with his beautiful Josselyn.

Chapter 41
AJAX

Ajax tried to force himself to his feet. His body was healing, but the extent of his injuries slowed the process. Arthur licked Letholdus's blood from his hand and smiled wickedly at Ajax before he began to advance. Oliver took a stance next to Ajax. "Get back, Oliver," Ajax said, getting to his feet.

Arthur's attention swung to the boy with a narrowed, calculating gaze. His scrutiny caused anger to flare over his features. "Oliver," he said maliciously. "I can see the resemblance to your father." Arthur pointed his sword at Oliver. "*You* will die, bastard son of King Brom Floros."

As Arthur advanced, Oliver met his blade with his own, but the force knocked him backward. Oliver regained his footing, struggling against the dark strength of Arthur. He managed a few hits before Arthur's closed fist met his face, dropping him to the ground, unconscious.

Ajax swung his sword to block Arthur's blade aimed at Oliver's still body. Although an exceptional fighter, Oliver was not strong enough to face the inhuman strength and speed that Arthur now possessed. Ajax could feel his own strength returning, matching Arthur's blows again and again. Ajax tore the remains of his tattered shirt from his body so it would not hinder his movements.

The battle raged on, every swing matched in kind. It now became a battle of endurance. Ajax leapt over Letholdus's fallen body; the momentary distraction gave him an opportunity. Ajax avoided Arthur's downswing but missed the flash of Arthur's knife that he brought down in his other hand, sinking it deep in Ajax's throat.

Lorelei screamed and ran toward them. Ajax could not deter her; his voice was stolen as he pulled the blade free from his neck. Arthur grabbed hold of Lorelei, seemingly amused by her attempt to attack him.

Lorelei unexpectedly jabbed the blade used to slay her own mother into Arthur's chest. His expression darkened immediately as he looked down to see crimson coating his shirt.

"He is injured!" Lorelei cried out when she realized the new development. Arthur brusquely tossed her back, and she met the ground with breathtaking force.

Ajax looked at the wound. Until now, Arthur's flesh had repelled all injury. Now, looking at the wound, he could see fear in Arthur's eyes for the first time since they began their battle.

"Mother..." Arthur's breathed was forced, his jaw clenched tightly as he withdrew the knife. He was looking at the blood coating his fingers, seeing his own mortality. Something had happened, changing the rules, leaving the once-confident Arthur terrified. The color leeched from his skin as he looked up Ajax.

Ajax took the opportunity to sink his blade deep in Arthur's chest. Arthur grasped at the sword. His eyes filled with fright as Ajax twisted the blade deep before withdrawing it. Arthur fell lifelessly to the ground, staring blankly up at the sky.

Ajax grabbed hold of Lorelei, kissing her briskly on the lips, smoothing her hair in search of injuries. "I am fine," she assured him with a smile. They both turned their attention to Oliver, still out cold. Lorelei pulled away from Ajax and knelt down beside Oliver. She placed her hands on him in a way that told Ajax she was drawing upon her healing ability. He stepped back to give her some room.

Ajax withdrew his sword, hearing someone approach. A familiar face came into view. "Have I missed all the fun?" Margas appeared before him. He took in Ajax's bloodied state and received his confirmation, despite Ajax's refusal to answer his question. Ajax was not in the mood to humor him.

"I will not let you hurt her," Ajax growled. He stepped forward aggressively, blocking Margas should he choose to seek out Lorelei.

Margas raised his hands in surrender. "I followed Prince Arthur's trail here in hopes of killing that piece of shite. I will not take up arms against you, Ajax. Your father filled me in on some of the details of the situation... I cannot say that I agree with your actions, but I will not betray you. I give you my word."

Ajax nodded his thanks. He knew the man's word was cast in stone, and he would not have to fight him on this matter. Margas looked over at Lorelei as she healed Oliver. "She is not what I expected a Siren to be. A part of me knows what she is, and that part of me would like nothing more than to crush her." Ajax's muscles tightened defensively, but Margas once again raised his hands. "Though part of me finds her intriguing. There is something different about her…"

"She is not a Siren in the sense that we know of them. She is something more, something worth saving," Ajax said defensively.

Oliver began stirring, and Lorelei helped him sit up.

"The little shite is still around, is he? He might outlive us all at this rate."

"I am counting on it." Ajax ran his fingers through his hair, realizing how much blood coated him.

"I have a letter signed by the king, given to me by his own hand, claiming Oliver is his true heir." Margas pulled the rolled parchment from his breast pocket. "Guess he did something right in the end. It does not make up for his errors, but it gives us hope for the future."

"It does," Ajax agreed, taking the scroll from Margas.

"You do not seem surprised by this? You already knew who Oliver was, then?" Margas said.

"Yes," Ajax conceded.

"He is the only surviving heir to the throne. Where is that grumpy bastard Letholdus, off finding the nearest tavern?"

Ajax turned his gaze toward his fallen father, and Margas made the connection. He placed his hand upon Ajax's shoulder. "Sorry, Jax, he was a brilliant warrior, stronger than the best of us."

Ajax nodded. "He saved my life." His father was always difficult, but he fought against the nature of the curse that was bound to their very blood and never once attempted to do Ajax any real harm. Ultimately, he gave his life for his son, and Ajax felt great sorrow at the loss.

"We will give him burial worthy of a great warrior." Margas gave Ajax's shoulder a comforting squeeze.

* * *

Ajax was lost in thought as he stared out over the bodies scattered before him. He pondered the death that was brought to Lorelei's home and the loss they had endured. He had taken her from the safety of her home and thrown her into a world of destruction and chaos.

He was pulled from his wandering thoughts when Lorelei's small hand grabbed hold of his with a reassuring squeeze. She did not say anything but looked up at him with bright eyes and a hesitant smile. "I tried to save Letholdus. I tried to save him, but I could not…"

"Come here." Ajax pulled her into his arms. "I know you tried. He is beyond our reach now. His suffering is over." He pulled her into a tight embrace and kissed the top of her head. "I am the reason you have known so much pain. I have brought this destruction to your home," he whispered, pouring his heart out to the one who had claimed it.

"I do not regret any of it, because it led me to you," Lorelei said.

Ajax leaned in, kissing her tenderly. "I love you, Lorelei."

Lorelei's smile lit up his world. "And I you, always."

Chapter 42
AJAX
Two months later...

The sun was casting comforting warmth upon all within its kingdom, though Ajax could not appreciate the beauty of the day; there was too much urgency.

His horse thundered over the earth at a fast gallop. Ajax did not slow its pace until he was at his intended destination. His heart was beating frantically, not from the thrill of the ride but from fear. It was the reason he had sought out Avina, the healer and Lorelei's grandmother. He and Lorelei had not returned here since the day Lorelei discovered the truth of her history; she needed time to adjust and mourn her mother.

He jumped from the saddle and charged toward the door of the small house nestled in the protection of the trees. He knocked abruptly before swinging the door open, not waiting for an answer.

"Avina!" Ajax called into the seemingly vacant house.

"I was wondering when you would return." Avina's voice came from behind him.

Ajax turned around and took in the sight of the elderly woman. Her gray hair was down in waves around her shoulders, making her appear younger than he remembered. She stepped around Ajax's large form, entering her house. Her hands were covered in dirt, and she held a basket of freshly picked herbs.

"Are you here about the baby?" Avina turned and looked back at him when she spoke, watching his reaction.

"You knew she was pregnant?" Ajax said in a mixture of accusation and surprise.

"I suspected." Avina shrugged. "I also suspect that the reason you fled across the land and into my home like a wild man is that you fear the curse will still affect her."

Ajax nodded, unable to form words. It was true; he had never experienced such raw fear as he did when Lorelei told him she was carrying his child. He was now facing what he dreaded the most, the possibility of Lorelei's death.

"It is true that when Lorelei's mother was laid to rest in the waters that birthed her, the curse was broken. Aisling was the last of the true-blood Sirens the curse was created for. Do you still bear the mark of the Savas?" Avina set her basket aside and looked up at him expectantly.

Ajax shook his head. The mark had disappeared when they cast Aisling's bones into the sea. "Although because the child was conceived before this, I regretfully must tell you that I do not know Lorelei's fate. I do not know if it wove its way into Lorelei's future, or not. Curses are such fickle things, and once cast they can bend and change the rules the longer they live. We both know that curse was ancient."

"That is not good enough!" Ajax demanded. He needed answers.

"You do not think that I have tried to seek her future through every source available? She is my granddaughter, the last of my bloodline, and I am struggling with this every bit as much as you, I assure you. Fate would have it that this truth not be known. All we can do now is have faith that there is a plan for her, like there is for your son."

"My son?" Ajax gasped.

"Yes, Ajax. Your son will be a king of waters in which his mother's Siren lineage was forged. His name will find its place in history, never to be forgotten." Her words were certain.

"A king? I do not understand." Ajax shook his head in disbelief.

"You do not need to. Go home to Lorelei and live each moment you are granted with her to the fullest. It is the only wisdom I can grant you."

Ajax's shoulders fell in defeat. He had sought Avina's counsel to reassure himself that Lorelei would survive this. He wanted to know that she would be granted the gift of motherhood; she would watch their child grow while giving him the gift of her love. As he stood before Avina, he found could not give him what he sought. She could not cast his fears aside. He could not escape the possible truth that Lorelei might die bringing their son into the world, like the mothers of all the Men of Savas before her. Ajax turned somberly and walked back out into the bright sunlight.

"Ajax!" Avina called out to him as he mounted his horse. "Whatever this world has planned for Lorelei and yourself, take comfort in the fact that your son will be loved. May that give you hope for the future." Avina disappeared back into her home and closed the door while he still looked on thoughtfully. Her parting words, although they did not ease his fear, lifted a great weight from him. He spurred his horse to start the journey home, back to his heart, to his true love.

EPILOGUE

The rolling waves crashed hungrily against the shore. The water churned and moved like a living thing as it extended far beyond the eye could perceive in its vast glory. The water was restless under the clear blue sky, calling to the young man standing just out of its reach. The salty smell carried up to him, enticing him to venture out into its depths with many promises, many unknowns that he yearned to experience. Sometimes when he concentrated, he thought he could hear the call of an alluring song carried on the waves, so faint he did not know if it was only his imagination. Closing his eyes, he felt the necklace in his hand. The white shell was smooth and familiar under his fingers. It was once his mother's, and he treasured it.

A large bird caught his attention as it circled overhead, screeching. The bird flew with complete certainty that it belonged in the sky, looking down at the world. He envied the bird's sureness as he watched its graceful flight.

"There you are, my son." The young man turned to see his father approaching, walking down the narrow incline that led to the beach. "I knew I would find you here." A smile spread across his father's face, a face that strongly resembled his own. His father still carried the weight of a warrior, with strength that most men could never hope for. The only thing that was noticeably different between the two other than their age was that he had his mother's eyes; one as blue as the clearest ocean and one as green as the lushest forest.

"Father." He sighed.

His father's expression turned to a sympathetic smile as he came to stand next to him, feet in the sand, staring out at the never-ending water.

"How will I know when I am ready?" the young man asked.

His father's large hand came to rest on his shoulder. "When you accept the fact that you will make mistakes and can live with them, when you can carry the weight of many and do not crumble from the force, and most importantly when you can accept the fact that you will never truly be ready." He gave the young man's shoulder an affectionate squeeze.

"What if I cannot do it?" His father was a man whose wisdom he respected above all others.

"It is normal to doubt the unknown. But there comes a time when we all have to accept our destiny. I can see your potential, and I can assure you that I have never doubted what you are capable of."

"I am scared."

"Without fear you cannot have courage, and without courage you cannot be great." His father smiled.

"Do you really think so?"

"I have it on good authority that the world will never forget you," his father said proudly. "Although today is not the day to ponder such decisions — today we celebrate a new life."

"Clara gave birth?"

"Yes, and it was a boy. After having six girls, it was a very pleasant surprise for Oliver." His father laughed. Even though there was no blood relation, Oliver was family in every other sense of the word.

"Though with six older sisters, that boy may never be able to fight his way to the crown."

"You might be right, Tritan." His father's rich laugh warmed him. "Come, let us not keep your beautiful mother waiting."

These were only words upon the pages
until you brought them to life.
Thank you

ACKNOWLEDGEMENTS

A huge thank-you to:

Ryan McNeil, my husband, for his unwavering support.
My parents, who are always my biggest fans.
Taylor McNeil, my daughter, who loves to point out my mistakes.
Allister Thompson, my editor, who took my words
and polished them to perfection.
Emma Dolan, my cover artist, who made my book beautiful.
J.L. Drake, author, who took the time to give me
invaluable information and guidance.

Aimee McNeil was born and raised in Nova Scotia, Canada, where she continues to live today with her husband and three children.

Alluring Song is her first novel, which she presented to the world after a lifetime of dreaming. Aimee writes fantasy because she does not like to be confined within the boundaries of reality. Other interests include reading, painting, and enjoying every moment with her family.

Aimee loves to hear from her readers. You can visit her online at:

aimeemcneilswriting.blogspot.ca
Instagram/@aimeemcneilswriting
Facebook.com/aimeemcneilswriting
Twitter/@aimeeswriting

Made in the USA
Lexington, KY
06 June 2015